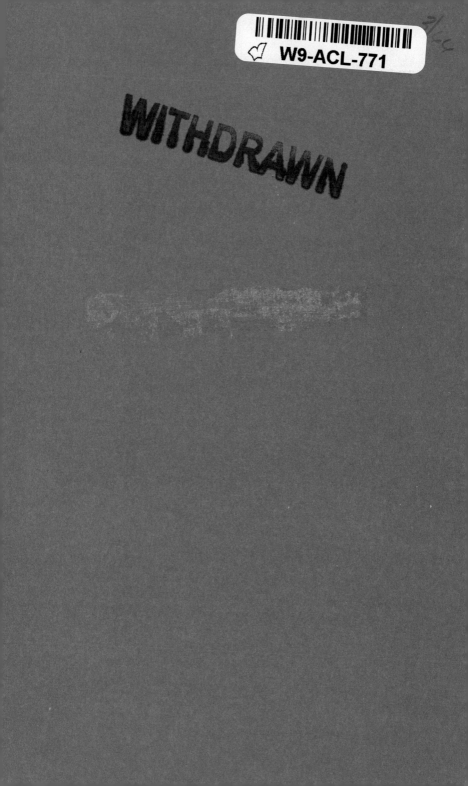

DOWN WHERE THE MOON IS SMALL

By Richard Llewellyn

DOWN WHERE THE MOON IS SMALL

SWEET MORN OF JUDAS' DAY

A MAN IN A MIRROR

UP, INTO THE SINGING MOUNTAIN

CHEZ PAVAN

MR. HAMISH GLEAVE

A FLAME FOR DOUBTING THOMAS

A FEW FLOWERS FOR SHINER

NONE BUT THE LONELY HEART

HOW GREEN WAS MY VALLEY

Juveniles

WARDEN OF THE SMOKE AND BELLS

THE FLAME OF HERCULES

THE WITCH OF MERTHYN

"And I shall sleep . . . Down Where the Moon Is Small"

RICHARD LLEWELLYN

1966

DOUBLEDAY & COMPANY, INC.

GARDEN CITY, NEW YORK

All of the characters in this book
are fictitious, and any resemblance
to actual persons, living or dead,
is purely coincidental.

Library of Congress Catalog Card Number 66–12205

Printed in the United States of America
First Edition

To the memory of
my sister
Gwladys,
Commandant, Royal Red Cross,
and her nieces
Ann and Sally,
and Marie, nicest of women,
killed in the bombing of
London, June 1944, ever,
with love.

Richard

DOWN WHERE THE MOON IS SMALL

1

Dearly touched a heart can be with proof of love from an absent one.

Many a happy minute you can have and a few sad as well only to think, and in memory live again, hearing and seeing all those years ago, and thankful even for the clock that brings back and yet takes you on.

Ceridwen, lovely old girl she was, must have packed these shirts and socks of mine and my best suit, and the little blue cloth my mother put about her hair to do the house, perhaps not willing to destroy or give them away and not knowing what else to do. The newspapers are all nearly ten years old and then it was that she left the Valley at last, and went with Blethyn to Angharad in South Africa. Camphor—you thought of moth, Ceridwen *fach-i!*—is still clear to the nose, and I wish we had brought back the lace basket from Mrs. Tom Harries over the mountain, but she said it was long since she saw one, and pretty, too, and keepsake or not, but Sûs gave it to her. Useful it would be to carry these little things for I will have to crawl and climb to be out of here, and slag is not the cleanest friend. Only by chance I found the parcel on the top shelf of the cupboard under the stairs where my mother kept special little treats, most for my father, and not to be looked into, much less touched, by any of us. Even then, all these years later, I still had a conscience to put my hand near the latch, and if Mama had spoken from behind there, no surprise would have been in me. So we are brought up, and the lessons stay.

The stairs had been boarded up by somebody to make a larger space with the wall taken out between the passage and the front room, but pressure on the roof must have snapped the planks, and I pulled a few away, and the cupboard was there, shining in varnish as I remembered it. A lot of our things I suppose were left in the house, but after everybody went from The Hill others lived there without paying rent until the slag was a danger, and they had to go. The rooms had been stripped except for two boxes, one I am sitting on, and the other tabling my bread and meat and thermos of tea. Eating as we did down in the colliery I am, and tasting coal with every bite. Steak and bread and wine in the open air was always daily with us in Patagonia and I suppose it always will be. Only sometimes we sat at table for the midday meal. Outside we were nearer the asado to cut and come again, and no need to dirty the house with workboots or wash plates and linen, or for anybody to be running in and out of the kitchen as the girls used to do here, Ceridwen especially after Angharad was married, for Olwen was still a baby, and most of us were at home, and nobody else to help my mother.

Those were my growing years so I remember more, and thinking of when we were small I suppose we remember in the words of the time, and sure it is I see and hear those days in the language of Cambria that we always spoke, and only sometimes in English. Later on I recall most in English, for only that we spoke in school. None of our books or lessons were in Cambrian, and I know my father must have told everybody to speak English in the house so that I could learn. Pain is in me, and deep understanding, to remember his anger when I wanted to go down the colliery with him instead of back to school.

"A scholar I wanted you to be," he said, on the way down The Hill. "You will never have a scholarship where we are going. No need. Only fools and cripples and blind ponies wanted."

"You are not a fool or a cripple, Dada," I said.

"Both," he said. "I should have been out years since. But there was your good Mama and all of you. Pay was in gold. Gold spoke. You will have silver now, and not much for your day's work. Later, if you are still a fool, you shall have pieces of paper. Instead to be a scholar, and a man of the head, you will be another kind of rabbit, making holes and throwing out the dirt."

"Ah, come on now, Dada," Ianto said. "There is a beautiful rabbit you are."

"What else?" my father said. "Born in the Image. But the truth was not in me. The coal was nearer to home, and so was the money. 'What Shall It Profit A Man To Gain The Whole World And Lose his youngest boy to the pit?' To Hell, and blind damnation. Go, you."

That must have been the only time I ever heard my father swear beyond a word and under the breath, or in a joke, and even going down in the cage with all the other men that morning I was still more frightened of his eyes than the speed of drop and the feeling of nothing under me. Never did I forget that fall, but again, I remember it in the Cambrian, every word, not in English. A few of these newspapers Ceridwen wrapped thick for packing are Cambrian, but the larger are English, that we spread to cover scrubbed floors, or tore in squares and strung for the hook out in the back. The first toilet roll I ever saw was in Evans, Sugar and Sand, and he used to keep them out in the fowlhouse because Mrs. Evans said they were rude, and for a long time buying one was thought to be a sin and you had to whisper for them, and I, the youngest, had to be pushed to go to the shop, for the girls turned their faces, and my brothers would have prayed never even to dream.

Strange to me, now, the way we thought then.

Looking at myself as a boy I remember plain as sitting here every word in Cambrian, always with thought of my mother and father because nothing much happened to me without them. As a young man in the Atlantic Colony, hearing myself speak, remembering what I did, I know I was rougher and the Cambrian I spoke was harsher, because I was a Southerner, and most of the pioneers were from the North. No longer was I home, but homesick, all the way over in Patagonia, with few friends and a strange life, at least for a time, so that I had to apply myself to the narrow way of work and thrift or I might have become the failure I thought I was.

Not until I reached the Andes, and working in shadow of the Cordilleras, was I sure.

But then, I was with Lal.

It took a long time to go down from the Singing Mountain, that first time, and we were digging most of the way, but the people in the Valley saw our fires that night and came to meet us and showed a better path. Many of them had been there long before Colonel Fontana led the pioneer wagon train over from the Atlantic Colony, and they still thought of themselves as part of New Cambria. They laughed at trouble with Indios. There was none, and with them there had been only friendship. Indios most of them had, working in the fields and out on the pampas, and some had two or three girls helping in the house. Others, of course, never allowed an Indio near the door and proud of it, though, strange, there were always plenty of girls and boys in the family to do the work without pay. Everything has a reason.

Most of us had a square league of land given by the Government, and mile on mile of common land nearby, though everywhere was forest except already cleared, either by fire, or cut down with the ax and burned for fuel or stacked for timber. Looking at what little had been done over the years, we knew we had work and to spare.

The people in the Andes were different in many ways from those over in the Atlantic Colony. They were so few, and spread across the leagues, and they seemed hardier, browner, thinner, and kinder with everybody because they had been through many bad years, and they knew we were going to have a good taste before we were much older, and sorry without saying so for not being able to do more for us.

Our place was miles along the river in thick forest. Gwenonwy and Donato were next up, Rhinberry across on the other side, and Vyrnwy furthest, and Doli and Solva in between. We knew we were there when Corianth Austin, next door to us, pointed to the end post of his bit of fence made of split trunks. For the next six miles, everything was Lal's and mine, and a wonderful feeling that is, too.

We were in early spring and new green was out and the sky was blue without a cloud, and beyond the forest the sun was hot, but by the time we had chosen a place to camp, the light was going. While a sheep was on the grill we sat down, Lal, Gwenonwy, Donato, Rhinberry, and me, and we made a plan. It was no use two of us trying to clear timber, pull up roots, plow and build a house all alone. Gwenonwy had to go back to her ranch in the Territory to look at the sheep and take stores for the peons, and Lal had to think about Maes Corwen and the flocks and herds at least twice a year. Gwenonwy had two peons with her, and Lal had three, so we would lose seven in work for weeks at a time.

We shook hands, all of us, on a plan to clear one space each for a house and garden as it came, starting with ours, going on to Donato's and over to Rhin's. First, we cut down the smallest trees except those useful for wind-breaks, stacked the trunks, and piled the branches for fuel. Once we had a space, Rhin went over it with a plow, and planted potatoes and small plots of vegetables. When the big area was clear of saplings and brush, then we started on the tall trees, most of cypress, maitén, and coihué. Sorry we were to see them come down, too, although we saved a fine stand where the house was going to be, and other islands of timber where the cattle and sheep would have shelter from snow.

If you have never cut through a bole with an ax, sawn it in plank lengths, roped and pulled the stack with oxen to the timber yard, and then gone back to dig out and pull up the root, you know nothing about work. We used to fall on our sheepskins at night many a time too tired to give a kiss, not because we forgot but because we slept. Bandsaw, ax, pick, shovel, all meant the same. If we were not sawing we were chopping, and if not chopping then picking into earth about the roots, and shoveling deep to get the chains under so that the oxen could pull. Good friends of ours those oxen were, too. Lal and Gwenonwy went in once or twice a month to get stores and always brought back a few sacks of corn for the animals. Most people never bothered, but that measure morning and night gave us good value in the work, and when one of them broke a leg under a falling root, Rhinberry and his Indios smoked the strips and we had tender meat almost through the winter. Pigs we bought and fattened for bacon and ham, sheep and cattle we smoked, and fish from the river, and that little smoke shed was filled long before the first heavy snow, and thank God, too. The others knew something about the country and stored against any chance. Donato and me, alone, well, we would have died. There were no roads, of course, and no tracks that a townsman's eye would see. In those first two years I went into the village once, to get a whetstone because mine broke when the horses stampeded and smashed the tool shed. Our houses were not built until after that first Christmas, the best and I think the strangest I ever had. The logs we trimmed and stacked, generally at night or on Sundays, but only when enough land had been cleared to plow late crops of potatoes, vegetables, and cereals. All that time, of course, Lal and I were not married. We built good toldos of logs for each of us to dress and bath in, but we slept in the wagons. Lal had hers next to mine with Rhin at one end, and Gwenonwy and Donato on the other, with a thatched place for the baby and the laundry in front. That baby was a little wonder. Never can I remember hearing him make a noise, but for most of the day he was off with the Indio girls to Rhin's where they were curing hides and carding wool and making carpets for the houses.

The village, or, as we called it, the City of the Mill, or the Colony of Sixteenth October, as it was known to the Government because of the day when the main column got there years before, had a long wide street with wooden houses here and there, and a corner shop, a couple of wine bars, a mill, a chapel, and a school, and that was all, but considering that everything had to be built in spare time by volunteers, it was a small miracle. While I was looking at it, I knew I ought to be back on our place with fifty things to do, and the guilt I felt to be sitting there doing nothing I knew was shared by others I saw waiting impatiently in the shop. They had a smile, and a greeting and a touch of the hat for everybody, and off. The women kissed each other, shouted something over their shoulders, and off, too, horseback, trap or wagon, all the same. Everybody had a conscience, a sense of duty and no time, but if they could have seen what was to happen after they went, perhaps more than one might have considered the luxury of a dawdle and a gentle word.

That place was a utilitarian marvel, and no wonder, because Moishe Levy owned it, him of the Everything Under the Sun, Twice, emporium over in the City of Lewis. Geza Paal managed, and his wife Tina kept the accounts and made a good cup of tea. Everything useful to a farm was there, and I found the nails I wanted and a set of blades and saws, wire and net, jute in rolls, cement, chimney pots, pipe, and best of all, big galvanized iron baths. Geza got me a wagon to carry them in but he refused any money.

"Mistress Corwen has credit," he said. "No good getting things tangled. Your name or hers, it's the same, and Moishe doesn't want money from here. Too much risk. Your account goes over there, and it's paid there. So have what you like."

"But don't you use money here, then?" I asked him. "I mean, for meat and bread, and things?"

He laughed.

"Look," he said. "Not one of these people here's sold an animal for the past two years. Nobody to buy. No money to pay. Who buys corn if he can grow it? Milk? They pour it in the ground. No road anywhere. No town anywhere. No market. So? No sale."

"A bright lookout," I said. "Are we building to starve?"

"Richest country on earth," he said. "Only the indolent starve. You can grow enough. You can clear land. Breed sheep. Cattle. That's meat and wool. With a road to the coast, there's your market. But if you take my advice, get a piece of the pampas, outside. Keep sheep there. They don't need much attention. Good rams, a little thought at the right time, you'll have a wool-clip. Fleeces. Carcasses? We need a freezing plant first. That's years off. But it'll take you the years to get settled, no?"

Years, yes. True words.

Even getting water to the houses was a beautiful joke that took months. Before I had always thought of water in a tap. They had running water in the City of Lewis, and many of the farms had pipes, though most used a well and a bucket, or the river. But to pipe water into a cistern in our clearing was something else again. Of course, Rhinberry was only watching me, and Lal and he enjoyed the joke.

"Poor Mr. South," Lal said. "How will you raise water to fill a cistern from a flat old river? A line of Indios with buckets? The water will cost gold for the glass. Better stick to a morning and night fill, yes?"

"No," I said. "I am sick of an outhouse, and a hole in the ground. I will have a pull-the-plug, and hot water for a good shave, and even enough for a bath. So wait, you."

Well, of course, Rhin had the secret. He and his Indios came in one Sunday morning with the oxen dragging tree trunks, split down the middle and hollowed with an ax, each about twenty foot long, so that they looked like half-canes. Even then I was dull.

"Look, boy," he said, and pointed to the waterfall higher up on the hillside. "Did you notice that patient little one, by there? He hasn't been dry all the summer. He will only fill more from now till spring. We put one of these hollowed logs in the water. Support it with a Y timber. Fit the end of the next under the lip, let it fall an inch, and fit the next and the next till the water runs in a wooden canal all the way down to pour in the cistern, here. Yes?"

Light.

We went out looking for branches with a fork strong enough to support a log, and we used crossed timbers for the shorter heights, but the comedy came when we had to fit the canal with just enough fall to bring water gently into the cistern. The waterfall was a good six hundred yards away and at least a hundred feet above us. It would have taken an engineer to do it right the first time, but of course, we got sopping and drowned because if there is one thing that will fall if you give it a chance, it is water, and if I never knew it before, then was when I was taught.

"Bath?" Lal said. "There is no need, boy. Just keep playing with your old logs, when will you ever need one? Wet through with you, all day, every day. There is nice and clean. But you could do with a clip. Like an old caracul ram, you are, boy. Come here and give me a bristler."

I had a beard below my chest and hair on my shoulders, but of course we all did, until the girls took sheep shears and gave us a clip. Lal gave me a couple of good ones, and I felt better, but I wanted to shave. I am one with a disgust for long hair and a beard. I feel dirty with a day's scrub on the chin and fit for the Pit with more. But in those days there was nothing to shave with, no place, and no time, and in any event, the women had no personal comfort, either, so it was unfair to take time from the day when they were loyal, and said nothing, and worked as if they were men.

Lal suffered as a woman.

Only once I saw her standing, head down, with an arm stiff against a tree, and I went to her, not knowing, and put a hand on her, and she turned as a cat.

"Go from here," she said, between teeth. "Leave me."

That night she came into the wagon and I woke, hearing the rustling, and I felt the weight of a hand on my shoulder.

"Huw," she whispered. "I couldn't sleep. Forgive me for this afternoon. There is a time, you see? Such pain, you could die."

"Darling mine," I said. "It's enough. Gone. Forgotten. A good cup of tea, now then?"

She lay back, and breathed out at the canopy.

"O, God, a cup of hot tea," she said. "Thin. Only a drop of milk. Almost no sugar. And hot. Yes. Yes, please."

In that time there were no pills, not much medicine, and a cup of tea was universal comfort, and for some of us it still is, and best of them all. Down I went, and blew sparks in the fire, and the kettle bubbled like a good one, and up I went with a cup of tea, and she was sleeping, O, a beautiful dream. Shame to wake her, and I was crawling out and my foot caught something, and there was a clatter to cross the eyes, and every half-bred cur in the Andes was barking forever, and I saw her move, and put the cup beside her, and she came up on her elbows and turned.

"I will drink this now and sleep here," she said. "I will sleep here always from tonight. Cold it is. And lonely. When shall we have the house ready?"

"The moment I can see a clear week," I said. "If I could find a preacher, we would marry before then."

"We are married now," she said. "Anybody who will make me a cup of tea this time of night, we are married. Not another word. Give me a kiss, boy. Angels' wings are warm above us. Sleep well."

From that moment, I was determined to have us under a roof before the next winter. Gwenonwy and Donato had to be first because of the baby, then us, and Rhinberry wanted to build his own place on the other side because of his Indios. A lot of people speak badly of Indios, but I believe they are only pointing at themselves. There are Indios and Indios, of course, just as there are whites and others, and I have seen whites without a bath from birth, with the dirt of generations on the floor, and the empty cans and weathered bones of a lifetime or two spread about the house. Those, it was, with most to say of Indios.

A lot of people in this world, it seems, take pleasure to have something to hate. Some I have met hate the Irish, others hate Jews, a lot hate us, and the Greeks, and Basques, and Poles, Negroes, and Chinians.

They hate, therefore they are.

Rhinberry's family of Indios had called in others, whether relations or friends, from both the Tehuelche and the Araucano. They were two different nations, in size, thought, and color, different as Africans from Arabs, and the best of them were people good as I ever met. Indio men have only one duty, to hunt food for their families, and they never did anything else except train ponies and make saddlery and weapons. Indio women looked after the children, gathered fuel and kept the fires alight, made clothes or tents from guanaco pelts, and cooked what was brought to them. No use to compare their lives with ours. They had no books, or knowledge of anything except what they were born to.

"I will trust a Tehuelche before the best white I ever knew," Rhinberry said. "You can be a little more careful with an Araucano because he's had to fight Europeans for three hundred years and he's learned a few lessons. But my people over there are gold. A hunting party is in now. Tell me what you want, and I will have all the men here for the next couple of weeks. Simply tell them. It is done."

Some of them cut the granite and rolled it down, and others chipped, sitting in the little quarry under the waterfall. They only had to be shown how to use the hammer once, and I never saw them stop for a rest or sit back for a few moments' chatter. They worked, but not because it was work. They had no idea what work was. Their business was hunting, and anything else was a waste of time. What we were doing, with chipping stone, and hollowing logs, and stacking timber, and plowing and planting, to them was madness. They were helping because Rhinberry asked Saiheque, their cacique, and he gave the orders. Even when they saw Donato and me filling the house foundations with rock, and squaring the outside with the rough-faced stone, they were still sure we were lunatics. We got the corner posts up, and Donato used the saw to cut key-notches in the logs and I smoothed them with the plane until they fitted, and then we began to stack them into four walls.

Well, when those men and women saw the timbers, cut to size long before, going up, wall by wall, and a doorway appearing front and back, and windows, and presently, a good big square house solid in front of them, we could barely stop from laughing. They could not be coaxed to understand how a pile of timber became a house with doors and windows. They were looking in, some at the front, some at the back, and not believing they could see each other, and running round there to make sure.

But when we bolted in the rafters and put planks across the tops of the walls to lift the rooftree, we had all the help we needed from some of the strongest men I have ever seen, all of them head and shoulders taller than us, and lifting that heavy trunk, trimmed smooth and oiled, as if it were a pole. Once it was in place, we notched the ribs in, and then came the time for hammer and nails. All the planks were handed up, and fitted to the ribs, Donato on one side, me on the other, knocking in two-inchers, each of us with a group watching those nails disappear as children watch a conjurer. They were putting their fingers where the nails had gone in, trying to see where they were.

Saiheque, taller, broader than the rest, never budged from my side. We had not a word between us, for he spoke only Arauco, but we did very well with signs, and when I gave him the hammer and my bag of nails I might have been giving him a thousand horses—the only gift they valued—and he started hitting nails in everywhere till I showed him that only one nail had to go through one place in the plank to one place in the rib, and on to the next. He never needed telling again. They all learned quickly and I can never remember telling any of them twice. They came in a group, and they stood, and they watched, and they might stand for hours, or days. Those with interest would stay. Others went off to find something else. In that way, Donato and I found our workmen, the first we employed in the valley, and each had one job, and only that job, and you would never get him to do another. Saiheque's job was anything to do with a hammer and nails, at first. He was extraordinary with that hammer, because he was strong and with a good eye. He could put a four-inch nail in flat with two hits, though I never could, and I never saw anybody else do it, either. But when I showed him what a plane could do in the way of smoothing and polishing, eh, then Saiheque seemed to grow feathers. He stared, and passed his hand, and laid his face flat to the board to see the sun reflecting, and picked up the plane, and turned it over and over, and looked up, then, at me.

And smiled.

As if we had a big secret between us, he smiled.

From that moment, no more hammer and nails.

Any planing to be done, Saiheque would do it, and God help anybody putting a nose in.

For months, in spare moments we had dragged in tree trunks fallen in forest fires of generations before, fine timber, twenty, thirty and forty foot long, that we band-sawed into planks and stacked, though they wanted little enough seasoning. A lot was cypress, and some alerces, a wonderful deep red wood that we marked for paneling and tiling. Well, when the roofboards were up, and the tarpaper was on and tacked, then we began setting good big tiles from alerces. It has the virtue of cutting straight, thin, and it will stand any weather through a lifetime. Donato did the cutting and he soon had more helpers than tools. Up went Saiheque again, inch-nails through the tile into the slat, working from the edge of the overhang, straight-legged, head down toward the ground, never straightening for a rest, simply taking a tile, knocking it in, pacing sideways to the next till he reached the edge of the roof, and then passing sideways the other way. He never stood straight till he finished, up on top of the rooftree, and then he ran down the slope of the roof and jumped off, and no harm.

"We could train these," Donato said, and very respectful. "We'd have no need sending to the City for help. Everybody we need is here, and better than we'd get from outside. How do we begin?"

Gwenonwy and Lal looked at each other and laughed.

"You are in sound sleep, boy," Gwenonwy said to him. "This is playtime for them. In a couple of days, when the scouts have marked guanaco, they will be off. They must have food. And in any event, they will be moving north for the winter. You won't get them to stay. Or work."

"If they earned a week's money, they will go off and buy bottles and you will never see them till they are empty," Lal said. "Perhaps yes, perhaps never."

"Rhinberry's people do well," I said.

"They are not true Indios," Lal said. "Not Araucano or Tehuelche. Not of the hunters, not of the fighters. These with Saiheque are *manzanero*. Among the best. But they will hunt and roam till they die. Work is not in them."

Saiheque and a dozen more at that time were always in the tool shed because I was planing timber to line the rooms. They stared to see the big plane take off the broad, fine shavings, and they had a name for each one of the set of eight, and the smallest, naturally, was favorite, the three-quarter inch, that peeled a surface fine as skin, they called *ujcha Domo*, the Little Virgin, and the biggest was *huilkar Haün*, or Big Mouth.

One day I came back from putting up a side of the living-room panels, and Saiheque had Big Mouth at work on a rough plank, and I stood there, watching him. He moved slowly, careful of his strength, and of the tool and the wood, but cursing in his throat because never mind how he put his head, there was no shine.

He had no notion of something flat, or of a level surface.

The idea was not in his mind, because it had never been in his time.

So there I had to start.

I picked up a piece of smooth board and held it toward the light so that he could see it shine. A piece of rough scantling held the same way gave no shine, but when I passed the Little Virgin down a couple of times, I made him see she had left a shining path.

He looked at me, and in his eyes, far at the back, I thought I could see a glint, perhaps almost a smile, and I thought I could be looking at a human mind back tens of thousands of years, feeling its way into light.

First, I found a couple of small rough places in the plank and put his finger on them to feel, and chose a number four blade. A couple of passes and they were smooth. I felt them, and rubbed his fingers across them, and looked at him, but I might just as well have looked at the wall. Nothing is so flat as an Indio face when that is what they want.

I found larger patches where he had dug, and passed his hand over them. Big Mouth smoothed them, and I passed my hand, and took his hand and pressed well down to make him feel it was flat. On and on, little places at a time, plane smooth and then touch, and each time I put the size of the shaving against the plane to show him that each had a different bite. When the plank was quite smooth, then I started to work on the final shave, the one that brings up the polish, though to make sure he would see, I took the lamp off the hook and put it down low where it would shine over the surface.

When the plank was smooth, I put a rough cut on the bench and passed his hand over it, and over the one just planed, and then I pulled him down until his eyes were level with both surfaces. In one, the lamp shone a pale splash, in the other, nothing. Again I passed his hand over the finished plank, and took him around to feel the other. For moments he rubbed his palms over the rough, and the smooth, and went to the other end, changing hands. The smooth one gave no sound, the other scratched. The lesson was finished when he walked down with the flat of his hand on the rough, and got a good splinter in the ball of his thumb. He took it out with his teeth, and spat, watched the blood bead, and rubbed it on the short leather apron about his waist.

He took Big Mouth from the rack, felt for rough places as I had done, and smoothed them, chose other planes by size of shaving, and one by one, feeling and planing, he smoothed the plank of rough places, and then began at the top and went down, fining. When he was finished, not before, he knelt to look. No need to tell me, because I knew it was well done, and good as I would ever want. Without a word to him, I picked up both planks and carried them out to the house, and put them in place against the wall, ran the brace in, put in the screws, and they were both part of the paneling, with nothing to tell the difference between his work and mine. Only to make all plain, I went round the three sides that were up, rubbing the flat of my hand over the surface, and looked at him and smiled.

He stood in the door, watching me.

Feeling can burst the Indio throat but the face will never show sign. A mask of wood will show more. Tears may run from the inside of their eyes, but the eyes will stay open, with no sound, no move anywhere, nothing to tell they feel, except the tears that run and run.

Saiheque's tears ran small rivers, amazing in such a big man.

With my hand out I went to him, and he drew the knife from the thong about his waist, and I thought it was all over with me. Without looking down he cut a gash in the fat at his thumb root, and clenched his fist to fill the palm with blood. He took my hand and cut a good one in the same place, and my palm filled. He slapped his hand into mine, and squeezed like a ton-press, and said something, and put fist to mouth, and slapped me on the back with the other hand, and screamed long, and whirled about almost not to be seen, and off, out.

"Well," Lal said, coming from the back. "What is Mr. South doing, all blood, here?"

"Some of it is mine," I said and tried to stop the flow.

"Leave it," she said. "It will go sticky and stop on its own. You must let the blood run. It's for him. His is for you. You are blood-brother to Saiheque. All that is his is yours. All that is yours is his. Well, that's what they say. I shall have a word or two, there. But you have got a true friend. Nothing you can want in this part of the land. It is yours."

"What I want is a preacher, and get married," I said.

"Well, Rhin is going in tomorrow because he thinks a preacher is in the Colony at last," she said. "Gwenonwy's baby will be two years old and he ought to be baptized. Would you like to be married at the same time?"

In that voice she could have asked me if I would like another rasher, but her eyes gave her away. I made a good grab, but she was off, laughing, and I had to wait there for the blood to stop, because the water trough was just outside the door.

No sound was in the house. The living-room walls were almost finished. The bricks were drying out in the bedroom and bathroom, and Donato had almost finished the piping. Gwenonwy and Lal were talking near the fire in the kitchen shed, and I could smell meat on the grill, and biscuits browning, and the wondrous breath of beef bone soup.

Perhaps it was a movement, though I will swear not.

A girl was looking at me from the window farthest from the firelight. The lamp was on a peg behind me. Perhaps she was fifteen feet away. For a few moments I took no notice. I simply looked, thinking she was one of the girls from Rhin's place, or somebody helping Gwenonwy with the baby.

But I knew she was more beautiful than any Indio I had ever seen. She was looking at me. Not only at, but in, and through me. I remembered the way the Indio girls looked at Beretroff. I saw Michaye again, and sun alive in ink silk.

Those eyes never faltered, never blinked, black and yet filled with light, in a face pale against the dark sky. They looked through and through me for long seconds on end, and what happened when I thought of Lal, or held her, was happening then to me, though only looking, no move, at a pair of eyes without smile or frown, and yet with all feeling, and leaving sign hard in my body.

In a turn of the head she was gone and no sound.

I stood there, and I knew that if that one crooked her finger, I must go.

2

Up, into many a singing mountain and down, through forests and river-cool green valleys I have walked joyous in a sighing dream, hearing always the Voice of my People raised to the Glory of God, and never clearer than now, all these years later, certain in my soul that we still have a good chance.

This couple of pairs of socks were knitted for me by Angharad in the last weeks I was at school, and darned by my mother—but you would have to look again to find those small demesnes of patience in hours of dear days—and the shirts sewn by Bronwen still have my initial over the heart in red and blue. My father said I was marked like a Town jail convict with me, and Bron laughed and said only an old thief would wear them except the one she made them for, and my mother told her not to listen, and she wished from the heart she had the time to embroider so beautifully.

But that was wrong again, and she sat back in the quick, savage silence, here, and Bron walked out, and my mother closed her eyes, because Ivor was dead, and in the house down The Hill was plenty of time, long days and unending nights, but no man. Perhaps it was for that my mother sent me down there and without knowing it, gave everything a twist. In those days men respected women, but today respect seems a joke, to be spoken about with a hand to the side of the mouth, and a nudge. Owen asked me how I could stay so long near her, and nothing.

"For Christ's sake," I said. "What do you mean, nothing? Many and many a time I could have smashed the door. But for what? To go in bed? And after a minute or two, what? Tell me, what?"

"Well," he said, and smiled. O, a man of the world, our Owen. "It might have done the pair of you no harm."

"Without it no harm was done," I said. "When she married again, she was herself, as she had been before she married Ivor. If I had been at fancy, would she have been as much?"

"Curious way to look at things," he said. "It's funny, but you've still got a lot of the Valley in you. For me, it's like another world. I think we took everything too romantically. Too radically. Now, we know a little more."

"And knowing a little more, we are more than a little less," I said. "Radical we were because we had a father and mother, and they stood no nonsense. We did as we were told. Radical? You chose the right word. Yes, from the root. And because of that, Bron was safe with me. But long before that, I was safe with her."

But there was time to grow, too.

It seems silly, now, to speak or even think in such a way, especially among the smart and clever, or the pigsfoot-and-dull, because they are all the same, one or other, some in cars or rented beds, and the others with bicycles and loose in a field, but no difference. The same it was for us to go up the mountain, if it was few and far, but in those days was real risk. I only knew Ceinwen and a couple of others and thank God, too. If there had been more, I might have thanked less, for then it would have been not sweet adventure but only dull opportunity, not dearly remembered marvel, but one fool after another, and to the Devil.

This suit is the first with long trews I ever had, made for me by Hwfa Williams and Old Twm and put together in such argument of tape and chalk that nine days of wonder it is how they came about me. Of course everybody thought they were deadliest enemies from the way they shouted at each other, but I found out it was only a little game to dab some color in the thread of days. Old Thomas the Mill was there that afternoon I went in for my first fitting. Very kind he was with everybody, but no mind for anything, and no memory, though since his sons kept the mill going, he and Mrs. Thomas lived well and he was always dressed for Town, gloves, stick, and if not a bowler, then a top hat, that Old Twm used the big brass goose on to bring up a shine to see yourself.

"There, you, Mr. Thomas, my little one," he said, and held out the hat with the brim between the tips of his middle fingers. "The Prince of Wales haven't got a bit better, I will bet you."

"Oh, yes, well, I suppose," Old Thomas said, and took the hat and gave it a rub with his sleeve, but the wrong way, and all the nap came up. "Who is he, now then? New with us, yes?"

"Prince of Wales," Old Twm said, staring at the nap. "Son of Queen Victoria. The next king, boy."

"Yes, yes," Mr. Thomas said, and put the hat on carefully in the middle of his head. "They had that place down there near the Miskin, isn't it? O, yes. Knew them years. Well, well. Very safe, yes. First of the month, money down, a pleasure, yes. And gone to live in the Miskin, is it? Sad loss, yes. Well, getting very dark. Good morning all."

"Wait for your ulster, Mr. Thomas, my little one," Hwfa said, from the corner, and a real proprietor's voice. "Another button, and you shall have it warm against the weather. Some old fools would send you off, and a pneumonia the least to expect. If it was them, good God, I would starve, here."

"We are come close, now, indeed to God," Old Twm said, eyes up, and very serious. "Ham we were having today, see. Pure knuckle. I was picking splinters from my teeth hours, here."

"It would still be a lie, even if he had any teeth," Hwfa, and no interest. "A splendid ham, it was."

"Was, yes," Old Twm said, threading a needle, one eye shut at Old Thomas. "A Beast of the Revelations did start at the snout and chew to the tail, and down all the knuckles. We had one. Bitten to polish, then. 'tatoes and points, us. A mouthful of 'tatoes, see, and point to the ghost of a good ham, aye."

"Thank God you have got blessings," Hwfa said, and bit off a cotton. "A dry crust and a cheese rind you would have it hard to find outside. Not like the succulence we were having here, today. Best animal in the Five Valleys, and a premium, indeed."

"His own family always first," Old Twm said. "Premium, the lot. Succulence? Good God, you could suck till you dropped dead, here. A mouthful of old spit you would be having."

"More than spit did swell that old belly by there," Hwfa shouted, and fisted the wooden shoulder to creak. "Never filled anywhere else except in by here, and that old Three Bells bar have never known the ring of one penny-piece from you that didn't come from in by here for the past forty-odd years, man and boy. Thousands from me gone into those pockets, and nothing back, except idleness and complaints and lies, morning till night, *ar diâwl ach-i*."

"And *diâwl*, he is from his breath with him," Old Twm whispered with spit in my ear, and basted long white stitches over the top of my arm. "Thousands to these pockets? Tens of thousands to those over by there. And no wonder. A knuckler? No cost to him. A glass of beer? Cost. To who? Me. And who have got a half interest in the Three Bells? Be so good to be putting your eyes over in the corner, by there. Old shy-of-lock. Out of one pocket, and in the other. Box and Cox."

"Very good, too," Old Thomas said. "I put some in. Years ago, yes. Best in the orchard, no doubt. There's another, I forget. But better in the oven."

Old Twm closed one eye at me.

"Cox's pippins, now, is it, Mr. Thomas?" he said, with

sweetness. "A beauty is in squat over by there. But only the Devil will oven him, *ar diâwl.*"

"She would like a cutting, indeed," Old Thomas said. "From everywhere I brought one. Some took. Some not. Apples, yes, you have got to know."

"Adam thought the same," Old Twm said, in a good Bible voice, looking at Hwfa. "Aprons of fig leaves? The first tailor started his business then and there. No surprise to anybody what the name was. Big letters, yes, over the Tree of Knowledge."

"I know one who would never read it, to begin," Hwfa said, and sewing very steady with him. "And if an old snake was poking his head, I will tell the name. Him, now, with the cuff of a sleeve level with the boy's shoulder. Forty-odd years in the business, thousands earned, and knowing less than on the first day."

"A splendid master," Old Twm said. "A credit, indeed. And the cuff will do where it is. He have got room to grow."

"And for another six like him," Hwfa said, and snapped thread. "Ready, Mr. Thomas. A touch with the brush, and the best ulster in the country, yes. Bill on the table beside you, sir."

"Yes, well, the Mrs. will have to have a look at that," Old Thomas said. "I am here very late, see. I will have my death from the damp."

"Not with a garment like this, Mr. Thomas," Hwfa said, and flicked the brush, a wand from other realms. "Now we will put it on, and I will step down the street to pay respects to Mrs. Thomas."

"Over the mountain today and tomorrow," Old Thomas said, quick, and off with his spectacles. "Not expected back till my youngest son's wife do get here, yes. So you have got a half with the Three Bells, is it? The Mrs. have always said you are a well-found little man, here."

"If I was paid for my owings, I would be found a bit sooner, too," Hwfa said. "Cloth and thread and work, and special lining, extra pockets, trimming, horn buttons, all extra, rent, heat, light, amice collar, and wages again, good God, where is the end, here? If I am in the workhouse, my debtors will have their names shouted from the courthouse steps, a fine thing, isn't it?"

"Morgan Howells, the same," Old Twm said, and Old Thomas leaned over the table, hooking his stick for the ulster but it was just out of reach. "A publican, too. Drank everything, like an old fish with him."

"Not a drop here to be drunk," Hwfa said, and a corner of the green baize apron to his nose and pretending to cry. "A good cup of tea we were going to have, now just. When bills are paid, and money seen, and enough to buy a bit of sugar, and a pinch of tea, and the wet of a drop of milk, here."

"If I haven't got the coat, can I be blamed to owe?" Old Thomas said, and breathless. "Have first, then owe, isn't it?"

"I will tell you what, then, Mr. Thomas," Hwfa said, and the shoe-button eyes going between my sleeve, the brush, and the clock. "Quarterly rental due the fifth, yes. I will take from that."

"Oh no, now wait," Old Thomas said, and coming in a fluster with him. "Spoil the books, that will. My poor eldest boy, see, regular trouble with the bank. Books wrong, money in lack? O, dam', no."

"Him or me, one of us, anyway," Hwfa said, looking through the window and waving at somebody very careless. "I would rather it was him, indeed. Big shoulders, and by proportion, bigger pockets."

"Well, now, wait you," Old Thomas said, and pecking finger and thumb in his waistcoat. "I believe the Mrs. gave me a couple of sovereigns for something for the house. Perhaps that will do for the time, see?"

"O, spoil the books, that will," Hwfa said, sharp and coming very practical, fingers in poke to work on my other sleeve. "To item, five-and-a-half-guineas, E and O E. Then the books will come beautiful with us, yes."

Only the sound of somebody walking on the cobbles outside, and the whisper of Hwfa's chalk marking the cloth on my back, and Mrs. Tossall calling chickens in the garden behind. Old Thomas stood, a rock, looking at the wall, but then he turned his back and across me Hwfa winked at Old Twm's wink, not winks really, but a focus of ancient eyes in knowledge universal beyond time.

"Well, now then, there you, five and a half, exact to the sixpence," Old Thomas said, and propped the roll of sovereigns, and put a half sovereign next, and two half crowns and six pennies. "Only today I have got it. Other days no. But the Mrs. said I might need some. She will be sending somebody to look for me, see. Late, yes. Where is the coat with you?"

"Please to turn and put out the arms, Mr. Thomas, my little one, if it is not greatly to inconvenience," Old Twm said, and his chins up with importance, holding out the ulster. "Never have I had the luck to put somebody better into a nobler garment, and every stitch and snip on the premises, yours truly in the help, and a real pleasure here, yes, indeed to God. One of the gentry you do look."

"Yes, well, everybody a good day, now then," Old Thomas said, and pushed the hat farther on with the flat of his hand, used the walking stick to carve the air in front, and walked out with the coat half-on, half-off, and Hwfa shut the door behind, and stood there watching him down the street.

"Twm," he said, and looked all the way round to where he stood. "Did you see what happened to that one when I mentioned names shouted from the courthouse? And no memory? A charm. A miracle. Give me a list, now, of the owers. We will do a little more."

"Good, you," Old Twm said, and grunting up, clouting dust off a long book. "I am in hopes to see the last knuckler on earth, here."

"You will go over the cliff just behind him," Hwfa said, and picked up the money. "Gold, silver, and copper. There is handy. And pretty, too. Huw, did you bring me something from your Dada?"

"One sovereign," I said, and gave it to him. "The remainder on delivery."

"Well, good God," Old Twm said. "We are come very commercial all of a sudden, isn't it? Is it polite to ask? The boy will be learning some strange manners, here, yes?"

Hwfa took a lump of my cheek and pinched.

"Do good work all your days," he said. "Then hold out your hand and ask for the money. That is the lesson I have learned in this establishment."

"Right," Twm said, and held out his hand. "A couple of weeks' extras owing, here."

"When the client is from the premises, then we will speak business," Hwfa said looking up at the roof.

"To Hell with the client," Old Twm shouted. "Two weeks' extras, alterations Lewis Prosser, trimming to Mrs. Mostyn, a mile of braid on Nan Mardy's three quarter—three quarter? —good God, a bloody tent it is—"

"Hisht your language, now," Hwfa whispered. "Huw, tell your Dada I will be ready Wednesday next, five of the clock, punctual, if the old Devil himself isn't here before to destroy us for mouths, aye, black as the Pit."

"My two weeks' first, and to Hell with the Devil," Old Twm whispered back, with his nose an inch away from Hwfa's. "What is for the goose is for the gander, so let's have you."

"The goose is by there," Hwfa shouted, and pointed to the big shining iron. "The gander we know from the mouths of babes and old sucklings. So let us be having a bit of charcoal in by there and ready to press Nan Mardy's in a bit of shape, and here in a moment, nothing done except old chat, with you. Greatly beloved, what did I do to have this old thing jumping on my back these years?"

Old Twm was hitting the goose on the board, throwing in charcoal and tossing sparks one end to another, and Hwfa screaming to him to stop in case to burn the house down, the Twm hitting twice as hard and shouting to Hell with the house, and the bell rang, and there was Nan, just in time to listen to Hwfa, and Twm held the goose quiet for her to hear, and Nan's hair that was straight as candles must have been in tight curls for months with her.

Out went Nan and closed the door very quiet to make it worse, and Old Twm lay back with his slippers in the air laughing himself hopeless, and Hwfa stood against the wall, hands clasped, face in twist, eyes tight shut.

Nan was on the corner when I went out, and I could see she was in black frown, which was no surprise to me, then. We have become used to gross language of any sort, but even a damn in those days was considered foul use, and if you forgot yourself in front of a woman you would be lucky not to have your mouth stopped by a fist or a boot. But those were the days of the Book, of the nicety, and discipline, and often I have wondered when they stopped, and why.

Cyfartha told me, the first time I came back, about Hwfa and Old Twm. For more than fifty years they worked in that little shop, and one morning Ellis the Post found Hwfa in his big chair, with the lamp still burning. Old Twm was too drunk to go to the funeral, and when he came sober, he was in such a sink of shame that never again did he touch a drop. Worse, it was, that Hwfa left him everything, cash and property—"to the best-hearted friend any man has ever had"—with land and houses all the way through the Five Valleys and, of course, the half-interest in the Three Bells.

"He was son of Williams, Surveyor, so he had an eye for property," Cyfartha said. "He told me he would rather have the peace of needle and thimble. Well, day after day we were waiting for Old Twm, but he never came near. So one night, here, Dai said we ought to stroll down and scrape a couple of barnacles, eh Dai?"

"Right, you," Dai said. "And off we went, middle of business, and there he was, under the lamp, still working. So I said, come you, now then. A good pint will work a wonder. No, he said. Only one here, and no time to waste. Get some help, I said. Bring back Hwfa, he said, and sewing away there, yes, and crying. Well, we went from there, eh, Cyfartha?"

"Sad couple, too," Cyfartha said. "Weeks nobody saw him, only Evans the Milk, and Tossal. Ellis the Post came in one night and said he couldn't get an answer. Business letters from the solicitors, yes. So Dai and me, hats on again, and down the road."

"Found him cross-legged there, leaning over the goose," Dai said. "Every bit of work in the shop folded tidy beside him, needle and cotton stuck in, and thimble beside. The racks were empty. He finished, and he went. Well, the old Coroner said it might be a suicide. Inhaling the smoke of charcoal, see. So Cyfartha and me, we had to have a quiet little word with him, too, eh, Cyfartha?"

"Private between us, my little one," Cyfartha said. "Not long in the lasting, but only to say the new Coroner would have comfort to know he was there because the one before him was doing a bit of inhaling somewhere on the mountain. With a couple behind the ear. So it was brought in Accidental, and we rolled a barrel down to the shop, and everybody came from everywhere to drink a good one, eh, Dai?"

"Splendid," Dai said. "And the doctor said he would have to cut the joints to lay him straight, but we said to Hell, cross-legged he worked, cross-legged he went, and cross-legged, by damn, he will go up there to Hwfa. So Cyfartha and me, we made a case from a couple of those boards in the bar, and he fitted beautiful, eh, Cyfartha?"

"Best bit of wood in the place, and French polish, a work of art, boy," Cyfartha said. "Well, they came from everywhere for the funeral. Thousands, then. You would think we were playing France for top of the table. A hill of flowers, see. And the singing was a wonder. Eighteen choirs, we had, and the boys on the early shift, here. But the shock was later. Eh, Dai?"

"Shock, yes," Dai said, and his eyes in blinks there. "Left everything to Cyfartha and me, mind. Everything, boy, For being trusting. A few pints a week? We never had a slate for

Old Twm. We said when he couldn't count, he'd had enough. He never did have enough, eh, Cyfartha? And never one pint out, for or against."

"A good one, him," Cyfartha said. "Couldn't read or write. A slate and pencil would have shamed him in front of everybody. So no slate for Old Twm. And all his property, and Hwfa's to us. For trust."

"Couple of wealthy men," I said, and surprised, because the Three Bells could have done with a coat of paint in and out, and their boots were hanging. "Haven't you thought of a trip, somewhere? Come with me. Have a look at London."

Well, they looked at each other and laughed.

"Here's all the London we want, in by here," Dai said, and nodded at the roof. "London? What can we do there? Drink better beer? I will bet a thousand, gold, not as good. See something? What, then? I haven't seen a good yard in front of me these years, eh, Cyfartha?"

"Right, you, my little one," Cyfartha said. "Once over the mountain and back is far enough for me. Besides, we haven't got the money. We told your sister's solicitors we wouldn't touch principal or interest for ten years, and after that, ten again, eh, Dai?"

"Not a halfpenny," Dai said, and hit the counter with that ram of a fist, looking no softer than I remembered those years ago in mornings on the mountain. "Yes, very kind she was. We were worried sick with all the property, so I said, who could help us, only Huw, if he was here. But you were off, and Cyfartha said there's Mrs. Iestyn Evans, London, Cardiff, and Capetown up at Tyn-Y-Coed. Angharad. So Ellis the Post took a letter, special delivery, and if I never move again, she was here the next morning, nine o'clock sharp, eh, Cyfartha?"

"Nine, on the tick, so she must have left the house not a moment after six forty-five," Cyfartha said. "And beautiful? Well, good God, we were hit to hell, here. Never anything more beautiful I have seen in my life, eh, Dai?"

"I will take an oath in my grave," Dai said, eyes to Heaven. "Beautiful. And kind? Well, she sent two solicitors of hers here. They made a company for us. They manage everything. Invest every penny. It's like having nothing. No worry to us, eh, Cyfartha?"

"Not a single worry in the world, Dai, my little one, except is the beer going flat with us, or not getting here in time," Cyfartha said. "Everything else a pleasure, and a wonder to live, yes, Dai?"

"A couple of selfish ones, isn't it?" Mrs. Tossall the Shop said, that morning. "Nothing they have done all their lives except old boxing and that pub. Quiet enough, mind. O, yes. Nothing wrong. But they could have married and had a family and be a bit of use. Selfish they are, and they will go lonely to the grave, poor boys. Not a tear except in drink."

"You never wanted to do something else, or go anywhere else?" I asked both of them, resting there on their elbows, in their sixties then, I suppose, though younger to look at, even with broken noses and filled ears. "Look now, there's a question I want to ask, if you won't think I am rude. Didn't you have a thought of a girl to look after you? Children? Two good ones, never married? Why?"

Dai rubbed his gums with thumb and forefinger.

"I thought I would be middleweight champion," he said. "You can't think of being married, and fight a champion, if you haven't got twenty rounds in you. No use to think of wearing a champion's belt. A woman will take five rounds away from you, any time. So I was very careful with women. But I didn't have a good manager. I had the wrong fights. Eight fights I had in London, see. I knocked them out in the first. So I was not a popular one. I didn't punish. I put them out. So they didn't let me fight. Here, I was fighting week in and out. Good money but no nearer the champion. One morning I got out of bed, and I was thirty-six. Yes. I never had a moment more solemn in my life, boy. Eh, Cyfartha? I knew the championship was gone from me. And without that, I was not who I thought I was. I was good enough only to open a school. But if you are training youngsters not to throw themselves away on a woman, can you run after women yourself? That's why. Nothing more to be said. Eh, Cyfartha?"

"The same, Dai, only I was a bigger fool," Cyfartha said. "If I could write, I would have been a good manager. I can hit, and I can talk. Women, yes. I had a lovely girl down there in Bridgend. She was worth more than five rounds. With her I was, before I went in with Young Gorbals. I did well to the tenth, but in the eleventh he knew I was tired. I stayed to the fifteenth. By praying. If I'd had that extra five rounds I'd have murdered him. He became the champion. From then, I never wanted to see a woman. Not even see one."

"But it never had effect on health?" I asked him. "Some there are who say if a man doesn't have a woman, it's unnatural. Unhealthy. Man born of woman, remember?"

Dai looked down the road to the winding wheel on the pithead, and Cyfartha looked up at the last little stunt of timber in sparse leaf on the mountain.

"I will tell you the sort of people they are," Cyfartha said, cold. "Eh, Dai?"

"Nothing more to be added," Dai said. "A nutshell, and gospel. As for being married, well, if you come up with the right girl, you have come very lucky with you. Some do, some don't. Me, I had good lodgings for years here. A bed, and a tub. Some do want a bit more. I didn't, and I still don't, eh, Cyfartha?"

"With you, boy," Cyfartha said. "A couple of nuns are coming up here every week for scraps. A new church down there. They've never been married, I suppose. Does anybody call them unhealthy? Better girls, you would have to go far. If people would put their snouts in business of their own, and leave everybody else's, we would be in a lovely world, indeed. A few women here never married. Who would call them unhealthy? Eh, Dai?"

"I have been looking back here," Dai said. "I don't remember a single woman, not one, who ever looked once at me. I don't remember one I would go to the chest for a clean collar to put on for. I was never in the way, see."

"Never in love," I said.

Cyfartha drank the beer in his glass, and waited for Dai to drink, and turned to the beer-pull.

"Love is in books," he said. "Read enough books, you will have wonderful ideas about love. Watcyn John used to read us chapters, here, every night. Beautiful, yes. If you acted like that outside here, somebody would hit a hole in you."

"But there is love," I said. "Not only in books, either. There is love, and people do suffer. Ordinary people. Wonderful to them. Ordinary to everybody else. Years they go on. Years they wait. Years they hope and pray. And for years after they curse what kept them apart. Curse every moment not together. Because of love."

Dai nodded, and made patterns on the counter with a little finger almost as thick as my wrist.

"I often think I would have liked to feel like that," he said. "But I wish I could have felt like a champion much more. Love suits some. It isn't much to run after girls. No trouble, boy. A shave and a box of chocolates, and good God, we're off."

He jabbed that short forefinger into his chest with sound of drums.

"This always did what I told it to," he said. "It never told me anything. Four o'clock out, five o'clock up the mountain. Six o'clock, back. Seven o'clock, work. Four o'clock, bath. Five o'clock, punchbag and skip. Six o'clock, a couple of pints and a plate of food, and eight o'clock in bed. Now, then. Where is the woman in that? Eh, Cyfartha?"

"Yes, boy," Cyfartha said. "No score. That one in Bridgend married a 'surance agent. Went to Australia with him. Fancy. Afraid of me. Will you marry again, Huw?"

"I don't know," I said. "Too soon to tell."

Too soon, yes, because I seemed to live in a desert, no light, no hope. Those days I will never forget. There was nothing.

Nothing.

3

Sure it is in my mind, now, that our Colony started real work, and steady building, when Vyrnwy Beris came by with the blacksmith's shop on seven wagons a little after three o'clock in a morning I remember well, filled with stars and the light of a young moon, and all the trees were silver and the new wheat flowed like the sea.

Everybody was out of bed in a moment, and shaking hands and dancing in circles, and the girls ran to get a kettle on, and Donato brought his special medicine to make a punch. Vyrnwy told his drivers to let the horses go, and make camp, and we gave him a bed of sheepskins on a pile of hay near the fire. There he told us he had come over with Idwin and forty families, most of them going up to the other end of the valley, and new stores for Moishe's place in the village, and two very nice girls, new to the area, but hoping to make a way.

"Hoping," Lal said, looking up from the fire with the toast on the end of the fork. "Two girls? From the Colony? Alone? Who are they, then? Did you hear their names?"

"I believe I did," Vyrnwy said, scratching the back of his neck. "What was it, now? Very likely couple, they were, yes. Well behaved, too. Even when the leaders broke a trace, not a word. No language. A wheel came off crossing the Camwy, there, and the stores went in the river. The smallest one only stamped her foot. Not a wrong word."

Lal threw down the fork.

"Solva," she whispered. "Solva and Doli. Vyrnwy, where are they?"

"A couple of miles behind, or less," he said. "Quite right. Corwen, the name was."

But he was late with his joke because Lal and Gwenonwy were in a scream, there, running for the horses, and no word to us, they were off, bareback, split gallop.

"Alwen is with them, and we brought a preacher with us, so she'll be Mrs. Mostyn Williams before I've got one anvil flat, here," he said. "Poor Tynant Lewis has gone. Biggest funeral I ever saw. Everybody was there. Because everybody knew."

"Knew what?" I asked him.

"With him, we all died," he said, very sad, almost to himself. "He was the voice. He had the brain. And the heart. Who is left?"

Thinking of him, I wondered. Some men take charge without uniform or medals. A note is in the voice, ideas are put in words that everybody knew they had thought, but without ever being able to say them.

"There are other men of substance in the community, surely," I said.

"I will tell you what the substance is called," Vyrnwy said. "Tynant was one by himself. He could go to Buenos Aires and talk to the President. In the same way, he would talk to me. Injustice, to him, was a curse. But that's a small matter. His dream, here, was a new land. New Cambria. Without interference from anybody. Hopeless. Not enough of us, to begin. He tried to bring in our own coinage. Nobody would use it. We went back to pesos. He wanted our own government. Not enough had the time to spare. Too much work to do. This, that, the other. Well, after years and years, he dropped the idea. Then he was one of the older generation. A dream gone past. And finish."

"Do you think it is finished?" I asked him.

He nodded.

"No doubt," he said. "We have cleared the land for others, and they aren't slow. Our old ones die, and the land is cut in shares for the children. A little piece each. Not enough to live. Not all of them have got the brains to do much. They sell. Or they go in debt and it's taken. Or the lawyers get it. Go you to the Colony, now. Tynant Lewis had the best property in the valley. Well, there's a lawyer to the north, south, east, and west of it. Now. Not before. How did they get it? How do they get anything?"

We could hear the girls coming for minutes before we saw them, everybody talking to everybody else and screams of laughter flattening under the trees and the shouts of the drivers helping tired horses and harness belling in a fat stew of sound. All the Indios seemed to come from the night. One moment I could swear we had the place to ourselves, and the next, a silent crowd, looking. Then I had Doli and Solva squeezing against me and pulling my beard, and then a handshake from Alwen, but the biggest surprise was shy, hands behind, looking down.

"Tegwyn," Lal said. "Go on, girl. Give him a kiss."

Not even a hug for me, but only the tips of her fingers, shyer still.

"Come on, now, Teg," Rhinberry called out. "You know you slept with him, months, there."

Well, if you had seen the dander in that one. If she could have found something, a broom, a shovel, anything, she would have brained him. The girls got round her and laughed and babbled and swilled away the temper, and we ringed the fire with Donato's medicine, and very good for the time of morning.

"Look now," Lal whispered to me. "We don't want Vyrnwy here. No dirty old blacksmith, and noise and smell, and old drunkards about the place. Let him go down there to his own league. The same to the rest. Our house next. Then we will clear Gwenonwy's place, and put their house down there, and we will be here, by ourselves, and married and in peace. Yes?"

There seemed something selfish about it, that irritated me, and yet I knew she wanted the peace and quiet and order of her own place, and for that she was working her days, so really there was no answer except yes. But whatever we thought, Vyrnwy had strong will of his own, and when it came light he called his Indios and off he went, about six miles down on the other side of Rhinberry, and most of the Indios went with him, because a blacksmith to them is the greatest man on earth, and revered as one working with fire and bending iron to the will. Even though more planing was to be done, Saiheque was greatly tempted to go, and he stood for minutes listening to the shouts while the wagons creaked off, but then he came in and I nodded at the bench, and he began work.

Well, it was surprising what a difference Doli and Solva, their six peons, and the five shepherds made to us. Gwenonwy and Donato had two peons and two men had joined them. Lal had her three peons, and five men had joined us, and there was Tegwyn, and Rhinberry and his men, so we were more than thirty people working there, to say nothing of the Indios. In the first days, everybody did a bit of everything, but soon the work went to those best fitted. Donato and I had our own jobs and enough to do. Lal had charge of the peons to cut timber and clear ground. Rhinberry plowed and planted when he was not taking out roots. Gwenonwy looked after the animals and poultry and brought in the milk and meat. Solva had the butter and cream and helped Doli with the cooking, and that was no small matter. Tegwyn did the laundry and cleaned the wagons where we slept, and she would have scrubbed every tree and the sky itself, that one, though even so, that area was clean to the last shaving, and if she saw somebody drop anything, she stood till it was picked up, and many an Indio twice her size got a good clip with the broom only for standing about the place and making it look, as she always said, very shabby with us.

Day after day the Indios were cutting stone in the quarry, but only because Saiheque told them, and a lot more worked in the forge up with Vyrnwy. Every morning they started when we did and finished with us, and hammers were in tap all day, and when timber thinned as it was cut, I could see them up on the hill, gold-brown and muscled for two, naked from the waist, long black hair bound flat above the forehead by a leather band, talking sometimes, laughing always in shine of big white teeth that would crack a bone quick as any dog's.

Saiheque showed a perfect set the morning he came in with three little boys, all of them his image, and put them to stand beside his bench. He took a rough board and made them look at it in the light, and as I had done with him, so he did with them, finding rough places, and passing each small hand, and talking, not as we do to children but as to men. Those three had to learn step by step, and they had the names of the tools being used perfect in their own language, each in a scamper to collect shavings and match them against the right plane, never with an error. But after Saiheque had finished fining, and they all bent down to look at the light on polished board, to see those eyes go wide in a new wonder, and the smallest, Foyel, screeching to pull teeth, and the three of them dancing ring-o'-roses round their Dada, the proudest man in the world, well, it was worth far more than the few minutes lost from work. Lal came in while they were still there and gave them homemade toffee, I suppose the first time they ever had a sweet.

"Not long," she said. "You will have three or four of your own to teach. I wish I was a hen to have a couple of dozen eggs under me. I am broody for babies. And I am in a lust for you."

"Here, or in the wagon, and now," I said.

She gave me the tip of her tongue and laughed.

"We are all going in this afternoon to see if we can find the preacher," she said. "Then we will have a date, and he shall come here, and we will have the finest asado this valley will see till my first boy is born. Only that one will be better. So patience a little longer, Huw."

Standing a moment in the doorway, leaning against the jamb, she turned, and her face that was lovely sun-brown came in flush of fever, and her eyes wide, sidelong, filled with a fainting, a gleaming mist, glorious to see.

"Eh, dear," she said. "Why is it a few words and a piece of old paper can mean so much? But. We are not Indios. Will you cleave to me, boy?"

Only the day before and I might have been on my knees in front of her, never mind Saiheque and his sons. But something strange had come to me. Since that Indio girl had looked, I could see those eyes wherever I went, whatever I did. Some part of me seemed to be with her, or looking for her, or calling for her without a voice. Where, before, Lal had been perfection and all my world, now she was half, and I could feel the emptiness, and it stopped the words I might have found, and instead I was out in a night, and cursing myself for being disloyal, dishonest, and at the same time, trying to think what madness or heartlessness or what type of animal stupidity could bring a little Indio into comparison with Lal, or what in God's name had come between me and sanity.

But the mind works faster than words and I suppose I spoke while I thought.

"As the ax plunged in green timber," I said, and felt myself to be worse hypocrite than all the Pharisees put together.

"They will have to pull hard more than once to have you out, is it?" she said, and such a smile. "Good. Huw, never leave me, will you, boy?"

Well, down with the tools and go to her, then, and miracles, but any notion of the Indio was gone, and there was nothing in the world but the warmth and softness of Lal, most beautiful, that crumbled and melted me.

The laugh was in the one eye seen through her hair.

"Look," she whispered. "Leave me, now, will you, or that old piece of paper will be a waste of money. Give the little boys the rest of the sweets. I love you, in rags and bits."

Saiheque nodded, watching Lal walking back to the fire,

and pointed to the three boys, and he meant she would become a mother, and I nodded. He held up his cut hand, and I held up mine, and we touched palms, and he pointed again to each of his sons, and at the racks of tools, and the bench, and at me. Again I nodded because I understood he wanted me to teach his sons, and I put my right hand on each of their heads, and we touched palms again.

The four of them looked at me, no smile, not the light of a thought in any of them. Even the small one, Foyel, was like a little baulk of wood, and without a word they turned, and went out, and trotted over to their ponies, and Saiheque took his youngest under one arm and vaulted up, and off.

"Time you had somebody to speak between you and the Indios, here," Rhinberry said, while we were eating. "I have thought, but there wasn't anybody to work, and you don't want some idler here only to talk. Will I send you a good boy to train for a carpenter? Half-Indio, he is, but good."

He spoke as if he would rather not, and I thought he might be afraid I would say no, but I said yes, and his face seemed to go smaller with relief.

"Well, of course, boy," Lal said, before she went. "It's his son. By one of the Indios. He's been to school in the Colony. If he's no good, out with him. Behave yourself till I get back, now, will you?"

"I will stay and watch over him," Solva said, in the little voice, each word a carved stone. "Nobody shall steal my brother."

"Except her, if she could," Doli said, putting on gloves. "If I wasn't a fat old thing, here, I might have a chance. Who will marry me? Will I cry pints forever, then?"

Often in quiet moments I have wondered if she knew who was waiting for her down there in the village, though I am sure, and so was Lal, that she had no tiniest notion and no warning. But I wish I had been there when Volde was coming out of Geza's and she was going in, and they saw each other, and stood. They had met once, I believe, in Old Tibbald's, and only then for a moment, but dreams are wonderful messengers and wishes are good as prayers. Volde dropped an armful of parcels, and bottles smashed, and he cared nothing and shouted "Doli!" and she shouted "Volde!" and they wrapped arms about each other, careless, and Volde was shouting Russian and Doli was bawling—I can hear her—in Cambrian, and the pair of them understanding nothing and everything, and then Volde asked her in careful Castellano if they could find a good place for a little cup of something to talk quietly, and she nodded.

Out there in the street two lonely ones were looking at each other, speaking the lonely language that has no words, telling the dear comfort that lonely ones need, and in a moment, no warning, middle of any street or out in the wide palladium of Heaven or not, Volde knelt, and looked up at her, and asked her to marry, and she said yes, and he raised a howl that stopped everything there, and started to dance a *gopak* and Doli was laughing herself senseless. By that time Geza and Tina saw what was happening, and they were not Hungarians for nothing, so first they shut the shop because the crowd was all outside, either cheering or scandalized, and then they brought out the wine. Everybody started drinking and dancing and after a couple of hours, people who never saw each other before were old friends, and Doli and Volde, Lal and Solva, Gwenonwy and Teg were arms about each other, there, and a hundred more, singing themselves scraped. Tina put on an asado, and after everybody had eaten plenty they opened the shop just before midnight, if you please, and when all were served, they slept where they were. The girls had the wagons, and they loaded fat-eyed in the morning and got back to us in the afternoon, just when we were becoming really worried.

"Did you think the old Indios had us, boy?" Lal said. "You ought to have been there."

"When is the preacher coming?" I asked her.

"Ten days, exact, and we have ordered everything, and half the world will be here," she said, and gave me a kiss to buzz in my ears. "If only Solva could find a good one, too."

The Lord God moves in quiet ways.

I am sure that Doli, dancing about on a cloud, prayed every moment for Solva, and I know that Lal did, and even considered putting aside our marriage till Solva was settled.

"Poor girl," she said. "She will be by herself. Only old peons. And married fools, and bed-linen jokes."

One afternoon we heard a trumpet, and a troop of cavalry galloped in, smothered in dust, ragged, and enough hair to make a barber go home. The young lieutenant came to me with his sabre dragging in the dust. He wanted meat, yerba, and a place where they could repair saddlery. While he spoke I knew I had seen him somewhere, but I was still very stiff with Castellano, and Rhinberry's boy came useful to help.

"Mr. Lieutenant is Porfirio Hernandez's son," he said. "The owner of the Nymph estancia near Port Madryn. He is sure you know his father. His name is Oracio."

Well, of course we all knew Porfirio. The son was at the university so I never met him. But when Lal saw him, there was another ceremony because he had ridden Tanfi a couple of times, and they had both won money on each other's horses. The troop was sent to the river, and peons took hay and clover bales, and he was invited to eat with us. That done, I went back to work and everybody seemed to need sleep, so the place was quiet.

Too quiet.

There was not an Indio anywhere.

Rhinberry's boy, Luis, sixteen and growing into a big man, saw me looking.

"They have gone, sir," he said. "Indios hate soldiers. They will hunt winter food and ride to the north. In the spring, perhaps, they will come here again."

I missed them about the place, missed the sound of the hammers, missed Saiheque, and the stands of ponies under the trees.

"Fewer to get drunk," Lal said. "They are all very well. But a lot of people don't like them. They carry disease. And when they have too much to drink, there is always trouble."

"They never had drink here, and we never had disease," I said. "They have cut tons of stone, and cleared many a good mile of timber, and not a penny to pay. And besides, you are talking about your blood-brother-in-law."

"I am blood-granddaughter to the greatest," she said. "The cacique Namüncurá. So between us we ought to do well. Of course they didn't take money. That work they were ordered to do."

"They did it, and it couldn't have been done better," I said. "How many white men would accept the order or the work? Who is always talking of laziness, and dirt, and no discipline?"

Lal shrugged, a beautiful movement with her, because it lifted her breasts and sharpened the points, and for some reason turned down her lower lip and showed it full, red.

"Be out here a little longer," she said. "You will learn. And be careful. Indios are not all the same."

Oracio told us that and plainly round the fire after the asado. Late twenties, then, and a fine, dark, good-looking man, very strict with his men and with himself. Not a spoonful of fat was on him, he was hollow under the eyes and in the cheeks, and still tender from a lance-wound of six months before. Two years he had been with the Army, after taking a bachelor's degree at Buenos Aires University, and every minute of it in the pampas between San Martín de los Andes and a little farther south than us, and in his last weeks of commission before going back to take charge of the estancia from his father.

"He's going to Spain to visit his father and mother," he said. "He wants them to come here. But they would rather stay in Seville. Personally, that's my opinion. I had three months there and left my heart."

"You are engaged, Oracio?" Doli asked, with no more guile than an unborn seraph, or so it seemed.

"No," Oracio said, and handed back the *maté*. "Not that type of heart."

Doli's sigh of relief could have put out the fire.

"Thank God, now then," she said. "And are you with us for how long?"

"Till the saddlery's repaired and we've got enough stores," Oracio said.

"Where will I have good blade and cut the lot to ribbons?" Doli asked everybody. "The lot, ribbons, here."

Oracio, of course, understood not a word of Cambrian, but we were in fits, and worse, unable to show it.

"How long will the war last, Lieutenant?" Rhinberry asked.

"It's over," Oracio said. "One or two bands made a nuisance of themselves and got others to join them. I'm in sympathy with a great deal of the Indio case. But they destroyed their chances by pillage and murder. Then we moved in. We had to. The settlers had to be protected."

"We lost very few in all these years," Rhinberry said. "We always worked well with the Indios over in the Atlantic Colony. Without their good help in the first years, we would have starved. My father's sister was one who went to Buenos Aires and saw the President to stop the killing. I think it a shame they have lost their land. Then to be killed, man, woman, and child in the bargain? Are we Christians?"

Oracio shook his head.

"No," he said. "Nothing in war is Christian. But it is sometimes necessary. Weapons must be fought with weapons. The land is quiet, now. People can build. Bring in the flocks. Begin to civilize."

"Since how long is the war over?" Rhinberry asked. "Did you fight weapon with weapon? Didn't you use rifles and revolvers?"

Oracio nodded.

"Of course," he said. "That's one reason the war's over. They found out that lances, and bows and arrows and *boleadores* don't go so far as the bullet. They became men of peace. They were taught."

"Ah, yes," Rhinberry said, and passed the *maté* back to Doli. "You were fighting every day, no?"

"Sometimes weeks apart, sometimes months," Oracio said. "Days without a sign. Following cold tracks."

"No better tracker than the Gaucho," Rhinberry said, in a long pull at the *bombilla*. "Sometimes you came on a camp of women and children? When the men were out hunting?"

Oracio nodded, at the fire.

"And sometimes you slaughtered every woman and child, and burned the tents," Rhinberry said, to the same place in the fire. "Other times, you burned the tents and stole the food, and took the horses, and left the women and children to freeze or starve? Yes?"

"It has happened," Oracio said. "Not in this company."

"But the colonels or the generals, whatever they are, they were cheered in Buenos Aires as heroes and emancipators," Rhinberry said. "The same people now owning the lands of the Indios they slaughtered or starved to death in winter cold?"

"Perhaps," Oracio said.

"And it has gone on years, and now it is over," Rhinberry said. "Nobody told us. I suppose we Cambrians should be thankful you didn't start on us?"

"Were you a threat?" Oracio said. "Without the Army, what could you have done?"

"The Army has never been here," Rhinberry said. "I was here, first, as a boy with my father. We never saw the Army. As a matter of pure fact, if the criminals in Buenos Aires hadn't seen profit in taking land that belonged to Indios, the Army would never have been here. The Indio War, or the Desert War, whichever you please, would never have been fought if those busy little men up there hadn't wanted title to lands not theirs. So there was a lot of flag-wag, and many heroes, and the scum of creation was recruited to murder in the name of civilization. But the real name is robbery. Don't get up, sir."

Rhinberry stood, and gave the *maté* to Lal.

We were all standing, and Doli and a couple of us slipped in front of Oracio.

"No use to keep silent," Rhinberry said, and his voice shaking. "My little one, up there, now, is looking down to me. Tehuelche she was. No lovelier girl ever sang a man to sleep. Her family was murdered. She had to collect her mother's bones. She is up there now, only because horror climbed in her spirit and she could see nothing except ashes and the filth of men. While you and your soldiers remain, I will not come here. You are not welcome where I am. From me, you shall have not a grain of salt. Mistress Lal, Gwenonwy, all, good night."

The whisper, and the white face, and staring red eyes went away in darkness.

"You can never tell what that one will say next," Lal said, and poured water in the *maté*. "He shouldn't have made a guest uncomfortable. I will have a word with him."

"Unfortunately, I sympathize with his point of view," Oracio said, and leaned, elbows on knees, nearer to the fire, sad, and distant, and tired. "There's been no need for a great deal of the hounding and slaughter. On our estancia we've got Tehuelche, so I was brought up with them, and I love them. I'm not sure how I can go back. We're known to have killed out many of their relatives. No use denying it. There was no sense in it. They offered no harm. They were simply living."

"You killed Indios only to kill them?" Gwenonwy asked him. "Families?"

Oracio stood.

"I thank God I didn't," he said. "This troop hasn't. They're good boys. All Gaucho. From Río Negro, Neuquen, Nahuel Huapí. But we've only been in a couple of years. When I joined, I thought it a duty. To help my Country before I went into my own business. I imagined God knows what terrible battles. With thousands of screaming savages. Instead I never saw a battle. Never saw more than a couple of hundred Indios anywhere. And a good half, women and children. And I saw the slaughter and the burning. That, yes. No denial. That's why I'm glad I'm leaving. I'm not a soldier. At any rate, that kind of soldier. This troop has been out a long time. We've roamed. Happily. It's a marvelous country to roam in. Roaming and singing. I don't know what the others have been doing. But that man was right. The Army has sometimes been made a tool of thieves."

Over the vegetable patch, flame stitched red rags under the trees, and men were singing to a guitar.

"You are welcome to stay," Lal said. "Everything you want, only ask."

Oracio listened to the singing.

"Who's that playing the guitar?" he asked.

"My sister," Doli said. "Come, you. Let's all have a good sing. Nothing better to blow old cobwebs."

Lal took a kettle and so did I, and we went behind the others, with the yerba tin and the *matés*.

"Is that Rhinberry going mad?" she whispered. "If Oracio wasn't friends with us, he could turn us off the place. Send us back. And terrible trouble when we got home."

"He knows the truth," I said.

"We all know the truth," she said. "But the truth and what you say about the Army are two different things. Thank God he is neighbor to us, and known for years. And a good boy, too."

We stopped behind the others, looking at a big fire, and a ring of soldiers singing round Solva, sitting on a black and white poncho spread on a log. She looked to be carved in white marble and the guitar flared, red in firelight.

"The poor boys were very lonely, and they were singing for the heart," she said, in that small voice, which made words plainer than any shout. "Who knows all the verses of 'Catamarca'?"

"I do," Oracio said, quietly, in the crowd.

Solva smiled, o, a pretty smile, and struck a chord.

"Sing, boy," she said.

4

With all these candles burning, this kitchen is brighter than I remember, and the flames have warmed the air. But I think of Mama, and the family. Except when she sat to darn or sew, this was a room restless with life. But I wish I knew where the furniture went, though that was only the big table and the small one, my father's chair, and the smaller chairs and the bench and stools. When we were all in there, somebody had to sit on the floor, and that was only me. The dresser and book shelves and two cupboards and some pictures, no, there was nothing much in there, and yet it was all at least a hundred years old, either from my father's family or my mother's, and worth a great deal today, though my mother was always threatening to burn it and buy new. Strange that the rubbish our mothers and grandmothers gave away, or threw away, today is worth money, according to little men with a reserve price and a mallet.

When I first came back here I wanted to buy the street and make a gift to the museum. Olwen thought it ridiculous to spend money only to show how four generations of us lived and died. I wanted the houses on The Hill furnished as they had been, with the clothes hanging, and the washing, and the barrels and buckets for the baths, everything, to the detail, as if the families had gone out for a minute and coming back to live again.

"What on earth use would it be?" Olwen said, in a voice like my mother's, but in the English of what is called the Educated Class, which is so different from the un-Educated, and meant to be. "At a time like this, when there's so much poverty? Why not a few scholarships? Bring some of them out of the mire, at least."

She was only a few years younger than me but she spoke as if I was dragging my little cart on a bit of string.

"If we had a street of houses as they were in the Roman or the Tudor times, it would teach more history in ten minutes that I ever learned in school," I said. "Our people have died. There are a few, but only a few more. And they are not as we were. Will you argue?"

"Absolutely not," she said. "Personally, I thank God. I was utterly thankful to leave. I only wish I could have had poor Mama with me. She deserved a few easy years. She never had them."

"Nothing is quite as we would like," I said. "But I think it a pity that a way of life that produced so much magnificence and wretchedness should disappear. People to come won't know. They'll wonder how a form of slavery flourished for so long. I'd like to show them how chained people can exist, and even achieve a certain degree of comfort when enough women like Mama cook good meals and provide good beds. Without her and many another thousand, there would never have been a coal industry. Not enough men would have tolerated the conditions. Mama, in the kitchen. That was the power. I'd like to show the tools she had to work with."

"But who's going to come here?" she said, looking about the Valley. "The most God-forsaken, frightful hole in this entire squalid country. Is that what you want to advertise?"

"Not particularly," I said. "The squalor's part of us. We came from here. We've known it was wrong. And hated it. What did we do besides hating it, and running?"

"But you want to perpetuate it," she said. "A museum? People'll think there's a virtue in living in this sort of surrounding. A couple of years and a garden about it, a few uniformed guides, utter rot about the heroism and all the other sentimental rubbish, and I suppose there'll be miners' societies and heaven knows what other nonsense bobbing up. Simply give them an excuse. You know what they are."

"A museum to show how people lived in different periods," I said. "What they wore, ate, spent, and what their money would buy. There's still plenty of old furniture and old clothes. In a hundred years, two hundred, it would be an important place. Because unless people saw it for themselves they would never believe it."

"I agree," Olwen said, and tears ready. "That's perfectly, horrifyingly true. You can go in if you like. I won't. I'll wait for you in Tossall's."

That was those years ago, and since then, all that changed is more paint coming off the walls, more damp in the floor, and the slag, that shifted overnight and buried everything below, chapel, school, shops, though they were empty and for years unused, so no damage or loss except to my idea, and this little house, that soon will be buried and nothing to save it. Nothing will be left of us, or of my mother and father. Even the cemetery, that holds them and their generation and those who bore them, is under the slag.

All of us are gone, without sign except in the mind.

The telegram from Oracio took me back from London that time, and no man has fretted so many weeks as I, over the ocean to Buenos Aires, at last, and by train to Bahia Blanca that night, and the ship, then, to Port Madryn, hardly changed from the first time I saw it. He met me in the Ford T, that old miracle, and we went out to the estancia, a big place, though the house was as his father had left it except that Solva put in a sun porch, and made a garden. She never greatly changed through the years, and that time she looked young as ever, even though she was Mama to four fine children, the three eldest, a boy and two girls exactly like her, and the youngest boy, still in her arms, exactly like his father.

"It's too late," Oracio said, when we were walking, that evening. "There's nothing we can do. I saw everybody. Not many people know much about it. It was done quietly. We were slow. Skeleton's probably going to be the railhead. That's where property values are going up. We're out in the cold. It's a political job, first to last. There's no merit, so far as we're concerned. Freight will have to come off the main line and reload on narrow gauge trucks. That's extra expense. If we load wool or anything else at Skeleton, it will have to be unloaded off the narrow on to the broad gauge, to reach Bahia Blanca or Buenos Aires. Any idea what that's going to put on the price of everything?"

"You're sure there's nothing to be done?" I asked him.

"If we'd got there in time, we might have offered the boys more money and more shares," Oracio said. "As it is, they've been paid, and the line will go to Skeleton. That'll be the main excuse for not continuing the route from the City of Lewis to the City of the Mill. They've cut us off from the Atlantic. Naturally. Cheaper freight, faster loading means a better price for wool, meat, hides, fleeces, tallow, everything. And cheaper food. Less cost. More supply. Greater competition. More people. More activity. Higher wages. Less profit for the vampire bats."

"We ought to be able to see or rouse somebody to get it done," I said. "It's a matter for the Country, not for a couple of cattle and sheep companies."

Oracio laughed.

"What about your compatriots in the Colony and in the Andes?" he asked. "Aren't there enough of them to start a battle? What's to be the argument? Opening up Patagonia from east to west? Populating the desert? Lower transport costs for a handful of sheepfarmers at cost of millions to the Treasury? Think of those *mascalzones* in Buenos Aires, and then listen to your argument. And the State Legislature? Is there a brain or pocket you could appeal to? No, Huw. Francisco Moreno is dead. Long Live Francisco Moreno. He gave us half our Country, and we spat in his face."

That was the last time I went back, by wagon and horse, with Gauchos and a flock of sheep, and a herd of fine cattle across the pampas to the Andes. Almost ten weeks it took us, in marvelous late spring weather, letting the animals set the pace to have them fat at the end as in the beginning, and giving lambs and calves, colts and foals, plenty of time to rest and find their legs.

The days are with me now, gold, and blue, and a wondrous silence out ahead of the animals, listening to El Pampero hum in the ears of each bush, watching them barely shake half-away as maidens from improper whispers. Feasting in the long days' miles of wildflowers in scattery bloom, and berries ripening, and armadillos leading their families, and flutters of ostrich in stretch and stamp, and a buck and mightly kick of guanaco, all in a broad land of many a happy dream since.

Some of those bushes and plants I can name, but most not, though all of them have been my companions in many a starry night's sleep, gentlest guardians of rest, modest in dress and dustier than most, but warm hedge before the dawn's unruly breeze and canopy against the rain. Flat, the land, not even a little rise or bump, only the grit and pebbles underfoot that once was sea bed even up to the tops of the mountains farther on. The road had been dug deep by our hoofs and wheels for fifty years, made wide enough for almost three columns abreast, all on hard ground except across the Camwy.

Huts of settlers were here and there, and sometimes a store and wineshop at about the place a troop might halt for the midday meal, or at night, all poor houses, of boards and a tin roof, with a bench or two and a barrel of wine. But to get the tin and timber out there cost their owners time and a fortune, and they worked the years of their lives in waiting for somebody to pass, so their business was far from an offering in charity. Indios went to such places and sold guanaco hides, ostrich feathers, leatherwork, or anything that would get them a few gulps of alcohol. Too many sold their women and children and horses and the rights to their lands only for a few bottles. We had plenty of stores with us, so there was no need to go in any of them, and that again, so often repeated, was another count against all of us Cambrians then, and certainly in years to come, because we were thought a little too high in the nose and far too fine in the finger. But it was never that, and never that we preferred our own company. It was simply that against grimed-in dirt, drabs, and bad wine, we chose fresh air and a cup of tea, or a *maté*, and if it had to be a good whisky, and it often was, and thank God, then it came from the bottle to a clean mug.

High song was in the sky that only Patagonia knows, that airy height so cleanly blue and always unmarked except by passing drift of a Gaucho's fire, or the sweat of cattle, or the bluish breath of frying bacon and a couple of eggs, and salty dough bubbling gold in fat, and coffee going mad for sugar. Many an hour I read the singing clouds, and much to my blessing, for even now the blue is above me and I shall never be without comfort of the silence, and peace, and ageless health that spreads across leagues without water, though a kingdom of diamonds in white surprise of morning dew, and in frost, before the sun is strong, an hour or two of paradise in million glitter of showering jewels. A sky there is of pale, pale blue, and a thousand small white clouds like the fists of babies in tint of pink at the knuckles, moving, without pause, and then a darker sky, and a couple of clouds up there, round, like washed butter-muslin, streaming smooth, breaking in small scud with the babies' fists, and the piling, eggwhite froth in float at midday, and the plain enamel blue, the pampas blue of the afternoon's heat, that brings the sweat to dry and sets crisp salt to rime the lips.

We had passed Ginbox, a place where one of our pioneers had left a case of gin and forgot it for years, and I was thinking of turning off, out of the animals' way to boil water for a cup of tea, but I thought I could hear a bagpipe, and I was thinking myself turned in the wits for a bagpipe has a sound all its own. The skirls were coming strong with the breeze, but below a rise, to the side, and I called the dogs away from the point of the animals, and rode to see.

Dugald Mael MacGrannoch piped at the head of a few of his peons walking in twos, with a draggle of about thirty women and children behind. I reined on the edge, almost not believing I was seeing him, tall, thin, bearded, wearing a black ostrich feather bonnet in a band about his head, and a red and blue tartan shawl with a silver badge on the shoulder, and a black velvet jacket with braid and silver buttons, and a red and blue kilt, and a belt with a purse and white tassels hanging, and boots of horses' hocks with his toes in show with him. He saw me, and finished the tune, and let the pipe settle on his shoulder, and called a good day.

"Your Castellano is good as mine," I said. "We are driving a flock and a few head to the Andes. Anything we can do for you?"

He came up and we shook hands, and a couple of his men chopped out roots for the fire while I went back to tell Sanchez where I was.

"Come up and stay the night," Dugald said. "Keep us company. I've plenty of everything. You can aye catch up the morn's morn. I just droned my wee wife. I'm no' a gay one."

I never heard an English with more music, or that I had such a hard job to understand, and after a little we started to speak Castellano, and we did very well. We were talking about sheep, and cattle, and prices, and the cost of everything, or any desperate matter not to talk about what was putting the big tears in his eyes, and his foreman said it was dark and we had better reach the estancia. We might have gone four or five miles, and then I saw the true difference between us—whether in the Atlantic or the Andes—and the other settlers in the pampas, and I remembered Gwenonwy.

In the Atlantic Colony of Port Madryn, Rawson, the City of Lewis, Dolavon, and Gaiman, we had been able to bring in supplies by ship, and when farming began to show rich harvest there was plenty of money for comfort and even a little for luxury. In the Andes, we were in straits for years, there, unable to sell a bushel of grain or a kilo of wool. But most had family or friends over in the Atlantic Colony to help with stores, and when more of us got on our feet, and Chilenos began coming over the peaks to buy animals, and wagon columns between the two colonies became profitable, then the Cooperative opened a depot. After that we could get anything we wanted with only a few weeks to wait, and Moishe and others supplied in variety. All we had to do was ride the miles and take a wagon, or a few packhorses, and be out and back the same day, as we wished.

Dugald and his wife never could.

They were at least two weeks hard journey from anywhere, and no guarantee they would find one stick or brick when they got back. He was never able to go off alone, because he had to supervise the peons and keep the flock together, and his wife was never fond of the country, nervous of distance and silence, and frightened of everything, though she pretended not to be, but in the late years, hating it and wanting to go from there.

When I saw the estancia, I thought I knew why, poor girl. Lal would never have permitted any peon of ours to live in such a place. Yet, considering the distance they had to go for timber of any kind, Dugald had done marvels with bricks of baked mud and cattle dung, branches of the larger pampas bushes, and whitewash. Three rooms they had of walls I could almost touch with my fingertips outstretched, and a roof he brushed with the feathers in his cap. In the kitchen, an earth floor that could be sprinkled to keep down dust, a fire in a ring of stones in the corner, a small oil lamp, two little benches, a chair made from bamboo, and a few pots on hooks. In the bedroom, a flat of boards with sheepskins, and clothes on a string. In the other room, a store for wool, fleeces and hides that made a smell in the place, even though the night was cool, so I knew what it would be on a hot day.

"If your people passing by here hadn't bought my wool off me and kept us supplied, we'd have starved or given up long ago," Dugald said. "I wish we'd gone. She'd still be alive, perhaps. But we wanted our own place. We didn't see how it was going to turn out, that's all. I started with seventy sheep. I've got more than three thousand. My neighbors gave up and left me some of their flocks. I can't fence. There's no timber. So I've got to have peons out there. That's money. I can't sell enough animals to buy wire. I took a point up to El Sombrero last year. No buyers. I had to give them away to pay the peons. I came back here with just a couple of kilos of yerba. You know what that does to a woman?"

"Gather your flock, now, and come to the Andes," I said. "You can sell a few, get some money in hand, take a league and settle with us. When you've saved, and got the timber and wire, then come back here as a second place."

He was staring at the floor.

"No," he said. "She died here. So will I. Only thing is, there'll be none to pipe me in. None of my own folk to say a comforting word. Not that I'm fearful. But your own kind make a grand difference. D'you know how good it is to come back with you, and knock heads, and have a drink tonight? I feared more than anything coming back to this place. My head's full of 'The Maid o' Skye' and 'Flowers of the Forest.' Only the littlest whispers of her. It's enough."

The littlest whispers, yes, those I knew, and I also knew I was not brave as Dugald. Never for any reward would I have lived under that roof, and even then I was itching to go from there.

"Tell you what," he said. "I'll have a Patagonian bargain with you. I've a flock of a thousand or more just outside. I'll not count. Take them with you. Sell them next spring. Take twenty-five percent of the price and half the lambs. With my share, I'll buy what I want for a new house. I'll have a water tank. I'll have enough for some of the wire, perhaps credit for all of it. I can fence. Will you do it?"

"Others have gone by for years," I said. "Why didn't you ask one of them?"

"You must drink with a man," he said. "A word or two at the roadside's no way to know anybody. There was no time and I couldn't invite anybody down here. We'd no tea, or cups."

My heart was with her that had wanted to queen it here, and with him, because well I knew what she had felt, and said, wanting so much to meet a woman and talk again, and yet ashamed of having nothing to offer. Those coming after in ease of mind and body are careless, but they should know it was not courage alone that sustained our pioneers, but the pride that came with their blood.

"Will you take the bargain?" he asked. "My name's MacGrannoch."

"Yes," I said. "My name's Morgan."

We shook hands, nothing to paper, and I put the other bottle on the table.

"I am off before light," I said. "I will sleep now. Outside. My peon has put a place. Have you told your peons to be ready?"

"They were on the road behind you before we got here," he said. "You can catch up with them."

"You are a trusting man," I said.

"No," he said. "I know you people from the Colony. I'll see you away. You've brought a happy hour to a spiritless one."

"Have you got a Bible?" I asked him.

"Buried it with her," he said, stone sober, and crying. "She had to have sustenance against the night."

"You shall have mine," I said. "It is in English. You will have a companion, and a Hand on your shoulder. Drink well, and sleep, now."

The estancia looked like two sleeping animals, humped and hunched, with water in the trough shining one silver eye when we went by in the morning, walking at first, and then galloping into a waning moon, up to the track, and on, until we reached Dugald's flock, and a little farther on, ours. All the time I was thinking of the difference between him and me, and how much more of everything had been given to me, and yet, in the end, as with him, taken wholly away.

Gwenonwy came in the tool shed that afternoon long before, and stood to touch, and pick, and look through the door, and drive me silly.

"Well, Gwen, my little one," I said, because she was never one to waste a moment. "Are you on coals, there, girl?"

"Huw, you won't be angry," she said, half-turned away.

"Never," I said. "Come, you. Empty the chest."

"Well, I was thinking if Donato and me could have our house on our own league instead of here," she said, a little rill of words in a run to be out. "I know you thought we could stay here in the workshop till our league is cleared. But there's a lovely space there, and water just beyond the door."

"The timber and everything else is ready," I said. "All you want is wagons, and you could be in tomorrow afternoon."

She was off, and she must have settled everything first, and asked after, because not an hour later, she had our wagons and Rhin's and Vyrnwy's outside, and we loaded timber, the pipes and the bath, and through the woods we went, singing. Our men and Oracio's Gauchos made small work of it. The Indios had cut stone enough for a city. Once the foundation was in, the timbers went up like child's blocks, then the rooftree and ribs, and the roofboards, and the slats and tar-paper, and about eleven o'clock that night, they had four walls and a roof, and two happier people never lived, and they were waltzing each other from door to door.

"When are you going to build one like this for us?" Doli said, pushing hair from her eyes. "I would poison these two, now, to have it."

"Everything is ready," I said. "Wagons tomorrow, and it will be here. But where will you find a place, girl?"

"Did you think we've been sliding down old haystacks with us?" Doli said, and put Volde's arm about her. "A dear little place we have found by the river. We were going to have a toldo there. But I'll have the wagons on the dot tomorrow, and the asado will be ours. Yes?"

All that time, poor Solva was very much out of it. The girl

was always quiet, but she seemed to go even quieter, though strangely enough, the quieter she became, the more beautiful she looked, and if she used working clothes in the morning, she was in regalia after midday, with long sighs, and slow movements, and suffering to see food.

"We are going to have a time with that one," Lal said, late one night, watching the white dress almost in float under the trees. "She has made up her mind. She will have what she wants, or everybody in the world will suffer. Us, most."

"What does she want?" I asked her, not thinking.

"A good smacked bottom will do, to begin," she said. "The airs we are having, here. But wait if somebody asks her to play the guitar. Then we'll see."

"After midnight?" I said. "What time work in the morning?"

"When Doli brings the wagons," she said, and put her arms about my waist, and leaned to walk. "Not a week more, and we shall be married. So who is thinking of work?"

"We haven't even thought about the honeymoon," I said. "Volde says there are beautiful lakes not far. Shall we take a packhorse, and go there by ourselves?"

"Yes," she said, and I can feel the squeeze to rob breath. "Always I have wanted to ride love naked under the stars. Leave it to me. I will prepare everything."

We were singing there till when, as we did most nights, and Doli playing, or Solva, and handing the guitar to a Gaucho for a new ballad, though Solva was the only real guitarist there, and they almost worshiped her for it. Gauchos are born with music in the blood, though the sound to us is strange to begin, but ever after a dear haunting through life. They played bone whistles to the male beat of horsehide drums, and with guitar chords, and those Indio voices that break in the throat in minor keys and harmonies, we knew many an hour there when it was shame and disgrace to say enough, and go off to bed.

Mistress Solva, of course, never gave Oracio a look, though she could be dripping sweetness to the sergeant and a couple more, and from the look of him, Oracio might not have known she was on earth. Night after night we sat after a hard day, and the troop was still there next morning. Not that we wanted them to leave, either. They were out, pulling roots, and felling timber, putting up fences, chopping wood, anything that came first, and Oracio showed himself to be a workman besides a scholar. But it had to come out sooner or later, and Doli, with all the stars of the firmament in her eyes, and happier than any dozen, came in the shop to wait for a few shelves, and told me.

"Solva doesn't want them to go," she said, a fact, and no nonsense. "They love her and her voice, and the guitar to them is their mother's love. So when Oracio tells them to saddle and take stores, two or three are too sick to move, there. So they stay on a couple of days more. Then a couple more are sick. Nobody can be so sick as an old Gaucho. They show teeth, like a dead horse. And she goes to nurse them. With eggs and wine. Eggs and wine, she is nursing them? They will be with us forever, boy."

"Why is this?" I asked her, because, of course, some of us with enough to do of our own can be dull.

She looked at me from the side, fair hair, almost gold, and the bluest eyes, and a mouth-shut smile.

"No wonder Lal could squash you flat to her," she said. "I could. But I've got somebody who can squash a lot harder, too. Don't you know our Solva is after Oracio? She could never do better. But when will she get him? He's been in the desert too long. He's shy. In old rags, with him. He tries to hide his feet, poor boy."

"We could lend him some boots or money, whatever he wanted," I said.

"Never do it," she said, and strict. "They are all Gaucho. Not peons. Never offer money or anything else. If they want, they will ask, and pay later. If not, they will turn their backs, and go off without. If you try to pay them for the work they've done, they will put everything where they found it, and leave. The roots they will put in, and stamp the earth flat. Gauchos work for no man, but only themselves. Money buys nothing. Besides, old Hernandez has got millions. Oracio's the only son. Their land and Maes Corwen is only a few leagues apart. If Solva marries him, and we give her the third part nearest, and we buy the land between for a wedding present, think what a property they will have."

"Still thinking of property?" I said.

"What use to live and work without?" Doli said, and surprised. "Will you be a peon and die in your idleness?"

"All right," I said. "I will be property, too. What shall I have for a wedding present?"

Her smile was like sunrise on the Camwy, everything in flashing light, it seemed, because she was in love, and not quite of this earth.

"Wait you, boy," she said. "From the first day you came to Maes Corwen we have been thinking. When you gave us that beautiful coffer for nothing? Wait a couple of days and see. I wish I could sleep, and wake up for the morning."

That afternoon Vyrnwy came down, bathed white and dressed to kill, and, good God, a bunch of flowers, pulled from the bushes and strung.

"What now, then?" I said. "Did I miss the Trump? A shave you have had, boy."

"Courting, I am," he said and giving his tie a bit of a pull. "Everybody is off, here, so damn, I closed down, and came for an answer, see."

"Who is to give it?" I asked him. "Everybody is booked up, here, solid, once we can have the preacher."

"I noticed," he said, and he was looking so sad, I could have run him to the shed for a glass of something. "It seemed to me, you see, that Rhin was the favorite. So I stayed away."

"We thought you were too tired to come down," I said. "Favorite with who?"

"Well, Tegwyn, of course," he said, as if I had forgotten the shape of an egg.

"Look you, Vyrnwy, my little one," I said. "Behind the

kitchen shed, beyond the firewood, go over the space and down the path of the garden and look for the potato field. Behind the laundry-blow, look for the little house. There you will find her. I would love to come with you."

"You have got your business, and I have got mine," he said, and off he went.

Those afternoons none of the girls were to be seen anywhere, but women have their affairs, and Donato and I had our days crammed. He was making heavy wheels, but twice the common circumference to go easily through deep mud and the river, and I was making the axles, wagon tongues and boards. Everybody wanted them, because everything had to be carried or dragged, whether solid trunks, or cut firewood, or roots and stone. All were not so lucky as we had been. A man and wife with children, and no money to pay a peon or two could do very little beyond clearing a place to live and putting up a toldo, digging land and planting potatoes and grains, cutting down a few trees, or digging a well, and piling firewood against the winter of five months. Most of the Colony were not nearly so far advanced as we were. They were living in huts or toldos, not only because there was no market, nothing being sold, and no money, but because there were no extra people to work. It is one thing to talk, but to go two and three years without selling produce, without stores except on credit, or good clothes, or anything except what is of the land, or seeing a coin, can be poison to the spirit, and it is testimony to their Faith that all of them about us were cheerful, each, whether man or woman, working as a demon, and the first building up with a roof was the school, and in rags or not, the girls and boys were sent there.

Often, all those years ago, when El Pampero fluted down the valley we could hear the childrens' morning hymn, and a wonderful start to the day. Tegwyn's children, of course, were two on a pony from the first day, and out before light to be there in time. They were crying the first couple of mornings when they passed my shop, but after that they were off in a gallop, and both were scholars because Teg asked questions when they came home, so they had to know. A hard woman, some thought her, and others said she was cruel, but we knew she was neither but only sensible to what was necessary, and with a heart—ah, Teg, my little one!—much bigger than herself.

Perhaps because Rhinberry had given her some help, or because she washed for him, or the affair of Nelya Peninnah, but everybody seemed to think they would marry. A fine pair they would have made, too, except that she would never have had the Indios anywhere near except to work, and Rhin would never have let them go, and in any event, his eyes were always on his love up at the waterfall.

Vyrnwy, of course, was the best man she could have had, a hard worker himself, and needing a woman exactly like her. Alwen had kept house for him as a sister, but everything was a penance because she was in a dream to be Mrs. Mostyn Williams, so nothing was ever right. If he had to finish shoeing and his dinner was cooked black, it was his fault, and if he had no white shirt for chapel, it was because he made them dirtier than three men, so after a few years of that, he shut his mouth and lived and slept most of his time in the forge.

Not long, and I saw them, over where his horse was tied, and Teg carried the flowers soft in her arms.

They kissed, a touch, and he went at a gallop, and she came running through the trees, and down to the shop. At the door she leaned, and I thought she was laughing, but she came to the bench, and her fists were in her cheeks, and the big tears were spurting, yes, spurting from her eyes.

"O, Huw," she said, in the quiver of a whisper. "How will I be married? Nothing nice to put on me. Nothing. Not even a little scrap of old ribbon for the boy."

She ran from there, and bumping blind into bushes, and I went from there, a bit blind, too, looking for Lal.

5

Late one hot afternoon, just after a little tight-eyed siesta, I had started work, and Oracio came in the shop quietly, and rude or not, but snow in summer, I had to stare.

Somebody had given him a good clip, head and cheeks, and his uniform was brushed, what was there of his boots had a good try at a shine, and his sabre was polished.

"What is this, now then?" I asked him. "Are you off?"

"When you are married, you will be head of the family," he said, no smile, and pale as sunburn would let. "I submit my name to you, sir. I wish to ask permission to request the hand of Miss Corwen the younger, in marriage. As to finance, guarantees of stability and other resources, I can present a list, signed in the presence of a notary."

"I shall be very happy," I said. "Her sisters will be even happier. But did you ask Solva?"

He shook his head.

"I'm very nervous," he said. "I cannot present her to my parents. It's not the usual thing to do, just walking in and asking. I don't want her to think I didn't take it in consideration. But I can't tolerate this inanition of the spirit any longer. From the moment I saw her, I've been insane. I understand madness."

"You are speaking to a brother," I said. "Tell you what. I'll find Solva, and I'll say you would like a stitch put in that tunic. Out at the elbows, both sides. One shoulder only wants a push, and you will be out. Wait, you."

He wanted to stop me, but I was round the back, beyond Donato's place, and in steam for the laundry shed.

And there all the girls were, sewing in white. The inside shone pale in their faces with all the white silk in billows over the tables, and Mistress Eirene Vaughan was fitting a shape.

"So this is why I can never find you," I said.

"Don't come in, and please not to look at anything, be so good," Lal said. "Private, with us."

"Good," I said. "My look will be a better one, later. There is a poor soldier falling out of his tunic, here. If any lady will be so kind, and thanks in advance, a thread or two in charity will serve the Country."

It is certain that nobody knew, but only Solva got up. "Send the boy to me in the kitchen to have a bit of shade," she said, in the smallest, clearest voice, and took her work-basket. "And remember my name when tea is ready. I have got a throat like an old funnel, here."

The kitchen was through the trees, too far to hear a voice. A couple of Rhin's girls were peeling vegetables when I passed, but nobody else was near, and everywhere was quiet in sun.

What I was thinking I cannot remember, but in a sudden, like fire, I could feel the eyes of the Indio girl in my back. No use to try arguing with myself. Eyes I could feel, and I knew whose.

Without turning to see, I went into the shop, deliberately picked a saw, and started to take a half-inch plank out of the bole, first to have the excuse of not looking about, and secondly to make all the noise I could. But I might just as well have sung psalms. The movement was in front of me when she passed, a shadow in the light, and then to the side.

There I looked, and she was looking at me, but such a look that goes to frighten, not with fear, but with feeling. Yet her face was calm. How long, a second, a minute, she stood there, I am unsure, but then she turned and I heard the pony's hoofs. How she was dressed, or if barefoot or not, I had no notion. The eyes I saw, and nothing else, and I was shaking for minutes. Why I never spoke is beyond me, but fact is fact, and the fact is, I never thought to.

Then I knew that without any more nonsense I must find out who she was, and what she was doing in the place, and Rhinberry was the one to ask. But he had kept his word and never came near. My horse was loose, but Luis had a pony beyond the firewood and I walked up there, past the kitchen. In the shadow of the roof, Solva sat on a bag of potatoes with green and red cabbage and a pile of apples all round her, and the tunic was on her lap, and the work-basket on the floor, and she had Oracio's cap on the back of her head, and he knelt beside her, looking up, and they both saw me.

"We are discussing the Indio War," she said. "I don't want to marry an old murderer, and have my blood everywhere."

"This troop has never gone out to kill or destroy, but we've had to fight and we did," Oracio said, but very calmly. "All my men are Gaucho, of Indio birth, Tehuelche and Araucano. They don't kill their own. Many times we found tracks, and rode across them. War? Only five thousand men are in the entire Army. Against a few families of Indios? War? Genocide, yes. For commerce. You wish to consider me such a barbarian?"

"Don't you love him when he's angry?" she said, to nobody. "We have got to have these old whiskers off him. And this uniform has got to be washed, and taken to pieces and stitched again. I believe Geza has got good English riding boots to fit him, so I'll send in. And shirts. Not one, whole, to his back, and that one I wouldn't clean a wagon with."

"Has any of this got something to do with me?" I asked her.

She sat up surprised, and with the cap just seen in a stook of ash-fair hair, and her eyes wide, so pale and gray, and her mouth open, only an angel might have been prettier, though from the glow of Oracio's adoration, he could have argued.

"Well, I'm not sure," she said. "We ought to write to the President and tell him, as we did in the Atlantic Colony, years ago. The killing was stopped, near us. If Saiheque mixed blood with you, wouldn't you do something?"

"If I ever hear Saiheque or any of his people have been harried about us, I will do more than write," I said. "There are plenty here to help."

"I have told you," Oracio said, still looking at Solva. "The war is finished. We are going back to Biedma to sign off and be paid. My men are entering into my employment. Could we work with my father's men, knowing we had killed their brothers and sisters and their children? You must believe me. Believe it of most of us in the Army. Never."

Solva put her arms about him, and no nonsense, and the ashy-fair hair was over his face.

"There is nice your old whiskers are, boy," she whispered. "Nobody is blaming you. Or let me hear them. When are you going back?"

"When you are ready to bear the weight of the marriage ring," Oracio said. "Then you will wear it, and come with me, and we shall be together. And never one moment apart. Remember this."

"Perhaps you will tell me something to keep me here?" Solva said, and sitting back.

"Your sisters," Oracio said. "Your family. Your duty."

"My duty is with what is mine," Solva said. "My sisters have got business enough without me. As to the ring, I have borne the weight, and no trouble."

She pulled a silk tape from the neck of her dress and swung the ring looped in it.

"The gold is from beyond the lakes, at the back here, dug out by Thomas the Peak," she said. "Vyrnwy made them for us. Look, how heavy, and beautiful. What else, now then?"

"Has Teg got one?" I asked her.

She stared.

"Well, of course, boy," she said. "The first. He brought it to show."

"Good," I said. "Will you tell Lal I have gone to Rhin's?"

"You tell him to be here tonight for the asado I will give," she shouted behind me, if that clear little voice was a shout. "He will drink a wine with us, or never come near me again."

Rhin's place at that time was in a forest of fine cypress, with about a dozen or more big toldos, well-made to stand the weather, all round a stone water tank filled by hollow tree trunks coming from the waterfall, and stacks of enough cut wood to warm ten winters. In some of the toldos Indio women were making carpets, and in others more were turning sticks in tubs full of colors to dye the wool, and men were cutting hides, and women sewed, and in the last three, men and boys made saddlery and plaited bridles and stirrup leathers. In the toldo at the back, Rhin made big, round, flat loaves of bread, with a dozen women helping between the dough board and a line of clay ovens.

"Why is it I never knew you were a baker, Rhin?" I asked him.

"I am anything needed," he said, flour to the elbows, and putting a dry cap on from one of the girls. "A lot of the families haven't time to bake, and no money, either. So a bit of credit will do no harm, see, and the children will go to school full."

"Our families?" I said.

"Of course, our families," he said. "Here. In the valley. And the Indios. And some Chilenos. They have all got children. And children eat. Didn't you know?"

"I didn't know so many were in such a condition," I said. "Can we help?"

"Yes," he said, flat. "Two bags of flour every week. One half bag of sugar for them to have a slice of cake Saturday and Sunday. Eggs I have got. You shall have it back when the springtime brings new blessing. We could do with smoked meat, twenty carcasses or more. Hams. Vegetables, I have got drying here, but we could do with more. It will be a hard winter. And long. So better to take care now, than beat the breast later."

"We shall help," I said. "Come to the asado tonight. Solva will marry Oracio. She'll go with him, but keep her league here. It could be put to good use."

"I swore not," Rhin said, sifting flour over the dough, and rolling.

"Harden not thy heart," I said. "He could have done a lot worse. After all, they are soldiers, boy. Come over tonight. For Solva. And Doli. And Lal. And Tegwyn."

"Swearing an oath, with me, is strange, so I will think," he said. "I missed you, yes, I did. And the singing is splendid with you. My girls and boys were sitting about here, in dreams with them. I never thought to have a feeling for a drum and guitar. Very foreign, I thought. But they have an excellence, indeed."

"Bring all the girls and boys, and join the asado," I said. "They will be nearer the music. And friendlier with everybody of our own over there. Why not? Have they ever done any harm?"

"Huw, you are making trouble for yourself," he said, and cutting more dough. "Some of us don't like Indios, and won't have Indios, and hate anybody that helps."

"They can hate us, then," I said. "Lal's had three guardians since she was a little girl. Better men you won't find. The other girls the same. Now, Rhin. I have never had any Indio to help, or as one to employ."

"I can send a dozen now, only say one syllable," Rhin said, and leaned on the board. "I have been wanting to offer. Luis was the first, with a reason to be interpreter. Is he behaving?"

"A good boy, and I believe he will be a good workman," I said. "He's taught me to say *mari-mari* with the best. I don't think there's a prettier way to say Good Morning. I am asking about something else."

He looked at me, and I knew that he knew.

"There's an Indio girl," I said. "She's been twice. She only stands there. A moment. A minute. I don't know how long. Then she goes. Who is she?"

He turned from me.

"Ah, Huw," he said, in mourn. "If I could save you. Where was Luis?"

"Out for timber," I said. "But she's only been twice. When I was alone. Who is she?"

"Half-sister to Lal," he said. "Sister to Ithel and the rest. Granddaughter to the greatest cacique in all Patagonia. The truest blood in the land on her mother's side. Her father, of course, was Vrann Corwen. Her name is Lliutro. A lily."

"Where is she, and how can she be told not to go near the shop again?" I said.

"Look, Huw," he said, and dusted his hands of flour. "Nail one idea in your head. Indios will do as they want, and not as you want. You have been trained to abide by our Law. Whatever the Law is. And you don't know a small part of it. Indios never heard of a law. Except the Indio ways they were taught. Our Law and our way of doing anything to them is a mystery. That girl will do exactly as she pleases. She's never done anything else. She is what we call Daughter of the House. A princess. She can do no wrong. I will send word to her. I have no hope she will give a dandelion-puff."

"Why should she come and stare?" I asked him.

"Ithel, remember, is your friend," Rhinberry said. "He's her brother. Saiheque cut himself with you. Indios have another idea, you see, about being a friend. It's not simply friendliness. It's part of their meat, their bones, their nerves. A friend is the other half of their souls. If you die before, you must wait at the Gates, and help them into Paradise. That's a friend."

"She is a friend, is that it?" I said.

Rhinberry rounded another big loaf, halved it, pressed and rolled it, and slid it to the women waiting with the tray.

"Yes," he said. "She is a friend. But be careful. I've told you. We think of a friend. That word is not in Arauco. Another word serves. It is not the same. They use their bodies as they use their minds. To us, the body is rude. To them the body is only a part. Is there necessity to say more?"

"Be over for the asado and make Solva happy," I said. "And tell that one."

Out, to find the pony, looking about to see if I could see Lliutro, a beautiful name that sounds nothing like the way it is spelled, and up, and off, without sight of anyone like her. What I felt at that time, I am not sure, because although the eyes, the dark stare, made me restless in mind for a woman, and ready in the body, yet I was full of the thought of Lal and impatient of anyone else.

A righteous one in love, I was, and a mule should have kicked me, both hoofs, because if I had thought a little more, and confided in Lal, a lot could have been done, perhaps. Those notions crawl in after. Then, I thought I wanted to save nuisance. In truth, I suppose I was saving that girl for myself.

Everything was knocked out of my head when I got back.

The noise I could hear before I was off the pony, but Volde was loudest.

"Never," he was shouting, when I walked through the elderberries. "It is impossible. I cannot think of it."

Lal saw me, and ran.

"The preacher is Roman Catholic," she said. "What shall we do?"

"Married, we want to be," I said. "Roman Catholic, or what? Where is the difference? We are married."

"But we must do a lot of things, first," she said, and starting to drop the tears. "Catechism. And our children must be Roman Catholics."

At that time, Roman Catholic, to me, was the best part of the Devil himself. Where the idea came from I am not sure, but I think in school, when we were taught about poor people burned at the stake. But I had met a few since that time, and they looked ordinary to me and doing harm to nobody.

"If there was a Justice here, we could have the paper, and a thick thumb to everybody," I said. "Where is the Roman Catholic? Let us talk first. Is his piece of paper any better than the Justice's?"

"They think more of God and less about the Government," she said. "It is a marriage in Heaven. Not only down here."

"Nothing wrong with that," I said. "Why is Volde angry?"

"Angry?" Volde shouted. "But there is nothing I can respect. It is not the true church. How could we marry in such a manner? And our children? To be Roman? No. I say, absolutely, no."

"Where is he?" I asked. "Let us have a word, and find out."

"The peons just came back with the stores and told us he is in the village," Doli said. "I don't care if it's an old Catholic or who. Only so long as we are right, and we can go in the house and straight in beautiful bed, then, and nobody with a bit to say. We can go to the Justice after. Then the children are safe."

"No, Doli," Solva said. "If you swear, and marry, the children will go to the Church. They must."

"No 'must' with me," Tegwyn said. "My children shall not be Catholic. I won't be married by an old Catholic, either. We will roast in Hell before the night is gone."

"Well, there is silly you are, girl," Gwenonwy said, and much too calm. "Donato is Roman Catholic. I married him in the Roman Catholic shrine, there. I am one. So is the baby. Am I different? Are we smelling, with us?"

"We are in a fool's way here," Lal said. "What, exactly, have we got to do?"

"Nothing more than you want," Gwenonwy said. "I was frightened, too. I thought I was in the road to Hell, for sure. And I was frightened for the baby. Frightened. The very words. Roman Catholic. In our house, it was a sin to say them. The mention was not allowed."

"Ours, too," Doli said. "What did they do to you?"

Gwenonwy looked at her, no surprise, but almost laughing, thin lips closed, thin nose high, hollow cheeks even hollower, and the big blue-green eyes having a light and the sunshine gold in the eyelashes.

"Well, what do you think, and I was helpless, here?" she said. "They made me take off all my clothes, not one stitch on me, and they beat me raw, top to toe, and they made Donato eat the baby, no salt."

Volde saw nothing to laugh at, and I was beginning to worry for Doli, because for her, any life without plenty of laughter was only death a little delayed.

"You cannot tergiversate, here," he said, with both hands upraised. "You must face all the consequences, now, and for the rest of your lives, and the lives of your children."

Certain it is that most of us had never heard that word before, but his voice and eyes made us aware that for him it was not a simple question of marriage.

"Volde," Solva said, in that small voice, that made any argument, as it were, smaller, and less violent. "You were willing to marry with the preacher. If he was Baptist, or Methodist, or what he was. Why is it different with a Roman Catholic?"

"The preacher, yes, he is evangelist," Volde said. "He brings us to God. It is well. He joins us with the simple Word. It is enough. It is indissoluble. Forever. It is what I most want with my luminous one, here."

"The priest will do exactly the same," Gwenonwy said.

"No," Volde said, flat. "We are brought to Rome. No farther. With our children."

Standing there, in the green shade of that timber in the valley, I have often wondered what we thought Rome was, especially the women. Tegwyn, of course, was a Baptist. No use trying to move her. The severity of her life had made her proof against any form of persuasion, and her prayers on the knees every morning and night she knew were about to be answered, and she was sure that the answer had come from nobody but the Baptist God. Anything beyond was only temptation of the Devil, and there was no way for him to tempt her.

No woman has ever been surer than Tegwyn, and most of us seemed to know.

"Everybody do what they want," she said. "For me, no Catholic. A preacher, yes, or a Justice, very well. Nothing else."

"I will be Roman Catholic," Solva said. "Oracio is. I will be. And our children."

"Nothing has happened to Gwenonwy," Lal said.

That was the biggest surprise, because she was standing there looking as she always had, but she was a Roman Catholic.

"Nothing will," she said. "I don't feel different than when the Reverend Armon Tudor used to give us a service."

"I wish to God he was here," Doli said. "Bring out the Book, say the words, and everybody off, and no fault in the world."

"Chile is not far, through the lakes," Volde said. "We could ride there in ten days, or less. In Peulla they must have a Justice. Or the German colony farther on will have a non-conformist. For me, the same."

"What has happened to our preacher?" I asked. "Did he fall in the river?"

"If he did, his own sire has claimed him," Tegwyn said. "He is with boiling fat, in Rome."

"As I am," Gwenonwy said. "And very comfortable too."

A group of people, all old enough to accept the responsibilities of marriage and children, wasting time to talk in such a manner seems ridiculous, but years had to pass after that before Tegwyn and Gwenonwy gave each other a civil word, yet a moment before they were as sisters. All the girls were near to tears, and Volde was carving a piece of wood and Doli leaning to watch. Lal rested against me, and I put an arm about her and sensed her beauty that was warm for me, but I was thinking about Lliutro, and what she might know of Roman Catholics, or if she could be more ignorant than any of us, and suddenly I knew how Beretroff had felt when the Indio women stared at him, and only then, after all that time, I was sorry.

"Well, are we going on preparing the big asado, or shall we tell everybody we are off piecemeal to find somebody?" Lal said. "Make up our minds, now."

"Chile," Volde said.

"I am not leaving everything here for two or three weeks," I said. "Too much to be done."

"Not to marry me, boy?" Lal asked, but smiling, because I knew she agreed.

"I will marry you on the day, if it is before fifty Roman Catholics in stink from the Pit," I said.

"That's it," she said, and loosed me, and rolled up her sleeves. "Now I am right. And everybody else, a thumb."

"And me?" Doli said.

"You will marry with Volde where you please, and Teg will marry, and come back, and you will both find everything will be the same," Lal said, and gave her a good kiss. "Solva will be married with us, and the baby will be christened. Not the same as all of us together, but still good. Now then, work, everybody."

Oracio and his troop were out at the time clearing timber, but when he came in Solva brought him to the shop.

"Why is this hatred for the Roman Catholic?" he said, no bones, before I could welcome them. "Two hundred years ago the priests were here. They were martyred here. Why does everybody make us such idiocies?"

"Make allowance for grown-up children," I said. "We only know what we were taught. The rest comes with a bit of living."

"Then you," he said. "Are you enemy or friend?"

"I am nothing and nobody," I said. "I well remember Mr. Elias, Snuff. He called me 'somebody Morgan, and covering expenses to carpenter.' I am nothing more, for the moment. So why should I worry if I am in chapel, or anywhere else?"

"But this Volde," he said. "He is Russian? But his church is the same as the Roman."

"Let everybody have his own idea," I said. "Any prayer in any church goes to God. Any chapel, the same. Once in a time, from a stable. Let the fools argue. We shall have the trees and the air and the Word. That's all I want. Then Lal is one with me."

Solva squeezed Oracio's arm between both her own and started to pull him away.

"The answer is there, solid," she said. "Come, you. Let the fools argue."

A selfish answer, too, but if I leave the earth this moment, I shall still say it, and I shall never understand why the fools argue. They have all got a different little hat, and different little buttons, and they all put their bottoms into different little trews and they all earn a little bit of money. They have all got God the Father, the Son, and the Holy Ghost, and Eternal Love, and the Sacrifice, and Salvation, and the Resurrection, and yet, Tegwyn and Gwenonwy, both good girls, of the best, must be next to enemies and years after, come together in tears and find the Love for themselves, and without help.

Teg and Vyrnwy worried me, because I knew he could never leave the smithy for more than a week, exactly like me, because we had more work than we could manage, and promises to keep, and people needing what we could do. Donato had rows of finished wheels there, only needing Vyrnwy's iron hoops, and with my wagon tongues, axles, and boards, the carts were ready. Volde had almost made enough yokes for the oxen pairs, and Rhin's Indios had plaited the rawhides, so a bit of hammering, and people could come and take away what they were praying for. But the moment they were gone, twice as many were in want, and we were first to know that without carts, plenty of families would have a harder winter.

There was no good excuse for more than a week off. I knew that Teg wanted to be married more than she had ever wanted to live, and Vyrnwy needed her, and she knew it well. But nothing would have got her under that toldo with him except the Word, from the Book, out loud in front of everybody, and the paper, signed.

Luis came in with an ox-cart piled high with fine timber and bellowed and howled the team into place to unload.

"Sir," he said at the door. "The preacher is at Mr. Rhinberry's, and he will be here at the falling sun."

With only a royal hope in me, I looked at him.

"The preacher?" I said. "How do you know? What's his name?"

Luis lifted both shoulders.

"Mr. Rhinberry brought us all in to kneel," he said. "We sang. His name, I don't know."

"Come now, Luis," I said. "Mr. Rhinberry is not a Catholic. Why did you kneel?"

"Mr. Rhinberry was kneeling," he said.

"Who is the preacher?" I asked him. "Do we know him, here?"

He shook his head, and sent the hair from his ears with spread fingers.

"I remember him two years ago, out at Quilfiltreu," he said. "Before that, with Nahuel Pan, my grandfather. He works with Moishe Levy and Geza Paal."

"Not a Roman Catholic?" I asked him, and knew what a fool I was, for the boy stared.

"He is *Küme Huenü,* sir," Luis said. "He is the best. The friend. He is Mr. Rhinberry's brother."

Out I went, calling for Lal, and they all came running from the kitchen, and their faces were plain with worry.

"The preacher is here, and not a Catholic," I said. "No need for any more trouble. He is coming from Rhinberry's now."

A few words, and an ordinary voice, and yet I might have been one with a Flaming Sword.

Tegwyn bumped on her knees and fell in sobs, and Doli beside her, and Solva knelt, and Lal put her arms about them.

Ponies were in gallop, coming along the track, and Rhinberry slid off, and Luis ran to take the reins.

One came, a shadow under the trees, and took off the hat to brush dust.

"God's blessing everywhere," Rhinberry said. "The preacher is here, at last."

Mouth like a fly trap I was standing there, staring.

"Well, Huw," Mr. Gruffydd said. "I was sent in good time, do you see? 'Let them be only thine own, and not strangers with thee. Let thy fountain be blessed, and rejoice with the wife of thy youth.' I am here at last. Eh, Huw?"

"Amen," Rhin said, and looked at the girls. "Not one drop would he drink till he was here. Will he perish then?"

"Perish?" Doli said, and wiping her eyes. "He shall have a drink of my blood, only say."

"The kettle," Teg shouted, and off her knees, and the light in her. "I have got tea-bread and -cakes. Where is the tea with you, girl?"

"Tea," Lal shouted with her. "Tea. Milk, Doli."

"Tea, milk, Doli, tea, sugar, tea," they all sang, harmonizing, and ran in rumple of skirts, and laughing, arms about, children again.

Mr. Gruffydd looked at me.

"Moishe told me you were desperate for a minister," he said. "I made an exception. The others were old for the journey. I came south of the river instead of north. A wash would be a pleasure, indeed."

"Wash," I said, hardly knowing what I had heard. "We were praying, and you were sent."

"Enough here to plant," Mr. Gruffydd said. "Is there a bucket and a bit of soap anywhere? I am like Adam, before the Breath. Of the earth, and not yet himself, and the Rib still in quietus with him. Do you know what song is in my spirit to be here, Huw?"

"The prayer was heard," I said. "Mama, it was. I know it better than the day. Mama sent you."

6

Those days before the wedding were shivery in the mornings, cold enough at night to look for a good fire, but at noon we broiled in a shouting sun. People began coming in a week before, because news was slow, and they were afraid to be late. Some had a point of sheep or a grunt of pigs, or poultry in a rope net, or a grown calf, or something they had cooked, but however many there were, they all sang and they all worked, either with us, or with Gwenonwy and Donato next door, or over at Rhinberry's, or farther on, at Vyrnwy's. Up there, they baked the tea-cakes and loaves and rolls and fruit cakes with the fire of the forge. At Gwenonwy's, they plucked and cleaned poultry and cut the joints of meat. Rhinberry had everything else, from salads, vegetables and fruits to round bread, and with us was the place of the asado, and the *curantó*.

There must have been more than three hundred of us there, not counting the Indios, so there had to be plenty of food for at least six days. With food goes drink, and the wagons were coming in loaded with barrels, and many a case of bottles though they came into my shop for safety and went under key. The asado pit had been dug by the peons, about a hundred feet round, and we had plenty of irons to grill the carcasses, and a dozen wire platforms for the small fry and sausages.

Curantó, ceremonial banquet of the Araucano, I liked most of all.

Rhinberry came over with all his men and women to prepare the fires and dress the food. They made six shallow pits, round, about three paces across, and two foot deep, with plenty of space between each. The men went to gather stone, all about the same size, a forearm, and half that in width and breadth. The women chipped laurel wood, chacai, and maitén, because they burn clear and hot without much smoke, and they heaped green branches of maqui with plenty of leaves, and piles of pea-stalks beside each dig. Boys and girls cut squares of turf, and brought baskets of earth, and the little ones were sent to ask for sacks and wagon canvas. In all of this, the girls were running between the kitchen shed and the bakehouse we had put up, for in the final days, Rhin was in there building a wedding cake so big that before it was finished we had to lift the roof to carry it out. They had their own clay ovens, and Lal and Doli made tarts and pies of meats, fruits, and jams, Solva made cream pastries, Gwenonwy came back to finish rolling and shaping molds of meat and sausage, and Tegwyn had two ovens to herself for *empanadas,* a pastry filled with meat, whether poultry, beef or lamb, with raisins, onions, olives and whatever is nearest a good woman's mind, and they came gold from the heat, and of a taste to make you dribble to think, especially with a glass of wine. All the Provinces of Argentina have their own special *empanada,* but of those I will choose Tegwyn's of New Cambria, and Mendoza wine, because one melts, and the other heats, and the two go splendidly hand in hand as lovers in passion, always in rich pleasure and never a moment's harm.

At first light on the day before the wedding, Indios lined the *curantó* digs with wood chips a few inches deep, and over them they put the stones in rings, starting in the middle and working out, close together, and when the digs were covered, they looked like concave wheels, and well set. Over the stones they piled trunks of laurel, chacai, and maitén, and set flame, and I timed the fires to burn high and hot for six hours, sometimes a little less, but they seemed to know when to stop putting on fuel, and when there was more ash than wood, they swept the fire from the stones and left them almost clean. Over the stones they matted the branches of leaves thick enough to cover, and on that green carpet they put the chickens, ducks, geese, turkeys, joints of pork, beef and lamb, sausage of every kind, liver, kidneys, vegetables, fruits, pies, puddings and stuffed breads, until all the space was filled with another sort of wheel. Armfuls of pea-stalks went over to hold off a roof of green branches, stems out, laid thick, and then the sacks and canvas, and the steam was blowing out, and more sacks and canvas to stop the holes, and then turf in tight pack, and shovelsful of earth on top to close any gap, and tamp down.

By many an age of men I suppose the time of cooking had been learned by heart, but though they never heard of a clock, the Indios seemed to allow between an hour and thirty-five to forty-five minutes before they scraped away the earth, scooped off the turf, pulled away the sacks and lifted the branches. The leaves were cooked yellow, and whether or not their juices ran into the meats below, but the taste of everything was different, in some way cleaner in the mouth, of a delicacy and tenderness not to be found in ovens, pans, or pots. Except that it took time to prepare stones and wood, and the wait of hours while the stones came hot, I never found a simpler kitchen than the Indio, with nothing to wash except the hands, nothing to clean except ash that the winds were always happy to lift in play, with only appetite for sauce, and gusto the best part of each morsel, whether meat, vegetables, fruit or pastries, and each a triumph to stay in the mind. Only men seemed to be in charge of the cooking, perhaps because in the hours of watching the women had to look after the children, though without any sign or call, the families were there just when the earth came off, ready. Where they had that sense of time I never found out. It is one thing to tell the day's quarter from a look at the sun, but to tell one hour and thirty-five minutes from one hour and forty-five is something else again. But I marked the time, and I never found them more than ten minutes out, and that might have been the difference between the dampness or dryness of the wood.

About a sense of time, Rhinberry said the Araucano believed they each had a ball of spiritual wool in their hearts, and while the seconds of their lives passed, the end was being pulled by *Ranginhüenüchäu,* their Creator, winding it back to Himself, until there was only the end, and with that they ran laughing off the earth and into the sky, and wonderful welcome from their family and all their friends.

Some, too often, I have heard saying that the Indio is crude, bestial, never far from the Stone Age. A look at the elegant simplicity of that kitchen, a moment's study of their language, and only an hour round the fire at night, while they tell stories of their God, and the Spirits that sing and smile even in the smallest stones and drips of water, might enlighten a few of them, though there is no hope it would, and Rhinberry was always in a trembling temper when somebody tried to treat his men and women as animals, or as less than us.

"I have been in rags and next to barefoot, here, for years, and I will never be different till I run at the end of my skein up to my little one," he said. "None of them has got more than me. None of us shall have more than the other. But if I hear more talk about my boys and girls, I will go. They shall not be dismayed by these whited sepulchres."

"Wait you, now, Rhin," I said. "We haven't had time for a cemetery, boy."

"You have got open tombs standing up and rotting with them," he whispered, and pointing outside. "Turning away from my boys and girls. Making them feel miserable. Nobody is more sensitive than the Araucano. They are blushing to be staying here. If I wasn't here, they would go. Go? They would be gone."

"You can't expect more," Lal said, careless. "Only a few

years ago we lost good boys. Murdered, there. We never did the Indios any harm, did we? We asked the President to stop killing them. But they mutilated our boys. It takes time to forget. The families haven't forgotten. That's all."

"But there are different Indios, girl," Rhinberry said. "Huilliches, Pehuenches, Puelches, Nguluches, Moluches."

"Any Indio is an Indio," Lal said. "Are you going to give lectures, then, on how many kinds of Indios there are? Which one is good, and which bad? You will talk for El Pampero. And have the same answer. They will still be Indios. Better take no notice and wait for time, and babies, and books."

Rhinberry nodded, and looked out toward the crowd under the trees.

"You will marry before the Christian God," he said. "Only that Word will give you comfort, isn't it? But the other Words pass your ears. A few words, and you are married. A few other words? Do Unto Others? The Least Of These? Suffer The Little Children? They are only in the Book. They sit comfortable on the page. They never rise up to rend you. Eat and drink, and tomorrow we will marry. And to Hell with everybody else."

"That is not true," Lal said, every word with equal weight. "You are first to know it. Mama loved Rayentrú as one of us. Except we were up at the dam when she went, and knowing nothing, we would have been with you. When were we turning our backs on Indios? Or anybody else? You blame us for a few out there. Talk to them."

"I'm sorry," Rhinberry said. "Now try to explain it to my boys and girls. Solomon was wise because he had a language and his people could understand. I have got half a language. In the other half is ignorance and confusion. What, then, is left?"

"You have got duty," Lal said. "Go, you."

He laughed suddenly, as a little boy, and nodded, and went out calling a group near the asado pit.

"A little wine in them, and we might have trouble," Lal said. "We shall have to watch those barrels. Our boys can get just as drunk as Indios, and almost as nasty. Except those who don't drink, and how many are there? Ten in a hundred?"

"We'll find them and put them in charge of the barrels, and these bottles in here," I said.

"And what is Lord Mr. South going to do?" Lal asked me. "Get married, and nothing else?"

"I'll give you two hours after the ceremony," I said. "Only for them to drink the health of the bride and wish us well. Two hours. Then you will be on your horse and on the way to the lakes."

"Long before that, boy," she said, and gave me a kiss on the cheek with the warm O of her mouth. "Three hours, at least, riding. You be ready the moment he closes the Book. And what a shame your sisters can't be here."

"No way for it," I said. "And your father."

"Thank God he's where he is," she said, stretching both arms up. "We are happy without."

"I am a bad influence," I said. "You wouldn't have told me that a couple of months ago."

She smiled, and squeezed her shoulders in a quiver of strength.

"No," she said. "We are too kind with everybody. And they use us like crockery, and never mind if we chip. But there is sense, too. Let him die with his drink, or come sober to us. We will never be second to a bottle any more."

Solva and Oracio were with us before Mr. Gruffydd to have the Word between them before going back across the pampas, and they were ready to have another service with the Hernandez family in the City of Lewis to put everything at peace with God, the Church, and themselves.

"It is well," Mr. Gruffydd told all of us, one evening, over in the cataract corner, under the big trees above white water. "Parents are entitled to be comforted and so we must be strict. This country is not like the one most of us came from. We try to use ourselves in the same way, but we fail. There's another language to be learned, at least. Other customs to be observed. Other temptations to be thrust aside. No doubt we've done a great deal to change the country. But the country has changed us. It is not what it was, even a short year ago. And we are far from being what we were. Each day we change. Compared with ten years ago, we are others behind the same pair of eyes. I know the change in myself. Once I thought myself called to practice another revival of the Spirit. The spirit which needed to be revived was my own, but I didn't realize it. That was when I came here. With nothing. Not faith, not hope, not an ideal. In that state, no man may advise another. I took sheep, instead. Time, and silence, and the company of sheep, dogs, horses, and nights beside a fire looking at the stars. Well, the change comes, do you see? Quicker than we think. Faith returns, stronger than before. Ideals, pristine. Hope, sacrosanct. The Father reaches down through our darkness. With light He bars our retreat. It would be simple for all of you to put your names in a book, sign, and go off. No. You know within you it would be wrong. Wrong for you, because you were taught better. For that reason, and only for that reason, I am here to bring you into the House as man and wife, and in that Blessing you shall be one, always in the power and the love of the Lord."

No doubt but he had changed, too, quieter, and yet stronger within, gentler, perhaps, but with more force, and still the smile, but happier, as though he smiled because he must, and not merely to give comfort. Well, and so clearly I remembered him those mornings up on the mountain, sitting on the green slope among the daffodils, looking along the Valley, holding his ankles, trying not to let the breeze blow his eyelids shut, and telling about the Celts, and Goidels, and Belgi, and the Romans, Saxons, Normans, and the rest.

"And you see, Huw, we are still here," he said. "We may not know what our Fathers of those days felt, then, or in the sad days after. But the Spirit is still with us, because the Spirit is with God. That is the Word and the Light. While those are with us, we shall be born again."

But there are many ready to run rather than listen, and the more schooling, it seems, the readier if not faster.

"No, Huw, no, no," Olwen said, in that voice so much like my mother's. "I simply cannot stand it, and that's all. That sort of thing's all very well down here, I suppose, and I don't doubt it does everybody lots of moral good to climb out in any weather and put their best clothes on and sit there. Not for me. Not the prayers, and dear God, not the sermons. Not anything."

"No religion," I said.

"My own," she said. "I've built up a quiet little one all on my own. Perfectly happy with it. I pass this way but once, etcetera, and so on. I don't miss the other, except, I suppose, with a feeling of unutterable relief. I'm very much like Mama in those last years. She never went to chapel after little Dada died. Not a word about it. After all, why? Put a Baptist and a Methody in the same room, they'll bite each other. No good reason. Some odd bit of nonsense in the service. Don't tell me you're still one of them? You're not. It's not in your eyes. Thank God."

She never wanted to come out to the Colony, and I begged her, but her work took every moment, and societies in London, and being secretary of this and that gave her no free time, so any thought of six months away she said was simply out of the question. The couple of days we had in the Valley was an honor to me, I suppose, but she had a meeting in Cardiff, so she broke two stones with one tap, and dancing with nervousness until we were back on the London train, and such a change when we crossed the Border. A different girl, almost the one I had known as a little bit of a thing, holding my hand to go to Tossall's for sweets. But looking at grown-ups, so set with opinions and so ready to condemn, it is almost impossible to think of them as babies, or to see what sort of blubs they were when they were six.

That feeling I had when Paco Barramendiz came in with a troop that afternoon.

"A Fat One from Buenos Aires, him, and a lawyer,"

Corianth Austin said, behind me. "He was in my place yesterday. Good job my wife was there. I'd have killed him."

"What, now?" Lal said. "Land, or titles?"

"Anything," Corianth said. "Willie Price heard he came in with the soldiers from north of Nahuel Huapí. He's buying their land grants. He swore my titles are no good."

"Good as anybody's," Lal said. "Keep away from a pen, and always talk to him with at least two witnesses of your own."

Barramendiz was the first rotten lawyer I ever met, and the difference between him and the two in the Colony was respect for the Law and any decency. He came in later that afternoon from a camp across the river, and walked up the length of the shop as if he owned it, no knock or if you please.

"My name," he said, and flicked a card on the bench, and without putting down the mallet and chisel, I pushed the pile of shavings and the card to the floor.

"When you enter under this roof, take your hat off," I said. "I am working. Go outside, and wait till I have finished."

He leaned on both hands across the bench.

"Be careful how you speak to me," he said. "I hold an Army commission. I am also an officer of the High Court. I'm here to give you and a few more some advice that can save you a lot of trouble."

"I don't need it," I said. "Go, now."

"Your title to this land is worthless," he said, still leaning. "Just as the rest are."

The mallet was the largest, and I hammered within an inch of his fingers, and he moved, too.

"Our titles are in the Governor's office in Rawson," I said. "We have nothing further to say. Tomorrow there will be a ceremony of marriage here. You are welcome to eat and drink with us. But no more about titles. Outside, if you please."

By good fortune, Oracio came in with two of his troopers carrying pack saddles for the wooden frames I had finished.

None of them were in uniform, and they looked like anyone else, sweating, bearded, dusty, and in torn rope-soles.

"An enquiry here," I said to Oracio. "I suppose you will have an interest. This man says our titles aren't worth the paper."

"Who are you?" Oracio asked him.

"My card," Barramendiz said, and pointed to the floor. "Who are you?"

A trooper picked up the card and held it upside down.

"Very pretty," Oracio said, without looking. "What's your business in this region?"

"Are you a settler here?" Barramendiz asked, because Oracio's speech, unlike ours, was pure, clipped Castellano which I tried to copy.

"I am Lieutenant of Fifth Gaucho Cavalry," Oracio said. "I command here. Go to my camp. I shall talk to you."

"Lieutenant?" Barramendiz said, and looked him up and down, but that was all.

A nod from Oracio, and the troopers dropped the saddles, took the fat one by the arm and trews and out he went, and they had him running within five paces.

"We've been looking for that kind," Oracio said. "Every soldier in the desert's entitled to a piece of land here, Non-Coms a little more, and officers more according to rank. These thieves have been giving them a few pesos, or a case of rotgut for the titles. Of course, that type of title is clear. Nothing to pay. No taxes. Buy the grants of, say, twenty men, and you've got an estate for almost nothing. Buy the grants of half a regiment? An empire. For a few bottles. That's what they've been doing. The General's going to stop it. In an hour's time, come to my camp. Give evidence of what he said."

An unknown Oracio, strict, and black in the eye, not the same man when I and everybody else went over there later, all dressed and shaved, and as well we were. Oracio's hair was off, and his uniform was sewn and washed and fitting like another skin, and new boots, and everything polished, buttons, badges, and sabre with him, and the lance stuck in the ground beside his table. The Gauchos' uniforms had all been washed and sewn by Rhin's Indios, so the troop was smarter than any I had seen until then, and the camp was squared and cleaned, with rock surrounds to the tents made of our wagon canvas, and an Argentinian flag on a tall, peeled sapling.

We were too far to hear more than a murmur, but poor Mr. Paco got a short clip, indeed. He tried to bow and scrape and wheedle his way into good graces, but Oracio's face was flat as any Indio's. We were not even called for evidence. Half a dozen of the troopers marched out to say they had been offered a case of bottles and a few pesos to make a mark on paper, and that was enough.

Oracio shouted an order and the troop turned and ran to a pile of cut timber. Some of them dug a trench about two foot deep and a foot wide around a square of two paces. The timbers went upright in the trench and earth was stamped in, and there, almost by magic, was a little house, no windows, door, or roof, about ten feet high. Mr. Paco was shoved inside, the two timbers were replaced, and Oracio marched the troop back to the camp and dismissed them.

"There is a cruel old thing you are, boy," Solva said, but looking at him in a different way, almost with more pride. "Will you let him out for the wedding?"

"Sooner a mad dog," he said. "That type of criminal has robbed the Army. Still robbing. He'll stay there till we leave. I give warning. Nobody may go near. The General will deal with him."

Nobody had to be told.

That is, except Mr. Rhinberry Wynn, and as always, he had his own notion of what was to be.

While all of us were at the singing meet that night, Rhin and a couple of his boys threw over some food and a bottle of tea, and told Mr. Paco to eat and drink and throw the sack and bottle back, and be sure to bury the crumbs. It was Solva, that one with the small voice, who argued and argued until Oracio ordered a guanaco pelt tossed over to keep out the cold, though he was not to know that Rhin had already thrown one in.

Those nights must have been the first meet of more than a hundred voices in the valley, and by a long way the best trained, and though there were others after, I never heard better. We sang every ballad and hymn we were ever taught, and each night a couple or more of the standard choral pieces, but we always finished with the guitar, pipes, and drum. Mr. Gruffydd had forgotten nothing as a choirmaster, and when it was seen that he knew a little about it, people crowded to their places, and stood, not as having a tune on an outing, but as choristers with a voice, ready to be told when and what, and singing to command of the baton.

From my place I often caught Lal's eye in the half-circle of contraltos, and when I heard them rise on a note, I thought my heart would break to think of my mother and father, and all of us, because voices are always the same, and in one place or another they sound the same, and they bring the same memories, so tender and beyond all words beautiful, and so often excruciating to a pitch where you feel you must run. There were times when I wanted to slip away and sit in the shop, or up on the stones, and stop the ache in my throat. But I was dull, because everybody was the same, with memories crowding, and eyes gone in drown, and hoping those roundabout would sing up to cover the shake, and having to sing, then, from shame. That was the reason for the wonderful sound we made, because we sang over dreams of home, over desire to return, over cares of winter and lonely days. We killed fear with the voice, as God Almighty meant, and took strength from each other, knowing that as voices blend, so would the Will, and if there was trouble, plenty would help, and there were doors to open just as readily as lungs.

We were never wrong through the years, never wholly without, never driven to the knees.

"You don't sing the national anthem of Argentina," Oracio said, while we were round the fire and trying some of Teg's *empanadas* and the black Mendoza wine. "I'd like to hear it sung by such a choir. Because it's difficult. Written for trumpets."

"You have no tradition of choral music," Mr. Gruffydd said. "The national voice, the average, isn't a singing voice, and isn't trained chorally. When you're grown up, you can't sing. You squeak. I've been trying to train children. I know."

"Why are Cambrian children born with such voices?" Oracio asked. "Is it a throat or a mouth?"

"They hear their parents," Mr. Gruffydd said. "Throats and mouths, yes, because the language demands the use of both. Our children sing from the cot. Without practice they are toneless as any other. Some of our families can't sing a note. They don't practice. But I know German families that sing as angels, there. Listen to Volde. Basso profundo. But he's singing all day. When he isn't eating everything Doli leaves beyond lock and key."

"Ah, give thanks," Volde said, and spoke at the stars with his mouth full. "A cook. In ten millions, not such another cook."

"A couple of months, there is fat you will be," Doli said. "Eat, and beg for more."

"A couple of months, I know who the fat one will be," Solva said. "Will you please to pass the *empanadas* to my lovely old thin one here, starving with him?"

"The anthem of Argentina, Mr. Gruffydd, when these two have finished," Lal said. "I never heard it."

"Born here, never heard it?" Mr. Gruffydd said, and surprised.

"Never," Lal said. "Perhaps Oracio will sing it for us?"

"I have no tune," Oracio said. "A voice for shouting. I am envious of you. But the words are very fine. Except, of course, I cannot remember them. The children are taught."

"They are taught to gabble through a lot of syllables," Mr. Gruffydd said. "So they'll gabble for the rest of their lives. Everybody pays lip service to patriotism. Nobody's prepared to work. Even with the muscles of their mouths."

"I don't think I've heard the Cambrian anthem," Oracio said.

"I'll sing you to sleep with it, boy," Solva said. "We sing it to close everything."

"'Land of My Fathers,' it's called, for some," Doli said. "Not all. But my father would never sing it. He always swore it ought to be 'Men of Rhyddlan' because he was from the North, not the South. What do you think, Mr. Gruffydd?"

"Where we shall live for the rest of our lives, neither will be an anthem but only items in repertory," Mr. Gruffydd said. "This part of the country will either belong to Chile, or to Argentina. And it looks as if they'll go to war. If they do, we shall have to wait to find out which to sing."

Oracio drank from Solva's glass, and gave it back with a little kiss of the lips.

"Have you any doubt of the outcome?" he asked.

"Personally, I have no doubt but only horror," Mr. Gruffydd said. "I've dealt for years with the Chileans. I find them of highest integrity. They give their word. It is kept. Most of them are Spanish by descent, with Araucano blood. Others are German, Austrian. Those I know, at least. They're coming in here now, farther north. And the Chilean priests have known this land for two hundred years. They have a claim, you see. Only a few years ago, Argentina's southern boundary was more than a thousand miles north of us now. It was the Cambrians coming in here that brought the boundary down. If we hadn't succeeded, it would still be up there. But we did. God was with us. In a blessed land."

"Therefore you have a debt to Argentina," Oracio said.

"If it is allowed that Argentina has a debt to me, of the same size, I shall acknowledge, yes," Mr. Gruffydd said. "I've built, cleared, and reared flocks and herds in the desert, without help of soldiers or credits. I employ thirty men and their families. Indios. I brought my type of civilization here. Indio children have been taught the Castellano language, taught to earn, taught that other people's property is not to be taken. I am not the only one. Therefore, before you speak of my debt, let's hear what the Country's done. The land is here. Do you say that your Government knows anything about it? Where are the schools? Where's the Justice? You protect your soldiers. Who protects what you call the 'tame' Indios? But, using your logic, they are the original owners of these lands. In their ignorance, they need protection. They were here centuries before your fathers got here. What of them? Which anthem shall they sing?"

It seemed to occur to everybody at the same time that Oracio was the only "real" Argentinian there. Yet his father had come from Spain. Most of the others' fathers had come from Cambria. But they had all been born in what came to be called Argentina, without for one moment thinking of themselves as anything but Cambrians.

"You people want to take Patagonia for yourselves, isn't that so?" Oracio asked, perhaps, the *empanada*. "Isn't that why so many of you are here?"

"Wrong," Tom, Tot, called, at the back of the crowd. "I am here to have more land for my family."

Everybody shifted, and murmured agreement.

"The Chilenos have given much more help than anybody else," Mostyn Williams said. "They've brought food over the passes. When we had nothing. And always a good price for our sheep and cattle. I have got a big debt to Chile."

Another movement, and a louder murmur.

"Not for me to say," Volde said, and put his arm about Doli. "I shall do exactly as my Tsarina cook tells me."

"Argentina," Doli said. "I was born here, boy."

"Argentina," Solva said. "Not long after my thin one, here, I was born. Somebody else will be born soon, too. What will he be?"

"Argentina," Lal said. "No use thinking of anything else. Huw?"

"As Solva says, our children will be born here," I said. "What this is, I am. But whatever we call them, can they be anything else but Cambrian? Will Volde's children be anything but Russians?"

Doli had her arms about him, and he was turned to her, and weeping into his hands.

He raised a face in a man's agony that pulls at the mouth.

"Ah, Doli," he said. "It's true. Blood is not changed by signatures. We are what we are. That is the Will of God, and only He can change us. I shall be Argentinian in my feeling for you and the land. But I am Russian. Or tell the eagle it's become a condor."

"Amen," Mr. Gruffydd said. "Come, my little ones, on your knees, now. Let us ask a Blessing, for all of us, and for this Country. Of ours."

7

Mr. Gruffydd had changed far more than I knew. We never seemed to have more than a few minutes talk because of the work to be done and the constant crowd about us, though most of the time he was with Vyrnwy as second smith at the forge and then for a few hours he went down to Rhin and the Indios. It was more than strange, I thought, that he spoke so little of Angharad, though when he did, a new gentleness was in his voice and his eyes were tender with distant yearn.

"I am impatient, I am devoured to be back," he said, that last afternoon. "It will take a good two weeks, hard going. No use to think of her coming here. A wagon would never go through. She isn't used to a horse. A couple of weeks it took me. She could never do it. It would kill her. It was quite exhausting enough for her coming across from Carmen de Patagones. That was five weeks and a couple of days, going slow over the flat by the river, and camping often, and she had a comfortable wagon. Down here, there are the mountains. Rivers. No. You will have to come to us."

"I would, now, with all my heart," I said. "But it's hopeless. Lal must go to the Colony. I've got to stay here. See for yourself. There's enough to do for six. I've written her a letter."

"I should have brought one for you," he said, and laughed.

"You know Angharad. She'd rather paint the corral than hold a pen. And yet a good head for business."

No need to tell me. Angharad had less schooling, perhaps, than any of us, and my father said her handwriting was not less than atrocity itself. But a girl cannot help her Mama in the kitchen and be a scholar. That was one reason why she sent Olwen to a good school, and on to Oxford, though pity, because then Olwen spoke another kind of English and not a word of Cambrian, but Angharad made beautiful use of it, and her English was only a little spiced with the Valley and a touch of the South African, though when I heard her, I thought it healthy and without finick. But sisters speaking two sorts of the same language are not in comfort, especially when a more majestic form of spiritual expression folds flame within them, seen in each others' eyes, heard in the voice, and yet denied.

"Perhaps we shall manage next year," I said. "But look at the times. Spring, summer, autumn, we have got to be here, or in the Colony. Getting up there to you and back, six weeks at least. When? In winter?"

"Too much snow," Mr. Gruffydd said. "And next year we shall be in the Cape. We're going to bring back pedigree sheep, cattle, and horses. Wonderful animals, they have. And some farming ideas. All I've got up there is a plain box of a house. When I get back I'm resigned to seeing a change. My dust was not flat at the gate when she had the workmen in there."

He finished a mortice, and put it aside.

"I'm not sorry now that Bronwen didn't come on," he said. "At first it was a big disappointment. A lot of tears, there. But the moment we left the train and they saw the horses and wagons, it was finished. A lot of people can't be taught another life. They had no idea, you see, how long it would take. No idea of distance. How should they? They had never been out of the Valley. She was worried about his business. No need, of course. But two happier ones when we put them back on the ship you will never, never see. They are very happy together. Nothing else has meaning."

Farewell, older love, other time, new wonder!

In those words was pain enough.

Dear memory came about me and settled soft in gray bloom of brushed cobwebs. Small boys cannot be in love, so they say, but yes, they can, and the sooner they feel love for a woman, the sooner they become as men, the more male, and loyal. Bron must have been fifteen when she came up The Hill with the green ribbons flipping in the warm west wind, and looked at me from the side, and I ran into the kitchen and Mama seemed to know who was there, and off with her apron, and looking, O, long, long moments until she opened her arms, wide. Kind, and beautiful, my Mama. But no use to wish, for when they are gone, that, and only that, is goodbye to most of infant love, and truest meaning of all farewell. If ten or more years were between us, then Bron was twenty-five when I was fourteen, and when I was twenty, she was thirty-one or so, though as I felt in the spirit she was never older, but even younger, if I ever remembered years, and I believe I never did, but only the woman. But I was held in thought of my brother, Ivor, up on the hill under white pebbles and a cross, and she was held by a woman's sense of right and wrong.

"Unhealthy," Ceridwen's sister-in-law said, that time, a district nurse, and in starch about the cap and cuffs. "It's time you got married, isn't it?"

"Is it?" I said, and put down the cup of tea.

"Wait, now, Huw," Ceridwen said, always the peacemaker and far more my father than any of us except Davy and Owen. "Meurig only wants to say something."

"Let her say it to Sami, Canal Water," I said, because I knew what was coming. "I am in that house because I want to be. When I have got enough saved I will build bigger somewhere else. Beyond all the advice, and far from those wanting to 'say' something."

"Have you thought you could be selfish?" Meurig asked

me, for the look from a gorgon would never have put that one down. "Don't forget, we grew up together, Bron and me, so I know a little, at least. Why not speak to her? A good girl, still well able to marry, and two growing boys, and more than one ready to take her to chapel, and a younger brother-in-law in the house? Think about her a little more, now. If you can't marry her, let somebody else."

Then it was, perhaps, that everything began to slip, like this slag outside here, and nothing to hold the weight, and day by day the sliding, until the night I went. We go on, I suppose, moment by moment, without thinking or giving it words, but sure that we are filled with duty, and without doubt indispensable. A pity it takes so long to reach good sense.

"Bronwen told Angharad a great deal about you in those years," Mr. Gruffydd said. "What began in that innocence. And she's so happy it ended still innocently. But was it, I wonder, the first, the blessed innocence? Or was it suppression of truth? Temptation was overcome. But then temptation and victory were turned into part of a game. They took the place of desire. Desire changed shape from a woman to a concept of moral strength and propriety. You were a monk, triumphant. Without a church. Your victim was a woman. On her strength of will you survived. If she had been weak, how long would you have lasted? These things I know very well. It was the same between Angharad and me. Except that we didn't live near each other. Or know each other for that time. We become blind, Huw. Blind with our feeling. Blind with desire. And we give desire another face, better to look at. Temptation and triumph, and what great ones we are. It was that meeting of the deacons that showed me. Her name, in those voices, those mouths. I went."

"Did Bron say all that?" I asked him.

He laughed the big, deep music.

"But of course not," he said. "Angharad simply pieced together all the moments of cooking and cleaning, and getting the boys to school, and having to go shopping, knowing well what people were saying. And looking through them. Triumphant over temptation. But she knew that one day the boys would be old enough to hear. That frightened her."

"Well, it sounds much more unlikely than anything I ever imagined, and yet I was part," I said. "I don't think I'd recognize it as what happened between us. But I suppose it will do. I was never a triumphant monk. I went up with Tiddi many a time, and a few more. Bron was the nun. Now I see it, too. Selfish. What should I have done? Push open the door?"

"Realize the circumstances and go, just as you did later," he said. "Life is too short for excuses. We never think of tomorrow if we like ourselves today. Angharad and I lost those years. But today is all the dearer. She will have the house as she wants it when I go back. Then we shall go to Buenos Aires to be married, and off to the Cape."

"I didn't ask," I said. "Are you living in the same house, now?"

He laughed again, but not aloud.

"No," he said. "There was no comfort in my house of any kind, except the chairs you made me. She's staying with the family we came with. In Vuriloche. A town on the other side of the lake from me. Now she's tearing the house to pieces. The family goes back to Buenos Aires for the winter. We shall go with them. Over the mid-thirties, Huw, there is no great bodily temptation. Except, I must say, these Indio girls. I'm not sure what it is. Is the animal stronger than the human? What? Is the civilizing process all that makes us human? Yet these people have a strong civilization. Among themselves, highly moral. What is it? Desire to mate and produce? But without a word of the language, there is temptation. Is. No question. Is. The sort that isn't in many women of ours."

From the way he said it I knew he had known the touch of ink silk.

I had not.

But I knew the power of those eyes, and the tremor was in me.

"What will stop temptation?" I asked him.

"Turn straight round, and go," he said, still working.

"In fear for the fall of virtue?" I asked the back of his head. "What, then, is virtue? What is destroyed when we fall?"

"What makes us what we are," he said. "Character. There's an erosion of the will. Are you thinking of these Indio girls? After all, what are we doing? They can get the same service from their own men. We are simply a toy to be taken. They are bodies to be used. Humankind isn't honored like that. A healthy world wasn't built on it. A man who throws himself everywhere isn't likely to have the substance to build firm foundations anywhere. Look about you. The best families, the best farms, are those men likely to chase Indios? They won't have them on the place. Whether it's Sheba in jeweled glory, or an Indio in grease and grime, there is still virtue, because we are human, of the Spirit, and we are able to say yes, or no. The rest is for people with time to waste in talk."

"We haven't stopped working," I said. "If it is so simple to turn the back, where is the strength of this temptation?"

"I didn't say it was simple," he said, and looked out at the trees. "It isn't. They don't tempt as we understand it. They wait. They have the knowledge. Rage and curse as you will, what is done is done. Time and again. That is temptation. That's why I'm glad of marriage. They never come near a man with a wife or a woman of his own. Never. That's a rule of theirs, too. It's one of the reasons I went to the Book again. To be able to join men and women in marriage. It's necessary. Because without churches, or chapels or schools, for many, the body is all. Erosion. Presently, no need to think of anything. No use to do anything. Woman. A bottle. A roof. A fire. Sheepskins. And nothing. Torpescence. Paralysis. Death. Nothing to save them. Nothing to be done."

In the valley at that time there was nobody I knew in that

condition, though over in the Colony were many. Their families and friends tried to help, but it was perfectly true, there was nothing to be done except wait for them to die. For some reason, wine makes a much worse drunkard than any other kind of alcohol, perhaps because men can drink more of it than whisky, and the effect is to madden before stupefying.

While we were talking we heard the shouts and screams, and we ran out, past the kitchen shed, over to the asado pit and beyond, to the rush-roof shelter for the wine barrels. At the side, two men were trying to fight Volde, but he had them in a grip with each hand at armslength, and they were kicking at him and he was doing well to sidestep. Doli ran with a pick helve and with two hits I thought she had cracked the skulls of both, because it sounded like a bat against a fast ball, and they dropped, one after another and lay without a move.

"A very good start," Lal said, from the end of the store shed. "Very well. We will have Idwal Griffiths in charge of the barrels. Moelwyn, will you take the cases? Everybody, one bottle of wine each meal, and no more. Two bottles at night, to last the night, and no more. Moelwyn, two drinks at night of whisky or brandy. No more. Anybody who looks well on the way, not one drop. Barrels locked at ten o'clock, tonight, midnight tomorrow, and the day after. Ten o'clock after that. Those are the rules. Anybody who doesn't like them, go now."

"No reason why the rest of us should suffer," Mervyn Rees said, a whine like a child without toffee. "A little drop while we are working, no harm, see?"

"Most of them aren't drinking except *maté*," Lal said. "A little drop, and a little drop, and you are drunk like these two. A disgrace. Did you come only to drink?"

"Well, it's part," Mervyn said. "Not Sunday school, is it? You are having a lot of free help here. Why can't we have a glass and no old nonsense? Is this something new with us, now then?"

For the first time I saw Lal not sure of herself, because large hospitality was tradition, and she was a Corwen.

"All right," she said. "Have your glass. But remember. First sign, no more."

The two in clout were standing, holding their heads and joking, and Solva came with towels and a bowl but they turned away, sending her off, laughing, and Idwal poured a glass for each, and for the dozen or more crowding to laugh and drink with them.

Lal took my hand, almost in tears.

"It's starting," she said. "These are the drovers. Not our people. If we aren't careful they'll cause trouble."

"Careful or not, they will still cause trouble," Rhin said. "Leave it to me."

At six o'clock, still in white daylight, they opened the first *curantó*, and I watched them taking off earth, and turf packing, branches and pea-vines. Lal and I shared a chicken that seemed made of its own cream, vegetables tasting as if they ripened in another world, and apples in honey direct from the Garden.

"We must have a *curantó* at least once a week," Lal said. "Every Sunday. So we shall need Indios from Rhin."

"Good," I said. "You choose them, and by the time you are back, they will be well trained."

She looked at me with those eyes the color of velvet in wallflowers, that might be deep red, or gold, or some of each.

"No girls," she said. "Claerwen Austin will send her two youngest to clean the house, and wash, and look after the cows, pigs, and chickens. If anything is wanted, ask them. Claerwen is coming every day to see that everything is right with you and Donato. When I am here, I will train a couple. But until, no."

She poured the kettle's water over the back of her third finger to see if it was the right heat, and filled the *maté*, and gave it to me.

"Doli is crying now to be going away and leaving Volde for so long," she said. "I could cry too, but I will be married first and have plenty to cry for. It won't be long, and there will be enough to do, God knows. We will have to go to Solva's wedding, and then Maes Corwen will need at least a month, and then my mother's property, and the other. Three months, between fences, ditches, and shearing, branding, plant new trees, well, anyway, enough, and in the spring, the lambs, and then back. Bring in Gwenonwy on the way, and the new furnishings, and you will have all the furniture ready, yes? And I will have a ship's stove for that kitchen, bigger than Tegwyn's, wait, you. I could stamp to hear her boasting. Come, let us see the house."

She never tired of strolling beyond the walls, and going in the back door, and pointing where the furniture would be in every room, standing here and there, touching the paneling, and out, then, slowly, almost sorrowfully, through the front. In those days I had added other rooms, and a big cellar, and a cold room for the summer that we badly needed, so the house was a fair size. There was a porch and windbreak long enough for a dozen to have tea outside, and the main room, paneled in pale, polished cypress, with a cypress floor, a small dining room paneled in red alerces, the kitchen half-tiled, bathroom tiled, and the big bath tiled in and squared, three bedrooms all in alerces, and a large withdrawing room for us alone, and a room each, on the end, for business and papers. Round about was dug for a garden, and Lal had a list of flowers, shrubs and trees to bring back, especially the hydrangea and roses.

In my shop, and stacked to season outside I had timber for years, and a reserve of tools in chests, so that if we had been cast away then and there we would not have lacked for a lifetime. Thinking back, of course, I am surprised that in those days we were content with so little. It was far from being because we were not used to very much. The girls, and most of the families had left a good, rich life in the Atlantic Colony, and comfortable houses, shops full of the world's best, and a thousand good friends to be seen on any day. In the valley we had friends, yes, a dozen in forty miles, and a day's ride there, and another back, and everything else was very rough, at least, by comparison with today, and I have often been asked why we stayed.

It was simply that we liked to work. We relished a bit of difficulty, and we knew what would be the outcome because we were blessed in the good black earth, and hundreds of miles of virgin forest, and the green run of many a river, all in shelter of kindly mountains, and Patagonia's sky cleansed by El Pampero, and the sun's glory and plentiful rain.

Donato and I were fitting tongues to the last pairs of wheels that late afternoon, and Luis came running to say a stranger was in the shop, and shouting bad language to Rhin's boys helping with the timber, and using his whip on them. We finished the last cart and pushed it in line with the others, well-pleased with work that would save the toil of shifting logs, roots and earth with bare hands, for though it seems unlikely today, many a square mile was cleared into milch glebes by a man and a woman, and no more than their will to work, and the help of God.

Donato came with me to see who was doing the shouting, and we could hear him before we got there. The voice I knew, small, thin, like Solva's, but without the force or clarity, and when I saw him, I stopped, and he turned and waved the brandy bottle.

"Well, Morgan, who would think, yes," he called, cracked in an octave, and another gulp at the bottle, and bubbles going into his throat.

Clais Corwen, brother of Vrann, uncle of the girls, and renegade. Tall and flab, with a vinous fat in shoulders and belly. Fair hair wisped about his face and ears, and if there were less rags on him than when last I had seen him, they were just as ready for soap and water, and he was readier, and his beard would have given him meals for a week.

"Enough," I said, and took the bottle from him easily as from a baby. "Outside, first. Who gave you permission to come in here and break open this crate?"

"Break, no," Clais said, and laughed, eyes in his lids. "Open, I did. Nephew, yes. Niece in marriage, well, well."

A little push had him outside. There was no sense in him to argue.

"Now, then," I said. "Your business?"

"A service of papers, yes," he said, and sitting on a log like folding a rule, one piece at a time. "My brother, see. Good old boy, too. I will have a share, no?"

"Share of what?" I asked.

He looked at me in craft of pale blue eyes, and the smile of a drunkard.

"Maes Corwen," he said. "Everything, then, yes."

"Say nothing to the girls," I told Donato. "Find Rhinberry. Up at the bakehouse."

He ran, and I stood Clais on the rags of his slippers. He could be pushed or pulled, and no answer, only the smile, and a fetor of sweat and alcohol about him.

"Now, tell me about Maes Corwen, and Vrann, and your share, and service of papers," I said. "First, where are they?"

"For Lal, nobody else," he said, and without holding him, he would have fallen. "My share of Maes Corwen. Summons in Buenos Aires. Pretenses. False witness. Murder, no?"

"Who was murdered?" I asked him.

"Well, who else, poor Matithias, yes, don't you remember?" he said, and surprised. "Well, who is wiser if you pay old Indios to do a murder? Dead, he is, with the Maker, no? With the Maker. No chance, poor Matti, fair play, too. No?"

"Who paid Indios to murder?" I asked, and shook him, a sheepskin, limp.

"Well, well, a thing to say," he said, head wagging. "Not sure, yes. Mr. Elias has got everything. With the lawyers. The advocates, no? My share. And the families'. Everybody will have rights. The Law."

Rhinberry came running, and Donato and Luis behind.

"I was finishing a ring of sugarplums and violets, there," Rhin said. "So it's this one, is it? And in the same filth."

"Well, Rhin, boy," Clais said, and crouching away, still with the smile, but afraid, too. "Look, I came only for the wedding, see."

Rhin poked him and he fell flat.

"Out with it, now," he said. "What papers, what shares?"

"Lal is the one," Clais said. "Lady of the land. Nobody to say. Only her, no?"

Rhin picked up a ten-foot bamboo ox-guide and whistled it in a green arc, and struck him on the haunch. Clais screamed high in his throat and clawed the timber to stand.

"You know me, don't you?" Rhin said. "Nonsense with everybody else, but not with me. The papers, quick."

Clais was late to move and the cane caught him over the shoulders and again the little scream, like a baby. He tore his shirt more to feel inside, and pulled out a bundle in a cloth. Rhinberry took it, pushed him to sit on the timber, and undid the knots. Papers were folded between two squares of wood to keep them flat. Rhin took out the knife to cut the twine and gave the square to me, and put the blade across Clais' eyes.

"Move, and I will slit you to the bone," he said.

The papers were all in Castellano except one in Cambrian, and that one I read, from Vrann, witnessed by a Justice, swearing that the list of names were all natural children of his, and entitled to a share in his own and his wife's estate.

"I must find Lal," I said. "Keep him here."

Up I went to the place where they had been sewing, but the girl told me they were all ironing at Tegwyn's, which was reason why Clais was unheard. Thankfully I went, and beyond the potatoes I called Lal, and she came out, a lovely red from the fire in there.

"Clais is here," I said, and held out the letters.

She looked at me, and saw a world through me. Each letter got a glance, and that was enough.

What I expected I am not sure, but she laughed closed eyes and white teeth at the sky, as at something funny.

"A prize collection," she said, and rested against me. "One

is from Vrann. He's claiming shares in his estate for his natural children and their mothers, and for dear Uncle Clais. But he hasn't got an estate, you see. Matti foreclosed, and it came as part of the marriage contract. The other part was the Matithias Morse estate which was mine when he died. He left Nelya Peninnah only the place at the end of the valley and the other pieces he bought for her. All stones and miles from water. So even in his grave he is still laughing. Now, you see, Elias, Snuff, is suing as Nelya Penninah's husband for annulment of the contract. He wants restitution of all Matti's property for Nelya, and they're pretending that a person or persons unknown paid drunken Indios to murder by riding Matti down, or over. The case is in the court in Buenos Aires."

"How will you answer?" I asked her, and waved to Doli looking out of the door.

"In the Governor's office in Rawson, with the two best advocates in the Colony," she said. "Mr. Elias, Snuff, will wish he had kept his snout in his snuffbox. I'll tell the girls first, and then I'll attend to dear Uncle Clais. Are you worried?"

"Property, again," I said. "That Elias, Snuff, is an animal, and his Nelya Penninah is another as bad."

"You forget Vrann," she said. "He will do anything to go back to Maes Corwen. And when he is sober, my dear father has got a brain. I am not worried about vice or snuff or Nelyas. Brains, yes. You have got brains. Less than twenty hours, we are married, boy. Give me a good kiss, now. And pray for a fine night tomorrow. Yes?"

Rhinberry was alone when I got back.

"Clais is at my place and a couple looking after him," he said. "He marked a few with the whip, so they will mark him. And he will be sober for the wedding. If you want him. Be careful of Vrann. Plenty of friends. He was foreclosed and dispossessed by a dead man. He is a lawyer's dream. They can write letters for years. One court to another. Until you get tired and pay what they want. Or use up everything, and then they have got it. Only for writing letters."

"No business of mine," I said. "This is my property, here. No interest anywhere else. Not concerned."

But I was wrong. It is strange how sure we can be, and yet we are wrong. Often I have wondered if those so sure of the love of God Almighty are also wrong.

That night, the asado pit was ringed with hundreds, far more than we had thought, because everybody able to spare a few days had come in to see their friends and talk. Being alone is terror for some, and the faces showed the relief to be in chatter of other peoples' voices again, and hear something new, and the laughing was high and oftener forced, but they wanted excuse to laugh and feel themselves alive, only to be ready to go back to the little house, and the winter, and months of white silence.

The barrels were there only for that reason, to loosen tongues and humor, and when the glasses had been filled a few times, Lal had to relax the rule, and let them have what they wanted, and sensible, for there were too many to refuse and spoil enjoyment. A few became loud, but they went quiet very quickly. A couple of fights started, but nobody knew why or where the fighters went. Rhin and his Indios could have told. They were waiting in the dark, and the moment anybody opened his mouth too wide, a lasso fell over him, and he was dragged out, tied, and left until the morning.

Everybody crowded about the brides-to-be, and if they had drunk every toast, they would never have found the choir, much less stood in place. The grooms could have been snoring, there, but we all had our own glasses to lift and drink, and Lal had filled them with plain tea, so we swilled and smiled for an hour or more, and then Volde, Oracio, Vyrnwy, Donato, Mr. Gruffydd and I went to the shop for a good drop from the cases.

"Well, Huw," Mr. Gruffydd said. "Everything you haven't put in words, I know. I wish everybody was here, too. But wherever they all are, more love could not be round them."

"I am interested in the people of my wife," Volde said. "She told me much of the history. But how was such a religious spirit kept alive? Every other nation seems not to maintain the religious force. But I hear it in the singing. It is so much like the Russian. But what is this emotion? Feeling, force, what?"

"You must look at history," Mr. Gruffydd said. "Persecution, first of all. Nowhere to lay a head. We were pursued and slaughtered as these Indios today. They have a deep religious sense but with no tradition of other than catastrophe ritual. Drought, earthquakes, epidemics, they gather for ritual. We in Britain had armies slaughtering or enslaving for more than a thousand years. We had a Druidic tradition. It was followed by the evangelists, possibly from Rome, or traveling with aid of Roman arms, or sometimes without, from the Mediterranean, somewhere. The Romans went and the Saxons came. More slaughter. Then the Normans. A few British people were left in the north, and in the west. With the Normans came the Roman Church in strength, and it lasted until Henry Tudor destroyed it and built another just as rich. More than a hundred years later, another man, Cromwell, took out the trappings and instead of a church, decreed a chapel. Then another king returned, and the church was put back. But the chapels had taken hold. They were plain places, without ornament, where ordinary men could worship and sing. There was no longer wholesale slaughter, but there was still persecution, and it made people pray harder, sing harder, to survive. And the voice improves with practice, and the musical sense improves with training. But its basis was survival. As with the Hebrews."

"It does not explain the force," Volde said.

"You had persecution in Russia," Mr. Gruffydd said. "Explain, then, Tolstoy."

"Explain genius," Volde said.

"But every nation has its own genius," Mr. Gruffydd said. "Not in somebody here and there, but part of the nation itself. We have a genius for harmony. Whether in the voice, or whatever we do. Harmony there must be, or we throw it up. If there is harmony, we will suffer to finish and gladly. Without, nothing. Besides, you see, we had the Bible. When it was published in Cambrian, the humble of that day could read its truths for the first time. Our fathers realized it was written by ordinary men, fishers and carpenters and masons, persecuted, too. Men lowly as themselves. It had a meaning. And hope. It was hope they needed. And the Word was with them."

"Huw, will you beauties be in there all night, then?" Solva's little voice said, from the darkness beyond. "We have still got the altar to build, and up at five o'clock, and ten o'clock, married. And two hours bath and dress? Standing there, painting old lilies you are. Oracio, have you sworn not to kiss me good night, here?"

Oracio listened, head on one side, with a couple of thick ones under his belt and his feet well in the way to be someone else's.

"My passion, my heart," he said, at the floor. "You are all my dreams, and the fairest flower of my life. If I move, I shall fall and spread my brains."

"You should have drunk tea with the others," Solva said, and with love's own scold, hurrying in. "You have been in bibble of old whisky all night with you. The great soldier's dignity is not for tea? *Ach-y-fi.* Come you, my little one."

8

With the prayers in the hearts of those girls, and all of us, it was no wonder to find a dawn, crystal to the nose, blue above the treetops, not a single cloud, and a breath from El Pampero to rock a baby's crib.

Maté kettles rattled, and shadows moved across the fires. Far over, Volde's mighty voice anthemed a morning hymn and we stood to listen in natural silence of leaves shaking from sleep, and the river's breath, and twigs snapping their fingers at sparks, and the far-off call of a cockerel, and a dog fox barking up on the hill. But one of Rhin's Indios, poor boy, caught the end of a dishcloth from Mistress Eirene Vaughan to bring him from clattering a bucket, and her spectacles fell off and she stood beside him, no move, until we all joined in a chorus, and then she was feeling about and cursing everybody not to come near in case to tread and break them.

"My grandada's, they were, *dammo diâwl,*" she was in a shriek, there. "Keep your old feet from here, now, till they are safe and giving me a bit of shape. Old Indios, a nuisance, yes. Well, well. Not a mark, see. If I smashed them, what would I do to look?"

A question, indeed, and for that reason, Lal took a list of people with spectacles and brought back spares, and more than useful they were, though how they could wear them without a test and say they were right is far from me.

By light in bluish slant from the trees the altar looked good enough for a big chapel. Everybody lent a hand so it went up in minutes, though the days of work with ax, chisel and plane had been of weeks before. Hollowed half-logs in overlap made the roof, with the point above the middle of the Table, made of polished red alerces, and the walls were pale cypress. A three-stair dais wide enough for five couples to kneel joined a railed platform on either side for the choir. Benches we made for the older men and women in three rows, and then the walls, of hurdles threaded with flowering branches, and Rhin's Indios had cut armfuls of rushes to lay crisscross over the ground to have a soft carpet and no dust.

An argument began, I shall never be sure how, about candles on the Table.

"No candles," Idris Bryn Gilfa said, and hit his fist on the bench. "We are halfway to the Devil now, with a lot of old bushes about the place. The House of God it is, and I never saw a bush or candle in one."

"Well, we do want a bit of light in there, man," Willie Prosser said, and standing surprised holding packets of candles with the sticks under his arm. "Are you going to put old oil dips in there, then?"

"Oil dips were good enough in the Colony," Idris said, staring the wide gray eyes, head forward, beard out. "We are going nearer to the Catholics every single day. Candles? Tace is Latin for candle. That's Roman, yes. They light them by the dozen, every one a soul burning in Hell. Is that what you want here?"

"Well, good God, no, boy, I never thought," Willie said, and almost looking over his shoulder to see if devils were in a jump somewhere. "Well, to Hell with the candles, is it?"

"Wait, you, now," Doli called, from the kitchen shed, and put down the teapot, and came over to take the candles and the sticks and the matches, and smile her warmer at Idris.

"Candles we are going to have. Dark it is, and light there shall be. Else he will be christening me, and marrying the baby. Nothing to do with Rome or Catholics, and neither are we. Candles, Willie."

"Not on the Table," Idris said, still in a stare, with him. "Not to embellish."

"In the walls, man," Willie said, and backing away. "If Mr. Gruffydd doesn't mind, why should you?"

"Mr. Gruffydd?" Idris said, in falsetto with scorn. "Him, with a cross on the wall, up there? A cross, mark you. A preacher?"

"Plain wood, it is," Tegwyn shouted, from the kitchen. "Nothing carved. Nothing wrong with it. I will have one. A reminder Who died for us."

"A reminder you want, is it?" Idris shouted back. "Your Mama didn't need reminding. Plain chapel was good enough for her. Nothing carved, yes? There is nothing carved on a match, either. But it will burn this forest and everything in it. We hearken not to the Voice of our Fathers. Wait, you, for the night draweth nigh."

"Let us have the day before to have the night, Idris, my little one," Doli said, soft as a Mama. "Is it true the night draweth nigh? Well, thank God. Overdue it is, and I have waited long enough. And when tonight is with us, I will think with love even of you. Go now, have your bacon and eggs, getting cold there."

Quiet came over the forest, and only the sound of cutlery in tin plates, and pans and kettles being chased across the stoves in the kitchen. Hens were laying and chanting, and all our ducks came through a patch of light, dabbing orange webs on the way down to the river. Beyond the trees our fields were pale green to the knee. Red poppies were budding there, and cornflowers, a small magic, of seeds brought in the wheat from home and living comfortable as us. The house was solid, wanting only glass for the windows, and fixtures inside, and hot and cold water, but that was my odd-hour work for the winter. The shop was filled with orders for doors and window frames, shelves, cupboards, and every type of furniture. Donato had a year's work in carts and traps alone, but orders for wagons were three times as many. The finished wagons we had at the back, behind a tangle of saplings that nested the turkeys, where very few of us ever went. Of those in line, we had four especially built, paneled inside, with a good soft bed and Indio blankets, a wardrobe, and chest, a roof to keep out any weather, a partition of cypress at the back to be closed at night instead of tying a canvas, and a square of bricks with a chimney where a small fire could be lit for the morning *maté* instead of going out in the cold. Lal's wagon, of course, had just a little more love than the others, and Rhin's Indios had made a guanaco cover for the bed, with black and white and red and white ponchos about the walls, and white goatskin rugs.

But its weight entire seemed on my heart to think of the months away.

Yet, no use to brood. The work had to be done, and only Lal and the girls could do it, and that was all, and it was the same for every one of us.

Small moments of that morning are set in memory, sure, to the sound of Vyrnwy and his helpers hitting a peal on the anvils, knowing El Pampero would bring it to us. Even now I hear the noise beyond the trees, and Jeff Smallcote and Alys riding in, and Volde shouting and dancing, and everybody asking who they were, and not caring much when we told them Alys Caerog Evans and Jeff Smallcote, the Londoner.

"Couldn't let you two get spliced and us not here," Jeff said, outside the kitchen with a mouthful of bacon and a good drink of tea in splash. "We only heard last week. Then we had to find somebody to look after the sheep, you know, you can't leave 'em, can you? All takes time. Come to a finish, we had to leave the baby with the Countess. Then we had to find you. What a job, eh? There's nobody about. They're all here. So we followed the path."

"Countess?" Lal said. "Who is this?"

"Big place this side of the river," Jeff said. "Couple of kids of her own. Widow. Very nice, she is. But very, you know. Bad as Alys' father and mother. I mean, sort of, well, not exactly uppish. Very nice. But sort of tight round the corsets, you might say."

"She is German, and very strict," Alys said. "Nobody better, and my baby will be looked after."

"Finish your breakfast," Lal said. "Come over where we are dressing. A zoo, it is. I wish you had brought your baby. I will call in on the way. I'm off back on the tenth."

"The tenth?" Alys said, and eyes in shine. "Will you have me with you? Mama and Dada haven't seen the baby and I couldn't go alone. Jeff wouldn't let."

"What, and Indios knocking about?" Jeff said. "Very sensible. No use me trying to leave. Couldn't. Month? Two months? Too much to get done. Any case, we'll have to get back tomorrow. Take us four days."

"I'll call in," Lal said. "We will be a big party. Have you got a wagon?"

"We have," Jeff said. "But it wants a pair of wheels."

"Take them from here, packhorse," I said. "A mother and baby must have a wagon."

"I'll have one, boy," Lal said, in surprise. "No trouble there, at all."

My heart went underfoot, because plain as a donkey's nose, I could see Alys in the new wagon, and Lal on sheepskins underneath, the very thing I had tried to stop. No use to say anything.

Vyrnwy was first of us dressed and first there, and in a shirt washed white to blind by Tegwyn and starched to grip, and he got off the horse as if a move too quick would be his last, and took his bowler hat out of a cloth bag.

"Well, I am done up here like a bloody polecat, aye," he said. "A shirt like this I never had, see. Beautiful, it is. I couldn't get the studs in. She'll have to have me out with the scissors. We had to do up the collar with a button hook, there. Three of us. Well, in sweats, then, indeed to God."

Volde, I suppose, looked best of all, in a black frock coat

and white waistcoat and a gray cravat with a pearl. Tegwyn had laundered all our shirts, so we were comfortable as Vyrnwy, and my cuffs alone would have slaughtered any bullock, so sharp and so solid, and Oracio had a collar under the tunic that made him lift his head or have it cut off.

There was a shout and a run when we walked out from where we had dressed, and bottles and glasses came for a health, but we were left staring when the cheer started on the other side and the crowd turned from us as from the measles, and ran to see the girls.

Under shadow of the trees, they came in a line between the waving hats and handkerchiefs. Tegwyn walked first, in a gray jacket and skirt and a puff of cream lace in the neck and wrists and a veiled gray hat almost larger than the gray parasol. Doli next, in white, with a long veil and white parasol, and Solva, smaller, in white with a veil and looking as if she might blow away, then Alwyn, in white and veiled, and then Lal. All the girls had tiny waists, and the dresses had soft pleats over the hips and a little bustle, but if I looked at the others it was only because Lal was last, the most beautiful, a woman held in white folds of shining silk, and it took time to be sure it was I standing there, within ten minutes of marrying her, and unbelieving.

Ten minutes, and we lit the candles in the chapel, and Volde carried over the big silver bowl for the christening, and Mr. Gruffydd came from Donato's house, but exactly as I remembered him coming from Gorphwsfa many a time, the same smile, perhaps the same suit, the same walk, and the Book under his arm, but browner and without the beard. Everybody crushed into the hurdle enclosure behind the brides, but the grooms had to use their arms to go through, and I bent a cuff, and Vyrnwy lost a stud, and Tegwyn had to pull his tie tighter to close the collar, but his bullneck and her starch mocked her, and while he was saying "I do" one end was under his ear, and he was far happier, and breathing, and his smile was a wonder.

Donato gave me the ring, and Mr. Gruffydd stood before us.

"Do you, Huw, take this woman, Milalai, to be your lawful wedded wife?" he said, and the voice raised echoes under the log roof and out in the timber, and that was the first time I ever heard Lal's correct name.

"No," somebody was shouting, not near, and not far. "No notice given, nothing to paper. Murderer. Thief."

The crowd murmured and moved, and Lal smiled at Mr. Gruffydd's glance to the side.

"Uncle Clais," she whispered.

"Stole the birthright," Clais screamed, almost like an owl. "They cheated their father. Their brothers and sisters are starving. Thieves."

The voice stopped, and I imagined a lasso.

Again the crowd murmured approval, moved again, and the ring was on Lal's finger, and she stood closer, and I could see only her eyes, that carried diamonds through the veil.

Solva and Oracio were last, and when Mr. Gruffydd had given the Blessing and closed the Book, the crowd was already pushing aside the hurdles, and buckets were busy over at the wine barrels. We stood in line to have our names in the register, with all the witnesses, and when it was Lal's turn, Mr. Gruffydd gave her a box, and one for me.

"From Angharad, as a special gift," he said. "And this is one of the special days of my life, Huw. You were a little pale one in that kitchen when I first saw you. Years in a place full of steam, and hanging clothes, and cooking. I swore then to have you out in the air. Now, you are out. And I am out, too. This is the last service of my Ministry. I give thanks it was to marry Lal and you."

The crowd was too big, too noisy to talk, and then I was kissing new sisters and shaking hands with new brothers, and whether we liked it or not we were being dragged, or pushed, or half-carried over to the tables near the barrels to eat and drink.

"Thirty minutes," Lal whispered, over our glass. "At the

back of the maitén the horses are. My peons will look for you."

Crowds separated us, and an excitement was in them, as if five marriages made five times more emotion than one, and everybody was shouting and singing, and it seemed we were living with a different people, joyous in another world. While I changed I could hear them, but they sounded like foreigners, and I wished I could always hear people so happy. Even Tegwyn, there, was not the drawn-mouthed starer of before, but a smiling, gentle one, with eyes only for Vyrnwy, sharing a glass beneath the trees, as if she had never done anything else, and it was hard to think that such a pretty woman, so graceful with the parasol, could have worked to the knees in mud to plant enough food for her children, apart from cleaning houses in the City of Lewis for extra cash, at any time ready to defend herself with claws and teeth so that no man would dream of going near unless to be brained. Even in that short time the country had changed her, and in all certainty, her worth. Money alone, never mind how much, had neither worth nor value. Only those able to work were worth anything, and Tegwyn above all others could work for a dozen whether on the farm or in the corral or out on the pampas or in the house. Vyrnwy seemed put in a muse to find somebody he had known all his life without more than a nod between them, that one, of rough speech and manner and no patience with anything, suddenly becoming a beauty and blossoming by the moment, with such a smile, and a trembling voice, and eyes only for him.

"I was wondering how long this will last," he said, frowning inside a smile. "Huw, have you seen her like this before?"

"No," I said. "But my name isn't Vyrnwy."

She laughed at the sky, arms out, and brought up the parasol to close it, looking at him. In that gesture, so unlike the old Tegwyn, she seemed to be born somebody else.

"Do you want to go with the others, now, and get drunk?" she asked him in that new, vibrant voice. "Married you are, first in your life, and nobody to say a word if you are silly for a week, here. Or do you want to go home?"

He took her free hand and held it under his chin.

"Ah, Teg, my beloved little one, home," he said, a prayer, and kissed the hand. "I have been waiting. I nearly came to the wagon last night."

"Huw is here," she whispered, smiling and caring nothing. "If you had, I would have kept you. Wait you while I change. Where are the horses, with you?"

"Over the bridge," he said. "There I will be. How long?"

"Everything I will tear off, and put mine on," she said. "Minutes. And we will gallop, boy."

She stamped her foot to say it, and off, and Vyrnwy looked after her, and at me.

"I used to be very free with God," he said, and crushed grass with a turning heel. "One night, I was sick of ash and soot. There was nothing to eat in the house. No hot water. I thought if my mother was there, it would be different. Cleaner, yes. And something to eat. And I prayed by the kitchen table. Then I swore to sell, and come over here. If I hadn't, well, I would never have found Teg. So I was answered. Have you seen my place? You should come, boy. Sit down at the table, and tell me when you had anything to eat, last. The place is like a pin. Huw, will you build us a house like yours? She came with me to see it. And she cried, there. We have got to have one. Got to. I promised."

"Wait till Lal and I are back, and we will have it on the wagons," I said. "I'm off. Tell everybody I went with Lal."

Her peon, Tamaño, the big one, laughed through the bushes by the shop, and I followed him through a stand of timber to a clearing planted in wheat, and Lal gave me the reins and a tip-toe kiss, and she was up and leading. By that time I could sit on a horse, but I was never a good rider, never within miles of Lal, but she was weaned on horseback. It surprised me to see our place from the top of the hill behind the house. At first I never thought we were in a valley, but in a forest. But then, I saw the trees stretching mile on mile to blue mountains far away, and mountain peaks both sides of us, and our river in broad run below and going into deep green. Even with the clearing that had been done, I saw only a little space where we and the others were, and then I realized the size of the task, and how lucky we were to have help.

Horseback riding is not best for talk, and the way was too rough to go in pairs, and Lal was mostly in a canter unless she was climbing, or galloping on the flat, so for hours, there, I was alone, and enjoying every moment. We were in another country, a glory of green, with few trees, or thick but scattered, and brooks we jumped, pools we splashed through, and mountains all about us with a tip of snow purest white in a blaze of blue sky, and the wonder of *amancay*, the mountain lily, swaying lazy gold everywhere.

Lal waited at the top of the hill and pointed the crop. "There is the Altar of the Gods," she called. "Right behind our house, it is. When all the trees are down we shall see it."

As if a mason had chipped and forgotten to finish, many tall shapes were cut in the rock up there, at that height and distance in clear blue sky so many people in long orange and brown capes, and little clouds white about them, lofting as the girls' bridal veils, showing them one moment, hiding the next, a group of saints it might have been, in prayer upon the mountaintop.

Over the rise of the next hill we started a gallop of guanaco on the scree, and down in the dip a sedge of heron went up in slow flap, and I knew we were near marsh. But turning a heap of rocks, a green marvel of water spread down the miles, and mountains rising from the edge, not a ripple, and fish in taste for flies poking silvering circles, and teams of duck in wheeling shadows, and ibis, of the long beak and wonderful plumage in flight of scores settling in the air on heavy wings, and a thousand wild geese cheering us from open beaks.

"Well, now then," Lal said, and turned again. "Would you like our camp here? Or go an hour more, where I want?"

"Go an hour more," I said, looking at the sun. "If you want to ride love naked under the stars, we have got time enough."

She laughed, eyes shut, teeth fast in her lower lip, and her mount went up on his hinds in the turn, and she was in gallop down there, but I was happy to go slowly, and look at country settling quiet in the soul, and I began to know what the Indios felt in being denied a place where their fathers had ridden through time. In shadow of a burned forest we picked a way past bare trunks, twisted ghosts shining white from the seasons of years, and I thought I felt the anguish of all the Indio dead, almost seeing them reach up to Heaven, headless and broken and hopeless. Always after that I could never see the burned bodies of trees without thinking of Saiheque's brothers and sisters and their children, sabred and in flame among their tents and left for carrion.

It was that afternoon when a new unit of time became part of my life. Lal's Hour, it was called, and in order to measure it, you would have to go from the top of that second hill and ride until our camp, and if you broke your neck and the horse's heart, it might be done in a little under three hours, though if you were one like me, with more respect for both and a wish to see the country, then it would be near five, without a stop. By the time I got there, in blue evening, but led by the shining gold of our fire on the trees above, and a couple of shouts, I found the canvas up, and water drawn in buckets, and tea ready, firewood chopped, and a lamb staked, almost grilled and ready to eat.

"Well, where were you, boy?" Lal asked me, from under the canvas, changed and washed and combing her hair. "Did you stop to have a sandwich?"

"I was looking for that hour of yours," I said. "A Country Mile and Lal's Hour are from the same class. I didn't see the peons, so I'm in front of them, anyway."

She laughed, with the long hair deep red in firelight over her shoulder and the comb flashing half-through.

"They were here before me," she said. "Who do you think

did all the work? They are down below now with their wives and children. Tomorrow we will all go fishing. The bucket is there, and your clothes are here, and go through the trees to the bathroom."

We might have stayed in a kiss for another Lal's Hour, but Tampoco came whistling through the bushes with bread and a tea pot. Off I went through the trees and almost fell off a ledge of rock into a deep gorge white with a tumbling waterfall that dropped from a lip above me, but so far that I could hear no more than a whisper. But I had to shout to find the path back, and Tampoco came and took me only a few steps to the fire that I suppose I might never have found for myself. Then, I believe it was, that I knew how truly dependent a townsman is, how helpless without a guide, how much he must owe to those he might condemn as ignorant.

"If there isn't a lamp post and a bit of a sign, I'm finished," I said, and ashamed. "I couldn't even smell the smoke to bring me here."

"Of course not, boy," Lal said, cutting the loaf. "The wind is away from you. What would you like to drink? Are you cold?"

"Cold, yes," I said, and shivering. "That water is cold as charity. Have I been as cold before? Is there a hot cup of tea?"

"Only a special cold cup," Lal said. "Only a cold cup you have ever had with me, isn't it? I do love a cold cup of tea, indeed. Make it, and leave to go cold. A pleasure."

She gave me a mug boiling hot, with about half of it rum and honey, and in a couple of sips she was three different Lals, each more beautiful than the other, but she drank *maté*, that I never got used to. The *maté* always seemed a teat, with the *bombilla* for a nipple, and the people like children sucking to think themselves back at their mothers.

"Twice I have been here before," Lal said, while we were eating the asado. "The first time with Thomas, the Peak, when I was seven or eight. We went far over, where he had the gold mine. We will go there in a couple of days and see if we can find some. The second time with Idwyn, before he started taking the wagon trains over. Then we went up to Lake Thomas. We'll do that after we've been to the gold mines. I always swore to come back here the night I was married. How did I know I could? If we were married in the Colony, we would have to wait. A month, at least, of journeying. Before today, there was no hope of a preacher here. How do we know?"

"Perhaps the wish is pure enough to be a good prayer," I said. "But why did you want to come back? The waterfall?"

She nibbled shreds off a bone, threw it to the dogs, and took the napkin to wipe her hands.

"What did you see, coming up?" she asked me.

"Trees," I said.

"Only trees?" she said, and ready to cry.

"I was looking where you had gone," I said. "A tracker, I was. And look, I found you."

"The horse followed the dogs," she said. "A splendid tracker. Come with me."

We went from there, not twenty paces, through the wild rose bushes, out to a slab of rock, and such space that comes in a dream wide about us, and mountains in snow everywhere, and the red and gold clouds of sunset lighting a necklace of lakes among the deep green velvet pile of forests darkening in night. Softly then, we heard the waterfall, a mother's breath above the child she carries, and an owl called, and one answered far away, and down below children chattered, and a woman's sharp voice told them to be quiet.

"This is why," Lal whispered, and we were close. "That's Lake Roberts, and Lake Evans. Up there, Lake Matthews and Lake Williams. Lake Thomas, farther, and Lake Griffiths."

"Where is Lake Corwen?" I asked her.

"I'll show you in four days' time," she said. "More beautiful than any of these. Why don't you make a boat, and let us go on the water? We could go for miles and nothing to see except ducks and geese and fish and trees and mountains. And nothing to hear except us. Make a boat, Huw."

"The last carpenter to make a boat was Noah, and you know what happened," I said. "To make a boat is an art of its own, next to the wheel. We will speak to Donato and find what he thinks."

"Do you know why I wanted to be here tonight?" she whispered.

"Yes," I said. "But shall we have stars?"

She put her arms tight about me.

"Don't you know we had to sit down with Geza, and the calendar to find out when we would have a moon?" she said. "That was when Mr. Gruffydd came in from Vuriloche. But if somebody hadn't mentioned you, I don't believe he'd have come."

"He seemed different," I said. "Not quieter, or less the man he was. Different, or changed in some way, and yet happier deeper down. Surer, is the word, I think. Perhaps because he's going to marry, and he can see some peace in his life at last."

We ran back to the fire's warmth because we were above the snowline and the changing night breeze turned soft from the south and froze.

"Did you open the parcel from your sister?" Lal asked, while we rubbed hands.

"I left it down there," I said. "Pleasure when I go back. Did you?"

She opened a saddlebag hanging from a branch. The satin glowed against a bracelet of sapphires and diamonds.

"Doli and Solva each had one, another design, with different stones, but lovely," she said, in a strange voice. "I would give anything to meet her. I had nothing to give Mr. Gruffydd for her. We all wrote a note to tell her. When did she know we'd be married?"

"Since I first came here," I said. "I told her about all of you. Pages."

"You never told me very much about her," she said, busy

at the asado, and cutting off a strip of steak. "Eat this, now. It's the tenderest part. Not so tender as me, but it will do for the moment."

"I am far from sure I want to eat," I said.

"You have got time before the moon comes," she said, still in that strange voice. "Why didn't you tell me Angharad was a Roman Catholic?"

Well, I put the bread and meat down and looked at her with the air gone from me.

"Roman Catholic, girl?" I said, when I could speak. "What nonsense are you talking?"

"Not nonsense," she said, and eating, no odds. "Mr. Gruffydd told me she had to be married in a Registry in London because her husband was Roman Catholic and she didn't want to shock your mother and father. Civil marriage before, and the real wedding in the Roman Catholic church."

While she spoke, I could see my mother and father reading the letter from her, over by the window here, in this kitchen.

Only then, all those years later, I knew the real reason for the Split.

"I didn't know that," I said. "She never told me. Nobody did. Is that why she and Mr. Gruffydd haven't married yet?"

"Mr. Gruffydd has finished as a preacher," she said. "He came to marry us. Then he'll marry Angharad. As a Roman Catholic. He's joining the Church in Buenos Aires."

9

No man could have had more of life, and I give thanks on the knees that none could have known more of beauty than I have been given, and I began to know it in those days up by the waterfall.

Lal had wanted to ride each day to a new lake, and camp for the night, and on to another. But after that first night we walked everywhere over the icefield on top of the mountain to gather plants, or rode down to the lakeside to catch a fish for breakfast, or all round the edge to the other lake, and then back before darkness came. Forest was thicker than with us in the valley, and most of the time we had to cut a way. Not a path did we find, and not one soul did we meet in the eight days, and had it not been for the peons coming up to the camp, and the voices of their children we heard only on that one night, we might never have known there were others on earth.

It was not that we had to cut a way or that it would take too long or be too tiring that we always came back to the waterfall, but only because wonder was there. We wanted every moment, from the time of the setting sun to the sudden light of the evening star, and wait, then, for night to waken and spread shadow, and lie down close together to watch for the rising moon.

Then was another silence, of dearness, of being alone with

love, of hearing love breathe, moving warm under the hand, those small motions that have no sound that yet are heard by love's ear, part of the rock's stress of muscle beneath us, and tattle from the wild rose, and snow in pall on the peaks, and the patience of kneeling mountains, a soothe of breeze across the lake, a fine gossip from the leaves' evening whisper in the valley, and far away, the waterfall's sigh.

Light was whitest in the trees down below when the moon came from behind us, first a rim over peaks in glitter, and then the glisten on miles of ice, and a half-face that might have been smiling, and then the moon herself, rising up and going a little to our left, across diamond snow, and we could have sworn many a time that the higher she went, the smaller she became, though certain it is that coming over the edge she was far bigger than I ever saw her before, big enough to frighten, and only then I understood what Rhin's Indios meant when they said they preferred to sleep Down Where The Moon Is Small.

We, too, slept where the moon is small, but after Lal had danced white in light, naked in black flame of hair flung up, a spiral flow in stream behind her laughter, cloaking by a shaken head, torn, that vital cape, by points of breasts, the marvel of a line of thigh, a fling of swirling shadow across a whitears kneaded by the saddle to rounds hardening into silken rocks when she thrust herself upon me, and rode love naked under the stars, and a moon high, and all of life a singing glory.

But when she cried, eyes shut and open-mouthed to heaven, and fainted in weight upon me, then I became rider, and tasted heavy stalks on moonwhite apples, and rode-a-cock-horse to that flowered place in the mind where life and death are one, and sleep comes quick and sweet.

"No horses today," she said next morning. "I'm going to lie down and do nothing. I never did it before."

"You never sat and did nothing?" I said. "Try it, now, and find a treat."

"Mama said idle hands are the Devil's tools," Lal said. "I

would love to know what Doli and Solva are doing at this moment."

"Having a *maté*, and saying 'no horses today,'" I said. "Feel the sun on you. Who would think it would be so hot? Do you feel homesick for Maes Corwen? Do you want to go back to the Colony? Or live here?"

"Here," she said. "I always wanted to live here from when I was a small girl. Mountains and lakes, nothing else. But I am sore. Don't come near me for ten days. Have you got sandpaper with you, boy?"

"It will teach you to ride barefront," I said. "All I could see was the tip of your nose, and your chin, and your beautiful throat, and everything else in a bounce with you, except me and the rock."

"Well, hisht, boy," Lal said, shocked. "You are talking like an old publican, with you."

"Are the words more than the act?" I asked her. "Should they be less? Remember, from this time, if you want to ride, very well. A quiet pony you shall have. I can put my neck on my hands and cross my ankles, and rest there, pretty as kine in time of famine. But when you have finished your little gambols about Ygdrasil, then pony will turn stallion. In this school I am better rider with or without the stars, moon or sun. Where is the sandpaper? Who is sore? Where is this pony? Who will ride love in the morning?"

"If the peons see us," she whispered.

"A splendid example," I said. "Where is this wonderful rider? She was going to gallop everywhere, and lo, no horses today? So sore, and so much sandpaper, and enough of Eve's balm in the run to drown the Garden? Ride, now, gallop in front, leave me far behind, *cariad fach-i*. And no horses today? Pity, too."

"You have got strength like an old blacksmith," she said, quiet, and near to tears, and smiling.

"An old carpenter," I said. "Saw through a trunk a few times. A few hours with a plane. You have got only silk, tip to toe. I don't know why. I thought you were strong, girl.

Throwing the *bolas* and the lasso. Stamping about like a bow-legged Gaucho, there. But you are pure silk."

"Mama was right, she spoke the truth," Lal said, sitting up and breathing out, once, deep, and pulling the poncho about herself. "Idle hands are the Devil's tools. I am sorer than ever. I feel wonderful. To be married is better than I had dreamed. It is simpler than I thought. And marvelously better. Come down to the waterfall, now."

We went on the ledge, and Lal took off the poncho and walked into the fall of green water, and called to me from behind there, so off with everything, and in I went to a freeze that stopped the breath, and then Lal was standing there, laughing in warm foam. We were on a wide lane of rock with falling water silent in rags of glistening green, icy near, with waterdrops like a wire brush, but a yard away warm and like steam. We soaped each other, and stood near the edge in icy needles to wash off, and lay on the thick moss to roll in foam, and when our hands slipped in squeaks over each other, Lal led through that freezing weight of water, and out to the hot sun, and grass underfoot, and a good cup of tea.

"This will always be our own," she said. "We will never tell anybody. When we are tired of faces and voices, here we will come."

"Why don't we put in a title?" I said. "We can afford to. A league here will take from above, almost to the flat down there."

Lal shook her head under the towel.

"This might be Chile," she said. "There's no map. They are quarreling over what is whose. They don't even know where the border is. Not enough people have ever been here. Missionaries came long ago from Chile, but the Indios killed them. Our people have been coming here for thirty years. It ought to be New Cambria. We could make a wonderful country of it. But they'll never let us. We need ten thousand more families. And no wine."

"Do you think wine has made such a difference to us?" I asked her.

She sat up, shook the hair down her back, and smiled, a rarest beauty, and nothing in her eyes to tell she was naked.

"All you need do is look at what my grandfather and the first men and women did, and look at what is being done," she said, careless, as if to cover shame. "Didn't they cultivate and ditch and drain from Rawson, up to the City of Lewis, down to Gaiman and Dolavon? What's been done since? They've only worked what they've got. A few have got land in the pampas. Not many. A few have got land here. A handful. When the old ones die, the holding will be shared among the children. How many of them work as their fathers and mothers did? But they drink as their fathers never did. Time spent in drink is time away from work. No work, no money. The wineshop gives credit. How many who owned land are working as peons? Or gone away? How many have copied the habits of Indios? Work a little while, take the money, and get drunk?"

"I didn't see much drinking among the women," I said.

"They don't," Lal said. "But they are sick of it in the house, and they marry the first thing that crawls past."

"Like me," I said.

"Well, of course," she said. "I waited a long time, too. And I am glad, glad, glad, and it was worth every moment. Kiss me, now, but don't let the old Devil see those hands, yes? A peon is coming up. Listen."

Tambien was rattling a bucket against rocks on the way, and whistling to scratch glass, and Lal shrieked only a tiny one, and ran long white legs under a towel to the tent, and I lay back in the sun.

Those moments of thought up there were some of the fullest in my life with raw memory of Lal's tears in my shoulder, weeping relief that no longer was there need for that note sharp in her voice, and the small fear in her eyes behind the smile, and the quick, almost ungraceful turn on the heel when goodbyes were said, and the brief, rough handshake, as if, without them or the effect she wanted them to have, the senses might riot and flood the mind beyond heed.

Times have changed since then, and if I have wondered why, in truth there is not far to look. It was not Chapel or fear of God which kept most men and women to themselves, that held a Tegwyn safe, and kept Lal and her sisters from being Nelya Penninahs or Indios.

Any man knew that open misbehavior toward a woman might be wealed out of his skin with rawhide, if he had luck and escaped a bullet, or the knife. The women from birth were warned what to expect.

There was a penalty, heartless often, always condign. Only those with money, able to travel or hide behind their families could thumb their noses, yet their money was an offense, basis of their contempt. But if the wealthier people did as they pleased without penalty, then the time came when the poorer copied and the rot started.

Much later I asked Lal what she and Doli and Solva had thought of the passions that cause such trouble among us, that from her love of being loved I knew must have been a distress often enough.

But she stared at me as if I had dropped from another world.

"Think?" she said. "What use to think? Work, and go to sleep. What else?"

"You once told me any man would do," I said. "What did you mean?"

She laughed, that quick, upward beautiful turn of the head.

"Any man, yes, for marriage and children," she said. "But not any man to be happy as I am. Marriage, that is one thing. Marriage and happiness, that's quite another."

"We are off on a turning log again," I said. "As a Lal Corwen, no marriage, no man, didn't you feel you wanted something more from living? To do with the body? For the senses? Didn't the seasons trouble you?"

She sat back, looking at me from under the brows, smiling in the eyes, and a little frown of further knowledge put a line more in her forehead.

"Seasons, yes," she said, quietly, reasonably. "Every season had plenty for us. Sheep to the pampas, and back. Cattle to winter feed, and back. Lambing and calving. Branding and shearing. Ditching and damming. Two weeks here, a month or six weeks there. Back home, clean the house, mend the fences, plow the fields, sow, cut, and thresh, make haystacks, get the butter and cheese made, gather and cook fruit for the jams and jellies, dry the meat, smoke the bacon, preserve the eggs and vegetables. Wash the wool, card it, put in on the loom. Knit, crochet, mend, and darn. Sleep, yes, when you can't keep your eyes open. Trouble? Yes, always plenty. But the senses, and wishing for a man in bed, it was a thought like waking up in summer and wishing for a piece of Christmas pudding. Very nice, but silly. And besides, love is with soap and water. Have you ever seen some who've been with love without? I have helped to bury them. No, Huw. Mama was strict. What she said has lasted. Idle hands, I told you. But an idle mind is the Devil's own. And besides, soap and water. And where was the time?"

"Supposing there had been soap and water?" I said. "And the time?"

"Perhaps you would have a different answer," she said, and laughed. "I'm not sure where. My peons would have had a word to say, I suppose."

"Peons?" I said. "What have they to do with anything?"

"Come on, now, boy," she said, and filling the tea pot. "Why do you think Mama gave each of us three peons before we were seven years old? Why do you think they are with us, still? When do you think us two have been together without them near? Only up here we have been alone. Never anywhere else. Who do you think, with all the time, and soap and water, could have come near? What would I say to them? 'Tamaño, Tampoco, Tambien, the seasons are a trouble to me. I want something for my senses. I have got soap and water, and strange to say, a little bit of time. Go from me, my little ones, I have got Christmas pudding in summer.' Shall I tell you what they would do? Slash him in strips, slowly, and grill each piece for him to sniff."

"You would have nothing to say?" I asked her.

"They have been better fathers to me than my own Dada," she said, and tears ready. "What could I say to them with clear eyes? What? Christmas pudding?"

But I was remembering an evening coming back from the choir, and walking along the river bank under the poplars, and all the stars in the water, and listening to Giacomo, only just from Italy and dying of homesickness, with a glorious tenor singing *O Sole Mio* across the quiet flow, so that stars, voice and the river seemed one, and Lal turned to me, and kissed with a dry mouth, hot, rough, and ran to jump for the saddle, and away, without Good Night or God With You.

It was then I wondered if the years with Bron had not been ruled by the same unfelt discipline, of plenty to do day after day, and not many moments to think, and at those times a dismissal ready in tiredness and a wish to sleep as a stone, or impatience with a silliness. Strange it is that lives are governed in such a way, and a shout of laughter for some, and a wide sneer for others, but so the world spun for many a year and few to question, and all of them disregarded.

After that I took more notice of the peons, three good men, Indios, most Tehuelche and part *manzanero* and Loluche, Tamaño well over six feet, Tampoco about a foot the shorter, and Tambien shorter still. They always wore Gaucho clothes, of wide trews wrapped into a boot made of horses' hocks, flayed warm from the animal and put on to dry to the shape of the foot, tied at the big toe, and trimmed after. A poncho, sometimes red, or blue, or with stripes, they folded exactly like a baby's napkin, and wrapped the ends about the waist, and over that, a broad leather belt studded with coins, a shirt made by their wives, sometimes with lace on the collar and cuffs, a short jacket, and a felt hat turned up in front. Their saddlery was a wonder of plaited bridle and reins, with stirrups in jointed arms of heavy silver hanging from Indio saddles made by Rhin's men on a framework of wood with a fleece, giving a far more comfortable ride than ours. That wide belt in stud of coins had good reason, too, but

I knew nothing about it until the day when I saw them put to use, and thanked God, but that was after.

A morning came with us, and we were cold in sheepskins under the canvas, and no wonder, because the rain had begun and up where we were, snow was only a puff of wind away. Tambien had lit the fire, and the kettle was on, and Lal leaned on an elbow and looked at me, the sad, beautiful look with a joke in it, and a shoulder showing through shining hair and pleading to be kissed.

"Off with our clothes and walk in the rain, is it?" she said.

"Two more sheepskins, me," I said. "And a good cup of tea, and then come close to me and we will sandpaper a bit of time, and sleep fat till noon."

"It isn't six o'clock yet," she said. "By noon we could be down in the valley, and home. It isn't raining, there. Mountain rain, this is. And it will pour for a week. In my house it is dry. Here, you will be green with mildew by tonight, and wet through. There is pretty."

No more to be said, and Tampoco brought the horses, and we packed everything, and not an hour later we were going down through the forest, seeing nothing in the gray of rain, sad to be gone, happy to be thinking of home. There was no time for a goodbye to the waterfall, and the lake was only mist, and there is nothing so foolish as standing in a pour and water running in your ears, and pretending to be sorry to leave, and pulling faces, then. So we looked, and nodded, and ran.

It was true as Lal said, the rain had stopped in the valley, but when we looked behind, the peaks were in fog. Our forest was warm in sun, and we went through the trees as if meeting friends, and most are still known by the names we gave them that day, for we never cut down or cleared along that path. We called it Our Way, and if it was a little longer to reach the road, very well, but we never went in or out by any other, and when Lal came back with the seeds and plants and we sowed the spaces between the trees, no road on earth, in years to come, was ever half so lovely with tint, and scent, and memory.

If we expected an arms-out shouting welcome, it went very flat with us. Everything was locked and the kitchen was empty and tidy, and nowhere is so sad of comfort as cold stoves and racks of scoured pots. Only in my tool shed was sign of the living, and Luis' shout was welcome enough. The boy had been told to cut planks and plane them ready, and from the size of the stack he could never have gone to bed since we went. A good boy, one to tell what to do and leave him, then, knowing it would be done to the detail and no nonsense.

"Everybody is up with Moishe Levy," he said. "A big asado. He came past two days ago with so many wagons, they were off my fingers. He has five leagues beyond Vyrnwy for an Army camp. And the Lieutenant Hernandez is a captain."

"Let us be there, quick," Lal said, and turned, but she reined. "Come, boy. We will ride together. You shall never say I galloped on and left you alone again. I was cut to the heart."

"It was pleasant to ride down with you," I said, and stretched over to kiss. "Why did you leave me, before?"

"To show you what a good horsewoman I was, of course," she said. "Selfish, vain, and a brat. But I always had plenty to do, and no time, in three places at once. So if I have got the horse, I go. No more. Riding barefront teaches lessons, too. I will soon be in a bounce with milk. Will you wait for me then, boy?"

Only one answer, and quick, but a kiss is an exercise on a horse, and in those days I could fall off without that, and she had to come halfway, and a kiss, a marvel of the mouth I shall always remember, in the green light of trees, and the scent of raw timber, and Lal in love, and whispering.

"See if you can gallop," she said. "Don't go over his head, now. Don't let him take your bottom out of the saddle. If he bucks, hold on, grip tight with the knees, and look only between his ears. Never take your eyes off. And never let him take your bottom from the saddle."

That was the first and the best lesson in riding I ever had. In those few years I had ridden everywhere, but nobody had told me anything about managing a horse. Everything I picked up from watching others. From that moment I could ride, and even the horse seemed to know it, because never mind what is said to the contrary, a horse can smell a fool and he will have a game of his own.

Along to Vyrnwy's forge we went, and I was surprised beyond words at the size of our place, alone. A league has a three-mile front, and I had forgotten that I had a league and so had Lal, so our property had a front of six miles of fine timber and deep soil, all of it on the river, and you cannot imagine six miles until you have ridden it. But it was also six miles deep, so we had thirty-six square miles to clear and bring into profit.

"It will be years," Lal said, and laughing. "Every year we shall be lucky to clear a square mile. So before we see clean land we have got thirty-six years of work. Can you live with me for thirty-six years? One clean mile a year, and how many babies? I would give everything for ten at once."

"Put in the order," I said. "I will see what there is in stock. Rough or sandpapered?"

"For me, there is no difference," she said, in distant tone of the outraged. "I will suffer for my milk. Not one sound will I make when you torture me. I am the prisoner of an old fiend, and I loathe him every moment of my life. What time is the next suffering, boy?"

"Gallop," I said. "If I catch you, I will put your bottom on these briars, here."

Off she went, and I was not far after, but as well try to catch El Pampero. We passed the end of our two leagues, and the start of Doli's and Volde's, another six miles, with Rhinberry's on the other side, and then Solva's, but Oracio had five leagues as a lieutenant, so between them they had three hundred and twenty-four square miles.

"Go in the Army," Lal said. "You shall have a hundred children, but when you die, each one will have only a little more than three square miles. Except that we still don't know if this is Chile or Argentina."

Gwenonwy and Donato's league was next, but only Donato had applied for the title so the property was his, with not a sapling cleared or a seed in the ground.

"We shall have to help them," Lal said. "Perhaps we can get a few of Oracio's men to work for extra money. I will bring more men from the Colony. But who will pay for the land here? If it belongs to Chile, we are working for nothing. That's the only reason we've been given a league. To put us here as proof we exist. For the benefit of those little fat ones in Buenos Aires. And they don't even know the names here."

Vyrnwy's forge was the busiest place I had seen since leaving the Colony. We came on it out of the trees, pulling up in surprise to see so many people and horses. It was near a foaming white branch of the river so that he had plenty of water, and in a curve of the mountain's forest which gave him fuel and shelter together, but the garden and potato fields were Tegwyn's and her touch was in all the toldos. Even in the big open sheds of the forge everywhere was clean, swept, with cinders crushed in all the paths to lift feet from mud and smother dust, and the wooden floors of their six rooms, all of axed logs, were waxed in a polish, and anywhere that lime wash would cover shone white. Those rooms were simple boxes joined by stone paths one after another, with roofs of rush and twigs, and we saw why she wanted a house.

Vyrnwy came in a run, but a changed man, livelier, with clean linen, no patches or rags in his trews, whole boots to his feet and even the leathern apron had been scrubbed.

"Well, dam', there is good to see you two old blessed-in-the-act, there," he shouted. "Are you sick of bed? Me, no. A siesta, us, every afternoon. O, there is good, aye. Do you see the work I have got? A cavalry regiment over the river. A hundred horses a day to be shod. Most never had a shoe on them. Ten helpers I have got, and for Donato's work, eight more. A year like this, I will pay ten times for the house, see. When shall we have it?"

Teg was another woman, walking on cushions, fair hair piled up, and a smile as if she had just come from sleep. Lal took her off somewhere, and I went with Vyrnwy to the shed where the hoops and axles for our wheels were made, and there I found Donato fitting two pair to a rough cart, and Moishe Levy sat on the wagon tongue watching.

"Pray to the Lord God, it's enough," he said, and came, arms wide to welcome. "To find you. To find you, that was the prayer. This is Moishe, Army contractor. Here, over the way, that's the base. Argentina and Chile, they like to have a war. If it's a war, they have to eat. I supply. They have to use wagons. Sheds. Roofs. You supply. I sub-contract. Pay me ten percent. I handle accounts, I guarantee payment. Date specified. Should we ratify?"

"Yes," I said, because I liked Moishe, and we could make wagons. "Supposing I wouldn't?"

"Then it's more simple," he said, and opened his hands. "Emergency. We take you in the Army. You work for nothing. It's why I'm here. Moishe works for Moishe. They're stupid, they want to go to war? Good. For Moishe it's the same. He says no? He's in the Army, a sergeant in supply? Me? You? Vyrnwy? Donato? So now, we work for each other. The Army, it's satisfied. We take the profit. It's sensible?"

"How many wagons do you want?" I asked him.

"The order comes for a thousand," Moishe said. "They want wagons from San Martin de los Andes down to Tierra del Fuego. This Army has no bases here. This is the first. The next follows, a hundred miles south. Then another, and another. All got to be supplied from the Atlantic coast. They got to have wagons, move food, ammunition. Who has the wagons?"

"A thousand wagons?" I said to Donato, and he laughed at me. "Without carpenters, it will take years."

"A thousand, it's to warm the tools," Moishe said. "When the wagon trains go, they go up, they go down. How many up, how many down? How many wagons, each train, to supply a thousand soldiers? How many thousand soldiers? So, how many wagons? Six-wheelers? Four-wheelers? How many depots? What roofing? Walls? Timber? How many square feet? For barracks. Garrisons. Headquarters. Hospitals. Take the pencil. Paper."

"Find me the carpenters," I said. "Somebody will have to go to the Colony and bring back at least a hundred."

"He should go now," Moishe said. "Perhaps in the Regiment they have men."

"Carpenters aren't trained overnight," I said. "They spoil more than they make. We must have a reputation for delivering the best."

"Why I should pray to the Lord God?" Moishe said, and looking up at the roof. "It's what I want. The best. No excuses. Come. We shall sit somewhere. Get the paper filled. Cost? No worry."

"The worst part will be finding seasoned timber and cutting it," I said, but I remembered the miles of trunks in burned forests all about us. "We need saws."

"If a steam engine drives a saw, that's on a couple of wagons over there," Moishe said. "Who knows engines?"

"I do," I said, and at last, the hours of helping Owen out in the back, here, made a splendid return. "If you have got an engine, the sawmill is almost cutting our first plank."

"Don't stand about," Moishe said, and put his hat on. "Vyrnwy, Donato, you work with Huw?"

"What Huw wants, that's what I want," Vyrnwy said.

"We are partners," Donato said. "He speaks for us."

"I should meet such men, it's the Will," Moishe said, at the roof. "At last I got family. Huw, I kiss first the hand of your lady. Then we take a pencil."

In those few little minutes, although it never entered my head, I had started being a millionaire.

10

If I had bought this land those years ago the museum would long have been open, and I might be sitting somewhere else instead of here, like a fool, and saying goodbye to so much that was good that has gone.

But if you want something done, you must do it yourself while the thought is warm, and you have the energy.

Everything would have been simple before the slag began to shift, but after that, there was no hope. Engineers could have done a thousand things, but once the weight was on the move and the fire started, that was the end. Most of the houses still had pieces of furniture in them, and clothes left to molder. Ceridwen had lived for years in this house, and left a lot when she moved, but Angharad had a great deal more up at Tyn-y-Coed until they pulled the place down, a shame if I never move again. A fine old house it was, of big rooms and wonderful views, but the arterial road had to be built, and a factory estate took most of the farmland, so down it came. Now there are rows of red brick sheds with sandblasted windows, asphalt paths and lamp posts and litter bins, and at the picnic yesterday, the mayor said a lot about progress. Unlucky, for I was too late there again, or I might have bought the place, but Iestyn's family were never very friendly, and I believe they insisted on selling to spite Angharad, because she only had a share but not control. She screamed curses at them, but no use. The house had gone into the builder's yard when she got there, heaps of brick and stone at takeaway prices, but she managed to get a few of the doors and lintels and some of the paneling and a couple of fireplaces, and sent them to Little Looking Glass, and they settled very well there, too.

But I doubt she will ever come back here to the Valley, and the children, of course, would far rather live in Argentina or the Cape, or anywhere else.

"It's so sad, Uncle," Gwynn said, on that first visit. "*Triste.* No? Stones and silence."

"Right you are," I said, and ashamed, and seeing it through other eyes for the first time. "When I was your age, there was life, and music, and green nearly everywhere. But a blade of grass here would deserve to be framed. And the only noise is the radio. Do they ever turn it off?"

"But how did it happen?" he asked me. "Was it the war?"

A fine question, and I wish I could have answered yes, and so have had the grand excuse. The change to oil over coal in ships and factories might have been a fair one. Outworked pits, low grade coal, cost of labor and transport, all might have provided reasons, in part.

But nothing explained those stony wens crawling unchanged for a century and more across the mountain.

He was used to our talk of the Valley as a place of song, and good food and splendid friends. All we found were streets of closed doors, a long boneyard of a tiredness that seemed to smell in the air, a lot of cheap little shops, and some of the worst fodder in Christendom.

But what I could not seem to put into his mind was that although Cambria was a country, it was ruled with far less thought than a Colony, not from anywhere inside the border, but from London, and by those willfully ignorant of anything Cambrian except statistics, that were of figures on paper, about tonnage or cubic feet, whether of steel, carrots, or human beings.

"How do people tolerate it?" he asked me. "Are they slaves?"

He was about ten, I suppose.

"No, not exactly slaves," I said. "They want to be left alone. They have got what they want, and they are content. Those who aren't can move out, and send back a post card or a shilling or two, now and again. It looks as if there have been plenty."

"These are your Indios, then," he said. "Indios want to be left alone. Mama said she will clean out the Devil's Poncho before we are back. Isn't this the same?"

That place was on Angharad's property, a hollow where the river broke in three, with a few small trees, and a pour of rocks down the hillside. About a hundred families lived there, of mixed Indio and Chilean and Argentinian blood, with not a thought in their minds except how to work the least for enough *maté*, meat, fried dough, and wine. The luckiest lived in caves that were there, and the others piled rock in walls roofed with beaten cans. The women might do some wool-cleaning and mending or laundry for enough *maté* and wine, and go back. The men did three or four weeks of digging or chopping wood or helping with shearing and branding for meat and flour and wine, and went back. Without spirit, with not a thought in them except to be drunk, so they lived. In many places were such pockets of blight, though only to our eyes and senses. For them, it was a comfortable life and nothing would have them from it.

Angharad tried to put the children in a school she had built, with a small hospital at the side, but the mothers screamed when the children had to be bathed, and always sold the new clothing.

"You waste your time and a fortune." Augustin Videla, her neighbor, told her. "You teach them manners at the table with clean linen? You bathe them in the morning? You teach them A.B.C.? 1-2-3? 2 and 2? Why? What use?"

"Each one will be a citizen, and I have got a big debt to this country," Angharad said. "It is one of the few places

I have found peace in the world. They are neglected by everybody. Everything was taken from them. They have grown up savage because we allowed it. We knew better. We should have done a great deal better. I shall try."

"That clean cloth will be stolen to be sold for a litre of wine," Augustin said, with not a spark of feeling. "They bathe in the morning and go back at night to present a clean head for voracious lice. A.B.C.? Enough to cut their names on any tree. Scrawl in any latrine. No, madam. That's for the Government. Or the Province. Not for you. You lavish your time on trash."

Augustin spoke from experience because there were hundreds of that type of Indio on his own place, some of the hundreds of thousands up and down the land, and nothing to be done for them because of the life in those dens.

The afternoon I signed the contract with Moishe, I went down to Rhinberry and asked him to send a man to find Saiheque and his people and bring them to work.

"Work?" Rhinberry said, and laughing. "In winter? When will they get their own work done? Blankets, pelts, rugs, weapons, everything they have got to make new for the year to come. And dry the meat. Where will they have their tents here? What will they do in snow? But they have got a pass signed by Oracio. It might save them."

"Might?" I said.

"Might, yes, because they have got troops of good horses and plenty of ponies," Rhin said. "It takes little time to kill people. Horses have more value. A pony is worth any three of their women."

"When will any of this stop?" I said.

Rhin shrugged as if it were no matter to anybody.

"When they are accepted as human, with us," he said. "I'll send a man. It will be two or three weeks before you will have word, yes or no. You have got time to make a camp for them. I will send my people over to you. Tell them what to do. It is done."

Lal and I chose a place across the river, flat, but above the line of spring floods, with plenty of trees for shelter and fuel, and Rhin's Indios put down stone for the floors, and hollowed logs for the roofs, and put up long sheds of three timber walls, leaving one side open for the big fire. When they had finished, it looked more comfortable than the soldiers' place down the valley, and when Major Vicente saw it, he ordered the same type of shelter for his company, and gave us all the men we needed.

Well, Donato and I were not slow. We chose the best men day by day, and at the end we had nearly a hundred good workmen to work the sawmill, cut and fine the planks, shape wagon tongues, turn the felly, and put everything together with some help from Donato, Luis and me, and when Saiheque came in, one night, with a hundred and twelve men, we took them round the place and showed them what to do. Next morning they were part of the job, because the soldiers were all Indios and Gaucho, and they all spoke the same language, so there was no trouble anywhere and they worked as if God Himself had oiled them.

A question of pay came up as a comedy. Saiheque wanted no money. The soldiers were not allowed to have any extra.

"The General will be angry if you pay a centavo," Moishe said. "He could take out the contract. The men earn from the Army. It is enough. They feed here, they have wine here, they sleep here. Better than the others. They work here? Good. But the others, they patrol in the mountains. That's rough. Ice and snow. These, here? They should be with their mothers. Tell you what we do. We put money one side, every man the name. When he leaves the Army, we pay. Saiheque, the same. One day he needs money? We got it."

We started by turning out eight four-wheel wagons a day, and those we passed to our neighbors until everybody had a wagon. Ox-carts we made by the dozen, and as fast as we put them outside, they were gone. When the men knew what to do, and we planned the work, then we started to make the six-wheel mule wagons, but Vyrnwy held us back because his men were slow with the wheel hoops and saddlery irons, even if they were working up there till they dropped. That was when I started three shifts a day, that nobody had ever heard of before.

"But the men must sleep," Donato said, and downcast. "Even with the best food, they will die, no?"

"Three shifts, each working ten hours," I said. "When they are not working, then they sleep. The first shift cuts timber. The second does the shaping. The third puts everything together. Some of Saiheque's men will go up to Vyrnwy. They will work the night shift to make hoops. The second shift will make the saddlery irons. The daytime shift will shoe horses. Now, everybody is doing everything in the same time. Let us try doing it in three parts. See if it works."

Of course it worked, and everybody better off, especially us.

In those days I saw Lal only when she came with food, or when I dropped in a chair and she helped me to undress and fall into bed.

One evening I was at the sawmill counting the day's cut and passing it to the shop, and the girl doing our laundry came to me in a run.

"The mistress Lal," she said, and breathless. "You are requested to hurry, if you please."

God knows what I thought, or what I had been thinking all that time, but in those moments I knew what Lal meant to me, and I kicked back the stool, and ran for the house. Darkness was coming, and our shutters were closed, and no light shone. I jumped the fence, and up to the porch, flung open the windbreak, and slammed open the inner door, and I stood there.

Three lamps were lit, covered by parchment shades, candles tickled the air about the walls and on the table laid for two, and flame from logs waved in the fireplace. The floor shone gold in polish about white rugs from Rhin's Indios, and a white goatskin spread between the two armchairs covered by guanaco pelts on either side of the mantel, and the walls were hung with ponchos in different colors. The surprise was to see all the furniture I had thought in the tool shed for a final touch, there, in place. Shrubs were cut in bowls, and branches of berries were on the table. Everywhere was the hand of Lal.

But the real beauty was Lal, herself, dressed in cream silk, hair down her back with a bow, standing in the door to the kitchen, hands joined in front, resting on a heel, and smiling.

"You seemed to have forgotten the furniture, so Saiheque and Luis and my peons finished it for me," she said. "I sent the girl because everybody else was too busy. With work. I thought if I came myself, you might be angry. And refuse me."

"What could I refuse you?" I asked her, and I was shocked to think of anything.

"To have dinner with me," she said. "Do you know what today was?"

Birthdays, and any other date slipped through the mill gate of my mind.

"No, indeed, I don't," I said. "The day you had a table to put a plate on, dearest mine, more shame to me?"

She looked, the long, dark, shining look that in a moment might become all tears, or a holding of the breasts in laughter.

"We have been married six months," she said. "Except for Sunday dinner and back to work after, you haven't even sat down with me. Am I ugly, or are you sorry you saw me, or what?"

Well.

What to say.

She put up her head in the sudden, beautiful, pitying laugh and came to me, arms out.

"Never mind, boy," she said. "Working, yes, I know. But there is time here, too. From now, listen to me, dinner at this time every night, and dressed. I watched you eating with the men over there at midday. You are like an old Gaucho with a knife and a steak. It will do no harm to sit down properly, once every day. With me."

From that night, we always sat down at the same time,

and I had untold benefit from a sane habit. That hour or so, at a table opposite a beauty, there was time to talk and find out many things, time to be reminded, time to love and be loved, and those have import in any life, and without them, joy can pass unknown, unnoticed. That night, some of the men played the guitar and sang, and we sat with candles shining in silver and china she had brought from Maes Corwen, that I had never seen before.

It came on me, then, that I was in my own house, and everything about me was ours.

For the first time in my life I was sitting at my own table.

There is no feeling to compare.

But I was sitting at a far better table than I had ever known. It was a piece of alerces, deep red, and polished so that the silver was doubled and the candlesticks and dips shone twice, and the silver bowl of berries had its partner, and the wineglasses and decanter shone other rubies.

Silver, glass, and china, of course, were Lal's, part of her life at Maes Corwen, even if she was just as happy with lasso, *bolas* or branding iron.

But except at Tyn-y-Coed, I had never seen that sort of table before. It was only for the wealthy. The single decoration on our table at home, here, was the cruet. But we were taught how to sit, how to use cutlery, how to eat, and what not to do. The small nicenesses of silver, crystal, and porcelain were supplements of courtesy, offshoots, not trunk, foliage, never tree.

That was secret my mother and father knew, and passed to us, so that wherever we were, we were comfortable.

"This is the prettiest table I ever saw," I said, when I came out dressed. "We will kneel down and give thanks."

"Good," she said. "It will be twice for me. I gave thanks that every piece came from the boxes and not a breakage or a crack. Now I'll have trouble to train a girl how to take care of them while I'm away. I ought to go at the end of the week. The weather is in the thaw. The tenth I should have gone. Will you think of me, boy?"

What the prayer was I am not sure because we were in a kiss for most of it, but it went from grateful hearts and with love, so there was not much missing, I suppose, except attention. But we came off our knees quick enough for a knocking at the front.

"If it is somebody with more work, I will tell them to push both thumbs," Lal said, and running to the door. "Nobody shall take you from this house tonight."

"If you were heard, nobody would believe it was you," I said. "Push thumbs, indeed. There is a lady."

"They can put three, and a good push from me," Lal said, and opened the door, and there was Moishe Levy, frock coat, top hat, beard trimmed, hair parted, and pressing a handkerchief to his nose not to laugh.

"Never heard a word," he said. "If I can come in? A talk. We packed, up there. Going day after tomorrow."

"Come in, and welcome, and have dinner," Lal said. "I shall be with you in a moment, only to put another place."

"Wonderful," Moishe said, and looked about. "What you did here, it's a miracle. I want a house, up there. We have five years' hard work. Maybe more. They have reinforcements coming the end of this month. The General, he wants barracks. I contracted to build. He wants roads. I contracted. He wants everything. I got it. Huw, you want to be a partner?"

Lal and I looked at each other, for we knew the worth of Moishe as a man.

She nodded, and put both hands on his shoulders, and kissed his cheek.

"Yes, for both," she said. "Partner in what?"

Moishe touched his beard where she had kissed.

"It should turn gold," he said. "Partner. That's it. Partner. Fifty percent. Huw takes charge here. Everything. Make the decision, say yes or no, get everything done. I supply from the other side. He asks. I send. Why am I here if he is here? So, Huw. Partner. Take charge. Everybody. Tomorrow. The morning, nine o'clock, meet the General. Smart man. Thinks no war. It's what I think. They fight for what? Anything here? Mountains. No people. Grazing? No animals. What's the fight?"

"The Fat Ones in Buenos Aires," Lal said. "They fight in the cafés. In the newspapers. But not here. That's for others. A glass of sherry before your dinner?"

"Wonderful," Moishe said. "Solva is with us. Tegwyn. That's a woman. Doli. You? Anybody going to be here? Except bachelors. They should drown."

"One bachelor will be here when I come back, or there will be trouble," Lal said. "I want ten wagonloads of things to bring back with me."

"A ship from Le Havre, this week," Moishe said. "From Naples in two weeks. From Marseilles in a month. Anything you want. End of next month, from Liverpool. Partner, you know we bought two ships? Not big. Enough to start. Buenos Aires to Port Madryn. Kills a lot of cost. Health to both. Happiness, and thoughts from the heart in this house. The Holy Love light you, and the one way to go."

That night should have been a happy one but I could only think of Lal going from me so soon, and when Moishe had gone to bed in the end room, she put her arms about me and weak with tears, and we sat on the rug by the fire, like children, and tried to have comfort. But the best place was bed, and she was glory, and sleep is sudden.

In the morning we were out at five, in the rattle of *maté* kettles by the score even before our chickens started choir practice. Moishe took tea and so did I, but Lal was used to *maté*, and when light came, I took them over to see the wagons for the girls. Lal's was on the end in shadow and she was looking at me, because Doli's and Solva's and Tegwyn's and Gwenonwy's got *Oh's!* and *Ah's!* from Moishe, and indeed, they looked even better than I had thought.

"Well, that's all," I said, and slapped my hands, finish.

"All?" Lal said. "What about mine?"

"Yours?" I said. "What, yours? Yours, you were going to give to Alys Caerog Smallcote. What is the use to make one for you?"

Well, the big tears came up, there, and she looked at Moishe.

"One for every bitch in the world except me," she said. "A husband, is it? A partner?"

"Well, there's a spare over here perhaps we could hammer up in time," I said. "It won't be the same, of course. The canvas is a bit worn. A patch or two, I suppose. The boards have had fair wear. Some splinters."

"*I—want—one—like—that,*" Lal said, and hit her fist on Gwenonwy's wagon with every word, and lips tight to her teeth. "Or I will burn everything here."

Moishe could see the other, and the tiled roof, chimney, and window, and he shut his eyes in a smile, and put his hands in his pockets and strolled over.

"Better look here," he called. "Else I could take it. For the doubts."

Lal was too angry to notice the outside, but when she saw the steps going up to a half-door, her shoulders came down and she turned to me with that smile.

"Another trick, is it?" she said. "I was so angry, I could fall flaming, here."

Moishe went up the stair, and looked for many moments, and came down, and Lal went up, and opened the door and went in.

"That's work," Moishe said. "That's the way to travel. I came across on horse. Or the four-wheeler. I know where my back is. You got one for me?"

"Send a six-horse team in the morning," I said. "It will be ready."

"A big favor, that's what I ask," he said. "Merlin. He can't go. Too much shaking. Worries about the harp. You going to see he got the food and a bed? He likes to hear some people. A place near the kitchen?"

"I'll put up a little house by the elderberries," I said. "He can listen all day. Everybody will have to pass there. A moment, please."

Up the stair I went to look for Lal. She lay on the bed, sobbing, with her.

"Hey," I said. "Good God, girl. What is this?"

"I was nasty to you, and O, Huw, it's so beautiful," she said. "My little house. All the time I'm away I won't stay anywhere else one moment. Not one."

"But you'll give it to Alys," I said.

The scorn would have put ice on the desert.

"That one will never see the inside except to wish," she said, on her way to the door. "I am proud, proud. Much prettier than the others, Huw. This is where I will dream of you. Will we sleep here tonight?"

"Yes," I said. "The new springs will let everybody know, too."

"I'll splash kilos of grease on them," she said. "And everybody can go to push. Breakfast, ten minutes."

She ran, and Moishe turned with me to Donato's.

"You got the pick," he said. "Did you hear Elias, Snuff, has a case against her and the sisters?"

"They aren't afraid," I said. "They are going over to see the Governor."

"Talk to the General," Moishe said. "Governor's a friend. Understand? This game, one hand shakes the other. Then get the camp up. It's needed."

When I saw it, I knew why. Rain had fallen up at that end, and the General's tent was wet, and he was over the ankles in mud and nowhere to keep his papers from the drops.

"The camp, General, my partner likes to know where?" Moishe said. "Not here."

"Under that hill," the General said, pointing about a mile away. "How long must I wait?"

"If you send the wagons this afternoon, I will have your quarters up and dry tomorrow evening," I said. "The camp a week later. Soldiers' shelters, four a day until complete."

The General smiled, and signed the papers Moishe had put

neatly on the table. He never spoke very much in all the time I knew him, but that little was never to be misunderstood.

"You are Cambrian," he said. "Not a Hebrew?"

"Not," I said. "Some believe we are joined to them, but anciently."

"Will you, now, vote for Argentina or Chile?" he asked me. "We shall soon have a referendum, here. I must assure myself of my contractors, at least."

"My wife is Argentinian and my children will be," I said. "I have no papers as a citizen. I came here only to travel."

"You are now a citizen by my order," he said. "Later, we shall have a ceremony."

"His wife has trouble about land, in the Atlantic Colony," Moishe said, and offered a cigar. "Somebody trying to nose in. She has to go to the Governor's office. I shall be there. Her husband has to stay here, make these camps. The wagons. Can't take care of her."

"I shall give you a letter to the Governor," the General said, and smiled a General's smile, as if all had been settled long before the letter was written, much less got there. "You will please join me in a glass of wine, and I shall wait for a dry roof until tomorrow."

That roof was up, as I promised, a solid flooring of stone and planks, walls of trunks with smooth planks for paneling, a stone fireplace and a chimney without a puff of smoke, doors without a squeak, no drafts, and a small bathroom. He walked about in socks, wondering.

"I see it was done," he said. "I cannot see how you did it. We have a great deal more work to do. See me here at ten o'clock."

Not a bit of use to say I had to see my wife off.

At ten o'clock I was there, and for hours through the day to late evening I had no chance to think of wallflower-velvet eyes and whispers, and heartbreak, but only papers, maps, areas. But at last it was over, and I rode back through the rain to the house as she had left it. Three of Rhin's girls were in the kitchen with Claerwen Austin. The dinner came on the table though I doubt if I tasted anything, and they said good night, and went.

The books I entered and totaled, and again I went over the plans and checked quantities and prices, anything to keep from a lonely bed. Our room seemed a cold barren without the lace-edged pillow on her side, and the nightdress in the case, and the gown hanging behind the door, and her brush and comb and the pretty bottles on the dressing table.

I had grown used to beauty.

The want for her seemed to scorch somewhere inside. All I wanted to do was lie on the goatskin by the fire, pull a rug over me, and sleep, and to Hell. But there was no sense in it. To bed I went, and turned this way, and wondering how far she had gone, and turned that way and wondered how far tomorrow, and to the ceiling to wonder if she was thinking of me, and altogether having a fine time, there, I suppose, until I went to sleep without knowing.

Night after night the same, and sometimes I listened to harp music in Merlin Afon's warm house, and went back, soothed a little, perhaps, though not much.

One night I half-woke, between a dream and a daze, and I thought Lal had come back.

A woman was with me, warm, of satin.

But the scent was not Lal's, of wild berries on the mountain, and the hair was heavier, longer than I could reach, and even in darkness I knew her eyes, and she laughed in her throat, and when I moved I knew she was with me, and nothing then except to hold her and know other grace, other marvel.

That further glory, of ink silk.

Lliutro.

11

Conscience is a better friend than anybody, but too close to the elbow, and easy to be pushed away.

Many an hour I argued with myself about Lliutro, but I never got far, perhaps because I could never talk to her. She came only in the darkness. The one memory I had of her for a long time was when she stood in the sun, and looked. Never once in those days did I see her in the light. The house was unlocked, with only wooden latches, and it seemed insult to everybody to put bars on the doors. Any thief was sure to be caught by the dozens of workmen and soldiers sleeping roundabout, and how she went past them without being heard was mystery itself until I was made to realize that every Indio in the zone had known from the beginning.

There was too much to be done to waste time on her, but I knew while I gave myself an easy excuse that I was far more than wrong. A wonder I have always had about the mind, that can present facets of probity to the everyday, and seem rich with knowledge and all competency, and yet be such a half-grown rig that a form of conduct which in another would be outrage, can be swallowed meek and without a word, if there is pleasure to the senses and assurance of secrecy.

But then, Lliutro was not an ordinary woman. Thinking now, I am not entirely sure what I mean by an ordinary woman. Perhaps the women I regard as ordinary are rare to the men they marry, or who know them. Lal was never ordinary, but one by herself and all joy and desire incarnate, giving because she had wanted to give for so long and the feeling was new and free beyond bounds, and she took because she had dreamed of taking, and every moment a marvel of greed.

Lliutro was with me, part of me, before I knew.

That, no other reason, was why it went on for so long, and why I sometimes argued the moral in front of the fire at night after a lonely dinner at Lal's table, and the carnal self beside me, silent, closing an eye, knowing.

Never mind that I denied, but I grew to want the visitation that was part of dream, and in the morning easy to put aside.

To rest a hand on the satin warmth of a woman is glory. Passing a hand over Lliutro was to caress the long deeps and rounded heights of the mountain, never in light, but in darkness, where touch is all, and the senses live free of sight, and there are no moral laws or any misgivings but only the wonder of being alive.

It was never every night or every other night or when I expected. Days went by, and I was hoping, and going to sleep in a smile, thinking I would wake and find her. But many a morning came, and nothing.

Then, some night, I felt her moving, with me, as a woman moves, secretly inside herself, where none might feel except the Adam in man, where the brain is drawn down, and life is in pause and words never were.

Lliutro knew nothing except what twenty years had taught, had no schooling, wore guanaco pelts, spoke only Arauco, and the soles of her feet were hard, abrased, and they rasped the bed linen to be heard, and yet a replete woman, lovely enough in herself, and of other hidden beauty, that caught the heart to bleed in tangle of gentle thorns, wanting nothing, taking nothing, refusing everything except the comfort of a man.

It seems nonsense, now, but Rhinberry was voice of my conscience.

He came in the shed one morning, and moved his head toward the trees to be away from ears.

"Huw," he said, sharp and unexpected. "You are going deep in the wrong here, boy. Before you say a word, remember. I am responsible for every Indio. A sign from me, and they will go. This girl going into your house. Why do you allow it?"

"Because it happens," I said, and nothing so soft was ever put in words.

"Happens, yes," he said, and looked up at the mountain. "Let me tell you, now. Lal, Doli and Solva have got nine peons between them. Those men are more than dedicated. They are with the girls. Their families are here with me. What will happen when they know?"

"Who will tell them?" I said, naked and helpless.

"Any dog sniffing between here and the Colony," he said. "If Lal doesn't know now, she will. There will be serious trouble. If she doesn't kill that girl, it will be a surprise. If the peons go after her, God help her. It's so wrong she should suffer."

"How shall I tell her?" I asked him. "She must not suffer. Not. Understand me. I could do a bit of killing, too."

He put a hand on my shoulder.

"I know, boy, I know," he said, and tears were in his eyes. "Indio women, they go deep into a man. They aren't like others. The truth. You are spoiled for a woman. It will take you long to forget. If you forget. That's why I'm here, now. It's got to stop. It is madness coming to murder."

"I can't speak to her," I said. "I never have. She doesn't understand. What, then?"

"She is daughter of Saiheque's sister," Rhinberry said. "He knows. I'll tell him to send her away. If there was trouble because of her, he would spin the small *bola* in the middle of her face, and the head would be torn from the neck."

"No," I said. "Tell him, no."

"Not because he doesn't want," Rhin said. "She comes, well, not exactly with his permission, but there's no woman in your house. That's the Indio way. But if Lal or the peons touch her, there would be enmity forever. Blood, certain. So he would kill her to have peace. I shall tell him, no more. Send her from here."

That morning I left for the end of the valley with Major Vicente, and we took the sawmill with us and all the soldiers. Saiheque had his own bench in the tool shed and I went in to tell Luis what they were to do.

From the way Saiheque looked at me I knew Rhin had already spoken, but I had no wish that Luis should translate for us and so bring another into knowledge. We shook hands and smiled, and I suppose he saw I was sorry. If only I had known how sorry I was going to be, I might have found plenty to say, but we never know until after.

There was no road, except for the ruts up to Vyrnwy's, and usually everyone went his own way through the timber. With the Major we rode in a column and a guide far in front, but we often had to stop to manhandle the stores over brooks and wide cracks in the ground, and down steep places sometimes a couple of hundred feet high, and over rivers. Big River was worst, for there we had to take the wheels off the wagons again, pack the stores on the mules and all the horses, swim them over and back until everything was on the other side, and then hitch each wagon to a dozen pair to be hauled over, and often the current was so strong that two dozen were needed for the extra pull. By then, night was coming and we made camp, and never have I had more pleasure of a fire. None of us had been out of water since early afternoon, either on horseback to guide the pack animals, or on the banks to help with the haul, and the water was freezing, with a racing current strong enough to take a man off his mount, and we lost two good boys, among the last over, going careless with cold and leaving everything to the horse. But unless a horse has got a pair of knees in him, he will suit himself, and in that width, about a hundred yards, with water frothing over the saddle, a horse will turn with the current if he is let, and so it was. We chased for miles along the bank but we never found them.

"You waste your time," Major Vicente said, when we came back. "Here is your responsibility, not down there. Those men didn't drown. They'll go home to the north. Two more nuisances. Here they might have been trained to be useful. A couple of years, they'd be masons or carpenters. Now they'll thieve till they're caught and shot."

"I'm sorry," I said. "I was thinking of human life."

"The men with you weren't," he said. "How many of them give a roll of dung for anybody's life? They went after the horses, not the men. Horses have value."

"How is it that life is so cheap?" I asked him. "With us, life is a sanctity."

"You are a Christian," he said. "These are not. Your own Army, is it Christian? It doesn't kill?"

"Well, yes, when they have to fight," I said. "But there must be a good excuse."

He poured a mug of wine for me.

"We shall drink to that," he said. "They've changed their minds, haven't they? They didn't make much excuse when they invaded us."

"Invaded you?" I said. "I never heard of it. Since when?"

"We beat you, and took your colors and your General prisoner," he said, with fine enjoyment. "In 1810. General Whitlock. You don't read history? Poor man, he was court-martialed. But they didn't send anyone else. We were left in peace."

"I never heard a word about it," I said.

"You carry your noses high by reason of it," he said. "Sanctity of life? Outside an area of civilization, no. Doesn't exist. Has no substance. Even within that area, only by expedience. You have never killed? Or wanted to kill?"

"Yes," I said.

"What prevented you?" he asked me.

"Somebody got in front, I suppose," I said. "Or else perhaps the thought of the police."

"There are no police here," he said. "Nobody will prevent you. They would much rather see the fight."

We worked together off and on for about a year, until he was sent to the Atlantic coast, down there at Port Desire. He kept strict order, and he obeyed to the letter and he went wherever he was sent, but the real difference between the General and the Major was in their attitude toward Indios, or anybody else. The Major treated everybody as if they were not Generals. He knew he had to be careful with me because I was a contractor and I could come and go when I wanted, and also because at that time I spoke poor Castellano. But with everybody else he was a ruler, except when he came up against Vyrnwy, or Moelwyn Pugh, those times, and the last time, Saiheque taught him a lesson.

We were building a road to the garrison post in the South at Futaleüfü, not a real road, but a track three yards wide with a hard surface for wagons, and bridges only where necessary. That sort of work I had never done before, but it seemed to me little more than common sense and sweat, and there is nothing much wrong with what we did, for the road is there to this day. When there were deeps and marshes we cut trees and filled, and stretches of road were built on tens of thousands of trunks all dropped in place by men or oxen. What we might have done without oxen, I am not sure, but certain it is we would have been years late. We had about fifty yoke taken from the farms, and each worth a weight in gold.

Moelwyn turned out of the line one afternoon with two carts, and going the other way.

"What are you doing?" the Major shouted. "Get back in line, that man."

"I am off home," Moelwyn said. "Today is the day. I have got work enough waiting for me."

"You'll finish here, first," the Major said. "Get back and start working."

"I am contracted up until now, today," Moelwyn said, and very quiet. "I am going nowhere except home."

"Then you'll leave your oxen here," the Major said, taking no notice of me. "They'll be just as useful without you."

"Well, certainly," Moelwyn said, and a look for me good as a wink. "Ask anybody to take them."

His oxen were trained only in Cambrian, and used to quiet words and a touch. But when some Gaucho took them and started screaming curses in Castellano and poking them with the cane goad, they stood blocking the track and nothing would move them, because for them, everything was noise and no sense, and they lifted their horns, and stared the big eyes, and opened their mouths and bawled, and all the others round them bawled, and we had to come away to hear ourselves.

"Those animals are fit for no more than the asado," the Major said, and angry.

"An expensive one," I said. "Mr. Pugh is on contract until today. The worst of this stretch is done. Farther on, we shall have Indios."

"Worthless," he said. "We shall keep those animals."

"On your charge, not mine," I said. "I shall pay him off and make a note for the General. It is against the contract."

"The contract is to build a road," he said.

"The contract is for each man's part," I said. "Farther on we cross desert. We can't use oxen. That's why we have Indios to meet us. Moelwyn, go home, and thank you."

"I have a good mind to keep him," the Major said.

"Each day extra will be money from somebody's pocket," I said. "The contract is with civilians. They have their own work to do."

"We should have our own engineers," the Major said.

"No doubt," I said. "We have all got enough to do without building roads to nowhere, and for nothing."

"When we are invaded you'll find out their worth," the Major said.

"Where, invade, and what use?" I asked him. "Mountains

here, and splendid trees, and twenty miles to the east, pampas. Invade, for what?"

"You people are here only to make some money and clear off," the Major said. "I always forget that. No respect for the Country, the people, or anything else."

Difficult to keep the mouth shut, but I had to tell him that making carts and wagons in my own place was far more profitable and less onerous than building roads, and in any event by making carts and wheels, some of us were doing as much for the Country and its people as anyone else, besides breeding herds and flocks, opening schools and trading if only with each other.

"You trade with Chileans," he said, as if disease touched us.

"If not for them, we would have had a far worse time in past years," I said. "We had no help from this Country. There was nobody here. There still is not. Not people, or which nation, but only trade makes a country to live in. Exchange of goods and money. If you want it flat, profit."

It had never occurred to me before, but the years I had been listening to my brothers talking about economics had laid a solid base in my mind, not of studious knowledge, but of broad theory so that without effort I had retained a fair view of the entire field, as railwaymen know the names of stations and the signals along miles of track without having to think.

"Is the General aware of your friendliness to the Chilotes?" the Major asked, and used a term of contempt.

"He is aware that his soldiers are eating Chilean beef and mutton," I said. "There isn't any here. There won't by any spare till next year. Your soup tonight will be Chilean dried beef and oats. Your *maté* is from Paraguay. Brought by us. Flour for your bread came from us in the Colony. Or where else would you have it?"

"Well, now, come along, Mr. Morgan, we mustn't quarrel," he said, and laughed as if he had been at play. "A drink of wine, and share the soup. The Chilote soap. Watery. Like their blood. It runs away."

As it happened, I had spoken to the cook the night before, and he used more oats, lentils, onions, and carrots from our garden, and a rarity, potatoes. The mutton was well fed, so that the soup was thick, rich and unusual. We all went up with cleaned plates and filled twice and again, until the pots were empty and nothing for the dogs.

"You will wake in the morning and your mouth stuck tight with jelly," I said. "Compliments from your Chilean friends over the mountain."

Three other officers were with us now and then, but only to report that night, and go off next morning with stores for the mountain patrols. They never saw anybody up there, and in all the time I was with the column we never saw anyone except our own Indios, and sometimes a Gaucho coming off the pampas with animals to sell. We never had any trouble except fights among the men, and they were soon over. The fighters were bound with rawhide and left to hang for a day and a night. Not many wanted to copy their groans, so fights became scarcer, and curses stayed in the mouth. The men tied up were sometimes a week or more before they could walk or lift anything, and I had them carried in the store carts and fed until they were able, or they could have died where they were cut down, and nobody troubling for them. Like that I made a few good friends, too, rough men, most from the North, with as much Castellano as I had, and just as much strangers to the Major, but their grandfathers had served with General San Martín, so that in loyalty as Argentinians they were able to give points to the best.

The road was over the stony stretch and going up the valley to Futaleüfü when I turned back. Without cutting into the cypresses, enough timber was stacked to make shelters, and I left the men to put them up under the eye of Rupayan, of Saiheque's people, a solid workman they all respected, and no wonder, because anyone arguing was never seen again. Luis told me he strangled them, and I can believe it, because he was over six foot six, and the only man I ever saw take a yoke of oxen in each hand, both pulling against him, and keep them on their ground.

Another treat was promised us on the night before we left, but I was happier with bread and butter. Some of the soldiers went out and caught nets full of ducks, and about a dozen ostriches that were almost as common there as sparrows with us. They plucked all the birds and cleaned them, and filled the ostriches with berries and whole ducks, and put them in round clay ovens to roast. Well, the ducks may have been very good by themselves, but with their own grease and the ostriches', one mouthful was enough to oil a wagon train, never mind that the ostrich has got a taste of his own in the class of putrid belly-flannel. Not to eat was an insult, so I insulted everybody and put on a good steak.

"You'd never do in the camp, Mr. Morgan," the Major said, with splashes when he bit into a carcass. "A little farther south, we shall be eating guanaco. When there's no firewood, raw. You haven't tried guanaco liver? Entrails? Ostrich liver? Crude? You get used to it."

"No doubt, if I had to," I said. "Next time you are near, come and share my table. You will see what sort of guanaco and ostrich we like to eat. When the first of us came here, they never had anything else. For years. We are luckier."

He remembered that invitation, too, and next time he was up, he stayed nearly a week, and I suppose he would be there yet, if Vyrnwy had taken his drink at the forge instead of with Geza up at the village.

In those days I understood Beretroff more and more.

"A man becomes used to the touch of a woman," he said, and in those words is purest truth.

Lal, in all surety, I missed with that constant notion of loss which sometimes, however silly it may be, can feel like a wound, at others a sore space in the mind where I often called her before remembering she was gone. I had a damp distaste of being alone that made the bed into a freezing ice-field, and the best blaze in the fireplace only half as warm. There was less pride in work, for never mind how others talked, there was nothing to take the place of that smile, and the kiss. Lal's kiss was fresh from the Garden. No dabs of a sloppy mouth, no wetness on the cheek, but a kiss that was of the woman, coin of love, and never long in exchange or she looked for the bed.

That notion of loss was held back in some degree by Lliutro, because no doubt if the body is calm, the mind is not so ready to dream. But while I was out those weeks, and after, without her, I knew the sharp temper of lonely men, the instant fret of irritation and the crowding dreams that can spill even into work. Then I began to know why Donato preferred working alone and living in the far house, and why Vyrnwy could be heard on the anvil well into the night, and how it was that whatever warmth of welcome I got, they were soon in sharp temper with their helpers and sorry after. It was not long before I heard it in myself.

"Vyrnwy, answer me, now," I said, one afternoon when he came with a wagonload of hoops and we sat to have a cup of tea. "Do you really miss Teg?"

"Miss her, well, good God, worse than I would miss both my bloody legs, man," he said. "She shall never go away again, for a start. She can lose everything over there and we shall fault nothing. I have been sleeping in the forge these weeks. I can't bear the house, I could go mad."

"How about an Indio girl?" I asked him.

He looked at me a long time, for moments, and his eyes were pale gray, and in pity.

"I've had plenty," he said. "My first girl was Tehuelche. Beautiful. A lot say they are ugly, but people like that have got ugly minds, see. It took long to get over them. They are a habit. And once they have got a baby, you will never be without them and a dozen more. But what good will it do to have an Indio, now? As a woman, yes. Nothing better in this life. But what will I say to Tegwyn? To her, an Indio is not even clean. They are. Yes, indeed they are. But you could never tell Teg. And where will it be? Can I take her in the house? Besides, Teg would know soon enough. You are worse off than before. So to hell. In the dregs of myself, I am better, and I will wait."

Dregs, yes, I knew the meaning.

But that afternoon, when he came in, well in wine, and saw the Major, we had the other side of the medal.

"Your last troop is shod," Vyrnwy told him, no greeting, not a word to me. "Don't send any more. I am off to the Colony to meet my wife."

"You will stay until I tell you," the Major said. "You are contracted to shoe until we move."

"Nobody gives orders to me," Vyrnwy said. "You have got nothing to say."

"I shall take your forge in charge," the Major said. "I shall arrest you. The contract is cancelled."

"The contract is with me," I said. "I can get another smith soon enough."

"Right," Vyrnwy said. "But there is no strap iron. No nails. Now let's see you shoe a mouse."

Not a word from me because I knew we had plenty of both. In any event, no great harm would have been done. The animals were used to going unshod, and many officers preferred to go without because there was less noise and often, with the bare hoof, safer going.

"You support him," the Major said, to me. "The Army presents you with a fortune, but you have no loyalty."

"I told you I will have a smith down there tonight," I said. "About strap iron and nails, I shall have to see. The question of my loyalty I will leave to the General. In the matter of a fortune, I must tell you that since I began, I have not seen one centavo."

"Same boat," Vyrnwy said. "Neither have I. Have you got a little glass with you, Huw?"

"A good cup of tea, yes," I said. "This is the first time I have ever seen you in drink during the day."

He seemed not to sit, but fall in the chair, and his chin went all the way down, and I thought him asleep.

"I will drive three nails in his head," he whispered. "Nails and a hammer I have got. Only to find him."

He spoke in Castellano, and the Major looked at me in surprise, and yet not.

"Why three nails?" I asked. "And who will you find?"

"Irrualde," Vyrnwy whispered, down at the floor.

"The Lieutenant Irrualde?" the Major asked, and smiled and rested the sabre between crossed boot tips. "Ah, yes, sir. He showed great favor to your wife, no? But he has taken his troop to Commodoro Rivadavia. I doubt he will come back."

Vyrnwy nodded as if at fact, and sat up.

"Showed favor, yes," he said. "Twice we asked him to have an asado with us. Instead to be lonely in his own camp. Then he was always about the place. Teg told me she didn't want to be nasty, see. He could cause trouble. For some, any woman is a mark. Well, in the end she told him. And after, I told him. Then he went."

"Well, is that something to get drunk about, then?" I asked him. "He's gone. Late with your nails, aren't you?"

Vyrnwy came out of the chair and lifted the Major on his feet in a clatter and held him upright in that farrier's grip.

"Don't you laugh at me," he whispered. "You know he didn't go to Commodoro. You knew he was going to Port Madryn. You knew he could catch up with our train very easily. Didn't you? Not a word to me? Till I had a word with old Crocket, just in. He met them, going over. Irrualde is riding with the wagons. Is that allowed?"

The Major shook his head, and looked down at the hand holding him, and Vyrnwy let go.

"You are fortunate I am not wearing a tunic, or I would have to kill you," the Major said. "Even so, I should."

"Try," Vyrnwy said, and folded his arms. "Raise that sword to me and I will break it across you. Or any dozen of you."

"Wait, now," I said. "You are not sober."

"Sober enough to know this one knew where Irrualde was

going, and knowing he would worry Teg," he said, and I thought he would hit the Major. "If his Gauchos tie the girl, what will she do?"

"He'd never do that," I said. "There are plenty there to stop it."

"Who will stop them if the order is given?" Vyrnwy shouted. "What can a girl do? Fight? These swine would kill everybody, and burn everything, and blame the Indios. Who will say the truth? Shall we see our girls again?"

"You have gone in a bad dream," I said. "Have a sleep, now, and think again."

"Think, Jesus Christ, I have done enough," Vyrnwy said. "I am off, now. My troop is outside. I came to tell this one the forge is shut, and shake hands with you. If anything has come to my girl, I will come back to find him. But be sure Irrualde or me will be in the grave."

He went, and the Major sat down on the arm of the chair, and wiped his face on a shirtsleeve.

"Which one is Irrualde?" I asked him. "Have I seen him?"

"He is young, from Corrientes," he said. "He had the patrol in the South. He is foolish. But Captain Hernandez is near the train. Irrualde might dare to visit the man's wife. If he is found, there would be serious consequences for him."

"Visit her?" I said. "You mean, force himself on her."

The Major smiled, and shrugged.

"Depending on which to believe," he said. "My information is that his visits were, let us say, friendly?"

"Not Teg," I said. "Before God, not."

"When you speak of women, take care," the Major said. "If this man is sure of his wife, why is he jealous?"

"Not jealous," I said. "Worried. About safety."

The Major laughed.

"But you are not worried about the 'safety' of your wife," he said. "Because you have an Indio companion. No?"

12

Some wonderful pears my father brought one night threw yellow light on the wall here, but one good bite showed the worms, and though we looked and looked, we never found how they got in. Each seemed a fine weight in the hand, with a sweet smell, though the taste was only fair near the peel, but the rest was home for rot, so they all went to the chickens and Mama said they never had such a treat.

Those pears I was thinking about after Vyrnwy had gone. He seemed a tidy man in mind, and healthy with the best, and as a workman beyond compare. Teg, I knew, was of the strictest in all she thought and did, and if I was sure, then with better reason Vyrnwy must have been far surer.

But the worm was in him, and must have been rotting all those weeks, and yet without sign.

The worm was also in me.

Not a notion was in my head until Corianth sent Maifron with a message from Idwyn to say that Lal had arrived at Maes Corwen, and everybody was safe. Maifron was not more than ten at that time and a pretty little girl, too. There was no use in asking her questions because she only knew what she had been told. But I can see her now, face in sprinkle of freckle over the nose in polish of soap, fair hair with a narrow pink bow in flop at the back, and a blue dress with a white collar and cuffs cut down from her mother, and a plaited whip in the right hand, and a milk can in the other. While I looked at her, I knew I was jealous. Lal had sent short letters by those they passed on the way, but at that time she had sent not even a word for a couple of months.

A strange feeling is jealousy. No use to call yourself a fool, or pretend to feel nothing, and go in a traipse about the place.

The worm is in you. It rots.

Lal's character was of essence the woman, without any weakness that I ever found except in quick temper when all was not as she wanted, and a tendency to play older sister to everybody that I suppose was habit. Nothing was there to cause jealousy. Other men she treated not even as her peons, for to them she was always kind, though as a mother. Why, then, jealousy should grow rot in my mind was a mystery, unless of course, I was putting myself in her place with Lliutro, and blaming her for being faithless instead of cursing myself.

But beyond words, Christ's thorns are worn again by all who suffer jealousy. Blood drips in the mind, in the ears and eyes, blood in the vision, in the hearing, bursting in the pulse, and well I understand the poor ones, and weak, who kill for jealousy.

The worm is inside, out of reach, beyond sight, but there is nobody to give you to the chickens.

Only the faithless and guilty are jealous.

Well I knew it on the night when Lliutro came back.

Letters I had written to Lal were carried by everybody going across, and little carvings I sent her, but nothing, not a word from her for more than two months, and I felt exactly like Vyrnwy except that I drank nothing except *maté* since tea was scarce, and we had no milk because the cows were in the mountains for the winter. If I had used my head or asked, I would have known that snow was thick over the pampas and nobody was coming across. But at those times we think least. Only the selfish thoughts have room, and they grow, and move, like worms.

Sitting in the chair by the fire one night, I was, and almost ready to go to bed, and I heard the door open and close, though if the fire had been in flame instead of settling I might never have heard a sound. No need to look, or any use to say a word. She was behind me and I could feel her eyes, and without summons the carnal one was at my side, knowing, smiling.

A terrible feeling it is, when you must choose between the one inside you, arguing a right and a wrong and pleading for a thought of Lal and keeping troth and faith, and the ruffian, risen and hungry, blind and mute, never deaf, but without interest only in pierce of a woman.

But I should have thought far more of Lliutro.

She had been told to go from there, and Saiheque had said she went over the peaks to Reloncavi, and up to Temuco, even farther north than Angharad, but for an Indio, no journey at all. To come back was a disobedience and she must have known the risk.

The girl was ready for death.

To be with me, or to please herself, I never found out.

Going out to the shop every day and working as carpenter, or sometimes as a roadbuilder, or putting up a bridge, or a barrack, or a house were all, to me, no more than parts of the same job, but to others they were proof of magic. It was understood that I might know how to make wheels, furniture or anything else in wood, but few guessed that years in a mine teach endless lessons in stone, and neither could they know the hours I worked with my father and brothers building walls and a bath house in brick, and the new sheds at my uncle's place in cement, a variety of tasks I had long forgotten, but the way to get them done never left me, and whether it was in the shop, or on the road, or at a bridge or barracks, I had no question to ask anybody.

They asked me, and I told them what to do, and it made me next to a god, especially with the Indios, though even among ourselves I knew I had a position which I never sought and never claimed, simply because I was capable in many fields, a contractor to the Government, partner of Moishe Levy, husband of Lal and therefore co-owner of the Maes Corwen property, though in my own right near to being a millionaire.

All those things I thought of after, but I should have been thinking of them when Lliutro stood in the doorway.

And looked.

In that way I must so often have looked at Bronwen.

Of all women born, Lliutro and all of her sisters in truth were defenceless except in their instincts and what their mothers taught them to protect themselves. By physical strength they could be taken against their will, but only at peril, and many a man found himself in comfort with a willing partner one moment, and the next, a screaming maniac with his testicles torn away on a long, twisted string. But they had no Law, or any Judge, or Police, or Civil power to help them, and little was in the minds of any of us to be careful of an Indio, and women, of course, always were nobody.

But when I looked at her that night, not a thought was extra, except that she was there.

She spoke to me in the whisper of a woman with a man, smiling, no smallest fear in eyes or voice, and her little hands were on me, as fond buyers touch silk, without weight or mark, dearly, and only from want.

At those times a man is in a trap. He could stamp his foot and shout and point to the door and kick her from the place, and afterward go back to the fire, a good one, of moral strength and upright in the spirit. But even though I knew far back in my mind the harm I was doing to Lal, there was nothing in me to deny Lliutro. She fed the pride in me, I suppose, and held the loneliness. But I should have realized that as daughter and granddaughter of caciques, she was offering herself to one she took to be kind of cacique, one from the white, unable to hunt or do much with a horse, but one to be obeyed not only by her own people, but even by soldiers. Besides, as I found later, none of the Indios understood why Lal and the others had gone away. If we, Donato and Vyrnwy and I, had been hunting for a week or two, and Lal, Doli, Gwenonwy and Tegwyn had stayed at home, all would have been well and in accord with Indio thought. But to see the men staying and working, and the women going and leaving others to do their work, was only to show we found them no good, and sent them off.

The guanaco cloak whispered to the floor. She always felt as if she had been fresh-ironed. That perfume they made of berries was about her, faint, and yet it would be on your hands in the morning and in the bed for many a night after, faint, always faint, but enough to make you close your eyes and stretch, and wish. Her body was a softness that seemed to have no bone or any muscle, though she threw a lasso or the *bolas* good as any man, and no horse had ever shied her from its back, saddled or not, and many a time I saw her lift more than her own weight. Yet no sign showed to the eye, and under the hand she felt as a warm coil of gloss that in a moment would tighten in a shuddering, drowning clutch, and a cry deep in the throat as a baby in waking. No harm was in her, I will swear on the Day, not one small notion, no passing drift of badness then, or ever, for if a woman ever lived to purify a man's time on earth, that one was Lliutro, and I will go on my knees, now, to say it.

After that she came to the house on most nights at the same time but when I woke in the morning she was gone. She was a dream, active and dearly sensed at the time, but on awakening, forgotten. It could be called a purest form of selfishness, very well, but at that time I never thought what it was, if I ever thought anything, because I had enough to do during the day, and at night, tiredness alone made me a drunkard filled with sleep.

Saiheque never said a word to me, and neither did Rhinberry. Donato worked day after day, but I was never over there, and he came now and again for the Sunday asado, and then we spoke mainly of business.

There was enough.

Not surfaced roads, but ox-wagon tracks we had built north

and south for hundreds of miles, and at the end of every day's ride, a shelter for men and cattle, and supply depots where a force might be caught for the winter and never be in lack of a meal or feed for their animals. Everything in those days was a detail that grew into a plan for the entire border, so that if an attack was made anywhere, enough supplies were ready to provide the Army with everything needed for defence. After that was done, by the General's order, every depot was supplied with enough to take the Army into attack, and that was a far greater problem, whether in finding the necessary stores, or in getting it all there and then keeping it dry with a roof.

At that time the talk was all of war. Not many newspapers reached us, but we got our news from people coming down from the North, or up from the South, or across from the Atlantic or over the peaks from Chile.

"What will you do?" I asked Rhinberry.

"I am in twenty minds to think," he said. "One thing is sure. If there is war, all the Indios will be with Chile. They have been just as cruel to Indios over there. But now they have got sense. They have given them land. A lot of Indios have gone over there for good. On this side some of them have stayed because these were the lands of their fathers. Or they have friends. You, Donato, Vyrnwy, Corianth, all of us. But if there is war, they will go. I will have to think. Argentina has been good to us. I was born here, see. When we were hungry, we were helped. By the Argentinian Government. But on this side, the ordinary Chileno helped us to live. Choose, then. Which?"

"Who is right?" I asked him. "For what will they fight?"

"Size," he said. "Never mind what is there. Or where. Or who. Only size. The bigger on the map, the bigger the little man looking at it. The Chilenos want all the land west of where the rivers flow toward the Pacific. From that place, the Chilenos say, must be Chile. The Argentinians say the border must be marked by the mountain peaks. Water shifts. Today it will flow here, but tomorrow there. Mountain peaks stay where they are. Draw a line from peak to peak. That is the boundary. The Chilenos say, no. The divide, east or west, of the rivers. Or we will fight to take all we can."

"Who will win?" I asked him.

He looked up at sunshine moting pale blue rain through the treetops, and shook his head, a sad one.

"Hard to say," he said. "One thing is sure. The end will come with time, not with fights. Araucanos have never been beaten by white men. If this Army had been fighting Araucanos, we would not be comfortable here, let me tell you. Indios of the pampas are another breed. Tehuelche were too few. But the Araucano are a million in Chile. They win, or they die. And another thing. Spanish blood in Chile is mostly pioneer. Different again. They are less mixed. If you add one to another, we will be better not to start."

About then the winter rain began.

Rain I have seen for days on end, the little rain that soaks, that makes even the walls run, here, in this Valley and many a time. But I never saw rain fall, day and night for weeks on end, as in the Andes. The ground was mud over the ankles, the tracks were mud to the fetlock, and the river came almost up to the tool shed, and still the rain fell to sting. We had fires going to dry the timber, and in all the fireplaces to keep damp from the houses, but verdigris crept, and bread tasted sour, and the roofs were in daylong drum, and butts filled and dribbled, and tools went to rust, beds felt damp and clothing could be wrung, and we were neither wet nor dry but clammy, and still the rain came down. There is no use to work with wood at those times, and not much sense in trying to work at anything except to keep warm, for to keep dry, or even feel dry, is reward of angels and not for us. We had plenty of firewood, but the smoke choked us, and boiling a kettle in the morning was endless penance, or it could have been, except for Lliutro.

After a couple of weeks, when Donato came over one morning to see if I had a spare box of dry matches, we shared a pile of laurel to make a fire start quickly, though of course we needed dry logs to make it burn and give heat. We had none. Square meters of timber we had, but wet through.

"For next winter, a roof over the firewood," I said. "And we will cut enough for the stoves and the fireplaces. A lesson for a lifetime."

Lliutro taught the lesson. She must have had it from Rhinberry that we had trouble with fires, for next morning I found the tool shed almost full of moss torn from the trees. Moss I had seen used by Indios and the soldiers to start a fire, but I never thought of using it myself, and I asked Luis why he had never been out for some.

"The kerosene," he said. "It lights as well."

"Kerosene costs money and work to get it here," I said. "Not to waste on fires of wet wood. Go you, now. Cut small sticks for the cooking stoves, and logs for the fireplace, and stack them in the kitchen and along the passage. In a week we will have fires and no smoke. And bring in moss. We are like a lot of old rolling stones, here."

Lliutro, again, showed us why Indios always had a good hot fire. We knew they had, for we could see the glow at night, far over. We thought they kept the wood in the toldos, but we never went near to see, perhaps because we had no wish to intrude, or more likely we felt a little too high and mighty to visit a people roofed and dressed in guanaco pelts.

Batancal came with an ox-cart from Rhin's a couple of days later, and Luis came to ask where the stone should be put.

What I felt when I saw it I cannot tell, but I remembered my Dada, and through him, Mama, and the Valley, and all of us so far away.

"Coal, this is," I said. "Not a good grade, but coal, and it will burn well. Pile it in the end of the kitchen. Fill a couple of buckets for the fireplaces in the house. Have you known about this before?"

He looked at me as if I had left sense.

"Yes, sir," he said. "We always use it for fires."

"You couldn't say something about it?" I asked him. "Knowing we were like a lot of old wet-drawers here?"

"Sir, I thought you had a reason for the smoke," he said, artless as that. "As they make smoke in the *Toquiguahue*."

He used the Arauco word for church, and he meant incense.

"You can't be such a fool," I said. "This smoke is different. For no purpose except to show we didn't think far enough in front. Why should we burn good wood, and waste, if we can have coal?"

"You do everything better than us," he said, and very quiet, looking at the ground. "I waited for the reason. Why should I impose?"

The boy was telling plain truth, and I could have put an arm about him.

"We have got lessons to learn from each other," I said. "Go now, take all the carts, bring in coal and pile it in the kitchen shed. No more wood is needed, except small sticks, and the moss. And next time, when you don't understand, ask. Always ask. That way I learned. That way we all learn. Ask."

My own lesson I had to learn not an hour later, when I took a sack of coal as a gift of jewels over to Donato. He had a big place over there, and a couple of dozen men, most of them Basques, working for him, with some Chilenos and a few of Saiheque's people. At that time he made wagons of four wheels to be pulled by a pair, or in heavy load by four, and ox-carts, and light traps for better going in summer, and his books were full.

Well, he looked at me and the coal as if Moses and the Tablets had come again.

"Good God," he said. "Where did you find this?"

"Somewhere near, and we have been slow," I said. "But we will have a few tons ready in the nearest future, and never again will we suffer smoke. Send twenty men over tomorrow, and we will find the mine. Indios have been using it and saying nothing. There could be an industry, here. Better fuel, and save timber."

"Come in the house," he said. "It is too long since you visited me. So long, I thought we were not friends."

Fact, and the only reason was work.

But I had a shock. The house was in turmoil, everything pushed here and there, floors thick with the mud of that day and shiny, or dried and dusty of weeks, dishes and pots on the table and floor, fireplace in fluff of ash, bones thrown about the surround, dirty curtains, crumpled clothes, and two Indio girls I had never seen squatting to flay a sheep in the middle of the floor that Gwenonwy had waxed to break a neck.

"Well," I said. "Helpers?"

"Of their own accord," he said, but not looking at me, and from the way they were smiling at him, there was no doubt.

"What will Gwenonwy say?" I asked him.

"Let her come back and say it, and I will listen," he said, and shoveled ash in clouds. "She makes herself one with her sheep. Very well. But I have no need of sheep except to eat. A woman, yes. But two, for safety."

"Not the women, alone, but the state of the house," I said. "Eat a sheep, yes, but live like a pig?"

"They don't understand a house," he said. "They are good women. It is enough."

"Not nearly enough," I said. "When we make up the books, and you have got your money in the bank, you will be rich. You are rich, now. Every day, every shaving off, you are richer. You cannot live in this manner. You have great responsibility to yourself and your wife and all of us."

"You have greater," he said, still not looking at me. "But you have an Indio."

"True," I said, and I began to feel the meaning of disgrace. "I have an Indio. But I have a clean house."

"Not important," he said. "These are clean in the spirit. Housekeeping is another matter. Of the broom and dishcloth.

They are not used to them. They don't understand. Cleanliness of the spirit, yes."

"Teach them," I said. "I thought Corianth was sending the girls over to keep everything well with you?"

"There was too much rain," he said. "They were wet through. I told them to stay home."

"Not to see the Indios," I said. "Does Rhinberry know?"

"I asked him to send them," he said, and looked at me, an angry man, but calm. "What are thousands of sheep to me? What is land in the pampas? I want my house and my woman. Enough. I work. Where is my woman? Looking after sheep? And me? The husband? Sign the paper. Marriage. It's enough? No, my friend. Gwenonwy can come back and see the price of pampas land and a few thousand sheep. These Indios are better women. They ask nothing. You don't find it so?"

Every word I had thought and said to myself about Lal, and many a time, and yet there was something about his way of saying it, and everything about the sight and the smell of that house which made me want to deny him. Perhaps it was then that I began to see the penalty of going against what I knew to be right, of being faithless to Lal, of allowing another in her house, in her place, and giving excuses whether to her or to others or to myself. The bed, I knew, must burn.

Strange, that to see a friend in error is to see yourself, but twice as clear, and with shame to destroy.

"Why did you think we were no longer friends?" I asked him, and not looking at the Indios or at the blood pooling over that floor. "We shook hands on an agreement. Can you have an agreement and not be friends?"

"Business," he said, but he was looking strangely at me, as if he was coming awake.

"Not in my language," I said. "Friends, agreements, and business, yes. Without, no. I haven't been here because I have got enough to do. Why did you stay away from me?"

"Why did you tell Lal I was living with Indios?" he asked me. "Is that a friend?"

"I have told Lal nothing because I didn't know anything," I said. "Did I know you had Indios here? Who told you I had an Indio?"

He hardly moved in a shrug.

"Everybody knew," he said. "Should I blame you? The best of all. Who wouldn't? In the condition we are in. But you see, somebody told Gwenonwy."

"Lal and the girls have got peons, and their families are here," I said. "That's who. And if they told about you, they certainly added a word or two about me. So that is why Lal hasn't written."

"Vyrnwy," he said.

"Vyrnwy knew nothing, and even if he did, hot iron to the gut would never have a word from him," I said. "It could be our friends, the soldiers."

"They were not here when the Indios came," Donato said. "They couldn't guess. Somebody told. Who?"

We had to go, then and there, to Rhinberry's to find out.

"Now, look here," he said. "Gags of sacking will never stop some from gossip. Plenty of Indios are going from here. Many are coming back. Wagon trains go when the weather allows. Mouths are in all of them. A word, a look, it's enough. Everybody knows the family of Lliutro. That second girl of Donato's is sister to Solva's first peon. What can you hide?"

"You came to me about Lliutro," I said. "You were sure Saiheque would kill her. But she is back. He hasn't done anything. Not a word to me. Why?"

"Indios have their way, and we have ours," Rhin said, and went on stitching the saddle. "Lal isn't here. None of them are. There is no news of when they will be back here. Nobody has been sent out to guard them on the way in. What does the Indio think?"

"The house is open," Donato said. "Enter, and live. That's all."

Rhinberry nodded and went on stitching. Something was strange with him, in the set of his head, in the rough way he spoke, unlike his usual happy self, if, because of Donato, he spoke in Castellano.

"So the moment we know they are coming back, we kick the Indios from the place," I said. "Who will tell us?"

"I doubt you will have warning," Rhin said, no pause in the stitch, loop, and pull. "They will be here at night. You will be asleep. So will the Indios. Nice?"

"Then there will be real trouble," I said.

Rhin waxed the twine, broke it, and threaded as if he could see trouble through the awl's eye.

"Have you thought what loss of life there might be?" he asked nobody. "I think you are dancing as if everything was very comfortable with you. And because with you, then with everybody. You are wrong. I have told you both. Work, very well, and great ones in your own place. But you are supposed to be Christians of a kind. Christians have another way to live and show faith. You are showing faith worse than Indios. They have got their way to live. Nothing wrong with them. You are living in this fashion because your stable is without a mare. So you take somebody else's because she is in stray. Are your wives the sort of women to be in stray? Would they accept a man only because he came in the house? Would you expect them to? Would you kiss their feet? Or cut their throats?"

"They prefer sheep and the pampas," Donato said.

"The sheep are theirs and so is the land," Rhin said. "Will you give them away? Every sheep here was bred at good cost by the pioneers. Every meter of land was fenced in sweat and deprivation. Shall it go to waste because your bed is cold and no woman to wait on you?"

"Not that," Donato said, and he looked as I felt. "We have no need of sheep or pampas."

"Because now you have a little of your own to keep a roof over, and something to boil in the pot," Rhin said. "But our girls have got more than that. They are strict to the memories of them gone before. Them to come. Strict. They will be strict to keep any other man from putting so much as his eyes on them. Those you have got, that creep in the house like rats, what have they to offer? A moment? Two moments? Give time, they will litter with the best. When the child is grown, will you face your wife? They are blood of your blood, flesh of your flesh. Will you deny them? Will you do what Vrann Corwen is trying to do?"

Every word in that quiet voice I can hear now, and the sharp whisper of twine pulled through saddle leather, and the little squeak of the awl making place for another stitch.

"Vrann has got nothing to say," I said. "Perhaps Clais has a claim. Not Vrann."

"He has got everything," Rhinberry said. "He is eldest son, and the papers are all with him. Who says he lost everything in gaming? Where is the proof? Matti Mumpo died very suddenly, you know. Mr. Elias, Snuff, is not the man to let a lawyer sit idle if there is a bit of pleading to be done that might bring in a peso or two. And dear Mrs. Elias, of course, knew as much of her father's business as he did. A lot of paper can be destroyed in only one little hour, isn't it? And they have had time."

"But didn't Tynant Lewis have everything in order, there?" I said. "Everything is in the archives with the Governor at Rawson, surely? Lal is a businesswoman, too, you know. Mr. Elias will have to be out of bed very early."

"Rawson is in Patagonia, but Buenos Aires is the first city of Argentina," Rhin said. "The lawyers in Buenos Aires can do plenty, and it will be weeks before anything is known in Rawson. By then, the damage is done. I believe you will have to prepare yourself for a shock."

The stitching I can hear now, and the small echo of his voice in the peak of the toldo and in float among the leaves of the trees outside. Rain came again to beat as a roared whisper on the hides over the logs, seeming to wash away the words.

"No shock for me," Donato said, louder. "She will come back and find Indios. I will tell her why."

"Gwenonwy will accept," Rhin said. "She knows the camp life. It will be surprise to me if she didn't choose them herself before she left. They are both good girls. When she comes back, they will be off, soon enough. Huw is different. He is of our people, and he knows better. Vyrnwy is a better man than both of you. He has said to Hell with business. I am off to find my wife."

"It is in my mind," I said. "I have been thinking these days."

"Late," Rhin said, and put down the awl. "Idwyn was here last night. He will be over to you later. Lal has gone to Buenos Aires with Doli and Solva. They are in sore danger of losing everything. You will be lucky to see them before the end of the year."

So it was, and my son was born in Buenos Aires, and I was far from him, and my Lal.

13

If I had thrown everything aside as Vyrnwy had, and gone to find Lal, sure it is that she would have been the last one to thank me. To her, devotion and duty and work were all one word, and to be alone or in discomfort was part, and nothing to be done except live through it to a better time. So she told me in a long letter she wrote before going to Buenos Aires, though it took months to reach me. By then it was middle of winter and snow everywhere, but there were bright days of sun on a land of white pillows, and pines shining in beards of icicles, and it was such a day when her letter came, and I was happier than anyone for there was not a word about Indios, but only about the baby she was going to have.

Strange it is that if you have been doing wrong and you are forgiven, and told you may do in the light what was done in the dark, the taste is gone and joy is not with you.

When I saw Lliutro again, after reading that letter, she seemed to me to have gone smaller, and I saw only a thin, dark girl, and I knew what a swine I had been. The heart was not in me to put her away, and by luck, I suppose, I was saved from having to ask Rhinberry to tell her, though I am sure she knew, on that very night, I was not as I had been. A man can pretend in words, but not with his body. Conscience will ruin the Adam better than buckets of cold water.

The luck came with Luigi Benedetti, sent by Moishe to draw and map the tracks we had made, and to make plans of the camps and storage depots, in building, or built. Only I knew where they all were, so we got the troop together and left the morning after. Lliutro had gone when I woke, and I told Rhinberry it was finished when he came over with rugs and stores to see us away.

"If there is anything she wants, see that she has it, never mind what," I said. "Tell Geza she has got the run of the shop. We shall be away three weeks at least. When I am back I'll be forgotten."

He laughed up at me in the darkness, and patted the horse's neck.

"Ah, Huw, Huw," he said. "You have got lessons to learn. About Indio women, that is certain. Careful on the road, and come back safe, and God the Father have you in warm fold, boy."

Three weeks I had thought, but Benedetti and his theodolite and chains and poles, and the measuring and drawing, and snow and rain when we were held in white blank or gray pour for days on end, well, anyway, at the end of the sixth week we were not even to the halfway, and I knew I must go back.

"I shall be sorry to see you go, sir," Benedetti said, in the tent that night. "I am not used to the country."

No need to tell him that if anybody was unused, it was me. But I understood what he meant. He was only a few months from Italy, a graduate of Florence, and sad in love with a girl from Rapallo, and I remember, because he used to stand in the doorway of the canvas roof, and whisper to her, Nicola, almost as a prayer, and I wondered why I was not calling Lal in the same way. Except, of course, that Lal would have given me a look, only one, and that would have been enough. It came to me then, that I was unsure if we had sentiment without emotion, or emotion without sentiment, but certain it is that Italians have got plenty of both, and they either live sad with hope, or happy with promise, but little in between.

In charge of everybody I put Rupayan, and no steadier man anywhere. In those weeks he had learned the compass and how to use the theodolite good as the next, and he was testimony that Indios in truth have got brains. When I told him I was leaving everything, and Benedetti, in his charge, you might have thought him in gift of a new race of horses. Yet, the man had nothing more than his guanaco hides, and his troop, and himself.

Others were like him.

All those months we had been working a few days here, a week there, to cut tracks, or clear timber, or put up sheds and shelters, but it was only when I saw it on paper that I realized how much had been done, and over what distance. When I left Benedetti we were not so far as El Bolson, and he still had days of hard riding to reach the Vuriloche Pass, even if work and the weather let him.

Going back was bad enough, but I had good cause to be thankful to Lliutro. She had made me a *chiripá* worn like a baby's napkin, from a shaven guanaco pelt, and a guanaco *chamanto*, almost twice my height with a slit to put the head through, so that in the saddle I was covered back and front. A wide-brimmed felt hat, then, and with hair to the shoulders and a long beard, it was no wonder I never felt the cold, and rain might fall in tons but not a drop touched me.

The Indios were always a surprise. A day could be howling with a snow wind and my fingers might be numb, but they rode and worked bare to the waist. Never can I remember hearing any of them complain of cold, and I never saw them even rub their hands. A healthy lot they were, first to start in the morning and always last to finish at night, and never asking for anything in return.

They wanted nothing except what they had.

Always, before, I had ridden with others of us, and we either followed a guide or a track. But then, I was with Indios for the first time and I was taught how they cover the ground.

Nüfcütun, one of the lesser caciques, led the way through country I would have thought impossible, up ledges in cliffs I still dream about, down crevices a dog might have thought twice before going in, gallop-jumping chasms that made me shut my eyes, hurdling hours long through forests of fallen trees, splashing across white rivers, cantering over glaciers that trembled under us, and if the ponies sweated lather, they were always ready to gallop and I was forced to mock my care of them. Nüfcütun never seemed to look for any one point to go for, and I tried to ride close to watch him. His head never turned from the front, but the others were looking about all the time. When he saw a herd of guanaco far out on the low ground near Cholilla, he stopped, and I could see he was arguing with himself whether or not to go down and knock a few over. But I was with him, and he swung the reins and jumped a log, riding on in that gallop that I came to believe would never stop. Every bone in my body had gone to sleep though I was wakeful enough and I looked about only to take my mind away from tiredness of the nerves and marrow, and I saw the Cordillera peaks and valleys for the first time as if with eyes gone clearer in knowledge and pain.

In that pounding of horse against man I believe that for a time, by some other Will, I was forced into another mold of life, to think with another mind, even to breathe differently. Those few days were all I needed to be sure I was glad to have been born to another people, hard in their way, well able to endure and not easy to be put down by adversity. Yet, with every good wish in the world, I knew, then, I could never live for long as an Indio. They seemed to want food only once a day and then they gobbled anything, but it had to be fresh-killed meat. If there was time, they roasted it over a fire, or if they were too hungry, it went down raw, meat, fat, liver, kidneys, entrails, and juice to the last lick of the fingers. Ostrich, hare, armadillo or guanaco were all poison to me, and only leather would be tougher to chew, except the armadillo, with a taste of oily glue when cooked by itself, and raw, then not to be spoken about. In my pouch was bacon. They wanted nothing better than the rind. Biscuits I made from flour and water, fried in fat, and then toasted. They never touched them. *Maté* they liked sometimes, though oftener they drank water, but they were all ready for coffee when I made it in the mornings, and they ran to push in a line where the wind was blowing to sniff the smell, and laugh like children. Their noses and ears were match for any dog's in fineness. Twice we were led to Indio tents by smoke from their fires, but miles from where Nüfcütun had pulled up to point a finger, and I was always last to know why, for of course, my nose was last to be warned. In the tents were families from Chiloé, not so well formed or as good-looking as Saiheque's people. Though the snow was deep, children ran naked, not much covered anybody, and their fires were only handfuls of sticks, but hares hung by the dozen and we were all offered one. A raw hare is a treat to an Indio, and I knew I was bruising hospitality by saying no, but Nüfcütun told them I was a sheep-eater, and I made coffee for everybody, and to finish we were all friends. Rough though their lives were, without the smallest comfort except for guanaco pelts to keep them warm, men and women were sensitive as flowers, and shock was in me to see tears in the eyes of the old woman, smoke-wrinkled in face and body, naked above the waist, holding out a hare to me and not wanting to understand the shake of my head. The others were crunching into the hide and meat, but I had not enough inside me to be sick.

Home.

It had a wonderful sound, then.

Mountains under snow went up to peaks all round us, a blue lake going into a green one beyond the bend of the river, trees showering frozen crystals, hour after hour, other cones of mountains, another lake, gray, not a ripple, hours more of darkness in thick forest, and out, almost in gulp of relief to sky so light it could scald, among miles of boulders, and letting the ponies pick a way, through rivers, across patches to the bellyband in soft ice, over more rivers, up and down more mountains, around other lakes, through forests of cypress, up to a crevice, down a watercourse, another river, more forest of tall alerces, around a blue lake, through a waterfall, swim a pool, splash through a river, and almost without warning the mind stops thinking of what is seen, is not remotely taken by pain or tiredness, feels nothing for anybody, begins to move in a way that must, frighteningly, be like the Indio's, and even as the thoughts come, they are known to be of the Indio, pure, as if the true self had died and an Indio had taken charge.

Trees become green persons, each with a warm voice, and stones call out, rivers move white limbs and whisper, and lakes are all in murmur of love for guardian mountains, and the sky unrolls a robe in care of all beneath. The pony moves as part of the self, hoofs rap in the brain in time with all the others, tails and manes flick as the eye blinks, and the earth is only rough hide to be scraped with the speed of a woman's shell-knife. No real sleeping or waking, or seeing or feeling, no thought of the body if tired or alert, no dreams of the future or visions of the past, no songs or words or any memory of music, no notion of the self or what is gone or to come, but only mastery of the moment, a sense of being part of space in action, vital, timeless, at one with everything and yet, in empty, terrible truth, alone.

Then it was that I was made to realize why the Indio finds no need to work as we do. Everything to me, then, with the horse stretching his sweating neck in front of me, and to him, always, was in perfect order.

To cut down trees was the same as murdering men and women. In using the plow, pain ran from wounds in the earth, and the smallest stones had the same value as people, and any drop of water was equal with himself. Far down, I seemed to understand the sad eyes of a tired horse. It no longer surprised me that Indios worked through the day without a break, or never worked at all, or had no use for money. Riding in search of food was noblest work, for without, their families would die. There was no other reason for men to live, and when they had provided enough, up they went among those gone before, and others were sent into women to take their places. Women, then, I saw, had special work, to produce and cherish the future hunters and their women, and I knew why Indio children were never taught to behave. The hunter was not to be curbed, and the woman was not to learn when or how to curb, and if children ran as brutes in Bedlam, I knew why.

In that short space I learned much more than I had ever felt or thought, and memory held fast, whatever the state of mind could be called, whether plain fever, or the effect of long days of cold riding, little sleep, and a sense of fatigue that seemed to run hot in every bone. Certain it is that we were riding down the slope to the river before I knew we were at the house, and I could have fallen off for joy. But there was not a move in me. My boots were jammed in the stirrups and my legs were pressed to the saddle, and they had to loose the bellyband and slide me, blankets and all, to the floor, and lift me off.

The house was padlocked, and Nüfcütun had me carried into the kitchen beside the warm stove, and I began trying to move legs and arms, and to fill my lungs with less pain. For some reason I was taking in long, long breaths, that I had never done before. My ribs felt like a balloon with too much air and ready to burst. Yet, even in the moment I knew I had been breathing as an Indio, long and slow, though why, for what reason, I had to wait to find out. But it did me no harm, and indeed it has been a help.

Rhinberry came running, and very anxious, but I suppose my hand grip showed him there was nothing in the world wrong, though he looked down at me as if I was somebody else.

"You have been held safe," he said, but speaking as if he still had a doubt or two. "Is your breath easier with you?"

"I feel as if I had run a thousand miles," I said. "No real pain. Only stretched."

"I will have a little word of explanation from Nüfcütun,"

he said. "This is not the way he should have brought you here. Did you meet an old Indio woman on the way?"

Well, of course, I remembered the one with the hare, and I told him, and he laughed as if it was funny.

"Nüfcütun is a bad boy," he said. "Good, but bad. He took you to a *machi*. A wisewoman. I ordered her away from here. They cause trouble, one with another. She collects crippled children, blind men, and the wandering. If she wouldn't make a nuisance, I would help her more."

"I saw some of the children," I said. "They didn't seem crippled to me."

"She cures them," he said, as if it was no matter. "She has got the power. I don't know how. But she does. If she would keep to that, I would give her a place. She's a wicked old thing, though. She makes drinks, and people go silly. She rules nature."

Immediately I remembered mountains and lakes and forests, and the rivers and pools and stones, each with life and a voice real as my own, that I could hear, and there was no surprise in me but only agreement, a small madness, I suppose, but then it seemed normal and proper.

"I have seen enough," I said. "But she didn't give me a drink of anything. I made coffee for them."

He leaned against the table and folded his arms, and nodded as if he knew more than I could tell him.

"Where did you have the water?" he asked me. "Who got it? Look at you, boy. Your eyes are like old saucers with you. Can you stand? Drunk? No. Tired? Perhaps. But half-poisoned? Yes. Into the house and sleep, now then."

"Why is the door padlocked?" I asked him. "This is something new, isn't it?"

"New, yes," he said. "To keep those out with no business in. Luis has gone to Chile. He told me you were angry with him. You shouted about the coal. So he is off to his mother's family. Pity. A good boy, too."

A pity, yes, indeed, and in that way, bare to the bone, Luis went from me, and only because I lost my temper and he was hurt. After that I was more careful with Indios, and perhaps with everybody else, too.

My legs had always been weak from the time I was pulled from the river and whether the cold got into them, again, or the rubbish of the old wisewoman, but I was a couple of weeks in bed, which did no harm, and a lot of letters and accounts and reports were put out of the way and I had chance to look about. Business was growing from week to week. There were never quite enough men to fill the jobs and the highest wages made no difference. Saiheque and all his people had left, but nobody knew where. Rhin said that if I had been in the place he would still be working, but somebody was in to tell of a herd of guanaco near Llangiñeu, and in a moment they were all gone.

No use to argue or complain, because I knew, or I thought I knew, why, and ridiculous though it seems, sitting here, now, but if I had been sound in the legs, no doubt I would have saddled and gone after them.

With far less excuse than any Indio I would have gone, though why, well, only God knows, and neither was it the only time, and even now, if I think of peaks and the forests' quiet, and rivers white between lakes, all held in tremble of my youth, then in quick of dearest memory I know the taste of the *kalafaté*, and I must go.

During those weeks Rhin's girls brought me soups and grills of meat, all very good, I suppose, though any taste for food at that time was not part of me and I could eat anything cooked or raw. But when I got up, I started to cook for myself and found I was having more benefit. The women seemed to think a handful of oats in hot water and a piece of any meat boiled in it for a few minutes made a soup good enough for anybody, or that a cut of mutton thrown on top of the stove with a slice of bread, then, would make a meal for caciques. Marrow bones I got, and onions, carrots, turnips, leeks, potatoes and parsley, and made what I call a soup, though nothing to touch my mother's, and nowhere near Lal's, but very good. After that, I roasted meats in the joint with potatoes, and boiled any kind of vegetable, and later, when the weather was better, I made salads of fresh vegetables. But I could never get the Indios to eat any, not the soups, or roasts or vegetables, cooked or fresh. Meat was all they wanted, and not beef or mutton, but guanaco, ostrich, hare or armadillo, and even tuco-tuco, a sort of mole, and rats.

"It is what they are used to," Rhinberry said. "They are frightened to eat beef or mutton. It is not part of their life. It costs money. They don't want to use money. It comes from somebody else. They want to be themselves. No help from anybody."

But far better than he could tell me, I could have told him. They wanted inside them only those creatures that were part of what they lived in and moved through, that were marked to be eaten in order to use their time until they were drawn up to *Ranginhüenüchaü*.

"I suppose it sounds silly to you," I said. "But I understand perfectly."

He turned his back to look at the men piling logs under the kitchen shelter.

"I know you do," he said. "Don't let it go too far, though. I don't know what to do to help. My prayers are not much good, do you see? I am too near my little one, up there. I have known the Indio way. You know it. I am glad in the hot salt of my heart that you do. They will have a friend when I am gone."

"Well, Rhin, boy, good God, you have got splendid time yet," I said, and shocked at the white stare in his eyes. "What would any of us do without you? Are you ill, or sickening for something?"

"Only for peace," he said, still up at the waterfall. "I am not in patience to be alive. I have never done what I want. No chance. No hope. I am like my father. Live in hope and faith. Die in failure. Thy Will be done. I only thank God I knew that one up there. She was my light. Nothing else in my life."

"No man has ever been less a failure," I said. "I tell you as your friend. In what have you failed?"

He lifted his hands in prayer and went to the door.

"As we wanted this land to be New Cambria, as my father and mother worked to make it, that is how I wanted a part here only for the Indios," he said. "Where they could have their own way to live, and govern. I wanted the Indios to have a part. Well, my father and mother never saw the dream except for a few years, and the best years, over in the Colony. Then the Argentinos sent in the soldiers and the police, and the rest came in, and that first flood of the Camwy took everything from us, and New Cambria was washed to the ocean. The dream was done. With that dream went the other one, for the Indios. I only came over here to see if they could have land. But the Law is against. Now, another flood is on us, and we shall be finished again."

"What flood is this?" I asked him.

"The Boundary Commission," he said. "They are coming here with somebody sent by the English. They will mark the border between here and Chile. Who will be interested in the Indios?"

"What have the English got to do with it?" I asked him.

"Their king is the arbitrator," he said. "He will give a decision, and everybody will abide. But nobody will think a single word for the Indios. For them, nothing. They will be sent from their own land. As we will be from ours."

"Who will send us?" I asked him, and I was cold in the neck, for the truth was in him, and I could hear it.

"Whoever is in charge, who wants what any of us have got," he said. "Only change the law and send the soldiers. What could we do?"

"Do you think we are wasting our time here, then?" I asked him.

"Yes," he said, and no man surer. "We are building for others to use. As we did over in the Colony. Without us, first, there would still be nothing to compare with what there is. We came to a desert. We left a city, and a railway up to the port, and a couple of towns, and roads, and hundreds of farms. For others. And the Indios who kept us all alive in the first years of starvation? Nothing. They have got nothing to show, except contempt and hate. We forgot our debt to them. As we will be forgotten."

Glad I was, then, that I had lived my little time over in the Atlantic Colony of the Camwy. It was different from anywhere I had ever been before. The people were far more of Cambria than those I had left here, in the Valley, even to the language of an older time and in purer form than I had ever heard, for they had been cut off from us in the South by lack of roads, and until I went to the Colony I can never remember meeting anybody from the North. Kindness itself most of them were, and never a gentler people, if, that is, you behaved as they thought you should. One step beyond, and you were finished, and if with one, then with most of them, for they were like a big family, and offend one, offend the lot. But I was used to a freer way and so I found plenty of thorns in the clover wherever I went, though the friends I made were better people than those huddled in righteousness, and there I believe, was source of weakness which should have been a strength. They were like a lot of ostriches, there, putting their heads in the ground. Some think it an old wives' tale, but they can never have been out on the pampas. Certain it is, if the ostrich sees you first, down goes the head, and because its body is about the height and not far from the color of pampas bush, you will have to look well to see it, if, that is, you know what you are looking for.

The ostriches of the Colony lived unseen, and unseeing, they were passed by.

But then I had to think about ourselves in the Andes, and I was not a bit happy to find that more Basques had come in during those months than there were of us, and almost as many Arabs, Slavs, Italians, and Spaniards. We were outnumbered, never mind adding Chileans or Indios. To make sure, I asked Geza to count his customers in the village, and he was just as surprised.

"Germans are coming in from Chile," he said. "Russians, Poles, Yugoslavs. More of my own people. You built a school. Roads. What do you expect? Most of them are not citizens. Therefore, Cambrian voting strength is higher, now. But in a few years, no."

"Rhin is right," I said. "We are finished unless we can get more of our people in here. How?"

"If you can't offer them more than they have at the moment, why should they move?" Geza said. "You know the life over in the Atlantic Colony. The most comfortable in the world, even for the poorest. Why should they come over here to work hard? They don't need the money. Who wants uncertain title to a league of land out in the wilds, away from family and happy meetings and so much good food? I tell you, my friend, my wife worries me to go back. She doesn't want to stay here. Neither do I."

Well, funny thing, but only then it was that I started to wonder why I was still there, or why I had gone there, to begin.

Perhaps, though partly, because of Lal, and wanting to be far away from her, about to marry a man she hated only to save her property. But I knew in myself that the day must have come when I would have gone for no other reason than to leave a place that was dying in the rot of its dreams, dying with the death of its pioneers, each with part of the dream, each death leaving less of the dream, until death took all of the dream and those who dreamed, and left only a compost of negligent habit and rustic thought, where memory of times gone were far brighter than any hope for the future.

Exactly the same could come more easily to us in the Andes, because we were of the same people, if most were children of the pioneers, or those like myself, late-comers, long after. The first of us might break our backs to cut down the forests, plant, and bring in cattle and sheep to flourish. But there was no guarantee that the children could be relied upon to work with the same sense of purpose.

The vision, if it was no more, that I had while riding with

the Indios, and the long days in bed, and the mental fight which rises from a sense of physical weakness, all might have come together to open my eyes, or to crack scales that had brittled in the years.

The Faith of our Fathers was not in us.

More certain than I could put in words, I knew I had not the Faith of my father and mother. It was not in me to go on my knees to thank God, out loud, in front of a room crowded with people all the way out to the street and up and down The Hill, outside here, as my father had. Thanking God from a full heart was not in me. In the depth of my wisdom I would have thought I was making a fool of myself. It seemed right and proper for my father and the men of his time, and while Mr. Gruffydd was with us, but not after.

People would laugh.

People.

Those very people rotting in the compost.

And of them, I was one.

Well, well.

A lot of old monkeys on a wheel, and not a thought above bananas and nuts, and a female now and again.

Where did it start, or how, is a question I have turned side to side many a time, but it was much later that I thought I had the answer.

On a morning, Corianth came to say that the General was coming down with his staff a few days in front of the Boundary Commission, and I rode out to meet him. He was going on to Futaleüfü to stay in the shelter there but I invited him to take the house, and offered the houses of Doli and Solva to anyone else.

"I accept," he said. "We have been a little unfortunate in showing hospitality to our guests. An asado and a canvas roof, sheepskins, and a fire has been the extent. This is an island of civilization I greatly appreciate. A hot bath is the most inordinate luxury. I envy you."

Out of his uniform you would never think him anybody

very much, except kind, and not much to say, and that night we sat at the fire, and I was only sorry Lal was not there to put her mark on the place, and I told him, and he laughed.

"It's more than two years since I saw my wife," he said. "It's hard, this life, for a woman. But I couldn't allow her down here. We could be at war in any moment. I couldn't release troops to guard her. And if she was allowed, then all the other wives would have to come. She stays in Cordoba. I'm here. That's all, until my tour of duty ends."

"You think there will be war?" I said.

"No, I don't," he said. "But who knows? Somebody could make a mistake. Insignificant at any other time. It's enough. The fire's lit. The Chileans and ourselves are brothers. We've fought together. We've won together. But the best of brothers can become the worst enemies. Especially over shares in a birthright. Our Presidents have promised not to fight. But they're both a long way from us. We could be fighting and neither would know for days. There's a heavy responsibility. On all of us. Will you vote at the referendum?"

"I might hope to," I said, because I was unsure. "Am I allowed to vote?"

"Your votes will decide," he said. "Every title-holder in the zone is a citizen. You were English citizens. Your king is the arbitrator."

"British, not English," I said. "We are four countries in one. Some here are English. Or Scots. Not many. Most of us are Cambrian. How did the English king become an arbitrator?"

"It was assumed he would make an honorable choice between the two claims," he said. "His representative will make a report. On that will be decided whether this is Chile or Argentina."

"How about the Indios?" I asked him.

He stood, and drank the last of the wine and put down the glass.

"Sir," he said. "I am deeply grateful for your hospitality

and the freedom of your house. Permit me to wish you a most heartfelt good night. Do not be alarmed if a sentry escorts you to your lodging. Everything that moves is followed. Or shot. You're not nervous?"

14

Even old Mrs. Sarah Ann Bedwellty was there on the morning of the vote, clapping her hands to the creak of the withe bed stretched on leather straps between four horses, and Ieuan and Gilberto trying to guide the leaders on a fair course, and she doing everything to keep them off. Seventy-four, she was, and like a little girl with jokes, but afraid of death, not because it was the end, but because she would be Judged.

"Huw," she shouted to me. "Come you. Have me in a place where I will see everything. I haven't come forty leagues to be pushed in some old hole, here. Where are we, with you?"

"Will you vote for Chile or Argentina?" I asked her, and gave her a kiss. "Everybody will vote for the flag they are under. Which one are you?"

"The Red Dragon, of course," she said, and frowning to wrinkle the veil. "For that my Dada came here. Will I vote to see it go?"

"I am afraid you have got a disappointment," I said. "Our Dragon is there only for show. But the Government will never allow it. The soldiers are there, and the General has let it be known. No hope."

"I will vote just the same," she said, and picking the fingers of her gloves. "If not for us, who would be voting here? For what?"

"The soldiers and the Law say no," Rhinberry said. "Nothing to be done. Argentina or Chile. Yes or no. Nothing else."

"Well, well," she said. "*Diâwch ifan.* Goodness to gracious me. Sure I was in the heart we would have our own land at last, here."

We were out on the green stretch between the marsh and the river. A fine morning it was, and the asado fires were already blowing woodsmoke and ash, the wine tables were crowded, a scream of children played among the lines of horses and wagons, and the women had begun opening the baskets to take edge from appetite.

Three flags ruffled on the hilltop against the sky. Donato and I had peeled and varnished the saplings, Rhin's Indios made the halyards, and soldiers dug them in the night before while the General watched.

"Immediately after the ceremony, take down the flagpoles," he said to me. "The flag of Argentina will fly to the right. Next Chile. The flag of Cambria I permit to be hoisted as a gesture of respect. But it has no official place. The referendum is between Argentina and Chile. There will be no discussion."

"Many of us will feel more than regret," I said.

"Naturally and properly," he said. "But it must be understood that the lives of our soldiers were not sacrificed merely to present the fruits to another people. Have you any doubt?"

"You have the soldiers," I said. "What is there to doubt?"

He smiled across at the blue uniforms of Gaucho cavalrymen in glitter of sabres, and blue and white pennons on lance-tips.

"They have their own language," he said. "I shall pray the day goes well for us. I am at least confident of your vote."

"If there was choice I would vote for New Cambria," I said. "Most of us would. As it is, I shall vote for Argentina."

"Let us hope that the Englishman is suitably impressed," he said. "A vote of this sort makes a difference. A great deal of sentiment. What do you think?"

"Some are bound to vote for Chile," I said. "To spite, for

not allowing a vote for New Cambria. But most will be for Argentina. Chile didn't give us the land, you see."

But there was a moment when I thought I was wrong, indeed.

We put Mrs. Sarah Ann near the Dragon flag, next to Mrs. Maudie Evans, and Mistress Eirene Vaughan made tea for both, and dozens more of the old ones came over to put blankets and sit comfortably in view of all that went on, and spoiling for a talk, there.

"Will that Englishman bring his old legs here while I will have a little word with him?" Mrs. Sarah Ann said. "Perhaps he have missed a fact or two."

"He is not to be approached by anybody," Madoc Pugh said. "No chat. He will make up his mind on evidence. The vote will only point. It will not decide."

"What is the use to waste time here, then?" Mrs. Sarah Ann said, and the veil slipping down in the way of the cup. "Eight days to come here, and only tea and old dust to finish?"

"Wait you, now, my little one," Mistress Eirene said. "I will be happy to know we are with Argentina. If it was Chile, would we have the land? Would they let us stay? What will happen to the flocks? Will they let us keep a cup and saucer? Only Indios I have seen from Chile. What shall we have from them? Another cup of tea, Mr. Griffiths?"

"Yes, and squeeze the pot, with you, girl," Mr. Griffiths said. "Somebody leaned down very hard with the water. Have you got a tea leaf on a bit of cotton in there?"

"Alban Griffiths, his name is," Mistress Eirene said. "If you never drink worse, give thanks."

"Drink?" Alban said. "A bit of soap, I'd have a wash."

"You would be too pretty, boy," Mistress Eirene said, and a wink for Mrs. Sarah Ann. "We are in shivers to think, here."

"Wait, you," Tom, Tot, called. "They are coming over, look."

A group came with the General, and a tall man in riding boots and raincoat, beard going gray at the tips, and a blue eye that told he was not the one to stand any nonsense. He listened to the General and raised his hat to some of the women he saw waving, but an air about the set of his head forbade approach even if everybody had not been warned by the picquets to keep off.

Arbitrator, he was, sent by King Edward VII to decide the extent of a boundary between two friendly countries, neither able to decide for themselves without fighting, but too much good sense to go to war. By some I heard him called Colonel, and by others Commander, and others addressed him as Captain. Holditch, his name was, and though we only saw him for those couple of hours and never found out if he was in the Army or the Navy, yet he deserves a laureled place in history, for it is sure that his advice to the king prevented a war, and certain it is that both countries were blessed, and everybody had profit of the land for all these years because of it.

More people were coming in and the picquets were telling them where to put the wagons and giving notice of the voting time and what they should do. A lawyer brought in by the Army had a table where we gave our names and the number of our property on the map, name of father and mother, where born, and residence over in the Atlantic Colony. Of course I had none of that, and the lawyer looked up at me and laughed.

"No documents?" he said. "Birth certificate?"

"The General made me a citizen," I said.

"Then he must answer for you and sign the register," he said, and left the entry blank. "Next."

Well, I went across and caught his eye and he nodded.

"Colonel, allow me to present Mr. Morgan, an Army contractor," he said. "He is of the Gallic people."

The hand was not hard or soft but only polite, though mine, I knew, was thick in callous.

"How do you do," he said. "You understand English, of course."

"Most of us do," I said. "Many of us speak English at home, at times, though Cambrian, mostly."

"Cambrian?" he said.

"What the English call Welsh," I said. "Welsh is an Anglo-Saxon word. Cambrian is our word. From the Old Celtic *combroges*, compatriots."

"Instructive," he said, and looked at the flags. "Perhaps you could tell me. How long have you been here? I mean, as a settler? From birth?"

"Almost a couple of years here, and more on the other side, in the Atlantic Colony," I said. "But many here have been coming and going for forty years. Robert Roberts, John Evans, Alban Griffiths and plenty more were digging gold before I was born. They are all here. They could tell you. The only Chileans I have seen here were *huaso*. Cattlemen. A dozen at most."

He smiled at the General.

"No partisan influence," he said. "I merely wanted to know if there's ever been distinctly Chilean settling here. Areas, or tracts, homesteads? Do you know any?"

"Futaleüfü, there are some huts, but poor," I said. "That's about forty miles south of us. They are Indios and mixed. They are there for loneliness. Nothing up this way till El Bolson and Vuriloche. I know the area well."

"Mr. Morgan built the roads," the General said. "You'll stay in his house tonight. I'm especially glad it's been brought out that Chilean interest is a recent growth. Since, perhaps, it was found that this Colony is producing better cattle, sheep and cereals than most parts of their country? This cleared land would make a welcome addition. These people would lose their rights, obviously."

"You make a persuasive case," the Colonel said.

"If I think of my Army's casualties over past years, I am sufficiently persuaded," the General said. "We cleared this land with blood. Without help. Now, I am asked to vacate it? You wished to speak to me, Mr. Morgan?"

"The lawyer wants you to sign the register," I said. "I haven't any documents as citizen."

He beckoned to a lieutenant and told him to bring the register and the lawyer.

"You intend to remain here, Mr. Morgan?" the Colonel asked.

"I shall be a citizen," I said. "A stamp on paper, it is, and if you have got it, you are what the paper says. Never mind what you feel."

"You don't like the prospect of changing nationality?" he said.

"What I am is what I shall always be," I said. "Paper has got nothing to say. It opens gates, nothing else. But my wife will vote for Argentina. Our children will be Argentinians. I shall, too."

"Pity," he said. "From my point of view, of course. It's tragic that so many of you must change, as it were. You appear to be a very close-knit community. Powerful."

"With more people and some help from Home, we could have been much more powerful," I said. "This land could have been ours. There was no argument between Chile and Argentina before we came here. We cleared the wilderness. Then the land had worth. Then the fat ones wanted it. Then there was argument. Not before."

"Fat ones," he said.

"Fat," I said. "You have got plenty in London. Not only in the belly."

"Always a possibility," he said, and turned to meet the General, coming back with the lawyer.

"You are now indisputably, if not indestructibly, a citizen of Argentina," the General told me, and held out his hand. "I welcome you as friend. I value your help as a colleague. You have been a tremendous help to our Country. I'm told that your wife has legal trouble in Buenos Aires. You didn't tell me?"

"It concerns title to lands in the Atlantic Colony," I said, looking at the lawyer. "I thought it improper to worry you."

"All to do with people under my command is a worry to me," he said. "Give the details to my Adjutant and I will dispose of it, once for all. My letter to the Governor at Rawson had no effect?"

"The case was transferred to Buenos Aires," I said. "Her baby will be born there next month."

"She will be here shortly after," he said quietly, and watched the Adjutant writing. "You will find the business at issue will be settled in her favor. I am acquainted with the details. Is there any other matter of immediate concern?"

"Yes," I said. "Indios of many peoples have worked for my partner and me. They have never taken a centavo in payment. If we had voted New Cambria into being, each one would be a citizen, and each with a credit. If the vote is for Argentina, will the Indios be citizens? Can they be paid? Will they have land of their own?"

"In this zone, most of the Indios come from Chile," he said. "The others are hunters from the South, or pampas clans eating out the pasture. They destroy all they touch."

"Chile or Argentina, it is the same for an Indio and his family," I said. "As his father did, so will he. There are no signs to tell what is yours or mine or his. What will he do? Truly, it is his land."

"I suggest that you concern yourself with the immediate problem of clearing and making the zone livable," the General said. "If the Indios wish to settle, they may apply for land in the normal way. But they must work to clear and plant. Do you think they will? We need productive citizens, not nomads."

"They should be given a chance," I said. "They have worked well for me. They worked well for us over in the Colony. They would work well for the Country if they were given hope."

The General nodded.

"Fortunately we are not here today to decide anything except whether the majority of the settlers are loyal, or not, to Argentina," he said. "Let that first be done."

Whether General or Colonel, but both left hanging in the air what was most to be said, and a great discomfort to the pride it was. Diplomacy it is called, to say so much and no more, and let others guess, or hop mumchance, or feel demeaned, or cheated, or stupid, and yet not without courtesy, and a pretense of good manners that were never more than gloss of soft-spoken ruffians, high in the nose and little finger, always in private contempt of those they held inferior by birth, or schooling, or cash value.

At that time I believe we all felt very poor, and especially on that day. There was little money among us, and our clothes had been patched over the patches, nothing to speak about among ourselves because we knew why and were used to it, but among strangers better dressed, then we felt the difference, and the difference, I suppose, made us a little bit sharp with the eye and tongue, that in some of us came to open affront. Later on, of course, we all had plenty of money and clothes and everything else, but in those early years it is true to say that most of us had very little except respect, and that we had earned for the way we worked. It was seen and known that work and only work, with plow, pick, and ax would bring that forest to a civilized land, and nobody else was there to do it, except us.

Perhaps, if we had known we were not to choose between Argentina, Chile, and New Cambria, most of us would have stayed at home. As it was, we were come there, but unknowing, to be traitors to our first men and women.

Their own people were made final destroyers of the dream of New Cambria.

Thunder of failure was in the air that day, and I believe most of us heard it in the spirit.

On any other day we would have had singing and dancing, and horse competitions, and races for the children, and the wine tables would never have known a space. But only a few were over there later on, and most families went to group among their neighbors just behind the Dragon flag, so that without any plain move, it was suddenly seen that the crowd was away from both Chile and Argentina and crammed in shadow of the Dragon.

It helped nothing.

A trumpet sounded for the asado, but instead of the shout and run, the crowd broke slowly to walk over to the pits.

There was no sense to be hungry and let food go to waste, and in any event, they had shown what they felt. But they were in lack of appetite and even wine was not the livener it always was, and a gathering which should have been a shouting joy became only a champ of dry jaws and a gulp to take soreness from the throat.

"Well, anyway, we are lucky enough," Arnold Williams said. "If there was a war, deuce knows what would happen. If Chile came in here, we would lose everything. If we don't vote for Argentina, we shall be sent from here, and perhaps out of the Colony, too. Pushed on a ship, and off. I would rather vote for Argentina, and have my land and my family in peace. A bit of peace is worth paying for."

"My father and mother thought so," Rhin said, and cut a crusty slice. "They paid in aches and hunger and suffered the years for a bit of peace. But they thought, of course, New Cambria was about them. They thought it was their country. A surprise it would be to them if they saw us today. We have given in without even a little word against. Only because soldiers are there?"

"Why don't you put the little word in the right place then, instead of here?" John Evans said, and whetted his knife on the table edge. "We would listen and know what to say."

"My Indios would suffer much more than me," Rhin said. "I don't mind what they do to me. But my Indios, yes. They don't care if it is called Argentina or Chile. For them, the same. For me, too. But my mother and father thought differently."

"If they could see you with your Indios, they would think better still," Deri Bryn Gilfa said, and not in good temper. "Cast forth the mote. You are afraid to speak because of your Indios? But we have got our families. It would take those Gauchos two minutes to cut our throats, and everything else. We know Gauchos. What about the women and children? Shall I tell you? Well, then. That is one reason why there is no 'little' word from me."

But never mind how they tried to excuse themselves, the nag was in them and cheer was not. The women had a lot more to say than the men, but they spoke in Cambrian so that only we understood, though the noise was loud enough.

The Colonel sat on a log near me, eating duck roasted on the spit. The General had invited him to have a duck cooked in an ostrich carcass but I told him what to expect and when he saw the oil he looked at me and I sent the boy to the fire for a couple, roast, with a pot of apple sauce, and I never tasted better, with a flaky crust but tender, and in smack of downland grass, and mountain air, and the lakes' sweet waters.

"Your people are not so animated today," the General said, helping himself to chitlings. "I told the Colonel you sing for any reason or none. He tells me you have that reputation."

"Well, we are silent to eat for the moment," I said. "Mainly we are not happy about the dismissal of New Cambria from the ballot. Most of these have shared that dream since they were born. The pioneers before them. 'Unto thy seed I will give this land. And there builded he an altar.' We have no Abraham. We built the altars wherever we have been, and we have a lot to be thankful for. But it seems the Lord God is not with us. How would you feel if your flag was not allowed to fly today? Or if you lost a battle before to start?"

The General swallowed, and wiped his mouth, and lifted the glass.

"Unhappy," he said, and the glass went a little higher, and he drank.

"You share our feeling," I said.

"I'm a little unsure about this New Cambria idea," the Colonel said. "Do you mean your people thought this part of the country was theirs?"

"Everything south, from the south bank of the Camwy, right through Patagonia, and in width from the Atlantic to the Andes," I said. "That's why the pioneers came here, and starved. They were dreaming. The men who brought them here were better educated, and they had more knowledge of the world. But the bait was a land of the sun, where ripe oranges fell off the trees and filled the rivers. Masons, and carpenters, shepherds, and farmers from the villages of North Wales, they were the ones who loved the idea. Simple and credulous. And dreaming. And not very happy where they were because of landlordism, and poor wages and general poverty. So they got on a little schooner and sailed the Atlantic and came to a desert, and starved till they could grow enough. Not twenty years after, they won a gold medal for the world's best wheat at the Chicago Exhibition. From a desert. Starvation to plenty by sweat. But then the land had value. They built ports and roads. They built a railway. Then, I think, somebody in Buenos Aires realized they might be strong enough to look after themselves. The soldiers came, the police came, a Justice and schoolteachers. Our own schools taught in Cambrian and English. The new schools taught Castellano. Up went the flag. Not ours, with the Dragon. Over on this side we thought we still had a chance. We were dreaming. New Cambria was a dream that we dreamt. The river we called Camwy is now the Chubut. The road from the Atlantic, worn over the years by us, and named Hirdraeth Idwyn for him who found the way, is called something else. The mountains named for our pioneers are somebody else's. The lakes named for our first men are now some other name. This village is called in Cambrian Trevelin, City of the Mill, because John Evans, him, over there, worked years of his life almost single-handed to dig and bank miles of canal to make the mill wheel work and grind flour. With flour was food, and then a school, and a chapel, and shops, streets, houses, neighbors. Any help from anybody? None. Public funds? None. We cleared, we created. As we did on the other side.

We were dreaming. Today we are awake. If you eat, they are our animals. We grew the wheat and baked the bread. We carted the wine. Eat and drink your good fill. All here, and the people, are of New Cambria. Dreamers, every one."

"I don't think I realized that sort of promise was inherent in the agreement between the settlers and the Government," the Colonel said, and dipped a slice of duck in apple sauce and sprinkled chopped mint. "I can well understand how you feel."

"There was no such promise," the General said, and poured wine for me. "The record of the agreement is in the archives. It makes no mention of any country except Argentina. Why should a Secretary of State be so inept? Do you suppose Congress would have agreed? Was it a verbal promise? Something tacit? And the Government on several occasions sending tools, seeds, animals, and stores? And troops of this Army at most times in garrison? I think the people became affluent, and then the idea grew. It never had the remotest substance."

"As I told you," I said. "We were dreaming. But before we came, your frontier was a thousand miles to the north."

A troop of soldiers and civilians galloped down to the picquet line, and left their mounts, and walked across. The Colonel stood, and went with the General to meet them.

Francisco Moreno, the Argentinian member on the Boundary Commission, I had known for long enough, and no better man to be found in a lifetime of Sundays. Short, and broad, with black hair and beard, and eyes always bright in twinkle, he came often through the south in study of mountains and lakes and rivers, keeping the talk going all night, with rich ideas of creating industry, but ignored where he was not hamstrung by the blindworms in Buenos Aires. Today, of course, there are statues of him everywhere, but in those days he was a laughingstock, held by many to be cracked, though his ideas are good to this day, most of them still where he left them, in the rich air of his vital breath.

He met the Colonel and the General as old friends and they

came back to the fire, talking about the number of wild cattle up in the forest below the mountain peaks.

"They ought to be rounded up," Francisco said. "Those bulls attack without warning. Almost as bad as the wild boars. Any number of them. And a surprising lot of puma. We didn't see anyone. Everybody's here. It mystifies me, the Chileans haven't sent patrols. Not a sign, not a track. Your soldiers report absolutely no movement."

"I've always maintained this is purely a lawyer's argument," the General said. "They got a lot in the courtroom they'd never get in the field, or anywhere else. Mr. Morgan, we shall round up those cattle and drive them down to your cleared area, breed from the best, and slaughter the remainder. We shall use your smokehouse on shares, and we'll both have smoked meat rations for the winter."

"Most of those cattle belong to Saiheque," I said. "He will have to be paid. What will his people do for food? They rely on cattle when guanaco are scarce."

"Those cattle, depend on it, are progeny of herds stolen by his father from ranches he burned in the Provinces of Buenos Aires and Neuquen," the General said. "His part of the booty. Our friend Francisco can tell you about Saiheque Senior. And about Catriel, and Yanquetrúz and Calvucurá, and the other thieves. Isn't it so?"

"We made them into thieves," Francisco said, cleaning a drumstick. "For years they were bribed with money, animals, and food. And impunity. They enjoyed the rank and uniform of general or colonel. What do you expect? Why should the uneducated and indisciplined obey any except their own desires?"

"Our advice was not accepted," the General said, cutting a steak. "It was a political responsibility. When it was seen to have failed, we were asked our advice. After that, command was given to the Army. You know the result."

"You allowed them to wear the uniform and use the rank," Francisco said, and seeming to enjoy the baiting as much as the thick collop of lamb. "General Calvucurá? No more impossible animal. Freebooter. Murderer. Attacked how many towns? Stole what amount? Raped how many dozens of our women? Kept a harem of them. For years. In a General's uniform? Each year, more gifts, more bribes. More raids. More women."

"The politicians speak, and we are silent," the General said. "It is not an illustrious chapter. It was expedience to point of suicide. But it also taught lessons. Never again will we permit politicians to dictate in matters which affect the destiny of our Country. The lesson was thoroughly learned then. It will never be forgotten."

He spoke quietly, cutting the steak on a slice of bread, eating as if nothing was in question. But I had known him for too long. He was not a man to show feeling of any kind.

Almost unseen he was shaking, and white patches were under his eyes in shadow of the braided cap's wide peak. But the knife hand was steady to cut a strip of steak, and the teeth bit, and a crumb settled in the beard, and while he lifted the glass he smiled, but not in the eyes.

Until then I had never known that Indios had been made generals and colonels in the Army, and given uniforms, and bribed not to attack the populous regions north of the Camwy. It was fine surprise to me that Indios had raided up so far as Rosario and Cordoba, for years on end, and not a word from the Army.

"I wonder if you could tell me," the Colonel began in his English manner, courteous almost to flatter and yet direct. "We've also had our frontier wars. To what do you attribute an end to armed resistance after so many years of indeterminate fighting? Better lines of communication? Better soldiers? More of them? Better horses? Less enemy resistance? A wearing down by superior force?"

The General shook his head and dabbed the napkin.

"None of those," he said. "Lances, bows and arrows and *boleadores* are no competition for men able to kill or disable with a small piece of lead. The Desert War was decided solely by the Remington carbine. That was our advantage. We used it."

The Colonel put aside a carcass and wiped his fingers.

"Your ducks, here, in the Argentine, really are in a class by themselves," he said.

15

Years afterward I often heard it said that the vote for Argentina was foregone, but there are many of us not so sure as all that. If the ballot had been allowed between the three choices, and New Cambria had won, then I suppose we would have had to vote a second time and perhaps Argentina would have run away with it because very few had any real confidence in a New Cambrian government, to begin, and we had no Army, for there were not many of us, and at that time none of us had any money to do anything except live as we were.

"What would you do without soldiers?" Tom, Tot, asked the crowd. "The Indios would be in here with a thousand lances and take us piecemeal one after the other. And what, then, about New Cambria? Who has got time from his work to do a bit of ruling? Ruling what? Twelve children I have got, here. Six working. But fourteen mouths are in my mind, day in and out. Will you think well of me if I put on my funeral suit and top hat to do a bit of ruling? Or will you push me with lunatics? Who else has got time? Huw Morgan has got the head, yes. No doubt. But what about his business? Can he leave it? Not even a little moment. What then of New Cambria? The same as on the other side. Everybody too busy. Those not busy, too old. So let us give thanks and go back to work."

Merlin Afon played wonderful, deep chords on the harp

near the asado pits, at any other time a tocsin, but nobody moved, and none sang.

"You were too long with the English," Bala Jones said, and looking in his pipebowl. "We would like our own government, for a change. Our own language. And schools. We had that for years on the other side, contrary to what you stated. We did very well, there. Too well. Better than all the rest of the country. For that, they sent in the soldiers. Then they took government from us. Have your facts right, to start. Then open your mouth."

Everybody shouted encouragement and moved closer.

"What are those men talking about?" the General asked me.

"They are in debate about a vote for Argentina," I said.

"The little man appears to have authority, but what does he say?" the Adjutant asked. "The language is like German. I can't pick up a word."

"The short one is Thomas Llywarch," I said. "He was Sergeant of Fusiliers with the English Army. I believe he served over half the world."

"Ask him here," the General said. "A useful man."

Tom, Tot, came over when I called and in a couple of minutes they were kneeling to draw diagrams on the ground, and the General was learning about the formation of troops at El Kebir.

But I was worried about the rest of us.

It is all very well to call a lot of people a crowd. Every man and woman there I knew as friends, and each was a responsible person, working hard, living the best life they could, and not one of them in default, or a shirker, or backward to say what was in the mind. They were honest, for their lives had taught them to be, and they were direct in thought and speech because there was no time in their days to waste in a shift from here to there.

New Cambria was in their souls, as it had been in their fathers' and mothers'. They were unwilling to see the idea perish by default of presentation. A sense of injustice would not be stifled, but much more, the loyalties of two generations of Cambrians, with full knowledge of all they had built and more still in the building, were strong, impelling their minds, bringing the blood to heat and forging tempers never mild to white revolt. The women shouted more than the men, and suddenly I was glad that Lal was not there, with Doli and Solva, for those three might have made the difference between noisy talk and a holy fight.

Holy, yes, because most were sure of themselves in God, and they believed, and they lived in the Faith of their Fathers.

In this day, it is no use trying to explain to anybody, even to myself.

Sitting here in this little kitchen that groans, now, under weight from outside, I remember my mother and father and all the other mothers and fathers on The Hill.

They were all the same.

"I'm not sure, either," Owen said, that night in Detroit. "I've been here a long time, and I know all of them at the plant, but it's not the same. I don't think it's changed since I came. There are plenty of churches and chapels and I certainly don't think people are less Christian. They don't show forth so much, I suppose. It's old-fashioned. Doesn't fit the time. Or the people."

"Well, would you say they are better people?" I asked him.

"No, not better," he said, quick, in surprise. "You could never have better people, well, not as I remember them. But they were simpler in their daily life. Look at me today, and think of me twenty-five years ago, up and down the colliery, there. Am I the same? I don't feel any difference, mind. But do you think I could go back to the Valley? Never. Or sit in chapel with the family as Dada used to do? Lead in the hymn? Pray extempore? Impossible. It's not only that I haven't the gift of words he had. I haven't got his heart. And only God knows, I haven't got his courage."

We were in his splendid white house outside Detroit, staying overnight on the way back from Chicago. My head was a lighthouse shining only for itself, and no other way to say it. Moishe had been to North America before, but not to New York and even he was surprised. We came up in the steamer we had bought in Newport News, and docked in the early morning, so that when the mist lifted and the sun shone over fingers of stone flashing light from a thousand windows, we thought we were in another world, and indeed we were. Many times I have been there since but I never got over the shock of pleasure I had that first time, though it is still not so much a city, as a complex of spiritual restlessness. We were there only two days but I never went to sleep except in the chair. In bed my eyes closed but my brain flamed and I had to get up. Moishe was the same, but he was like a father to me, and the more nervous me, the calmer him. Well, anyway, it was not the traffic of horse buses and carriages, and victorias and broughams and some of the finest coachwork and horseflesh I ever saw, or the lights at night, or the wonderful shops, even if at any other time they would have been enough.

The automobiles put everything else a bad second.

The moment I remember well.

That first morning, we had just come from the barber's shop, and a shave to remember, with a wrap of hot towels, and a rub of grease and a razor like a woman's palm, and we were crossing from Fifth Avenue to Madison, and I heard the noise, and in that moment I was out in the back, here, in the bath house, helping Owen with his engine. It was the same sound, and the same smell of petrol, and Moishe slapped hands together, and the two of us stood there, with our eyes fat on the ends of our eyelashes.

"The Lord God look down," Moishe said, in a marvel. "What is this?"

A black body was on four wheels, and the man sat high to guide it, but it was gone before we had a good look. A policeman stood beside a lamp post, and smiled at us.

"It's a Lizzie," he said, and I can hear him now. "She'll go all of thirty miles an hour. Not in the city, though."

"Where could we see one?" Moishe asked him. "We like to buy it."

The policeman put his mouth down.

"Well, now, say," he said and looked about, and pointed the stick. "Go down here to 42nd and Lexington. The hardware store? I seen'm there. Where they buy the gasoline. Maybe he'll tell you."

The manager was very helpful but he showed us a book full of orders and said there was no hope of buying one for months to come, and gave us the address of Henry Ford in Detroit. But I had heard that name before, from Olwen, telling me that Owen was there and doing well as an engineer. It never was in my mind to see him, but when we asked, they said at the railway station we could go to Chicago, and come back via Detroit. Up we went to Chicago to see the stockyards, and the packing and icing units and we bought one complete, and sent Owen a telegram, and there he was, on the station with his wife to meet us. Her family had come from Poland only a few years when she met Owen and her English was still not much, but they only had to look at each other and they knew, so words were no odds. No man ever found a lovelier girl, and the five children were as much like her as him, and he told me nobody had less to complain about.

"I landed in Philadelphia with nothing," he said. "I had all the jobs you can think of. But I never went without something to eat and I always managed to find a roof. I was in Des Moines, there, and one afternoon a man came in with a broken spring. It was the first automobile I had seen close to. So I mended the spring and came up with him to his place just outside here. He gave me a letter to Mr. Ford, and I started on the spot, that morning. The rest you can say is work, and meeting this one, and enjoying every moment. I only wish I could have had Mama here. No other wish in the world."

We went with him to the Ford plant, a big place, and even though it was before six in the morning, Mr. Ford was on the assembly floor working with a dozen men, all of them opening and slamming doors.

"Testing a new door handle," Owen said. "They wear out. It's the metal."

Mr. Ford took us in his office, every bit as bare as mine, and we had a cup of coffee and talked about Patagonia in loud voices over clamor in the shop that never stopped. We had to catch the train that afternoon to be back in New York in time to take delivery of the freezing units.

"We would like to buy one of your automobiles to take back," I said. "We think it's the very thing we need. Horses don't go fast enough for us. Will they go on tracks? That's all we've got."

"All she asks for is a fair surface," Mr. Ford said. "Got lots of mud down there?"

"Our fair share, I believe," I said. "But a shovel and a few stones work wonders."

"Tell you what I'll do," he said. "Buy two and I'll give you one."

"That's three," Moishe said. "We buy four, you give us two? Cash?"

"You have a deal," Mr. Ford said. "Owen, take these gentlemen to the cashier."

"We want them on the train with us," Moishe said. "That's now."

"They'll be there," Mr. Ford said. "You'll need spares. Tires. Plugs. I'll put in an assortment. Tell Mr. Keller to check with me."

"Yes, sir," Owen said. "And I take the commission."

Mr. Ford laughed.

"On four," he said. "All right."

Well, the seven cases were on trucks behind the train when we left, and we were taught the difference between grain-fed and grass-fed cattle in the best steak in the world in the restaurant car, that must have cost a fortune in carved walnut, with mirrors. We had good trains in Argentina, but nothing to compare. We sat like a couple of caciques in armchairs, and newspapers came on at every stop, and everything in the world we wanted was handy, and we were sorry to get off. If the ship had looked tremendous when we first saw her, we seemed to have grown other eyes only in those few days. She was a good tonnage and right for our needs but we knew we would have to have another three times as big, at least, so we ordered her, and a larger sister to follow.

"We can't use her, we sell her," Moishe said. "Now we buy the soaps and perfumes, good cloth, lace. Come with. You learn, maybe."

Buying and selling sounds very simple in two words, and so does profit and loss, but nearly always we forget the brain in between.

Moishe was the greatest merchant of them all. He seemed to know the cost of every article he touched, and he bargained his buying price at that cost plus a fair percentage profit margin for the seller, which always allowed him to sell for at least three times as much and still be well under any competitor in Argentina.

"Remember, we have big transport costs," he said. "All the way here from down there, that's money. Take the stuff back there, that's money. That money got to get warm in the selling price. So buy a lot, lowest price. Bargain. See the blood. Pay cash. That's the secret. Cash."

We had a lot of money with us, most of it in gold bars and coins of many countries that we changed at banks and counting houses. In New York we opened an account and then we paid with checks, the first I had seen, though in those days not many would take them in exchange except with a month's wait to verify.

"We have to open our own bank," Moishe said, that night, while we waited for a warehouseman to make up his mind if he would take a check or no business. "We got wool, meat, hides, cereals. That's money. Most, it's credit. We don't waste time after this. No more we hang about. Our own ships, our own business, our own bank. And our own insurance. See what I say."

He was a prophet, and I suppose it was not five years before we had the bank and insurance business well in health and agents in New York, London, Paris, and Hamburg, with our own offices in Buenos Aires, and branches in the City of Lewis and most of the towns in Patagonia all the way to Ushuaia. All I did was attend quarterly meetings when I was able, and sign balance sheets as a director, and vote for this or that. My own business took every moment and I could have wished for a forty-eight-hour day many a time.

It started with the arrival of the Fords.

The moment we were alongside at Port Madryn, which seemed not to have changed by so much as an extra plank or a coat of paint since I first got there, we had a dozen buyers for each, money in hand, and shouting. Moishe sold three for five times what we paid, but I kept mine, and one for Oracio and Solva, and one for Volde and Doli, but they paid the same price, brothers and sisters or not.

"In business, no relations," Moishe said. "The price, it's cheap. Next time, twice as much. We turn her round, she brings back thirty. We open the account. Tomorrow, they're sold, cash."

He was right. We had orders for a hundred only from the men in town at the time. Within the year we had sold a thousand, cash down for all of them, and the ship voyaged on a two day turn-around laden, going up, with wool, hides, and cereals, and came back with Fords, spares, and general goods pushed in the spaces.

Four wheels and a motor shrank the country, made a fool of space, brought everybody and everything months nearer, lengthened the calendar, put the horses back on the ranch, and sent the mules into limbo with the wagons, the traps, governess carts and carriages.

That first drive across was a hymn, every mile, from Port Madryn, through the City of Lewis and everybody out to see us and cheer, all the way over Hirdraeth Idwyn, through The Feathers, and Ginbox, and Tin Roofs, and stopping every couple of hours to give the radiator a drink, or wait until they cooled down, but flashing across—or so we thought, then—at twenty and thirty miles an hour and on the first day, when the sun was going, we were almost at Indio Stones.

Even we could hardly believe it. It seems funny now, but we were frightened of the speed. Twenty miles an hour, and frightened. Next morning, we thought we would have trouble at the river, but Lizzie was high off the ground, and we chose the shallowest part of Gwenonwy's Bridge, and went through dry as ducks.

Moishe got down and kissed the Ford label on the bonnet.

"They should make a saint," he said, in raptures, there. "This road, for me, it's Avenida Henry Ford. We make our office back there, it's Number One, Avenida Henry Ford."

To this day, that road, for me, is Avenida Henry Ford.

We cut a new, straighter track, because we had no use for water holes to give animals a drink and no need to look for pasture.

We pointed Lizzie's bonnet for the Andes, and went, direct.

Two and a half days it took us that first time, instead of three weeks by wagon express. But we could hardly believe it, and the people to meet us had a much harder job, and most of them gave us The Eye, in doubt.

Only the Countess accepted what we said, and readily, because she had seen pictures in the magazines she got from Europe. We crossed her place at Hualjaina on the evening of the second day, with the Andes' blue teeth biting at the horizon, and stopped near the ranch house, on the other side of the brook, and bapped the horn's black rubber bulb.

A funny little sound, that seems to have flown with Evans, the Mill's, yodel, and the Muffin Man's bell on The Hill.

The ranch house was built of branches laced to hold a thick plaster of mud, with a galvanized iron roof painted red and steadied from strong winds by stones. The windows were small to discourage flies and night visitors, and the door opened on a thick chain, with a dozen big dogs, kept hungry, in a howl and slaver just outside.

The Countess at that time had a little boy and girl looking

beyond her skirts, both fair as her plaits, that hung below the bullet belt and .45 Colt she always carried. Her husband died before she turned nineteen in a country that still thought of a woman without a man as anyone's sweet. But that notion she cured many a time, until it became rote that the quickest way to the cemetery was a Wrong Move at Hualjaina. She let all riders come to about forty paces from the house, or just past the clump of elderberry. Then she opened the door and told him, or them, that fodder and drink for the animals were to be had beyond the cookhouse, and lodging at the men's bunkhouse on the other side of the paddock. If the arrival did as she told him and accepted distant hospitality, well and good. But many a whoreshop prince thought himself omnipotent, and swaggered on, sure that a few compliments and a twirl of mustachios would put him beside her.

That .45 Colt never missed. She always shot twice, and about a half mile from the house she had a fine private cemetery, watered morning and night, with flowering shrubs and little trees, and a bench in shadow to rest the corpse on while the grave was dug, giving the mourners time to think of proper behavior in the presence of true women.

We had better luck, and she invited us in. She had known Moishe for years, and me since I went with the General to see how many sheep she could supply for winter rations. The house was small but clean as a pin and filled with furniture and porcelain she brought from Europe. She wanted to go back for a holiday, but the children were too young for the journey, so it had been almost ten years, then, since she built the house, but she was sure in mind to go that year, and Moishe promised to take her and the children in the Ford to Port Madryn, and arranged their passage in our ship to Buenos Aires.

"But you have a wide interest in business, Mr. Levy," she said.

"Me, and Huw, and who else?" Moishe said. "We could die, here. What have we? Sheep?"

"If we use them correctly, it's enough," she said. "They bring an excellent livelihood. I feel grateful for my flock. We haven't anything else."

Moishe shook his head, and I have never forgotten his eyes, in denial, with contempt.

"Wrong," he said. "Water, we got. A pump-house each lake, we put water in canals to the pampas. Water in the pampas? A garden. A garden, that's cereals and fruits and vegetables, and grass for beef. That's money. That's new people. That's Patagonia in business. What business we got, now? Nothing. How many people? Nobody. Who's talking? Nobody."

"Many a long year," the Countess said. "Pumps cost money."

"Money, we got enough," Moishe said. "Brains? Nothing. Politicos? How many? Who wants a garden? In the pampas? The more garden, less sheep. Less sheep, less money for the sheep companies and families. Sheep companies and families, they control. Wool business, they control. So? No pumps. No gardens. No people. No people, no wages. No wages, no market. No market, no movement. And? We are dead."

"We have the fortune to be alive and enjoying breath," the Countess said. "The country is young. When I came there was nothing."

"You have twenty, thirty, fifty peons?" Moishe said. "Fifty like you, forty peons each, two thousand. And the families. Who else? Indios. Fifty of you earn the gold. You spend where? In Buenos Aires. In Europe. But here? Groceries. Nothing."

"But you and Mr. Morgan have done well enough," the Countess said.

"Government contracts, roads, bridges, barracks," Moishe said. "That's payment. Not movement. Roads for soldiers. Should be for people. But why they should come? How much they earn? What profit? Sheep, sheep, sheep. Wool, meat, fat. Profit? For a few."

"But you and Mr. Morgan have sheep," she said, and

turned the mutton steaks. "Why do you hate them so much?"

"I don't hate," Moishe said, and took the little girl on his knee. "I never hate. But we waste country, waste time, waste brains. Water we got. Use it."

Almost the same words, with even more force I heard those years before, on the day of the vote, when Francisco Moreno argued with the General, and the English arbitrator, Colonel or Commander whatever-he-was Holditch sucked a pipe, and looked as if he were not listening to every word.

"A single track rail from the Atlantic, here, will open almost the entire pampas," he said. "It's necessary for development. This boundary will never be accepted as a firm line. Whatever line we decide, it will always be encroached on. The majority living here are Indios. Argentina and Chile, what are they to Araucanos? In a generation or two who'll accept what we marked? More infringements. More talk of fighting. We need emigrants. Centers of work. Not soldiers, but farmers, cattlemen, industrialists. More arable land for cultivation. More people. More citizens. More claim to what we say is ours."

"More, more, more," the General said, joking. "So far, we've got nothing except foothold. We've got to keep it by force of arms, if necessary. One step at a time. What could you bring on a rail line? What industry?"

"Iron and coal is all round us in abundance," Francisco said. "Steel foundries come next. Copper, lead, tin, all the primaries are here. All we need is people. And power. These lakes, a chain of a thousand miles, and the rivers will give us all the power we need. Hydraulic pumps, that's all. In Buenos Aires they won't listen. Why should they? They are paid well enough not to."

"You don't suggest bribes?" the General said, sternly, still joking.

"Bribes?" Francisco said. "Who speaks of bribes? Time confers dignity. They are called perquisites of office. The cattle companies in the North, the sheep companies down here. They pay for what they'd never get legally. Why not?

Saves time and trouble. How many hundreds of soldiers have sold their land grants? Enormous areas bought for nothing. The rest taken on nominal rent or none at all. Sketches, but no maps. When maps are available, who'll question a fence-line? In how many years? Which Law Court will deny it? Silk-mouthed thieves. 'But these are honorable men?' How long since Indio assassins were granted the rank and uniform of general? Your rank, and your uniform?"

"I am forced to agree," the General said. "You suggest that the boundary, whatever it may be, will not be accepted?"

"I suggest nothing," Francisco said. "I asseverate. The decision of His Britannic Majesty will be respected. Certainly. Now tell the Indios, and keep that line inviolate. How? They can cross these mountains at a thousand places unknown to us. They can build, breed cattle, bring up a family. Who'll stop them? How many soldiers do you need?"

"Obviously you have a solution," the General said. "I confess I haven't. Any thought of defending this southern line is nothing less than nightmare. We can only deny the more accessible gaps. What else?"

"Make a natural cushion," Francisco said. "Create a neutral strip from San Martín down to the Magellan Straits. Inaugurate a National Park. By law. Keep it under government control. Let it be kept as it is now. A mountainous garden. Primeval. Permit no settlers. No herds or flocks. An area devoted to nature, as it was, and as it will be in a hundred years or a thousand. Who could complain? What need of armies? That's the natural boundary."

None of us standing there, I suppose, looking at Francisco in worn boots, threadbare clothes, blowing hair and beard, and the General in brushed blue with a gold laced cap, thought for any moment that we were listening to history in course of dictation. It was years later that the dream was given meat, but on that afternoon I doubt if many of us agreed. We had never heard of a National Park, to start, and park, to us meant a public garden, and any thought of so much land going idle was almost sacrilegious, besides that the mountain forests made the best cover and feed for animals through the winter.

We were interested only in land, sheep and cattle, though his mind and noble spirit looked for means to prevent war.

Whatever we might have been thinking was knocked out of our heads by Tom, Tot.

He stood on a barrel, and the General watched from below, hands folded on the sabre, with his officers round about.

"I will speak in Castellano," Tom, Tot, called out, not in a shout but loud enough for all to hear. "Not long ago, some of us were in beautiful trouble over in the Atlantic Colony, remember? Mr. Justice Dab and Blow asked us if we would one day be as loyal to Argentina as we were to our own people, yes? I said then, the day will come. This is the day. Plain and bright about us. The talk about New Cambria can wait. There is time. This vote is between Argentina and Chile. They both claim this land which our pioneers were living in almost forty years ago. We have a debt to Argentina. Our wives are Argentinian. Our children were born and baptized here. Argentina gave us land in the Atlantic Colony. Argentina gives us more land, here. Chile never gave me anything. I have never seen anybody from Chile, except Indios. Will you vote for them? Or will you vote for the flag that protects all of us, and the country you stand on? How will you pay your debt for all you have? Have you been asked for money, or an animal, or even the smallest twist of wool? You are asked only for a vote. What use to argue? The way home is far enough. The wife has got fourteen to cook for. Thank God, all in good health. We are blessed with wonderful families, and a free land. All we pay is loyalty. Vote now, of free will. Who is for Argentina?"

A few arms went up, others faltered up, more joined, and while the meaning of the words went into bone, dozens more, and then all the arms were up, but in silence.

"By acclamation, sir," Tom, Tot, said, down at the General, and took an egg from his pocket and threw it high and pulled a revolver from under his coat and fired, and the egg became a yellow star.

The flag of Chile, and the Dragon were being hauled down. Bala Jones folded the Dragon and gave it to Mistress Eirene Vaughan, and everybody was shouting and moving toward the wine barrels, and the trumpeters were splitting the ears with a fanfaronade.

A galloping horse made the crowd run and the rider was bareback, leaning far out to snatch the Chilean flag from the sergeant, and galloping on lick split without pause, up the rise and away.

No doubt about the bare feet and bangles and the guanaco robe and flying plaits.

Lliutro.

16

If I had been asked at any time until then what I thought about Lliutro, I suppose I would have given an excuse, the first in mind, any of those selfish tries to put the blame for misconduct somewhere else, a mental wriggle to appear upright in the eyes of the godly, or nearer home, to bring relief and a small smile to the maw of the hypocrite in bob and nod within.

But when I saw her shake out Chile's flag, the white and red bar and white star in a blue triangle and carry it flying over her shoulder, four hoofs in patter and scatter, up the rise and over, as if forever into brilliant sky, then it was that I knew I must follow. If I had been told only a minute before that I would have a feeling of madness to see her gallop away, I suppose I would have laughed. But that feeling of loss for a woman is tragedy. She is only what she is, and you are no more than what you are, and the pair of you matter nothing anywhere, and yet the world can go to Hell, but you must be with her, arms about her, in or out of flame, and the Devil himself can scratch. To others comedy, but to you, only tragedy.

So I felt, and I was calm with surprise, and without a word to anybody I went down to the lines to find my horse, and I rode up the slope, jumping fallen trees to the rise, and looked into the dip, and over the river, and up the mountainside, but in those ricks of forest as well look for a needle.

In my throat, in my lungs, I could hear her name, but the mountain breeze whined, and all the trees whispered, and there was nothing except whining and whispering, and memory of a woman's satin, and muscle, and a cry without voice that even now can close my eyes to think.

Nothing to do except turn and ride down to Rhin's, because the General and members of the Boundary Commission had our house for that night, and I had no wish to act host and listen to their talk, and be lonely.

Rhin was still at the balloting but his head woman came to meet me, a tall Araucana-Tehuelche, one of the few I ever saw with a lot of white hair among the black. Kalata might have been thirty or seventy, though there was no way to tell. She was thin as a lath, not a wrinkle in her face and she walked almost without touching the ground. Rhin made them all wear our clothes, perhaps because of chance visitors, but when they were working alone neither men nor women wore anything except a leather strap with a little apron, though even so I never saw the smallest impropriety, and when visitors came the women put on the guanaco cloak that covered them neck to ankles.

Kalata wore only the apron when I went in. She made no move toward the cloak, but put aside the embroidery and went over to make tea as Rhin always did.

"Kalata," I said. "Where shall I find Lliutro?"

She shook her head without turning.

"Nobody will find her," she said. "She will go into the bamboo. When the blood is dry, then you will find her."

"Blood?" I said.

"Her mother is *manzanera,*" she said. "They are of Chile. Of the family of Queupoliquen. That was their flag."

"What does it matter, which flag, to Araucanos?" I asked her. "Does the land change because of a flag?"

"I live in my own house," she said. "Does a man put his saddle inside my door? Am I his woman? This flag, who puts it in my house? Who asks? Does he bring guanaco meat? Which family does he serve?"

"But Kalata, this flag is sign of a country, not a man," I said. "If it has nothing for you, why did Lliutro ride away with it? Why does she hide in the bamboo with her wounds? If a flag is nothing to you, why is it more to her?"

"Our fathers fought against the *Yanque*," she said, still without turning. "That was their flag. This was their country. Why should other flags be seen here? Who shall own a woman's house without her word?"

"Soldiers do as they are told by the Government," I said. "They don't ask to own a woman's house, or anything of hers. They want to be sure where it is right for all their people to live. Where their animals can graze without taking from somebody else. A flag is sign of justice in defence of all men."

"If there is to be a flag, it must be Lliutro's," she said. "It was the flag of my grandfather. They were of the blood of Queupoliquen. This is their country. Who disobeys the dead?"

"Those alive must decide their own laws and the way they want to live," I said. "The people of my blood also do not want this flag. Neither do they want Chile's. But there must be authority. Every man must obey a cacique. Caciques obey their *toqui*. In my country we have no *toqui*. We have a government. But we have no soldiers here. Therefore we must obey."

"You obey because you are told?" she said, over her shoulder. "Who tells a man against his will?"

"No use to fight," I said. "Men die. Who looks after the woman and children?"

"If the woman has a knife, nobody," she said. "Children die with a touch of the *bolas*. She dies at the wrists and neck. What is a man to obey? Should he also kneel for the foot on his head?"

"Ideas change," I said, and I barely believed it, for her voice held the contempt of her race. "If men and women die, there will be no children. Where is the use in this?"

"The land will be richer," she said. "Is a mountain smaller because a flag flies? Why is a man? But a mountain thinks nothing of flags or men. It moves when *Ranginhüenüchaü* turns in sleep, or never. Why should a man?"

"He thinks," I said. "Does a mountain?"

She looked over her shoulder and laughed, and surely never was a lovelier sound.

"It has its life," she said. "Of course it thinks. Or how would it live?"

But I had been in that place before in talks with Rhin. He believed, and I was halfway to believing with him, that all things have life, all things feel, and all things can think, and it is a man's business to find out how and use the knowledge for the good of all. There was nothing much I could say against because I remembered too well what I had felt while I rode with them, and that feeling had never been far from me. Even now, I feel the life in this house, in these stones, in flame, even in the slag outside.

It was strange to talk to a woman almost naked about matters which I had never thought much of. Yet she seemed to have made up her mind, and it was from that afternoon that I had far more respect for her. Before, she was only an Indio helping Rhin. After, I had many reasons to think she was a real power behind him, and certainly her advice to me when I needed it was the best I could have had. Long after, I found out why. But it is still strange to think back, seeing the brown body, the long black hair with white bands, and straight legs and spread toes, and yet a voice of such authority, with pity, too, and never far from laughter.

"Where is she?" I asked. "I want to go to her."

"Nobody will," she said.

"How did you know she had gone?" I asked again. "There was not time for a messenger to come here."

"When have we needed messengers?" she said, and poured the tea.

"Could somebody tell her I am waiting, ready to go to her?" I asked, helpless.

"Which ear will listen?" she said. "Above the voice of Queupoliquen, which voice will she hear?"

"I am brother to Saiheque," I said.

"You let his flag go with her," she said.

"Did I know he had a flag?" I said. "He should have told me. Lliutro should have told me."

"They should have told you of Queupoliquen," she said. "He died with his feet in a slow fire. He hung from a tree. With a heavy stone on his shoulders. His arms tore from his body. He smiled."

"Which of the Indio people treat their *toqui* in such a manner?" I asked her.

"*Yanque*," she said. "These, with their flag, are still *Yanque*. They burn and kill. They are *Yanque*. They destroy. We shall follow Lliutro."

"What of her, up at the waterfall?" I asked. "Will she be left there?"

"There are many waterfalls," she said. "We shall find one on the side of the evening sun."

"On the side of the evening sun, there are no guanaco," I said. "How will you live?"

She laughed again, a lovely sound, of calmness and peace and perfect trust, and her back was a girl's, with no hang or raddle to tell of age.

"How have we lived?" she said, looking beyond the doorway. "Do you think we are poor? We hunt guanaco because we must. It trains our men. In winter we go north to the cattle country, or to the cattle and sheep on the side of the evening sun. These are not for men."

"But you work with Rhinberry Wynn," I said. "He is not a guanaco hunter."

"He teaches us what is to come," she said. "When it is here, we shall be ready."

"What is this that comes?" I asked her. "Why will you be ready? Rhinberry has never spoken of this to me, and I am his friend."

"It comes for us, not for you," she said, but so sadly.

"Saiheque gave you his sons because he knows. His father took him to Buenos Aires. He came back as a child without a tongue. Without eyes, except to see our faults. All he thinks we ought to be. Rhinberry believes as he does."

"I thought he wanted you to live your own lives," I said, disturbed much more by her calmness than by the words, even if they were surprise enough. "After all this time, I know nothing of this?"

"Why should you?" she said. "You are *pichi huinca.*"

She called me a little white man, not exactly in the sense of being small, but only of being one, alone, without family or friends, and helpless except in the strength of brothers.

"Rhinberry is also *pichi huinca,*" I said.

She shook the strange fall of black hair with wide and narrow bands of white.

"No," she said, staring out of the window. "He thinks and lives as we do. But he teaches us his ways. He is *Küme Huenü.*"

"So was the preacher," I said. "How was this?"

"They are brothers," she said. "They are of our family."

"And I, not?" I said. "Or any of us?"

"You work with soldiers," she said, as if nothing more was needed.

"They will make the land safe for everybody," I said, but not sure of my excuse. "There will never be any more burning or shooting or killing. No more robbery. There will be justice, and peace."

Again she laughed, as a Mama laughs at something funny her child has said, more with love and pity than from any amusement, and I had the same helpless feeling as a child, knowing something is wrong but unable to see the right.

"We shall go tonight or tomorrow," she said, and put the tea on the table. "Some have already gone. They will follow Lliutro. Two things you must remember. If you need help, Saiheque will be here. If you need the *Küme Huenü,* light a fire at the waterfall."

"How will Saiheque know?" I asked her.

"Eyes will be near to see," she said, and I knew she meant Lliutro, though I never asked, but at least I had an empty feeling of comfort.

We heard them coming back in a gallop, and Rhin was among the last.

He came in, and saw me with the old smile, no surprise, but I knew it was all over.

"Well, we are finished here," he said, as if everything was settled. "I will put the land in your name. Whatever is left is yours. Use it as you please."

We think of stupid things to say at such times.

"What about bread for the children?" I asked.

"Everything I have sent to Miss Lewis, and she will find a couple of the mothers to do the baking," he said. "I had a word with the General, and some of his men will put a bake-house there."

"He couldn't have been pleased," I said.

"He agreed it was wisest," Rhin said. "We won't be able to cross this border after this. Well, not openly. Soldiers will stop any movement. Especially of cattle. I told him you will be in charge of our affairs, and I will send a man to deal with accounts, let us say, six months from now."

"It will bring sad hearts to many," I said. "Why must you go?"

"As these are treated, so I will be," he said, and took the cup from Kalata. "I am thinking of leaving this one here with some of the younger children at school."

"They will be looked after," I said. "I will see to it."

"I will have to ask her, first," he said. "She is not a pile of hides to be pushed from here to there. But pity to take the little ones when they are learning well."

"But why must they go?" I asked him, feeling an impatience. "Why does some boundary you can't see, a line on a map, interfere with what you are doing?"

He put the cup down and smashed the saucer and turned the white face of rage.

"The line is in the heart, in the blood," he said. "This is

their land. Will they let any other stop them? They will fight. And then? Blood. They will raid and burn. Be thankful Saiheque is your friend. You could all burn tonight. I am taking these away to be from temptation and trouble. They will go back to their own family grounds. If they want to come back, there are plenty of places where a few can go through with none to see them. The General gave me leave to pass with packhorses when I want. Him and his leave. I told him I could pass with all the Indios on the other side of the peaks whenever I wanted, and he would never see one of them. That's why I'm going. He agreed."

"But is the boundary made this very night?" I asked him. "Has somebody made the law? The English king has got to decide first, hasn't he?"

"Time is not with us," Rhin said. "Spring is on us, then summer and winter. Plenty to do. If we wait, we lose good building time, planting and growing time. Wait too long, and they brood in black blood. They saw the flag carried. It is the only one they know. As well ask them to serve another cacique. We shall go before sunrise."

I could hardly tell him I wanted to sleep there that night.

"Before sunrise?" I said. "In darkness?"

"I have got to go to the waterfall tonight," he said. "They will meet me tomorrow. There is a lot to be done."

Nothing is so sad as trying to say a goodbye that cannot find the words.

"I am only sorry to be leaving you," he said. "If I find a few good ones there, will I send them to you? It will be the only chance they will have. There is nothing over there."

"Then, good God, why are you taking these?" I asked him. "What will they do there?"

"It is their land and they can go as they please," he said. "Here, they are only Indios, and nothing. I will come over twice a year, if I can, with ponchos, rugs, cloth, anything that will sell. Will you buy?"

"Everything you bring," I said. "Is there anything you want to take?"

"Yes," he said. "A good press of your hand, boy. God Almighty turned me to you in darkness over the waters. I have never forgotten. She is up there, safe, because of you. Because of her, I will take these safe from here. They must not be left in temptation. They are not as we are. Law isn't in them. They will take to the lance and flames. But I will keep them in work. They must learn to know what it will bring."

"Is that what you are doing, then?" I said. "Teaching them to work?"

"Yes," he said, and no man surer. "Work is peace. I will take you down to the track."

"Stay here," I said. "You have got plenty to do. I will think of all of you. But. We shall be empty. 'Sent empty away.' Goodbye, now."

He nodded, and stood, without moving, and I went.

Evening was blue when I walked toward the water tank. Indios were everywhere, like shadows, moving among the toldos with bundles. Nobody stopped or called and I was sadder then, because they were all friends, and at any other time they would have been in a crowd to hear me speak a few words of Arauco and laugh, and try to teach me more.

But my horse was not under the tree, and then somebody waved, and my heart seemed to bump through my gullet for I thought Lliutro was holding him out there. A girl, about her size, held a cleft stick with a piece of bark stuck in, so back I went to Kalata's toldo.

Rhinberry sat in the chair with his back to me, round-shouldered at the fire.

"Far from me to worry you," I said, and gave him the stick. "What is this?"

He looked at it, and up at me.

"It is a wife's message to a hunter," he said. "She is worried for you. Everything is well. Huw, think, now. Lal is coming back."

"When she does, I will tell her," I said. "She knows from my letters."

"Why don't you go, now, to Buenos Aires," he said. "No trouble for you. What is business beside the threat of this?"

"Threat?" I said.

"She will claim you," he said. "To her, Lal is only another woman. Nobody. Has Lal been with you for as long as Lliutro? Therefore, by Indio thought, Lliutro is mistress of the toldo. Lal has got nothing to say. Neither have you. You are hers to claim."

A couple of hours before, and I had been ready to follow Lliutro to the ends of everywhere and no care for anybody. But to hear that I was to be claimed as anything, or that Lal had to take another place, well, I could see the living room in the house, and the fireplace, and the polished floors and the glass and silver as Lal had left it, and Gwenonwy's living room as Donato and his Indios had made it, and instantly I had a feeling of illness, a disgust without words, a fury.

"Never," I said. "Give this to somebody, and tell her to stay where she is. I am finished."

"Good, you," he said, not moving. "It is the best. I will pray you will be held to stay strong."

But I was too angry, a sudden rage that made me breathless, and running sweat, and I could think of nothing, even to thank him, and I went from there and found the horse, and off, down to Corianth's place to ask for a meal and a bed.

The family was still out, and I went in the barn and found a good bundle of dried clover for the horse, and went up to the house. An Indio girl came out with a candle, and in two minutes she had a steak and a loaf in front of me and a jug of wine.

But what a difference between Lal's house and that one.

A difference of money, some might say, but they would be wrong.

Rhin had no money, but his place was comfortable and in gay colors with furniture he made, and the rugs and carpets of the Indios, and plenty of soap and water.

Corianth's family had a stove, a table and six chairs and the bare walls. The stove had never been cleaned, the table was in rickets, the chairs should have been firewood long since, and the walls were grimed in smoke, cobwebbed, and streaked by dirty hands.

Out to the barn I went, and brought back a couple of sacks and some bricks.

"Rake out the fire," I told the girls. "Light one outside, and put on a couple of buckets of water."

Chairs and table I put beyond the door. We got the stove cool with water, and scraped the top free of grease. Hot water and soda and a good scrub brought the floor clean. With a brick held in a sack we got some polish in the stove, and I left them to finish, and rode over to my place for whitewash, and paint, and some tools, nails and screws. In a couple of hours we had the place whitewashed, walls and ceiling, woodwork scraped and painted, tables and chairs planed new, scrubbed and all steady on the ground, and the stove shone.

But what pleased me was the pleasure of the two Indio girls.

"Keep it like this," I said. "It is just as easy as the other. But better to the eye and nose."

The family came while we were lighting the fire.

The children came to the door, and stood. The two eldest girls helped their mother to carry Corianth snoring to bed. No need to ask why. The smell of drunkenness is enough. Claerwen came in and opened her mouth to say something, and saw the stove, and the walls and floor, and sat down, looking at the clean, shining top of the table.

"I don't know what you must think of us," she said.

"Time," I said. "You haven't got time. Children to school, cows to milk, plowing, chop wood, don't I know? But what do these Indios do?"

"Cook," she said. "I am up in the big field. We have got to get the 'tatoes in, see."

"After that, everything else," I said. "But as long as they make bread and grill a bit of steak, and look after the babies, they have earned keep, is it? But you send two girls to clean my place, and they come back to this? Do you know why I am always complaining they don't work well? They don't know. These two Indios have seen what I did. Tell them to keep it like this. Send your girls to me tomorrow, and I will show them what to do in future."

She tapped the pads of her fingers on the table, dry and cracked, with the shreds of black nails, and the poor girl was weary enough to fall.

"I am 'shamed," she said. "You have got to be reminded. It didn't seem to matter, then? But it will. If he would keep from the drink, we would be better, see. Good, he is. But two drinks, and a bigger fool is not on the earth."

"Go to bed," I told the children. "I will sleep in the barn. In the morning we will talk again."

"All very well for you," she said, in the same tired voice. "You have got help. Four children under eight. Eldest, twelve. I have got to get the 'tatoes in. Cabbage next. Plow the middle patch. I would like a few onions, indeed."

She was talking almost in her sleep, not seeing me or anybody else.

The two girls came from behind the stove as if they were used to it, and lifted her, and took her out to the next room, and when they passed me she was gone from the world.

"How often is she like that?" I asked the older Indio, when she came back.

"Every night," she said.

"And the husband?" I said.

She poked a thumb at her mouth to say he drank.

"Go to bed," I said. "I will be gone with the sun."

The barn rustled with rats, but the hay was dry, and I was almost sleeping when I heard steps, and I saw the two girls go past the door, each with a bundle. Before they were far I was up to them.

"Where are you going?" I said.

"Down to our families," the elder said. "We are leaving."

"I will pay you well to stay," I said. "This woman needs your help. There's no need for you to go."

"They will kill us," she said, and the younger girl stared fright.

"Who?" I asked her.

"The soldiers," she said. "We would be slaves. They would sell us."

"Nonsense," I said, but I knew it was hopeless. "I will pay you well, and I will buy you new clothes, and everything you want. Go back there and help in the house."

"What use, clothes, if we are dead?" she asked the younger, and pushed her. "Go, run."

They went to the elderberry clump and came out with their ponies, and up, and off, and I listened to the gallop, low in spirit as I have ever been.

A few hours later, before the sun was over the peaks, I was at Donato's place. No need to ask, because his face said everything. The house was even worse than I remembered, though his tool shed was swept and in order, and his men sat on planks about the fire, eating the morning asado.

"Everybody, gone," he said. "Not one Indio. Nobody to help. Not even one."

He looked at the men.

"Some of these are talking of going," he said. "What will they do without a woman?"

Perhaps we become sick of what we have thought, or what we have done, and perhaps we have been sick for a long time without knowing it, and then, suddenly, a word or a look will bring it all in spew, and the strength of disgust surprises us.

"Let them get on, or go," I said, and turned for my house. "Wages and keep, that's the bargain. If they want women, they will have to find them. Make up your mind. The Indios have gone. Thank God."

17

A time, I suppose, is in every life when the spirit seems to ask what we are doing with our days on earth, if we have done the best till then, or if there is something else we ought to be doing before it is too late.

About when Rhinberry left us, that was how I felt, though who asked, or why the question came to haunt me, I am not sure.

But it haunted, as a ghost, as a voice from the dead.

No use to tell myself that in worldly goods I had more than any of our family, except, of course, Angharad, that came to her in marriage. No peace was in thought of miles of roads built, dozens of bridges, barracks, depots, and living quarters in use, all from my brain and hand. My bank account did nothing to ease unease. Nothing I did, or was asked to do had any taste of pleasure, or brought peace from a sense of hurry, without direction or any real reason, to be off and doing something else, better, more useful, of higher purpose, though what, only God Almighty could know. But the days were full, and there was time to think only at night.

Twenty-two children were left behind with Kalata and three older girls, and we carted them along to Miss Lewis at the school. Five of Rhin's big toldos we pulled down and rebuilt a little way off, near the river, with the biggest for a chapel to say prayers morning and night and march two and two, in and out, to classes or for meals.

"This is the only way, Mr. Morgan, and we are blessed, indeed," Miss Lewis said, happy as anybody could be. "They must be from those dens they are living in. Away from their parents. They must be washed, and in clean clothes, and eat from a plate on a clean cloth, and learn to use a knife and fork. A few years, and they won't go back to the old ways. The best boys shall go to Buenos Aires or the City of Lewis. Girls, the same. The rest, a good trade. In a few years, we will have less talk of dirty Indios."

"Are they capable of learning?" I asked her, because I had heard stories.

"Young enough, bright as sparrows," she said, and polished the spectacles. "Only a few weeks, it seems, over six years of age, they are useless. Nothing to be done. Their parents are in them. Indio ideas. Nothing we say or do has sense. I will not waste time with them. Out they go."

But with the Indios all gone, she had no help except Kalata and the three girls. It was all very well to say a couple of the mothers would bake bread, but the mothers had to work, and it was a long way to come. The Major sent an Army cook, but when the troop left, so did he, and Kalata baked, but it was hours every day, to wash children, and launder, and cook, and keep the place clean.

"We have got to have help, Mr. Morgan," Miss Lewis said, that afternoon, when I passed through. "There isn't a spare pair of hands anywhere. I have got eighty-eight childen well, and five in bed. I need a minimum of twenty to give everybody spare time. Next month, twenty more children will be joining. How?"

She was too thin, dark under the eyes, and papery in the face, and her hands were sticks, but she was the sort of woman to drop before to give in, and I knew she was not far from it.

Kalata put us right. Another thin one, worked to the bone, and tired to the roots of her hair, plaited round her head in bands of black and white, very strange and pretty, and a white overall.

"Futaleüfü, and Palenque, and up north in El Bolson," she said. "You could call women from the island. Chiloé. They serve the families, there. They are not our people."

As it happened, I was putting rock markers at the points where the Boundary Commission judged the dividing line passed between Chile and Argentina. Only the Devil himself could have thought of such a job, on the tops of mountains, most in snow, or under centuries of ice, but ice or snow, Devil or not, the General insisted that the marker should go on the point, not a foot this way or that, and damn your neck, or frostbite and everything else. Up on the peaks we went, with ponies where they would go, but where it was too steep we had to go alone, and I was never one for heights. Certain it is that without Rupayan I could never have started, far less finish. Beside that one, a goat was no more than a sleeping beauty. He would climb anywhere and anything, and come back for the instruments, and cement, and me, and Benedetti. We went up all the peaks marked for us, though the soldiers never did, and I was glad after, because then nobody could tell me about the land or any detail, and it served me well.

Rupayan might have followed Saiheque, but I found he was not of the same people.

"If you are Huilliche of the south, why should you go to the west?" I asked him, that morning. "You and your men are being well-paid and fed, and you will have a flock of sheep when you finish. Why would you go where you are not known? Which family will take you? Stay with me, and you will have free land. Your children are in school. Will you take them away? Shall others read signs and write, and add numbers? Are your children slaves of the Araucano?"

He nodded on bent shoulders, looking away, hands behind, still.

"I am Indio," he said. "We shall be sent away. Our women taken. We are told these things. It will be soon."

"Never," I said. "My hand, never."

We shook hands, no more, and back he went to work.

But I told the General somebody was putting the word about that Indios were to be killed, and their women and children made into slaves.

"If I find them, they will be shot," he said, without feeling. "I shall enquire. Meanwhile, those men deserve a half league. You may tell them so."

In that way I kept Rupayan and his Huilliche team, and with them I reached Futaleüfü, The Wide River, and rough. The first evening I went along the valley, and saw the huts and toldos of the Chilean settlers, far smaller, poorer places than ours, though the people looked healthy and cheerful enough, and the children could not be matched for apples in the cheeks, groups of them, shy, peeping from the bushes. Many spaces were planted in vegetables and wheat, and flowers were in bloom, and the biggest blackberries I ever saw were not yet ripe, but I had an eye on them, because the blackberry is royalest gift in a jam or a tart, and dear reminder of home. There were none up with us, so I had a few dozen canes loaded, and they did very well but never so well as there, if it was soil, or more sun or rain, or less wind, but everything seems to grow better on the Chilean side, no doubt, except bone-idleness.

That night we camped in the valley, near the place of the marker. A sub-officer of the Chilean Carabiniers came to the fire and saluted, and told me very civil we were on the wrong side of the border, and please to sleep there in comfort, and go peacefully in the morning.

"Thank you," I said. "But we are putting a few stones to mark a place for the Boundary Commission. They are not sure where the line is. But they know the dispute is over an area about here. We are marking it so that it can be seen from your side and from Argentina's. Then somebody will make up his mind which side of it the line goes."

"I will make up his mind," he said, and pointed back the way we had come. "Put it down there. This is Chile."

"On the map it is nothing," I said, and unrolled the big

chart with Benedetti's scribble on it. "This is where we are. The line is drawn from this peak. It goes from here to this peak. To the east is Argentina. The other side is Chile."

"I was born here," he said, and pointed to a light. "This is Chile. Put your marker down there."

"Soldiers will come and there will be trouble," I said. "Is it worth it for a few hundred square meters?"

"It took my father and mother years of work to clear a few hundred square meters," he said. "They cleared the land you are on. I permit you to sleep here. It is Chile. Enjoy our hospitality. Tomorrow I shall come again."

Well, no use to argue with that one. He was too dark in the eye, too much happy smile, and too hospitable to be played with, and next morning, before the sun, we put up a pile of stones and rode across the river. Sure enough, while we were having breakfast, he came to the ford, and I crossed halfway to meet him, in deep, fast green water, and the horses plunged to keep foothold.

"You put up the stones," he said, still smiling. "I knocked them down."

"That is your business," I said. "Ours is finished, here. Except, there is a question I would like to ask. Have you got any men or women wanting work? From Chiloé, or anywhere, if they are not shy of the plow and the ax?"

He stared such surprise that I laughed.

"You offend hospitality, and ask for help?" he said. "Why should anybody trust you?"

"No reason," I said. "I am doing my job. You are doing yours. Down the road here, many families would do a better job with more help. Good wages and board. A bonus if they work seedtime to harvest. My name is Morgan. This side of the City of the Mill."

"How many?" he asked, and turning for the other bank.

"A hundred," I said, almost in a dare. "Men and women. Husbands and wives. Bring the children. There's a school. Two hundred. As many as you please. They will all find good work."

By the time I was back in the valley, the first couples were there, with dozens riding by on some days, dribs and drabs others, but they all found a place. Donato and I had forty couples clearing, and I put twenty each on Doli and Solva's place, and twenty more up at Vyrnwy's, and in the weeks after, we were able to find which were the ones able to work or not. But they were all hard workers. Never did we find a bad pair among those first arrivals. The difficult part was in putting them up, and paying them. Men like Corianth had no money, but they were the ones most in need of help. A dozen of us got together in Geza's office to find some way of getting enough cash for wages, and to decide on a system to give them credit in the shop without going too far in debt. But the biggest problem was where they would live.

"You can't stop them building a shed for themselves," Tom, Tot, said. "Married people are 'titled to a bit of privacy. An old barn is all very well. These are going to work for months, I hope. I will keep mine years if they will stay. But they will do as they did in the Colony. Build a few posts and a straw roof. Add planks. Then mud bricks. One day you will find two or three women. And an outhouse. A planting of potatoes. Vegetables. A fruit tree or two. Before the words are from you, acres of good land is theirs. How many are working for you? How much of your best land is gone *rrrrp!* in a couple of years, and nothing you can say?"

"They will live off my land," Elidyr Jones said. "Work, yes. Live, no. There is plenty of land round about."

"They won't work as hard," Idris Bryn Gilfa said. "Or as long. Mine will get so much per ten meters of clear, clean land. Without burning. They can live where they like. But off my land."

"Most won't work on those terms," Milton Roberts said. "They know what they want. They aren't fools."

"Use Rhinberry's place and the toldos," I said. "We can put up more. Water is there, and fuel. It is built. They can stay there for as long as they please. They'll know who it belongs to. They'll know Saiheque. They won't take advantage. But if they want, I don't see why they can't have a league of their own if they work well for a couple of years."

"They would have to become citizens," the Major said. "No colonists will be permitted, be sure of that."

"Can they be colonists if they were born here?" I said. "Within a few kilometers? Citizens of what? Buenos Aires? A couple of thousand kilometers or more north, they have more right than the people who live here? Work here? Bring the land clean for use?"

"They are Chilotes," the Major said, using a term of small disdain. "Let them work, pay them, and let them go. Enough of them, and they could claim it for Chile."

"Pity a few of us didn't claim it for New Cambria," I said. "We have a better claim than anyone in Buenos Aires, to begin. These people all do a thorough day's work. Soon there will be hundreds of them. They will buy goods here. They will create a new market. Land will be clean for miles in a couple of years. Property will have value. There will be trade to the coast. By whose work? Buenos Aires? Or the few of us, and the Chileans we support?"

"It seems to me you should be a citizen of Chile," the Major said, not agreeably.

"I am a citizen of Argentina, but it doesn't take from me a sense of justice," I said. "People in the rest of the country never heard of us. They'll never see us. But they have more right to the land than the people born here?"

"Born in Chile," the Major said.

"An invention of Santiago, and Argentina was invented in Buenos Aires," I said. "Not even a hundred years ago. Those we are talking about were here long before anybody. Their people are buried about the place. They make the best markers. The true boundary is where a man loved a woman, and a child was born. If you want a frontier, there it is. Very well. I will arrange with Moishe a sum in cash every three months. It is agreed that employers will sign Geza's book once a month for a half of a month's wage in goods for each man and woman in work. All owings to be paid at the end of three months. No interest. Any of us unable to pay because of conditions will earmark animals, feed, grains, hides, wool or fleeces to the amount. Anything else?"

"What rent shall they pay for living at Rhin's place?" Tom, Tot, asked. "It's going to be far, for some."

"No rent," I said. "Rhin would never allow it. They will pay their work in the garden, and clearing timber. You are right about being far for many. We will build on other ground up the other end of the valley. If more are needed elsewhere, we will build again. In that way they will be together in companionship. Geza can open a branch in each. So can others. If the Major has no objection?"

"The best idea I've yet heard," he said. "I'll have a patrol round all of them. Then they'll know we're about. In that case, I'll permit no extra building. They'll live in those groups, or go."

That was how the Indio villages came to life, with the little shops and wine bars coming later, though looking at remnants now, nobody would dream what happened to make them so.

"I'm thinking to start a wagon train with Idwyn," Mog, Moke, said, outside. "On the day he starts from the City of Lewis, I will start from here. I'm no good on the farm. My hands are stubborn, with them."

The hands were still black, and eaten with frostbite in twists.

"Contract with me for all goods for the next two years," I said, and I saw the big light in his eyes. "Start, and the best of fortune. What else?"

"Will I be having three wagons, credit, pay quarterly?" he asked, poor boy, afraid I would say no. "Forty mules I can buy if I have got the cash. But I haven't. No wagons, or mules, or cash. Only me, and stubborn old hands, no good with the plow. Useless, I am."

In a moment I could see him, over the fire at night, knowing his mother was growing older and working for two, and cursing those hands that had helped to save all of us, and I was in his place and wondering how I would feel.

"You have got wagons, and mules and saddlery, and feed and stores," I said, and nodded to Geza. "You have got heart and courage. That is more than money. When will you start?"

"Now, just," he said. "Thank you, Mr. Morgan. I will never forget."

True, too.

But that sense of hurry, of standing still and doing little, of wasting time, was in me, and nothing gave any peace. The house was joy to walk in, everything in place and shining. There was always hot water, and a big fire, and green branches in the vases to bring Lal warm in the room. Bathing and shaving and dressing with collar and tie only to sit down to a plate of food by myself seemed silly enough, and yet it did good and stopped a lot of laziness, and after, I dealt with accounts and paper, and there was always more than enough of it, so it was late when I went to bed, sometimes to sleep, other times to twist and turn, and get up to make a cup of tea and sleep in the chair till Rupayan's boy lit the fire. One morning I woke, and he was standing in a grin, watching me, and I knew from a dry throat I had been snoring.

That moment I remember.

It seemed to me then, that I was only dozing in chairs and waiting for somebody to light fires, and all my life I had never done anything else except wait for somebody to light a fire, or do something or other before I was awake. I think I wakened then.

It seems strange that I had never thought seriously of going to Buenos Aires. Perhaps I was used to the thought of Lal as self-reliant, capable of looking after herself and resenting any help as interference. I had been used to women able to make up their own minds, and Lal had never given me any reason to change.

But before I came out of that chair I had settled everything to be done, and the way held clear for Beunos Aires. The troop was ready after midday with stores for a month, and I took six of the men with the packhorses and spare mounts, and off we went. At Donato's I left messages for everybody, gave him a list of things to be done, and told him to leave Rupayan in charge of the workmen. It was a bad year for floods, and snow had filled the lakes, and swelled the rivers to wide, rushing seas that we had to go around for we could never have crossed. Up on the high shoulder we went, through the skirt of the forest, and I realized we were on the way to Lal's waterfall, but going over between the peaks instead of beside the lake. Snow was still deep, and wild boar tracks were everywhere, with puma sometimes, all fresh, so we knew we must be careful with the horses, even if the dogs had not spoken plainly enough, running close to us, hackles up, in a long growl. By that time I was used to riding anywhere and mountains meant no more than the pampas, yet at the top I had to pull in.

Not a track, but a fault in the rock went down almost sheer for about a mile, never more than a couple of feet wide and littered with stones.

Batancal led the bellmare, and the other horses followed her, and the men went behind. Nobody asked any questions, nobody looked at anybody, so down I went with them. A dozen times I thought we were gone, with rock splintering under hoofs and chunks falling to break branches in the treetops below, and pack-animals slithering on hinds for yards, and us getting bumped against the cliff hard enough to fling us off, but the horses snuffled and plodded as if it was nothing out of the usual, even when they had to jump a six-foot gap, no rider, and only a chirrup to send them over. Morro, a good gray, went across with no help from me, and when we landed, and I opened my eyes, we were at the back of the waterfall's rim, and the fall was just below us, a diamond curtain of thick icicles glittering in rainbow flashes all the way down to a break above the pool's crystal cone of broken ice.

Light was going, and I was glad. A sleep up there, in a place of such memory seemed a good start to the journey.

The men made a camp farther down, and I lit a big fire among the rose briars, and hung the canvas over tall loops, and I was never more comfortable, lying on my sheepskins, with a space to see out across the lake, though mist covered most of the water and all the mountains on the other side. The asado came up, and I made coffee, and sat down at the fireside in gray evening, listening to drizzle starting, not feeling lonely, exactly, but more than ready to be in Buenos Aires with Lal.

If the wish moved, and Lliutro came in mind, or if I thought of her, and what she was doing, and where, as I had a thousand times, but I felt no surprise to see a hand and an arm in firelight holding up a cleft stick with a piece of bark in it.

An older woman looked in, and smiled. Somewhere I had seen her, and when she motioned me to follow I had no worry, but only eagerness to find Lliutro, and we went up, behind the waterfall, not far, across two tree trunks over the drop, into a forest of pine and coihué, so thick that only now and then we heard a raindrop slip through, and walking made no sound in an age of leaf fall, and the air held fragrance of a pine cob fire.

Through the trees I saw her, sitting chin on hand, barely out of the flame, in front of a low toldo built under the branches. She wore a guanaco cloak and her plait hung on the right shoulder with a new leather band about the brow, a silver ornament on a pendant at the throat, and boots of guanaco fleece. Inside the toldo were sheepskins on a pile of green cane, a pig's belly water bag, her saddlery and blankets, and a sheep's carcass hung in cloth.

"I was told you were in Chile," I said.

"I have been, but tonight I waited here for you," she said, and made room on the log, and I knew somebody had been teaching her Castellano. "I shall go with you to Vuriloche, and back through the lakes. Saiheque holds you as a brother. His sons will go to you when the snows finish."

"Why are you here?" I asked her. "The soldiers could find you. What then?"

The barest smile she gave me.

"Thirty men are in lance throw," she said. "I am not in the soldier's country. My country is where the toldo ends at the east. The line is from this peak across to that one. I am this side."

Rupayan, of course, showed her where the line went. His smoke signals warned her I was on the way, and no doubt Batancal was told to take the mountain path to make sure we met. But I was far from wanting her to come with us to Vuriloche. Army patrols were everywhere, and so were my workmen. Davies, Tom Tiddler's, had charge of the depot at El Bolson, and Idris Richards had a team clearing the track from Epuyen, and their wives were with them. To ignore talk was all very well, but I was coming back with Lal, and I had to be careful.

"There will be trouble if I am seen with you," I said.

"We shall go my way," she said, as if it were done. "Nobody will see us. We shall be near Vuriloche in five days."

"I want to visit my manager in El Bolson," I said.

"Tomorrow night," she said.

"I will not ride like an Indio," I said. "I want to go with time. No *lefi-luan*."

"The horses will take us," she said. "We shall sit. As now. No *lefi-luan*. No hurry. Quiet water."

"Who taught you Castellano?" I asked her.

"Moyamachi," she said, nodding at the older woman. "I study every day. I shall go to school three months. If I speak well, it's enough. If not, three months more."

"In which school?" I asked.

"In Santiago," she said. "Before the snows finish, when we pick strawberries, then I shall speak. Now I am a canoe. Others take me."

"You speak better than I do," I said. "Nobody has used me for a canoe."

"You are a man, and you make wood and iron obey," she

said. "Other men obey you even without words. Not so many as a baby. This is strange to me. Our caciques speak many hours for a small thing. You speak little, but much is done. You are *Ulmain* among your people. I learn Castellano to speak to you, and you will speak for us as *Küme Huenü.*"

"I am happy to be *Küme Huenü,*" I said. "Why should I speak for you?"

"For us," she said. "We have no man to speak. No old man has patience to learn. The young hunters have no time. The boys are too small. Who teaches them? I must learn. I must speak with the soldiers. Their *toqui.* In Santiago I shall speak. I want to know why the flag of the family of Queupoliquen is not permitted."

"I shall speak, and it will interest me to know what reason they give," I said, but I was surprised she spoke so fluently. "I would be more interested to know how you were taught to speak such good Castellano. In a few weeks?"

"While I sleep," she said. "In the day I say the words. At night, sleep again, learn more."

"Wait, now," I said. "While you sleep you learn? How?"

"Moyamachi," she said as if there was no need for another word. "I sleep. She teaches."

The woman came with two small wooden bowls full of thin liquid, like tea, and Lliutro nodded to me to take one.

"It is *paico,*" she said, and raised the bowl in both hands. "We shall make a promise. When I come back from Santiago, you will take me to the soldier's *toqui.*"

"Very well," I said, and watched her drinking, and I drank.

Cool, not sugary or sour, but like the taste of unripe damsons just below the skin, and we touched empty bowls, and she sat chin in hand again, watching me, turning the bowl on the tips of her fingers, but mine fell and rolled, and I wanted to pick it up, but my arms were stone, to the fingers, not a move.

As a block, without any feeling, though I could see and hear but not think, so I was held.

Clear as now, I saw every detail, and heard what they said

when they carried me in the toldo and put me on the sheepskins. Nothing seemed strange to me, even that beyond sight and hearing and the sense that joins the two, nothing in me seemed to live, except that I knew I was clearly and plainly and most surely me. Calm I was, at peace eternal, with not a notion of my name, or who I was, or where I had ever been. Every detail in the roof of the toldo I saw, and I can remember, to this day, the shining edges of the leaves of maitén, and a spider making a web on the guanaco pelt and the carcass swinging in the fly cloth. How long it was that I stayed awake I cannot tell, but I can remember drinking, and eating, and sitting up and somebody pulling my ankles and then being warm in the sheepskins again. Memories are with me of talking, though I cannot remember to whom, and hearing voices but not whose, and not a word remains but only the sound and a shaking in the body when the voice is used, and seeing light in places, perhaps of flame, though it floated as a long veil, soon gone.

I woke to daylight, still in the toldo, and there was shine beyond the leaves, a surprise because winter has no sun. There was nothing in the place except my clothes hanging from the roof, and my boots in glisten of grease, and the sheepskins over me and a fine poncho woven of guanaco wool. My head was perfectly clear, and I felt better in body and soul than at any time in my life, without weakness or the smallest laxity in any muscle. My clothes went on in moments, and I was pulling on the boots, and I missed seeing the ends of my beard.

My face was smooth, and my hair was cut to the lobes of my ears like an Indio. But a shave so close would have made me sore, and then I knew I had been plucked by an Indio woman. The fire was out, the ash was cold, and there were no bones about the place, or anything to tell how long I had been there. The poncho went over my shoulder, and off I went.

Well, I remember laughing while I walked through the trees. No worry was in me, not a care, and I felt a giant in strength and coldly sane in mind. It surprised me though, to walk from the forest into bright sunlight.

Wild rose was breaking in bud, first green smiled everywhere, and I heard the river before I crossed the tree-trunk bridge, and saw the white rush below, and sun shone in the powder of water and a rainbow grew like a flower.

My canvas was still there, and my sheepskins, and a good fire had just been lit and the coffee pot shone.

Batancal came round the rock and looked at me, and the smile in his eyes said Yes I Know, And I Am Sorry, But It Is Funny. He wore a leather band about the head, a sheared hide poncho to the waist, *bombachos* and horse-hock boots, not the clothes of winter.

In the sun I was warm, and I saw it was about nine in the morning.

"How long have we been here?" I asked him, and laughed.

"Seven weeks and two days," he said, eyes sideways to have it right, and looking up, very innocent, and down, then, to me.

We both sat, and we laughed till the tears ran, but I shall never be sure why.

18

A silk hat, starched linen and a frock coat and white waistcoat make a difference if only in manners, there can be no doubt, and many a time, sitting under the *ombú*, looking over the strong milky tea of the River Plate I thought of myself in a toldo, or under a pampas bush, or in the carpenter's shop, and then in Buenos Aires, as a wealthy one, married to a beauty of a girl, with a fine son, many friends, and on terms with ministers of the government, and even with the President.

But from this little kitchen I came, and in that space, where the wall bed used to be, I learned most of what I know to be the truth about living. Even the Lord Christ had to ask what Truth was, but I think a part can be found in the decent instinct of a woman, and a boy shall have most from his mother, as I had it, and all of us, from Mama, though not in fat books or sayings of wisdom, but in a way of looking at everything, and thinking about them, and doing there and then what has to be done.

On The Hill that morning I was sunning with my father out on the front step, and I saw Mama coming up with two shopping bags full from the market, and the wind was sharp and I knew she would have white fingers, so I was off to help her. In front of Iorwerth Richard's garden the girls were playing hopscotch and I ran through them, a yard from anybody, but Mab was hopping and my shadow frightened her and she tripped over Ness and they both fell in a soft bump, as girls fall, and Mab had a scratched knee and both of them bawled to open a tomb, but I ran on to help Mama though I knew something was wrong from the look.

"Go back and help Mab to the house," Mama said. "How long have you been knocking down little girls?"

"I didn't touch them," I said, and I nearly cried from rage and shame. "Old girls, they are always falling down, and shouting, then. For nothing."

"I am another old girl," Mama said. "Shall I expect to be pushed over by Master Huw Morgan and roll down The Hill with the potatoes and sprouts? Go, you."

Back I went and pulled Mab up and dragged her in the back to Mrs. Richards, and she thanked me and said I was a real little gentleman and told Mab to give me a kiss, but I was off before that, and when I came out, my Dada had taken the bags, and he and Mama were going in the house.

Never did I live it down, and every time I went from the door I had a reminder.

"Out, now then, to push over more little girls to hurt, is it?" Mama said, darning a shirt, she was, and I can see the needle going in and out, flat to the cloth. "You are doing well, indeed. It will be no surprise to see the policeman here, either. Pushing little girls, big old boy you are, good gracious. There is brave."

It used to make me so angry I could crack my head against a stone. But I was always very careful with girls after that. Perhaps it had effect in everything I ever had to do with women, for I was never able to deal with them as if they were men, or had another type of sex in wearing trousers, or as anything but little girls grown up, and still, if they fell down, making a soft bump. Even the Widow Glyn I saw as a little girl and tried to treat with kindness, and did, for a time, though thank God that kindness never made me marry her. Lal said I should have owned up to sleeping with her, in the bed I was paying rent for, and make her confess she came in my room of her own will. Yet that would have been taking advantage of a weakness, which in any event, was always an enjoyment, and I was last to complain.

"She was perfectly willing to take advantage of you," Lal said. "And spiteful after. Nobody thanks you for courtesy. You should have told the Council straight that you had her and she was very good, and part of the furniture. Paying, you were, for her and the room and shop. Only your laundry and sundries were extra. They would have thought more of you."

"Marital bed, she stated in the complaint," I said. "It was not. It was an ordinary bed, and a bit bumpy. After she had been in a few times, she changed the mattress."

"Nothing like a bit of suffering to open the purse," Lal said. "I should have done a lot more. Uncle Tynant called it verging on the deceitful. He was first to know she would go with anybody. If they had money. No charge. She liked the feel of money."

"Uncle Tynant should have asked the right question," I said. "There was no marital bed. Just a plain bed. And nothing approaching the connubial. Why should I give her all the blame? Or any blame? I had the right to turn her out. She turned me out, instead, and I feel grateful to her. We are quits. Her legs were beautiful, indeed. White. I suppose I should have told the Council that?"

"No need, boy," Lal said. "They had known, years. There before you."

About all those little things I used to think when I drove down to sit under the *ombú* those mornings, only to breathe fresh air before the day's heat, and think for a few minutes before going to one of the Ministeries, or to the merchants' quarter to buy for the company. Every day was full, for Lal and for me, though our time was spent very differently.

The night I got to Buenos Aires in a train from Azul, everybody was there to meet me, but I will swear before God I had to stare at Lal for seconds like a fool before I knew her, so beautiful she was, so calm, though the fever only

I knew was in her eyes, and when we kissed she might have fallen. Everybody was there, and nobody ever felt more beggarly than me, really in rags, without a good wash for days except for a sluice on the train. Well, we all went to the comfortable place Lal had rented from a family then in Europe, a little house in the French style in Belgrano we tried to buy, though I was glad enough they refused, for I could never have lived there afterward and never would I have sold it.

We had supper in the dining room of mirrors, and coffee in the drawing room looking out over the garden, and nobody would let me change my clothes or even comb my hair because they said I reminded them of the South, and they were homesick and ready to go.

But my son was in my heart and mind, a big, heavy fellow, with Lal's eyes and a laugh that went deep enough to bring tears. Doli and Solva both were expecting, and pretending to be jealous that Lal had become Mama first.

"We should have been in a line together," Doli said. "What did you do, boy"?

"Ask Lal," I said.

"We were looking at the waterfall," Lal said, busy with coffee. "It might have been because we had no sugar up there. The only mistake Tambien made. Plenty of tea and coffee. No sugar."

"I am the only one taking sugar, and I never noticed it," I said. "I had plenty."

"I wonder did you have time to make a cup of anything," Solva said. "And coffee is very bad for keeping you awake."

"Nothing will keep me awake tonight," Lal said. "I have never been so happy. Huw, you have grown, or changed, or something. What is it?"

"Forgot the sugar, girl," Doli said.

"Middle-aged spread," Solva said. "Oracio is getting one, too."

"Volde always had one," Doli said. "And very comfortable."

"I'm thinner," I said. "And thicker soles. And shaved."

Even there, in that warm room, in laughter, and with Lal, so beautiful, looking at me with the flush I knew and loved, but I could see the eyes of Lliutro, and thought I heard her voice, and behind I saw the smile of Moyamachi, plain and real as anybody there.

Lal's woman's sense of their presence, I was sure was the change she felt in me, and while I was not exactly afraid, or even worried, I was still in a waking wonder because I could think in Arauco, and I could speak and understand every word with the best. Before, I had known a few words, and I could pronounce a fair try. But on the ride across from Vuriloche I spoke as an Indio, far better than in Castellano, and strange, I saw everything as an Araucano. That was the mystery, but I told only Lal and she put her arms strong about me and said it was a dream, and she had been from me too long, but never again. Easy to say, and close in bed, soonest to forget, but the mark I never lost. No other soul on earth knew about it except Rhinberry and the Indios, though nobody thought much about them, and more the pity.

"*Relqué marí epú,*" Batancal said, and I knew he meant fifty-two, or seven weeks and three days, and I answered him as an Indio, and while we laughed he knew, and his eyes began a stare, and from then he treated me with quick feet as a true *Ulmain,* and the others, more. Nobody mentioned Lliutro, but she was never far from me. My mind was like a tuning fork, a touch, and she was there, a pure note.

In many ways I am glad I had to go to Buenos Aires at that time. Meeting Lal seemed to restore a balance, and having to behave as one with some idea of himself, as much as being with her and our son, did a great deal to pull me out of one sort of life, and into another, just as strange to me, but simpler, where I could use what I had been taught, whether in the Valley, or in the Atlantic Colony, and again in the Andes.

That first day was comical for me. A breakfast of porridge, bacon and eggs, and tea brought me back to the Valley with a bump, and very good, too. The carriage was there on the dot of eight o'clock, and off we went to the tailor, the shirtmaker, the shoemaker and the hatter. Shame is a funny thing to feel, but Lal went in, no nonsense, in a cherry dress with lace, and a wide hat with cherries and a veil, and I will put money there was no lovelier girl anywhere in the world, and everybody knew it. But I louted in with boots in bits, trousers torn, shirt in rags, coat without elbows, and a hat from the bin, but nobody seemed to notice except me. The measuring was the same as with Hwfa and Old Twm, and I thought of them while the tape lashed and tightened. Both were alive at that time, and I could imagine what they would have said to hear Lal looking at patterns and ordering, not one, but a dozen suits, morning, afternoon, evening and for the camp.

"When will I wear them?" I said, and laughing to think of me with a dozen suits.

"The time will come," Lal said, chin down, so I knew it was no use.

Shirtmakers, the same story of dozens, and shoes, half a dozen, and hats, and she bought me a walking stick with my initials on the gold band.

It was then I began to know that many of our people in the Atlantic Colony were much more than wealthy, and far from being the simple ones they appeared. From respect for the memory of their fathers and mothers they made a life in Patagonia in much the same way as the old ones toward the end of their days, making a difference between what they called The Camp, that part of the pampas they had brought to green riches, and the other life of ease they were able to enjoy in the city.

In their homes in the Colony they lived simply enough though well and wanting for nothing. But in Buenos Aires they were city people. Maes Corwen was a plain stretch of miles everywhere of farm, and the cereals alone would have made a rich living. Yet apart altogether were the cattle, in meat, hides, tallow, butter, and cheese, and the sheep in meat, fleeces, and wool, beside the yield of flocks by the thousands out on the pampas. It was only when I saw the figures that I realized how much the three girls owned, and I began to understand why Lal would go to any extreme to save it for Doli and Solva and herself. The biggest shock was to see what Matithias Morse had left her in the marriage contract. Even without liquid cash, the holdings in property were enormous, and I could understand why Mr. and Mrs. Elias, Snuff, would go to law if only to have a fraction back.

But the General had proved a good friend, and I never forgot, and yet even with all his help, and the proof of documents and scores of witnesses, the case went from judge to judge into weeks and months, and Lal was in one court or another, or in the advocates' offices for hours every day, and on Saturdays she was in the anteroom until six at night to read the pages, written in copperplate, of all that had been said that week, and what was to be pleaded in the week to come.

A wonderful girl, Lal.

In those months she had become as good a lawyer as anybody, and the lawyers said so, and waited for her to decide the next move, because she knew the land and the people, but they knew only the Law, at that time not so tempered as now, and those on the other side took all the rope they might, because every moment their fees fattened.

Monday to Friday, then, except for that first day, I took Lal to the Court in our carriage driven by Benoit, a Frenchman of an older day, a great respecter of all persons respecting him, or otherwise a fat spit and nothing. At the Court I left her with a kiss on the veiled cheek, that always held the perfume of the bedroom, and a kiss in the gloved hand, which blessed perfume in my palm and on my fingers, that I loved, and I watched her met by the lawyers, at least four of them, to take her into Court, and I went to the office. Perhaps Lal was too wrapped in her own business at that time to give a thought to mine, but I had more than enough to do. Moishe sent me the reports by our weekly ship, with balances to date, bank statements, credits to be signed in the Ministeries and put to our joint account, and the items to be loaded for the voyage down. In the early days it had been sacks of this and dozens of that, but now it was tons and cases, and thousands of tons when there were a couple before, and tens of thousands of cubic feet instead of a few. Coal we began supplying for the naval bases, and metals for the repair yards, and railway trucks and passenger cars. Gas pipe and water ducts, lamp posts and telegraph line, hospital beds and linen, blankets, paint, desks, window glass, every mortal thing humans ever wanted was in those lists, and I had to find them, buy at the best price, and get them delivered to dockside. Very soon I got tired of being promised wagons and waiting a couple of days for nothing. Early on I bought my own horses and wagons and I soon had a transport company to take anything and send it anywhere, first inside the borders, and then worldwide. Almost anybody in every business I got to know over the months, and I suppose it was not a year till we had our company quoted on the Stock Exchange. By then we had three steamers and eight sailing vessels, not large, but more tonnage went up and down for us than for anyone else, and we became the first name for imports and exports to the interior, by far the most important wool and hide brokers, and we made the first long-term contract for live and frozen meat and put up half the capital for a freezing plant, first, and then, later installed the plant we bought in Chicago.

Lal knew little of all that. Whether she thought I was only strolling about in my finery, or following Benoit in a trot about the city, I am not sure, but she could talk only about victories in Court, or agreements in the lawyers' offices, or how much heavier the boy was since the month before, or who was coming to the house next week, all a pleasure over dinner at night, or coffee after, or in bed, the best place of all for speaking about anything.

It was not until she saw my name as guest of the Minister of War in *La Prensa* that she looked at me as if I had a life apart from the house and herself.

"Why didn't you tell me you were having luncheon?" she said, thin, looking as though I had insulted her.

"I didn't know until he invited me," I said.

"But it was yesterday," she said. "Why didn't you tell me last night?"

"Too many people here," I said. "And I didn't think of it. In a small room, it was."

"A minister," she said. "How was that?"

"Contracts," I said. "We will supply for the new naval base. We shall build a road from Bahia Blanca to Neuquen, and down, to join the track going to the south. We will buy a sewage system for the city. We are going to explore an underground railway here. I have an appointment with the President next week. I'd better tell you about that and save trouble."

"Appointment with the President, what for?" she said, in whispers, unbelieving.

"Army contracts," I said. "Except for the General and a few of his staff, I know that zone better than anyone else. If it is quantities or distances or requirements, better than all of them. I'm going to save the Country some money."

She nodded.

"Careful, now," she said. "Learn your lessons. Saving the Country some money means taking profit away from somebody. At the top. You could make enemies."

"No odds," I said. "And no interest."

"Will you remember I have got a case?" Lal said, and very pretty. "Wheels are within wheels, here. You never know which buyer is friend of who, or if the judge is the uncle or cousin of somebody. Careful about profit. Money is a touchstone."

Only a few minutes with the President were enough to see the extent of his main worry, and endless smaller, every one of them important but with no hope of being dealt with because of a lack of brains, materials, and money.

"That frontier is a constant preoccupation," he said, while we looked at the map. "It cannot be guarded along its extent.

We can only do the best with what we have. For that reason, Army conscription is vital, or we would never have the men. We haven't the money to pay volunteers. They can earn more on any farm. That's why I'm very grateful to men like yourself for working down in the south. If we'd had to pay contractors in the city to go down there, it would have cost a hundred or a thousand times more. Who knows? And not as well done. The General Staff is very pleased with the reports. That's why we'd like you to undertake further contracts. My ministers have the details. Have you, at any time, had difficulty with the Chileans?"

"None whatever, sir," I said. "I've only met about fifty or less all the time I've been there. They came in to buy animals. It's the Indios making the difficulty."

"Ah, the Indios," he said, and put his hands together. "What's to be done? They do nothing they are told. They take advantage of goodwill. Kindness is weakness. Is it true they understand nothing but force?"

"No, sir," I said, point-blank. "I have lived with them. The moment they are treated simply as men and women, and not as wild animals, they will obey. Most of the work you say I did well was the work of Indios. Not one centavo in payment. But we put the money aside. When they need it, it's there. For schools or anything else. We shall do the same with these contracts. Employ all the Indios we can find. If they will go. They can't be driven. They are men and women. It would serve better if they knew they were all citizens. Indios are not less than us. They live as they want. We, as we want. That's all. Take the children from the parents and put them to school. In fifteen years you will have a new nation. We have started down there."

The President shook his head, ran a hand down the gray beard singed at the tips.

"Money," he said, and sad. "No money. Schools are nearest my heart. We must have them. How? With what? If I could indulge in abracadabra, I would. But the facts must be faced.

No money. We must finish a railway to the north and west. It will take years. We must build ports. Roads. How?"

He walked to the window, and looked over the river, that went to the horizon, and a steamer blew black smoke over a fourmaster and a schooner.

"We are a young nation, and small," he said. "In the past few years, we've done a great deal. If we do more we shall go heavily in debt. I will not permit it. Therefore, some things must suffer. In patience. If we could save the cost of that Army down there, we might put the money to better use."

"Francisco Moreno has the idea," I said. "The mountains and lakes are natural barriers against attack. But there are dozens of passes over, known and unknown. An Army would go mad trying to guard them. But if the zone on our side of the mountains, let us say, to a depth of thirty kilometers is taken as neutral ground, no farming, no settling, then perhaps it would be respected as a true frontier. The territory would be no gain to either side. Not worth fighting for."

"He's been putting the idea forward, yes, I know," the President said. "A parkland? I'm not sure how it would be received. Wouldn't they come through just the same? What is gained?"

"It will remain as it was," I said. "Indios can live there if they want. They move every few days. Nobody will interfere. No roads or tracks will pass through the mountains. A few men at the passes will be enough. Even if they are wanted. It will be virgin land forever. A wonderful place to go for a week or two. Nothing like trees and rivers and mountains. And no people."

"You make me envious," he said. "Meantime, you have appointments. I want to see those budgets. My ministers know my wishes. When you have finished business, I shall want to see you again. Be good enough to repeat to them what you told me about the Indios."

A good man, I found him, and the ministers and secretaries were no less, and after, I was not so ready to talk about the Fat Ones of Buenos Aires. They had a great deal to do, and not much to do anything with, and the Minister of Education had tears in his eyes when I told how Miss Lewis taught a hundred children with nothing except what she could collect from us.

Soon after I had to take an office to deal with the mass of business, and my working day was longer. But I always went down to the *ombú* to sit in green shadow, and feel cool for a couple of minutes, and not exactly think, but only let my mind have a rest and turn in its own oil, and remember this and that, like a freewheel downhill. But in that way I got some very good ideas, too, though how they came, or where from, only God knows. That *ombú* looked like a tree, but it was really a plant left over from before the Flood, perhaps before the Stone Age, somebody told me, but even now I can feel the cool breeze, and in those days, without electric fans or ice, a few breaths of fresh air every day was a blessing nobody could afford to miss. When at last Moishe came up we both used to sit under the *ombú*, and I suppose most of our policies were made there. If I was startled at the size of our commitments, he was not.

"Question of multiples," he said, that morning. "Multiply by two, it's doubled. By two again, doubled again. That way, two meters become four, and eight, and sixteen. All you do? Multiply. Price? Multiply with it. Cheaper for more? No. Why? Transport. Remember transport. If the government takes responsibility for transport? Take the cost off the price, add fifteen per cent. Why? Thieves. You sign only down there. What's delivered you sign for. What's bought here, they pay for. Everything else, it's multiples."

A couple of weeks he spent with us, but never could I get him to meet any of the ministers or their staffs, never would he wear anything except the brownish swallow tail and kneed-out trousers, and we never got him to dinner to meet anybody. He stayed in the office or at the hotel, or in the merchants quarter buying, buying. Only Lal could pretty him into coming home for a meal and then the guests had to be of the family.

Solva asked him why he was so unwilling to be social.

"First, I don't speak the language," he said. "After forty years good life, it's disgrace. Words, I got. Can't write a letter. Can't talk. Business? Certainly. Anything else? Nothing. And who likes talk? Too many ideas, the head. Talk, it's time to waste. Me, I work. Go to sleep. Wake up, work. For me, it's enough."

"But it's a very stuffy old way to live, isn't it?" Solva said. "Work, sleep, work? I thought you liked music? There's the Opera in ten days, look. We will have a party to go, is it?"

"Ten days, I'm aboard going back," Moishe said. "First when I came here, no language. No money. A tray, couple pencils, pins, needles, cotton. Supplied credit. From this, I eat. I sleep in the street. Months. One day, it's a funeral. My supplier. I'm in the synagogue. No cantor. But I know. I am a cantor. I sing. For him. Soon everybody wants I should sing. So I sing. From the money I have a stall. Women's wear. A shop. Men and women's wear. Children. Shirts, that's big. I have four women for shirts. Thirty. A hundred twenty women make shirts. I buy textiles. Sell the shirt factory. But I have bigger profit in the scrap than the shirts, factory, machines, everything. So I buy scrap iron. And I sing. In the afternoon, at night. In the synagogue, in the halls. Business, it comes in the dressing room. Much. I am happy? No. Why? Ask it the wind why should it blow. We are going to marry. Fine educated girl, good family, the best. I have got house, property, carriage. Good business. Money. Sing every night. One night I come home. Not tired. Feel sick, the head. I walk. I come down the streets where I sell with the tray. Where I sleep. So many more sleeping. I walk to the port. To a small ship, she's going out. To the master I ask, where. Bahia, San Antonio, Port Madryn, he says. Got room for one more, cash? Come aboard, he says. So. Three weeks, Port Madryn. City of Lewis. Start business."

He sat back in the chair, crossed his feet, and we all looked at him.

"What became of the girl, and everything here?" Solva asked.

Moishe lifted that shoulder, and we waited for him to speak but he looked across scarlet flowers in the garden.

"You mean you left everything and never heard again?" Doli asked, eyes from her head.

"Nothing," Moishe said. "No interest. Don't want it."

"There is a funny old boy, you are," Solva said, in the little voice. "I'm sorry for the poor girl."

"She could marry better," Moishe said. "Not worse."

"You won't go to a concert but you've got Merlin Afon playing the harp all day," Lal said. "You must love music, then?"

"Merlin, he's like Moishe," he said. "Blind. Never saw music. But it's in the heart. The music, it's natural. Me, born in prison. Father, mother, they die. Me? Clean the prison. Run for everybody. Kicks. I'm twenty, it's a revolution. I'm out. A new brain. I like to go back to prison. Instead I get a ship, in the hold. Dirty water. Go to Algiers. No language. Sell fruit. Dates. But my nose, it shouts. More kicks. Another ship. Marseilles. Three days, no food. Another ship. Buenos Aires. And here."

"Where did you learn to sing?" Solva asked.

"My father," Moishe said. "He was chief cantor. He sang for us. Soft. But I learned."

"Why are you like Merlin?" Lal asked.

"He never saw beauty," Moishe said. "He makes his own. For me, too."

That night Lal had a quiet cry in my shoulder, thinking about Moishe and how many more in prison only for being themselves, so after good comfort there was nothing to do except slip out of bed to make us a cup of tea. Down to the white kitchen I went, and put the kettle on, and took out the tea canister, and the pot caddy, and milk from the window sill and I caught a flash of yellow from the laundry room next door. Light shone in, on a cluster of yellow lilies growing in a tin.

Amancay.

Instantly I was in the Andes, instantly I wanted to be back, instantly I thought of Lliutro and even of Moyamachi, and instantly, and stupidly wild, I could have walked from the house, down to the port, as Moishe had, and gone aboard, leaving everything, unconcerned, without interest, except to go.

The shadow behind me was Lal, in a pale blue dressing gown, half-sleepy and wholly beautiful, and I felt ashamed through to the soles of my feet.

"Oh, did you see the *amancay?*" she said, so happily. "Two Indios brought them this afternoon. I'll plant them tomorrow. The government brought a few of them up. The families of some of the caciques. They will have some house-training in the Institute, here. They got our address from the Superior, they told Tonietta. A mother and daughter. They must know us. I'll find them, and see. I wonder which family? Or did Rhinberry send them?"

Frightened as a fool, I stood there with the milk jug, looking at yellow petals.

I could have told her.

19

Lal wore a dress of pale apricot that seemed to have a faint pink shadow, and I always remember her, one bright morning outside the Court, when we kissed goodbye leaving with me the perfume of her beauty, turning for the stair, taking the long skirt in the left hand, making a shining woman's line with the tight waist and bodice, lace at wrists and high neck, wide, rose-flowered hat and loop of veil, and the curve of her cheek in a smile, tapping the parasol between the come-and-go of black patent toes with buckles, walking up to meet the lawyers, skirts of palest apricot, shadows moving faintly pink, long white gloves, gold mesh bag, high shoulders, tiny waist, in sunlight at the top a cloud of a woman turning to wave, and gone, in darkness.

Most of the younger men she met were in love with her, I suppose—why do I see so clearly the white rose in ramble over our fence at the back here, those years ago?—and with Doli and Solva as with any other, but as Lal and the girls always said, they "looked" at them. I know the look, not angry, not sorrowful, but as a dead fish might be looked at. Most of them behaved, but many sent bouquets day after day, and little notes in red ink. The senior partners were all serious, and if they were told by the clerks that gallant conduct was in the air, mistaken juniors were never seen again. It happened often, and Lal was sorry for them, but she had no time to waste. After all those months the case came to a final judgment, and in that time she was nervous, looking at each paper, reading the depositions, testimonies, and arguments all over again to make sure nothing had been left out, and our drawing room and bedroom were like a lawyer's office with paper, and seals, and tape.

One Saturday afternoon, I left the boy and his nurse and went to the office to meet her. The anteroom was crowded and the main office looked much more like a school, with about twenty men all writing on long sheets of folio, and a man in the corner taking off copies on purple jelly and a roller. The chief clerk showed me in next door, a small office with a roll-top desk, a portrait of President Mitre, and red-velvet chairs. The door was a little open. The next office held a smell of cigars but the desks were shut. In the office farther on, a man seemed to be dictating, and I took no notice till I heard Lal's voice.

Castellano is a good language for love, and I had been sitting there thinking about my own affairs when I heard a different tone and very different words, but Lal's voice seemed weighted for less than business with the law, and she laughed, and that was when I got up, and pushed the door wider.

"If I am needed, I am here," I said, loud enough, and stood.

A scuffle in the other room and in moments Lal came to the door, laughing, head back, hand to bosom, one arm high on the jamb.

"Well, Huw, my little one," she said barely. "Why didn't you come in, boy?"

"You are grown up," I said. "You shouldn't need any help. Or be told what to do. Why should I intrude?"

"You're taking it too seriously, aren't you?" she said, quieter. "You don't think there was anything wrong, surely?"

"He was in the middle of a bit of passion," I said. "You didn't disturb him. And if you didn't, then who am I? You're well able to protect yourself. If you don't, then you want him to go on. If that's what you want, it will lead somewhere. If it does, you don't need a husband. And I don't need that sort of wife."

"Wait, wait, now," she said, and looked into the room, and turned to me, laughing again. "He's gone. That's how serious it was. If I had a quarrel every time one of them offered a dab of sugar, I would be in fights all day. They know it does no good. I listen, and I read. He knew I was expecting you. Spice, that's all. For him, not me."

"He'd get spice," I said.

She was turning, but she looked at me from the side. "And what about your Indio?" she said, but still in half a laugh. "Our little *Qoya Hualnlliutromeü Antün Milla Queupoliquen?* What about that little misery? Wait till I find her. Only wait, that's all."

"Not her fault," I said. "Mine. I should have told you before. She is not to blame. I won't have a word against her."

"No need," she said, and went in the room, and came out with a parcel of documents that I tried to take, but she turned from me. "Thank you. I'll carry them."

"I came here to meet you to carry that package," I said.

"I'm perfectly capable, thank you," she said, and walked through the main office and everybody stood and called Good Night, and I followed, shaking.

Outside, Benoit opened the door of the carriage, and she got in.

"I shall walk," I told Benoit, and raised my hat.

Off I went, down San Martín, up into Florida, and along to the first bar. Half a dozen traders in there I knew, and if we met with pleasure, my drink tasted only of rage, and I was wet with sweat and in no mood to listen to jokes. Drink as a pacifier never did me any good. After two or three I can be sick. They served small sandwiches, cheese, biscuits, celery, olives, cold meats, hot mincemeats, and *empanadas* with any drink in those days, so I ate plenty, drank my couple, paid for the rounds, and went out, strolling.

The night held the day's sun, and the pavement was hot to my feet. A good soak in our bathroom prayed in the back of my mind. A hotel would have a bath, but no clean change, and I needed it. A porter could have taken a cab and a note for a suitcase, but that seemed too much. At that time there was nowhere to go except to a bar, or a house, and I was half in mind to go to a house but then I thought of our office, and there I went. The door was fresh painted blue, with the warehouse front, and our names in white letters, and the yard walls were in whitewash, with all the wagons, shafts up, in pools from a scrub and everything quiet and tidy. Up the stairs, to the right, and I put the key in my door, but it was open.

Lal sat in my chair.

She was in tears like a little girl and she half-held out her arms, and I was round there, crushing her, and she almost strangled me with my collar.

"A beautiful boy waiting for us at home and we must quarrel and stay from him, and for what?" she whispered. "Old lawyers and Indios. No more quarrels, Huw. Not worth it. I will hold up my hands. Will you?"

"Flat," I said. "Before to start."

"Good," she said, and used the handkerchief. "Glad I am for the veil. I have got eyes like an old frog, here."

"Come you, my wonder," I said. "Dark it is, and cabs are not often down here. Why didn't you keep Benoit?"

"His night off, and the mare has gone to be shoed, and time, too," she said. "I told him to give her a special feed, and have the chestnut tomorrow. We have got a garden party next week. Mother Geralda sent a message. She's got about fifty Indios over there. All of us have been asked. Will you go, this time?"

"No," I said. "Send money."

"Some of Saiheque's family are there, and some from Yanquetruz's and the family of Namüncurá," Lal said, and put the cover on the inkpot. "They are blood relations. If we think anything of them we ought to go. Saiheque thinks of you as a brother. Shouldn't you be there?"

No need for her to tell me, but she wanted to see Lliutro and me together.

"What harm if I don't?" I said. "Money is what they want, not me."

"Think about it," she said, and took gloves and parasol to go. "Remember, the General will be there. Many of the Ministers. It's a government scheme. The Church is in it because they've got the buildings, and the nuns are looking after the girls. The men are in the barracks."

"If it is Government, why is money needed?" I asked. "Why not apply to me, here?"

"Money for better clothes and shoes," Lal said. "Better food, this, that and the other. There is always something to be bought for two people, never mind fifty."

"Can you tell me anything they buy down with us?" I asked her. "When did you ever see an Indio buy anything? Except spirits or wine? If the Government is paying, I won't give a centavo. They've got plenty of money in credit of their own. I'll see the General tomorrow and tell him. Bringing them up here does nothing but harm, anyway."

"You are giving plenty of excuses, there," Lal said. "What is the real reason you don't want to go?"

What, indeed.

Only that fear, freezing in the back of my neck, no different from ice put there, and just as real, only to think for a moment that I would see any of them, or have to talk to them, or worse still, to see Lliutro and have to talk to her.

No use to argue, but I could not, for all the gold or the General or anyone else on earth.

"I believe you think much more of her," Lal said, in shadow, back to me. "Why don't you say?"

"Wrong," I said. "If you want to know, I'll tell you. I could be a much better Indio than any of them. But it's got nothing to do with us. I am living as I want. Working as I want. There is nothing in this world I want more than you and the boy and what I am doing. Will you leave it, now? I will not go."

Her eyes were in wet of tears, looking at me.

"You knew who I meant," she said. "Tell me truthfully, now. What is between you?"

What in God's name to say was not in me. Anger because of that distrust, and knowledge of guilt melting anger, and shame for everything even for being alive, that without doubt, I felt. But even more was hate that she should question me, or that she could dare to say anything I did or had done, was wrong.

I knew then I had begun to think as an Indio, not as myself. There seemed to be two of me but I still knew which one was the real me, though I was unsure how long I would last.

"Is there anything with her you couldn't have with me?" she said, at the door.

"Nothing," I said. "And nobody is in the same universe."

"What is the difference between a street woman and your Indio?" she asked, and started to walk to the stairs.

"Well, Lal, good God," I nearly shouted. "Another world again. They take money to be used. By anybody. Used. And payment in cash. Lliutro made a decision. No money. Nothing. And she's not 'my' Indio, either."

"But what is the difference between them, and the Indio, and me?" she insisted, and her voice doubled in the stairwell. "As women, what?"

"Whether you mean what you do, or not," I said, and stayed where I was. "That's the difference. The feeling is the same, I think. But if you mean in your heart and soul all you feel, that's the difference. With you, I mean it. With others, not."

"Then why do it?" Lal asked, shakily, in the doorway. "If you don't mean it, whatever that is, why do you bother?"

"Well, if you will have everything flat, there is a lot of

mustard with the beef if you go with a woman you don't know," I said. "She is new to you. Her feeling is strange to you. Her body is the same, perhaps. Curiosity is just as important. Everything to be done is the same. No difference. If I have got everything a bit mixed here, I'm sorry. There's no difference. And all the difference in wide creation. The difference is, if you mean what you feel, or if you are thinking only of yourself. To enjoy what you are doing. For your own sake. Not for hers. And please to remember. Some women take for themselves, too. No thought for anybody else."

Plain as the crystal square of the inkpot I could see Lliutro. Whether I was afraid that Lal and she might meet, or what, I am not sure but I was cold at any thought of going near, of seeing or hearing or even looking at any Indio, man or woman. No use to deny, a freeze was in the back of my head and down my spine, and I was in shivers, knowing that I could tear my clothes off and be an Indio. I seemed to be half in the air, wide awake and yet in a dream.

"Put your arms round me," I said. "Quick. Hold me, Lal. Hold me, girl."

The strength in her I felt, and her voice in whispers I heard, and she lifted me almost off my feet, and that was probably the saving touch, because at the back of somewhere far away in my mind I was angry that she should try to carry me, and I could see my suits tidy on hangers, and the polish of my shoes and boots on the rack, and my hats on the hallstand, and Tonietta serving porridge in the morning, and I could smell bacon, and the pages of *La Prensa,* and Lal's soap and powder in the bathroom, but over them I was reaching for the leather apron and the guanaco cloak, and I had an appetite for the taste of crude meats, and the pounding heave of a pony in gallop, hunger, desire, yearn, appetite, thirst, together were in me, and nothing to answer except anger that a woman should try to carry me and I woke up, struggling as from sleep.

We were kneeling and Lal's arms were tight about me and she was praying in whispers.

"Nothing the matter," I said, and in truth I never felt better or stronger, exactly as I had felt on waking in the toldo. "Hisht, now, will you?"

"Will you see a doctor, Huw?" she said, in my shoulder, and frightened. "You have worked too hard. Done too much. A couple of days in bed will do a world of good."

"Rather a day in the tomb," I said. "Nothing wrong with me. And no doctors, if you please. We could have a couple of days at the sea, yes. Would you like that? We could take the train tomorrow."

She looked at me, and turned to get her bag and parasol.

"Listen to me, now," she said. "Moishe has noticed the difference in you this long time. So have I. You are not the old Huw. Something is wrong. I knew I would never get you to a doctor, so I asked him. He will come to the house to take you. I will send a message. No more of this. Wait."

Well, I would have said enough, but Lal held up the flat of her hands and looked at me, chin down, beautiful.

Nothing else to do except give her a kiss, and go.

Moishe came for me at seven, and we took a fiacre to the Avenida Santa Fé, and a big house with double doors and a marble staircase smelling of wax.

"People pay not to die," Moishe said, while we walked up. "Fifty years I know him. We eat together the same plate, here. If it's heaven, he should cure God the headaches. Magreb Kasanevich, the same town we are born. So two millionaires? I think the father and mother. I ask it. Why not in time? They die poor. We live rich. It's right?"

We went into a drawing room with heavy furniture and gold-framed pictures, dark because the shutters kept out the sun.

Dr. Kasanevich came in, white, and they met as brothers, in laughter, talking a language I had never heard. Moishe leaped into a new man. Words came from him in a shaking stream and his hands and face were alive for the first time since I had known him, for generally he kept his hands behind, and only his eyes moved in the bearded face, and the clip of words was held always on a level near a whisper. But then I heard the timbre of a real voice and the lungs of a singer, and light on nose and cheeks, touching the eyes, bringing gold in whiskers and hair made him for those moments into a suppliant in appeal to Heaven, and I knew him to be more than buyer, seller, merchant, great friend of mine and how many thousands more, but a soul and spirit in might and truth.

"You see, Mr. Morgan?" Dr. Kasanevich said, in Castellano. "You see how it is? Suddenly it comes out. Suddenly it spills. If he had a wife, he'd be healthier. Take the words from him. Sit down, Moishe. We'll take coffee after."

We went in a room honored with books on all the walls, nothing to tell of medicine, and he touched a chair, and sat behind a table.

"We shall talk of a time spent with your Indio friends," he said, without any other word. "Your wife told me, Moishe told me, and now you tell me. How did you get there?"

To start in a sudden like that, in a strange room, I suppose, was the best that could have happened, and I told him all I could remember, and he listened, looking at me, never using the pencil.

"Why are you afraid to meet this girl?" he asked.

"Afraid is a heavy word," I said. "I am only afraid of being an Indio."

"What is it you fear?" he asked. "Leaving your wife and friends? Making a fool of yourself?"

"Yes," I said.

"Why do you want to be an Indio?" he asked me, and began to write. "What do you find so satisfactory about that life?"

"I don't find any satisfaction," I said. "I know I would have to. It's not what I want."

"Do you dream?" he asked.

"I can never remember a single dream in my life," I said.

"Perhaps I dream. I've always slept tired, or stayed awake."

"This girl told you she was taught Castellano in sleep," Dr. Kasanevich said. "You both drank this tea, or what was in the bowl?"

"She told me it was *paico*," I said. "It's a brew of herbs. I'm not sure what sort."

"That's where we should begin," he said, and put down the pencil. "I'm seriously interested here. You must make it your early business to see this girl. Find out what these herbs are, and what happened while you were drugged."

"Drugged?" I said, and scandalized to the roots, because I had never once thought of it.

"Of course, drugged," he said, and very cheerful. "You must know that all Indio peoples have a wide knowledge of herbs and their use in specific cases. They are not behind anyone in knowledge of the mind. In that area, we in the cities are just beginning to learn. You must find the girl, and if necessary force her to give you an account of the herbs and their preparation, and just as importantly, what system was followed while you were in the drugged state. Will you do that?"

"I suppose I shall have to," I said.

He laughed and smoothed the white hair, and nipped off the pince-nez in a round move that stayed in my mind, as if he lifted sight to see further.

"You are correct," he said. "You will have to. This extra knowledge doesn't interfere with your normal work?"

"No," I said. "I'm working harder now than at any time in my life."

"You don't feel uncomfortable in what you are doing?" he asked. "Is there any other work you'd rather do? In any other country?"

"Not exactly that," I said. "I often feel I ought to be doing something better. More useful. I have the feeling I am being pushed. By time. But I'm quite comfortable in this country."

He nodded, and wrote, and stood, bent over the desk.

"That's all for this morning," he said. "Now we'll have a cup of coffee. See that girl. Make her tell you. Bring her here, if you must. If she won't come, I'll see what I can do."

Instantly I could have killed him, and I was half out of the chair. As he stood, in the long white coat, looking down at the pad, I wanted to kill him.

He looked up at me.

"Don't try it," he said. "Take the idea out of your head."

"How do you know?" I said, drained, and in wonder.

"It's why I'm here, and why you are here," he said. "I don't disguise from you the seriousness of your condition. Try to keep that in focus. You are well-balanced. That's in your favor. But there's no easy treatment for the mind. You are a religious man? Which church do you attend?"

"Any," I said. "Every Sunday we go to one or the other. Not really religious. But brought up strictly enough."

"It's helped," he said, and opened the door. "It always does. Prayer brings the self together with the conscience. Moishe, your friend's a healthy man. Have no fears."

They spoke together over coffee as if I were not there, not the most miserable creature on earth, picked clean by the crows of worry, though not one single worry could I put solid in front of me, except what might happen to Lliutro. It never entered my head that I had to worry about Lal.

That afternoon Moishe came with me down to Bahia Blanca to look at the work to be done there, and at the new naval base, and we came back on a warship a couple of days before Mother Geralda's party. In that time Moishe said nothing, and neither did I, for we had more than enough to do. But when I left him at his hotel he put his hands on my shoulders.

"Fact," he said, smiling. "You look better. Work, it's the medicine, like Magreb says. You got to live right. You got to like the way you live. We get you right, I take a drink."

"I want to see you drink," I said. "I will have the date in gold on the wall, and frame the glass."

Suddenly, then, I knew I liked the way we lived.

If I was not taking Lal to Court I was up at five o'clock on summer mornings, breakfasting at half past, and walking through Belgrano when the bells pealed six. Streets were washed clean, not a scrap of paper anywhere, all the way down, past the Congress building, and through to our place on Alem, beside the wharfs. By then the city had been busy for an hour. If the flowers were coming in, I had a carnation or a rose buttonhole from old Donna Hecuba O'Higgins, a fourth generation Irishwoman, she told me, and even so, barely a word of Castellano, and an English I often never understood, except that she called the strawberries she sold in the punnets Red Weskits, and water, to her, was Wah-thur, and her new potatoes, and I never tasted better, were pray-tees. She had a stand on the corner near the Cathedral and if she went in for the Mass, you could take what you liked and leave the money. The docks at that time were in timber, and carts with ten-foot wheels went out to the ships a long way over the mud flats to bring passengers and cargo ashore. Our ships were smaller and anchored nearer, and our wharf was nearly always cleared on the first day or else we worked all night. Nobody thought of overtime or extra time in those days. Work was work, and it had to be done, and they were paid. If they wanted the work and the pay, very well, but if not they could say no, and go.

If Lal was going to Court I got up at the same time but after breakfast I walked down to the *ombú* and waited until Benoit picked me up on the way.

That *ombú* is with me now, a great sprawl of thick limbs coiling from the ground as if in sudden spasm of life, and then, shocked by what it saw, staying there, with leaves bursting, never a flower, no scent, but only cool shade, and a look about it to say In The Spirit I Have Lasted, And So Shall You.

Perhaps that was why I sat there.

Nobody else ever sat or stood or paused while I was there, though many gave me a look as if they were wondering what I was doing, sitting on a great root, and one morning it came to me that I was in a private chapel with a green roof and quick walls, and traffic all round making busy choir, and I never after felt it to be anything else. There, it was, that I thought about myself and my place in life, though most of that thinking was much more of prayer, rarely in Cambrian, and not often in English, but almost wholly in Castellano that I had learned to speak well with Lal for teacher, though with an accent I never lost, that the Minister told me was badge of honor, like the scarred feet of a barefoot pilgrim.

Mostly, I suppose, along with nearly everybody else in those days I wore the frock coat, starched linen and top hat, and only on the hottest days white linen, though I never felt the same, and Moishe refused to change anything for sake of the weather.

"I sweat, it's healthy," he said, in dismissal. "I don't sweat, it's usual. I should worry?"

Sometimes we both sat beneath the *ombú* and discussed what might be done in Patagonia to bring the country to life. Our great dream was a dam on the river we christened Camwy, which the Tehuelche called Chupat, and called Chubut by the mapmakers. Chupat, in Tehuelche, means a rope in loops, and Camwy, in Cambrian, means a river that winds, but only the one who thought of Chubut knows its meaning, and much of that blindness was in the way of working down there. The dam would have cost a few millions at that time, and by now would have saved thousands of millions and created thousands more. Nobody wanted to listen, not the Government, or the State Legislature, or any of the banks, and talking to private capital, of course, was like having a nice little chat with a wall. Nobody could see profit, much less getting their money back. The cereal growers to the north could see only the glean of superior harvests with less in price for themselves. Not for nothing we took gold medals in Chicago and Paris for best wheat. The northern cattlemen knew we would breed finer herds and so supply a better quality of animal. For sheep and wool, of course, we had never been equaled, and a cross-country system of canals could only help to multiply the flocks by giving water and making desert into grazing land, and creating areas where new towns and homesteads would follow the roads. Even a railway to join the Andes to the Atlantic was denied as uneconomic, because it would take many a lifetime to pay back capital, besides making the yearly loss a State debt with heavy taxes falling mostly on non-users.

"We have too much to do with our money," the Minister said, kindlily enough. "We have tens of thousands of square miles of excellent land that requires opening up. Desert must take its turn. We don't build to cheapen prices for a handful of sheep farmers. Imagine the uproar?"

"Put it out of your mind, Mr. Morgan," Mr. Clavering, the banker, said. "You collateral isn't anywhere near enough. If you lose a ship, for example, or have a drought, or a bad year for wool, where are you? It's the worst form of risk capital. I doubt you'd get London or anywhere else to look at it. You could try, of course. Even then, too much depends on circumstances. And few in favor."

Politics, in a word, one I began to hate, for it seemed to mean everything that kept people in a natural prison.

Moishe listened, never speaking, smoking that small cigar of twisted leaves, looking far away, he once told me, at the Promised Land, and when he sensed that all the talk was done, he lifted the right shoulder an inch, and let it fall.

Speech could never say so much.

"We don't have a country," he said, one morning. "A place, we got. People, they live comfortable. A country, a place, for them, the same. A flag they got. So once a year, raise the hat. Sing. Eat the asado. Get drunk. Next year, the same. So we supply. Make a living. A place, a country, to us, profit. It's enough?"

"I'm ashamed not to do more," I said.

Moishe took out the cigar to laugh, a little breathy shake, eyes shut, rubbing his chin with two fingers.

"Conscience," he said. "Only men born poor got conscience.

Conscience, what is? You should get crucified? For what? You're rich?"

I had to laugh with him.

"If I'm rich it's your fault," I said.

He shook his head, still eyes shut, serious.

"You got brains, you work twenty hours, that's why," he said. "Rich, that's profit. Brains, that's God. Work, that's you. Together, it's money. Look, I tell you. Me, I'm too old. You should take the cash. Everything. Go to North America. Use it. That's a country. You can help. To invest, we got plenty."

"How about you?" I said. "'Everything's' a lot of money. Half is yours."

"Cut me in," he said. "Money, for me, it's easy. I spend how much? I eat how much? In a palace I should live? Why? A tent, wagon, roof, from the office a mattress, what's the difference? I wake up the same. Ships, they sail the same. People, they eat the same. Want the same. I supply. I cut you in. You cut me in. So?"

"I'll have to talk to Lal," I said.

He looked away and nodded, and shook his head, and looked again at me, and raised his eyebrows.

"For a woman, a country, a place, it's the same," he said, and got up to go. "A man, a home, a baby, that's a woman. Eat, drink, sleep, money in the bank, clean floors, pretty hat, everything good. Why you should go somewhere else? For the same you got here? So a woman says yes? Which woman?"

It surprised me how absolutely correct he was.

"Do you mean to tell me, after you have become a very successful man here, with a wonderful future everybody is talking about, that you will take everything and go?" Lal almost whispered, that night when I told her. "For what? You make money out of a country, and take it out to spend, is it?"

"No," I said. "I take capital and start where business is understood. We are only trading, here."

"Fancy," she said, with tooth powder round her lips, and

the brush held ready, and her hair down her back in plaits, and her body a lovely statue plain in the white nightdress. "You take capital. Did you have any to begin?"

"Only what Moishe supplied," I said. "Brains and work, the rest. There's no farther to go down there. Nobody wants to go farther."

"You can't expect everything you want immediately," she said. "The dam will have to be talked into being built. So will the railway. People don't know what they want till they are told. Will you go away just because of that?"

"I didn't say I was going away," I said. "I simply told you what Moishe and I were talking about this morning."

"Oh, only talking, is it?" she said. "I've heard some before. You have got a lot to finish down there. A lot in the Atlantic Colony. The new port. The roads. How could you dream of leaving everything half-finished?"

"Nothing is half-finished," I said. "I wasn't speaking of leaving. I only told you. I wish I hadn't. That's all."

Lal put down the tooth brush and glass, and held up both hands, palms out.

I put mine up.

"Moishe must be going mad," she said, and started brushing her teeth again, turning into the bathroom. "What would he do without you? What would anybody do? Who built that business? Who built it here? Does he want to get rid of you? Does he think you're getting too much credit? Always with Ministers, and twice with the President? Does he think he could do it? You are too soft-hearted, Huw. People impose."

"*Tawsôn, ne'di?*" I said, as my father sometimes said to my mother, chattering there. "Give it a breather, now then."

"I can see I will have to take a stricter hand, here," Lal said. "They will all be riding rough-shod."

"Let's see it, first," I said. "When shall we take the boy to the sea?"

"Only say when, and we are ready," she said. "I would love to taste salt in a good breeze again. And I would love more to see a mountain. And wet my hair in the waterfall.

Are we going to stay here in the winter? Or go down there in the snow?"

"Make up your mind," I said. "I shall have to go soon to meet the General. I can come back, or we can stay there."

"I am only sorry to leave this house," she said, looking about. "Happy, it is. Let us have the case finished first. Then I will tell you. That night I will tell you."

20

Well, I had never seen Lal deep in tears, really and truly sobbing as a woman. Tears would come in her eyes quickly enough if she was gentled in feeling by good singing or talking of friends, or in pity for somebody, though she was cold as butcher's meat at any other time. Crying or weeping or letting tears run nowadays are become sign of worse than weakness, it appears, though in those days anybody could have a cry and nobody with a word to say, but we were a lot healthier, then, and none more than Lal.

The moment I went in, she fell on her knees on the blue carpet and sobbed to break my heart.

"We must leave," she said. "Leave. They are back. At the hotel. Oh, Huw. What, now?"

I lifted her, and I had been away almost a week, and she knew I was home.

"It will be late spring in the Andes," I said. "We will leave, yes, and go down there. Only to go down to our little house. Little? Bigger than this. Go shopping, now. Buy what you like. We'll take it down with us. Good land we have got not far away, on the park, even better than this. When we come back the house will be built. New. Ready for you to go in. Your own. Nobody will tell you when to come or go. Tomorrow I will buy the front-door lock, and give you the key. Well?"

But the tears went on, and I took not much notice because I knew she loved the house and so did I, and we had been happy there, and it seemed a natural compliment to a roof that had only been friendly, and felt by us both to be truly dear.

Yet I have often wondered, thinking back.

Those tears came so suddenly, and the sobs shook us both while I held her, and I wondered at the depth of her sorrow for leaving a house, and whispered all the nonsense to soothe her.

Remembering now, I wonder, and I am sure.

She knew.

Then the painters were there and the carpenters, and moving men, and tears were forgotten in detail of packing, and I was thankful enough to go back to the office, even happy that we were out that day instead of having a date to think about, with hours of wishing to live through.

Seeing the Indios at Mother Geralda's fiesta was almost like being south of the Camwy again, and because our minds were on going back we met them with greater pleasure though only Lal knew some of them, and I none. But I had no trouble in making good friends and not only because of Saiheque. Talking to them was enough for I spoke without fault or pause, and soon they were all round me, men and women, and asking me to plead for them with the Government. They wanted right of lands, rivers, lakes, and mountains, only for themselves.

"The whites have their land," Yanquetruz said. "We want ours."

He came from a people farther north than Saiheque's, not so tall or well-formed, but he had the face of a man to be obeyed, and a condor's eyes that glinted all the contempt an Indio would care to show and yet held friendliness. All the people with him, most in odds of European dress, wore guanaco cloaks and leather headbands, huddling together as if afraid of being lost, and their eyes ghost me now, so sad, so desolate. Yet all of them not long before had burned farms and villages, made prisoners of women and children, murdered the men without mercy, stripped the pampas of sheep and cattle, and more than once defeated the Army hand to hand.

The moment we went in the garden they came to meet and ring us, all calling out as if they knew me, though I had never seen any of them. Lal went off to find Mother Geralda, and I stood to listen to one and another, but then Yanquetruz came through them and said everything in fewest words. He was no fool. The Government had invited him up with his caciques and their families to see the city and buy what they wanted, and leave their children in school. But he had begun to think it was an excuse to take his authority from the South, for nobody would listen when he said they all wanted to go back, and too many soldiers were on guard to try breaking out, never mind that the women and children were in the convent apart from the men.

"I shall speak to the General," I said. "But I have no hope."

He spat and walked away, and his women followed, looking at me as if I were cause of their sorrow.

But I believe I was proof against any feeling that afternoon, for I was hot with surpise to find that though I had not forgotten a word of the language, that feeling of changing into somebody else, of being an Indio among them, of wanting to tear off clothes and gallop, the strange, dead sense of living someone else's life had not flung ice upon me.

Nowhere could I see Lliutro.

The afternoon blew late winter's fine rain and gray clouds hung, and under top hats and bowlers most noses were red, mufflers were wrapped, astrakhan collars were frogged to the neck, and women crowded the marquees to be out of the mud. Lal waved to me from one, and took me through the crush to Mother Geralda, in a brown habit, with a lawn headdress about her face and a point hanging between the eyebrows, so that she looked out from a heart-shaped frame of white that shocked with quiet beauty.

"The girl is in the infirmary, Mr. Morgan," she said, in English. "She is not a tractable patient. The city doesn't suit everybody, especially the Indio. It's either lungs or digestive disorders, generally. They don't get the food they're used to. This girl, Queupoliquen, has studied in Santiago, perhaps you know? I'd like her to stay, but I don't think I can keep her. She smashes rather too much. It's expensive. Really a mad thing."

"I shall pay for the damage," I said. "If there is anything she wants, I shall be glad to supply it. Perhaps she would be calmer if I could speak to her?"

"I was only telling Mrs. Morgan," Mother Geralda said, and looked at Lal. "You may see her, if you wish? Mr. Morgan cannot be admitted. The wing is *in clausura*.

Lal went with a nun, and I went off to see if I could find anyone from Saiheque's people, or any sign of Moyamachi. From group to group, and puddle to puddle, and through every patch of mud in the area I went cold to the bone, and at last I found the General over in a tent, talking to a few priests round a fire, and the smell of coffee was almost as good as the taste, and his welcome as warm.

"Nobody expects or wants war," he said, through the steam. "We shall have time to plan proper garrison buildings at the right places, but we shan't get the money for years. I'd like to see a few churches and schools down there if only for the sake of the children. We can't do everything at once, but we'll have some of the families with us this year, and I don't want savages growing up."

"A suggestion to the Cathedral," one of the priests said. "Any light word travels."

"I shall leave it to you," the General said. "I've never suggested or complained. But we need schools. Especially for the girls. They've got to be house-trained. We can't get a servant down there. Nobody wants to leave the city. On any terms. The everyday process of living for any properly brought up woman is simply impossible. They won't work."

"You mean the Indios, sir," I said.

"Of course, the Indios," he said, and laughed. "Touchy? You Cambrians wouldn't part with a girl."

"To be servants, no," I said. "To help about the house as one of the family, perhaps. There's a difference."

"Find me one or two," the General said, quick. "We'll treat them as daughters, I promise you. My wife and I will be in your debt evermore. Months of dark winter. We're not looking forward to it."

"We shall be there in the middle of next month," I said. "I'll see what I can do. Pardon me."

The stairway door had opened and Lal put up the umbrella, and the nuns took an arm either side and while they hurried through the rain to the marquee I jumped the pools after them.

"Well," I said, in shelter, and wonderful sweet from the perfume of so many women in the heat of all the lamps and candles. "Is the girl better?"

Lal looked at me, chin down, angry.

"She tried to claw me," she said. "They had to hold her. I want nothing more to do with Indios. As the nuns have told me, there is nothing to be done with them. As Miss Lewis said. As I have always known. Finish. Is that understood?"

"Yes," I said.

"She will be taken to Dr. Kasanevich tomorrow," Lal said. "Let us find Benoit and go home."

21

Dr. Kasanevich was a great judge of coffee and I often went in for a cup on the way to the office, taking him different kinds we imported, and a porcelain service from Stafford, in white and gold, that I had given him was shards in a dustpan on his desk when I went in that morning.

"Miss Queupoliquen," he said, without a smile. "She's always behaved before. But I had the other woman here yesterday. It took all of us to hold them. This room was a bullring."

"A mistake to bring them here," I said. "They are used to toldos. They are not slow to break anything. Heads or bones or coffee pots, the same. For what reward?"

"A few minor," he said, and looked at coffee-stained notes. "I haven't fully studied these. I had to go to bed quite early. Men of my age shouldn't wrestle with young women."

"She wasn't hurt?" I asked him.

He smiled at the pages, and shook his head.

"The older woman is cause of the trouble," he was saying more to himself than to me. "Without her the girl behaves normally. In her presence, an immediate restlessness. A type of hypnosis, probably. I should know much more. Even with a nurse between them, obstructing line of sight, still she became more hysterical. Neither spoke to each other at any time. Diet at the Convent is the same for everyone. They had no opportunity of eating or drinking anything extraneous, solid or liquid. They have nothing hidden in their clothing or their cubicles. Both are kept apart. A building between them. Yet they communicate."

"Indios seem to read the mind," I said. "They seem to know from far away."

"I've never been able to get the girl to talk about this *paico*," he said. "That led to the outbreak."

"Rhinberry's bound to tell me," I said. "I'll be after him the moment I get there."

"I'm interested to see that you are no longer disturbed," he said. "No feeling of any sort? Beyond pity?"

"Pity, yes, I suppose," I said. "None of them should be here. I believe it's proposed to send them all back in the next couple of weeks. There will be big sighs of relief at the Convent. They've tried everything. Even with the children. No good."

"When they return, will you be meeting this girl again?" Dr. Kasanevich asked, but looking out of the window. "There's great danger, there, you know. Both of them are raging animals. Three of my people needed stitches."

"I'm sorry I couldn't be here when they came," I said.

"The accompanying nuns wouldn't have permitted it," he said. "They came here only for clinical study. My men weren't allowed in until it was obvious they were homicidal."

He tapped the pages.

"This is the Indio problem first to last," he said. "No discipline or upbringing as we understand it. But they have just as much right to their system. It suits them. I can give no advice. This isn't a matter of treating patients. It's the structure of a type of society. Every creature in it must be trained to another way of thinking. I have no hope of success. If it were tried, I would predict disaster."

"And what for me?" I asked him.

He shrugged, but unlike Moishe, with both shoulders.

"You'd be unwise to meet this girl," he said. "There's no treatment, so far as I know, for your particular malady. It is perhaps a hypnosis, or a possession of a mind while in the drugged state, by means which can only be guessed. Fortunately, your personality is formed in a mold which clearly does not fully respond to newer pressures. They operate only fitfully at times when perhaps you are overtired, or when the subject of your work requires that you think in consonance. I was greatly relieved when you showed no effect from meeting Indios again. Yet you should be warned. You didn't meet this girl, or the woman. Perhaps I should try to warn you against return to that area. Against any chance of meeting them."

"I shall go," I said. "I believe I am over it. My wife has done wonders. In any case it is only for a couple of months. And I shall be very careful."

Olwen has told me since that the poor man had a hopeless task, that even in these days the most expert might take years to pull me together. The only reason I was well as I was at that time must have been the different life I was having with Lal, the new sort of work I was doing, and not least, the time I spent with the boy, and he took my mind away from everything. Or so I thought.

The afternoon I knew I was wrong, we were over at the racecourse.

It had to happen at some time if we stayed long enough, I suppose, for they lived in the city and went to most of the places open to people with money to spend, so it was barely a shock to walk into the horse ring and find ourselves looking at Mr. and Mrs. Elias, Snuff, him in a white frock coat and panama, and she in a flare of mustard crêpe-de-chine.

We had little enough to say to each other but Nelya Penninah had to disturb the sand in trailing skirts over to us, and Elias tapped snuff where he was. Her corset was not so tight, but it brimmed, and she had another chin though still creamy.

"Well, Lal, well you are looking," she said. "Back this minute from Europe we are. Come and see us. We are staying in the Alvear. A suite first floor, and pink velvet everything. Huw, you are bigger, boy. So handsome, indeed. I hear business is splendid with you, yes?"

"Fair," I said.

"And how is Maes Corwen looking?" Nelya Penninah asked.

"You took trouble for nothing," Lal said. "The case will cost you enough."

"O, that," Nelya Penninah said, and flipped the gloves and twirled the parasol. "Mr. Elias thought it was worth a gamble, nothing else. Plenty of friends made among the lawyers, money spent not wasted, and favors to come. Five big contracts already. We hear you have gone in the coasting trade? Very good. We are starting a line to Europe, first one next month. If you want a good night or two in Paris, let me know. You shall have the best cabin, free, yes, all oak."

"Thank you," Lal said.

"I hear your sister isn't very well after the baby," Nelya Penninah said. "Doli, is it?"

"Doli and Solva are both very well," Lal said. "Nothing the matter anywhere."

"O, well, different to what I heard," Nelya Penninah said. "I was told he was struck, there."

"I will tell you who will be struck in one moment," Lal said. "Go from here."

"Only I was told," Nelya Penninah said, and bounced both hips, and turned. "Thank God, my two are beautiful, indeed. And I haven't got to worry about Mr. Elias and some old Indio, either. And no foreigners, or big heads in the family."

Lal's arm shook hard in mine but I held her. Doli's baby was born deformed and not expected to live and Voldi seemed to think it was some fault of his. They were living in the City, but we saw them only once or twice a month because Moishe and I had capitalized his business in exporting to Russia, the Baltic States and the Middle East, and the ships were all over the docks in Buenos Aires, up at Rosario and down in Bahia Blanca, and if he was at home three days in a month, Doli thought herself lucky. Neither wanted to go back to the Andes, and Solva agreed with them that perhaps every two or three years they would all go for a month or two of picnics, and for the rest leave their property to a manager.

But we soon found out that the Elias, Snuff, pair meant to annoy us. We had an eye on saddle and wagon horses for the journey down. There were some Shires, Percherons and Clydesdales in the list we thought we might buy, and of the saddle horses, Lal had chosen several, but not one came our way. We started to bid on a few but the price went over sense and Tampoco pushed through to tell us that Elias, Snuff, had bought the animals we ticked, or offered the auctioneer twenty per cent over any price we would pay. Tampoco heard, of course, from the other Gauchos looking after the place.

"Good," Lal said. "Now let us go about and buy what comes. He can have everything at twenty per cent more."

The afternoon must have cost The Snuffs a good night's rest because Lal earmarked anything on four legs, bid in any ring she could reach, if it was saddle or wagon horses, ponies or bulls, calves, cows, pigs, sheep or champion rams. Sure enough her bid was always topped, so she never bought anything, and people were saying they had never seen such prices, and the one auctioneer we talked to said it was only money doing the talking and sensible people were keeping away. But again Tampoco had a prize for us, and we went with him to a stable near the course and Tamaño and Tambien waited to show a dozen fine *criollo* horses.

Claws gripped, and I stood there while they trotted, one by one.

That first moment should have warned me.

To see the shape of the *criollo's* head, a square-nosed hammer, brought the freeze of ice to the back of my neck, and I could hear Araucano screams and I knew the smell of guanaco pelts and the warm air of the toldo. Only because Lal was with me, talking to me, I stood there, or else I would have vaulted on the first, and away, and I knew the **Indio** was not so far off, and I was not by any means safe as I had thought.

If only I had made my mind firm, then. Or if I had listened to Dr. Kasanevich.

Or told Lal.

But I stood there like a fool in cold fright though not afraid of anything, but unable to say the words to show I had changed my mind, or to explain why I would rather not go south, and every instant I stood arguing with another nature, that Indio feeling was leaving me, until I became angry with myself for being such a dolt, and immediately I was of one mind again, and certain to go, and ashamed to say a word to Lal or anybody.

As well try to explain why at some moment I have gone into a place to drink a cup of tea, or a glass of something or other, exactly like everybody else in there, wanting a cup or a glass, and knowing why, and yet not knowing, but going in anyway, and coming out, drink drunk, money paid, not satisfied really, but only held for the moment.

Somebody ought to study that one moment, and the couple just before, because thirst is rarely the reason. Why, or for what reason I stood next to Lal, pretending to look at animals, and agreeing with all she said, and yet thinking a thousand miles to the south, with the people, sounds, smells, all plainer than those about me, I suppose I shall never know, and even less that I could love her as much as any man could love a woman, and yet keep from her what she had all right to be told.

Anyway, we bought the horses and went home, and found Barres from the office waiting for me with an urgent message from the General's adjutant. Lal went in, and Benoit turned round and back I went to the docks. Major Von Gelsbach and I were old friends by then, so we had no formality and he sat at the other desk in shirt sleeves, with the coffee almost made, and a mountain of paper he sheafed in order.

"Armaments," he said. "Unload at these wharves, use your

carts, your labor. Take on men you can trust. Work all night. All carts will travel together. Police guides."

"No trouble?" I said. "War?"

"Not yet," he said. "If there is, we are ready. I chose this site because it's out of the way. My staff will be here in half an hour. The General and the High Command later tonight. Say nothing to anybody. You realize this is an honor for you?"

Our wharves were on the far side of the main dock, away from the liners, and hidden from anyone unless they were curious and liked a long walk on cobbles, with all the rubbish of years to climb over or around, and piled cargoes ready to load, and hundreds of shouting stevedores in a cursing hurry, and always handy with a knife, and sailing ships by the score, either tied up, or out a little way in the water, or if they were too big, beyond the mud.

Mountain artillery, pack saddlery, ammunition, and other items were all marked in areas on the wharf and in the warehouses, and the carts were told off by place and time. By night we had finished, and the waiter was clearing away dinner when the foreman shouted that ship's lights were off shore, and I sent out the gangs to meet them. Unloading went as usual with us, and when the General came in with a dozen others, all in plain clothes, the first column of carts was ready to go. Von Gelsbach took the party to the warehouse and showed them a piece of artillery put together and taken apart, and they came back to the office for a glass of wine.

"Your stevedores are mostly Italians," the General said.

"All except two Serbians," I said. "All hard workers. No complaint, never an absence."

"Immigrants," the General said.

"None of them here more than a year," I said. "I shall take some of them with me to Patagonia. The rest don't want to go. All of them are rough workmen in carpentry or stone. Gardening. Farming. And homesick. Barely a word of the language. We tried to start a class, but only a few would attend."

"They're coming in by the hundred thousand," General Flores said, and looked at the wine in lamplight, with red patching his face. "Give them two generations, they'll rule the country."

"I don't know what the policy is," General Martinez said. "No selection, no plan when they get here. Labor for building the railways? But they aren't sent there. They all congregate here. Live in warrens. The city's becoming dangerous at night, you know?"

"They should all be put in a uniform and drafted by companies for a couple of years to work on national projects," Von Gelsbach said. "Women and children housed and schooled, taught the language. Two years, we'd have people earning correctly, living decently. As it is, they're less useful than dogs."

"That's the German in you," General Uriaga said, and laughed with the others. "Imagine the outcry in La Bella Italia. 'Our glorious sons made captive, sent to forced labor in the desert? Our daughters and little children sold into slavery.' It would never do. Free will. Yes or no. They want to come here? Very well. They paid passage. Now find a level."

"Basically of a Neapolitan slum," General Martinez said. "They will construct their slums wherever they go. But it won't be far from a town. Buenos Aires will be another Naples. With that philosophy."

"Which philosophy do you find in Naples?" the General asked.

"See us, and die," General Martinez said, and emptied the glass. "If we aren't careful, it is we who will die. Engulfed in macaroni."

"We need the hands," the General said.

General Martinez turned his glass upside down.

"Not that sort, or at that eventual price," he said. "They'll breed a million like themselves. Principles? Morals? Ideals?"

"They have a strong guardian in the Church," General

Flores said. "I am not entirely in agreement with your point of view."

"I speak of the future and swarming families," General Martinez said. "They'll never be hungry. That's certain. Their children will at least be healthy. In millions. To do what? Breed others? Other millions? Where is the integral Argentinian? Or our principles, our ideals? Where? You speak of priests? You visualize the country in sacerdotal control?"

"But, Carlos, you take everything too far," General Flores said, turning away in impatience. "If we have to recruit an army, all these can bear arms. Each will be useful. Was the Revolutionary Army such a cultural phenomenon?"

"They were patriots," General Martinez said. "They fought, died or survived as patriots. Of the soil. That was their ultimate strength in all contingency. The land, the people, the flag. What have these to offer? Beads, idols, dogma? They'll make us a colony of the Vatican."

"Beyond our time, and therefore debatable," the General said. "Major Von Gelsbach, attend me at midday tomorrow. Mr. Morgan, my thanks for your service and hospitality. Do you wish to join my column for the journey south?"

"We shall go by ship to Bahia Blanca and on, in our own wagons," I said.

"You have no confidence in a military line of march," the General said.

"Confidence, yes, but there's too much dust, and very little comfort," I said. "I like to travel my own way, in my own time, and breathe good air and drink clean water. Dust and mud, I have had enough."

They went off in their carriages, and the younger officers looked at me as if I was somebody, and when I went back to the office, Von Gelsbach took off his coat and laughed, rolling the cuffs of his shirt.

"He's not used to being talked to like that," he said and cut the end of a cigar. "You know you'd travel à la Prince if you were part of his retinue."

"My wife will be with me," I said. "I know too much about the Army and women."

He put the cigar down, and waved the match out.

"Explain that," he said, staring, direct.

"All very well," I said. "No use to be high and mighty. When my wife came over from the Andes, they were bothered by an officer. One of the women had a lot of trouble with him. I don't want it repeated."

"Did Mrs. Morgan make a complaint?" Von Gelsbach asked, and took a pad.

"To the Governor, in Rawson, with witnesses," I said. "His name was Irrualde. A lieutenant to Major Vicente. We never heard a word after."

"Irrualde," Von Gelsbach said, friendlier. "Sometimes there's an animal. But if people don't complain in the proper quarter, we can't do anything. I'll make it my business to look into this. We are jealous of our uniform. It has been insulted in the past. No more."

In voice and manner he had a lot of the general when speaking of Yanquetruz and other impostors given Army rank, not a hate exactly, or confidence, but a sense of inner faith that even put a shake in the voice. In those moments a man is dangerous, and I knew I had to tread lightly.

Grethe, his wife, and Lal went to afternoon parties together, walked the children in the park, tried each other's cooking recipes, rode horseback, chose hats and dresses, almost like sisters though two more unlike have never been. Yet in nature they were flowers of the same pollen. Grethe came from the cattlelands of San Luis to the north, of a German family in third generation but still with the disciplines of the first. Everything in Grethe's house and all about had to be exactly so, and since Lal was of the same bolt, they got along as sisters. They had plenty of friends, of course, and a dozen clubs and circles to take spare time, so that they were rarely at home during the day, and there was generally somewhere to go in the evening.

That midday when I got home, whiskery and a bit dull

from no sleep, everybody was out. Nearly everything of ours was packed, ready to go, and the lower rooms had been painted and closed, so that we lived in the glass-paned patio with the kitchen a few steps away, and the bedroom, bathroom and nursery upstairs. In a way I was glad to be alone, to shave and bath and make coffee and lounge as I pleased. The nurse was a good woman, though I am not sure we spoke a dozen words, but she was out, and the house was sunny enough to hear a fly buzz, and quiet.

The garden door squeaked, and down the flags came Mrs. Tressid Maule in float of veils, silks, and feather boa.

There was no time to run or hide, but I was in a towel and uncombed, and she walked in, waving to me through the glass as if a half-naked man was usual with her.

"Oh, Huw—mm—is Lal there?" she called. "I simply must see her."

She was younger than Lal, not so tall, but beautiful in a helpless way that would make you bleed to do anything for her. If there was something to lean against, she leaned, and if not she lolled, and even in walking her hands were in wilt like the petals of a fainting daisy. Her husband was engineer of Light & Power, and well enough off, but she always complained of having no money, though Lal said she was never out of shops, and certainly I never saw her in the same dress. She spoke as though the words were pushed out of her, each one a sulk on its own, and her voice ran down at the end of a sentence as a clock out of winding, and often failed in the middle, so that half she said never came out, and you had to keep an eye on her to see what you might be missing.

Whether her own name was Tressid or her husband's I never knew but everybody called her Paf, because she blew out her breath—ppf!—not much of a blow, but enough to tell anybody she was tired of life, in mid-speech or after two or three words—ppf!—though on one of the few times I met Mr. Maule at their house, he called her everything else loud and clear and in engineer's English. That house was a museum of indolence, but now I believe I understand why. Everything was good, for the Buenos Aires shops are not behind anywhere else for quality, but nothing was in place, and meals must have been eaten on every stick in the house from the stains, and carpets were marked, and dark patches were over the silken walls. Lal asked me what I thought they could do there, or if instead of eating their food, they threw it at each other. He was not a big man, but strong from the way he moved, red in the face, gingery and light blue in the eye, always in dark suits and starch, and never speaking much to anybody, as if he was not in the right place. But then Moylan O'Hann told me that his state of quiet was advanced drunkenness, and lack of speech was simple inability, or toper's wisdom.

Mrs. Maule leaned in the doorway and looked at a point only a little way from my right foot. Her underlip was out, and a ppf! was on the way and she had parasol and gloves in droop of hands, everything pale blue and gray except for white egret feathers in the hat.

"You must excuse me," I said. "I'm expecting Lal at any moment. I am just home from work."

"Getting like Reg," she said in a pout, without moving. "Comes home whene'—pff!—know where I'd find her?"

"Perhaps the German Club," I said.

"I'm not a member—ppf!—hot today isn't—pff!" she said, and pulled the boa from her neck downward so that the end fell on the floor almost where I was. The braid link and frilling feathers led direct from me to her right hand and she looked at it with no move. What she intended I am not sure, but it was like a red rag to a bull. If she had notions that I was a little dog on the end of a string or that she could use her sulks with me, they went soon enough. In two steps I was over there and I had the dress open in a ttrrrtt! of snaps undone and it fell about her ankles. She wore a white corset with a frill of pale blue lace and her breasts lay as two eggs in a nest, showing the nipples, pink and in glisten. Her hands went to push my shoulders, and then, when I held, she raised them to the hat, drawing out both pins in little sighs, and the hat went away in a white sweep of an arm and the pins rattled on the floor. She lifted easy, and light, and the corset gave a small, hard waist but her legs were warm, heavy, and she took the lobe of my ear between her teeth and the flip of the tip of her tongue brought shivers. Over in the corner, curtains, sheets, blankets were stacked ready, and there I took her, in shadow, and put her down. The towel fell and I was with her in the moment and her mouth was warm.

If one woman has more wonder than any other I am not sure, but there are moments when any woman is more wonderful than all others on earth, and Paf taught me that, and also that all women in those moments of marvel are not the same. Lal was stronger, and had her own ways and knew what she wanted, and Lliutro was never with me waking, but only out of sleep, and if it seems treason or worse but there can be no doubt that Paf taught me that little, and most marvelous, more. Where others took, she gave, and where they wanted, she made a gift, and in the crushing gold of moments when all light was mine and I sang as Son of God in The Garden, then she took me wholly to herself in dear protection, and I feel her arms even now, and kiss in thought wherever she is.

"Would you mind if I told my husband?" she said, when she came down, dressed, from the bathroom.

"No," I said. "Exactly as you will."

"Will you tell Lal?" she asked me, buttoning the gloves and dragging down her mouth.

"No," I said. "Unless you want me to."

She turned up her eyes, that were smiling, and dull with faraway sorrow.

"Ah, Lal," she whispered. "How am I to meet you?"

Her left hand reached to touch my shoulder, and she walked quickly to the glass door.

"We shall meet soon, Huw," she said, without turning. "I'm going now, while I can. I'd rather stay."

No lean or loll, no ppf! or sign of helplessness, but only gray and pale blue in rustle along the flags and a white flash of egret plumes before the door closed quietly, and a small gray feather from the boa in lilt across the floor.

That night, working late, Rodriguez came in to say that somebody wished to see me, a friend, about a private matter.

Maule came in, slowly, holding both sides of the doorway, nodding the smile of the serenely drunk.

"Evening," he said, and sat carefully in the chair. "Shan't take y' time. Busy man. Listen, uh. Paf told me. Straight's a gun barrel. Wouldn't be kept. Ready to pack up. Leave. Wanted to know how I felt. Me?"

He sat back, breathed in, tried to pull the trouser over his knee.

"Glad it's over with," he said, still in a smile of pale blue eyes, but with heat too near. "I'm no good, y' see? No good. Been to doctors. No go. Like a woman, no hole. Blocked up. Can't do, that's me. Can't get a beat. Finish. I told her, I says, find yourself somebody. Married, she says. But I'll tell you when. Tell you who. Best electrical engineer in the country. Mm? Earn good money. Mm? 's use? I'm no good."

His eyes closed and he might have been asleep, but suddenly he sat forward, staring the palest blue ruin of grief.

"Wanted you to know, that's all," he said. "In a way I'm glad. Don't blame you. You're better than a lot. They'd talk. I'd, by Christ, I would, I'd murder the lot. She's worth 'em all."

He got up and leaned on the desk for a moment, turned on one arm, and pushed himself away to the door, blundered against the jamb.

"Now the police," he said. "Best thing. Get it over."

"Police?" I said, and went over to him. "Why, police?"

"Got my hands round her neck," he whispered, smiling the blue, serene stare and tears bright on cheekbones. "Heard it go. Told you. I'm finished. Get it over."

22

As a flourish from the quill of mighty Cervantes, Brother Little Mountain came from the forest, speaking soft to Hasdrubal in hoof and thrash over fallen timber, sliding on hinds down to the froth of stony shallows to cross the Pichileufu.

We had just dragged the last wagon out on the other side, going toward Vuriloche to buy stores for the few days between us and home, and we shouted to him, and he waved, and sat there, reins loose, a big man in a black cassock and shovel-brimmed hat, with a cowhide bundle tied both sides of the saddle, reading a little book in the palm of his hand, waiting until Hasdrubal, with her muzzle in the stream, was quite sure she had drunk enough, and his patience a wonder of saints to see.

There was a mule for you.

Eighteen hands of patchy gray and every bone in show, with teeth to pull a screamer from Hell, and a long tail she kept still until you were near enough for a flick that would knock you silly, nobody could do anything with her, not the peons with lovetalk, or Lal with dips of honey, and surely not Brother Little Mountain.

"She is the world of original sin," he said, when he slid off. "A hoof in each corner, and watch them. A thoroughly dangerous, ungrateful, ridiculous animal. Obdurate. A sly talent for comedy. The laugh of an idiot. And wholly lovable.

In her own time, but remark this, she takes me where I wish to go. How could I ask for more? I give her nothing except weight, and work."

"Hasdrubal," Lal said. "Why did you call her that? And how does an 'it' become 'she'? Mules are not one or the other, are they, poor things?"

"She is undoubtedly handmaiden of Baal," Brother Little Mountain said. "Or, let us say, a helpmeet. 'It,' but certainly not. 'She,' without equivocation. An 'it' could not assert itself. But she has five hats and two wreaths. She must wear one every day, or not a move. 'She,' beyond question."

That day she had her ears pushed through a little straw hat with three black and white eagle feathers in the band, and nothing would have it off till the sun was red, and Tamaño had let the bellmare go with the troop to night pasture. Only then, she put her head down, and Brother Little Mountain took off the hat, careful to let her see he put it into one of the hide bundles, and talking his nonsense to her the whole time.

"Dog Latin," he said. "It soothes her, though it wouldn't surprise me if she knew what I was saying. As I told you, she's an idiot. But I have learned to be careful of idiots. I am one myself."

"Well, good gracious," Lal said. "How are you an idiot?"

He had a smile to make you ashamed of something, a soft knife in the heart.

"Here is my parish," he said, and raised his arms to the pampas all round us. "Where are my people? Where are the souls who need me? I must build my church. Where? The enquiry of an idiot."

"Come, you," Lal said. "A special asado tonight. Quail we caught today. And I have made a rice pudding with dates and raisins and ginger and honey. Do you like Turkish coffee?"

Brother Little Mountain sat back on the bundle and laughed quietly at the sky.

"You fill my mouth before I eat," he said. "Where do you find dates and Turkish coffee?"

"My husband is an importer," Lal said. "If there is anything you would like, only say. We have got a little of everything. But we are not Roman Catholics. I am sorry."

"You have a Church," he said. "Or you would not give so much respect to mine."

"I am Church of Cambria," Lal said. "My husband is Baptist."

"Anglo-Saxons," he said.

"Not," I said.

"English," he said, bending forward, open-eyed, a large shadow in sunset.

"Not," I said.

He sat back, and the smile was felt, even in darkness.

"Then somewhere in the British workbox," he said. "Steam, iron, noise."

"Good," Lal said. "Cambria. One of the countries of Britain."

"Ah," he said, and put the back of his hand up to his forehead. "*Pais de Gales.*"

"*Galenses* they call us here," Lal said. "Originally of Gaul. But I wonder."

He stood, but he seemed larger than the hills behind.

"I shall swim," he said. "When the quail are ready, I shall be here. Permit me."

"A good one," Lal said, listening to him scraping through loose stones. "I wish we were something, too."

"Well, aren't we?" I said. "Good God, what more do we want? I have got you and the boy. What more? Baptist, Church of Cambria, where are we different? Really, what more do we want?"

"I wish we were something, that's all," Lal said, and sprinkling the birds with salted water and herbs. "A chapel we have got, and who is in it? Where is the preacher? Can't afford one. They have all got to have their pay. I wonder how much pay this one gets."

"Ask him," I said.

"Rude," she said. "But I like the Roman Catholic churches

we went to. You did, too. Grethe told me the priests have no pay. Only an allowance from the collection. Some of them were fat, indeed."

"This one isn't small about the barrel, either," I said.

"I told Tamaño to wash for him," Lal said. "His hat was an inch in dust. His coat isn't better. Why do they wear black? It shows."

"It tells everybody who he is," I said. "Some of ours wear anything. Who knows who they are? A collar back to front on Sundays. And everything back to front for the rest of the week. Until you can't believe them. It isn't in their lives. Why should it be in yours?"

"Well, I wish we were something, anyway," Lal said. "We used to go to chapel with Mama. Very good, too. But I think she would have enjoyed the Roman Catholic church much more. I enjoyed those early mornings with Grethe. I felt cleaner. She isn't Catholic, either. She's Lutheran. A sin, I suppose, to go. But we didn't care. You didn't, either, did you, those couple of times?"

"You are coming nearer every day," I said, and surprised.

"No," Lal said. "We never took Communion there, and we never confessed. We only enjoyed it. I only missed our singing. But I felt much nearer to God. And if it isn't that, then what takes you there?"

"Do you want to be a Catholic?" I asked her, straight.

"I wouldn't mind," she said. "Only a few minutes more for the potatoes and you can call everybody."

But she was too careless in speaking of something else in the same tone, so I knew she had thought long, and even worried, though not a word to me. Then was not the time to talk, and I am not sure what we might have decided, except that the memory has always been a small comfort, anyway.

While we picked the quail, Brother Little Mountain told us he had ridden south and east for months, looking for a good place to start a school, but with small hope. Families were stretched with leagues between, the few Army camps had no use for schools, though makeshift classes were looked after by officers' wives, and in the villages not many had interest in putting their children to books.

"Why is it so necessary to have a school, first?" Lal asked him. "Isn't a church more useful?"

"A church, you mean a building," Brother Little Mountain said. "I am the Church here. I don't need a building. I need children to teach. But there's great use in building for a school. It becomes a church. Ten children are ten souls. Ten souls will each create a better world about them, and only ten times ten are a hundred. Where, anywhere in this land do you find a hundred educated souls? On the coast, among your people? But they don't want me. Where else? In Vuriloche? A seasonal flow of Indios. For more than half the year the school would be empty. Protestants and nonconformists close their eyes to me. That's why I was unprepared for this hospitality. Many pass by. Such a pleasant surprise. It's uncommon, may I say?"

"You must feel disappointed," Lal said. "Are you often discouraged? Or sad?"

Brother Little Mountain laughed, picking a drumstick clean.

"We learn to weep for the correct reasons," he said. "Discouraged, no. Sad, never. Somewhere I am needed. That's why I'm here. Searching. All that saddens me is passing time. But have no doubt Hasdrubal will someday take me there. It's her duty. After all, a half-brother of hers took the Son up to Jerusalem."

Lal looked at me across the fire, the stare that seemed to go darker with a smile somewhere, an amaze, a small joy, and a question.

"Miss Lewis," she said quietly, and turned to him. "Have you been down to the City of the Mill? It's the Colony of Sixteenth October. Ours. Cambrian. One of our teachers has got a school there."

"That side, no, I haven't been," he said, but he stopped chewing and no smile. "If the pupils are Cambrian, would I be welcome?"

Lal took the big pie-dish from Tampoco.

"You could try," she said. "She's only a small one. I doubt if she would eat you."

Before light next morning, Tambien brought the coffee and a kettle of water for Lal's *maté*, and said the Reverend Brother thanked us for our generosity, and implored our forgiveness for not saying thanks in person, but he was going direct to the Colony.

Lal smiled, a sleepy one, and stretched, a beauty.

"I knew he would," she said. "And you'll see, Miss Lewis won't send him off."

We got to Vuriloche, a little place, of a few flat fronts in wood and a couple of wine shops and warehouses in those days, and we were tempted to ride the extra miles north to Little Looking Glass and Angharad's house, but it would have made us a month late at home, so we bought stores, and shoed the teams, and south we went. Lake Nahuel Huapi was always a love of Lal's, and the morning we reached the hillbrow we looked back to keep it in memory, almost green, miles across, and flowing west toward deep blue islands and the mountains still violet in early light. All day we bumped over the track in the forest beside Lake Gutierrez, and then Mascardi, named for the martyrs, and we made camp beside a waterfall, and Tamaño pointed out where the priests could have crossed between the peaks from Chile.

"They must have been brave men," Lal said, looking at the forest dark about us, and the lake white in moonlight. "They had nobody, and nothing to eat anywhere. And those Indios, too. They did terrible things to men in those days. Give them a chance, they still do."

"We returned their gifts, Mistress," Tamaño said, one of the few times I ever heard a hint of argument, and the only time I heard any of them confess to Indio blood. "They even took our children."

"Yes, very well," Lal said, to stop it. "But a priest is a priest."

"Not to us, Mistress," Tamaño said. "My father told us

they were spies. His father told him. They go first to touch the children's heads and heal the sick. Then the others come to kill. Who knows the difference?"

"Well, not in our time," Lal said. "Would you call Brother Little Mountain anybody's spy?"

Tamaño nodded at the peak.

"Who rides a mule is fit for anything," he said. "I offered him a good horse of mine."

"What did he say?" Lal asked.

"The mule would take him twice as far and cost half as much," Tamaño said. "Which father sends his child to be taught by one who rides a mule?"

"Hopeless," Lal said, when he walked off. "About horses, there is no snob to compare with a Gaucho. But I am afraid he will have a hard time down there. Everybody isn't like us. And that old mule will put everybody against him."

But we had a bad surprise, too. Davies, Tom Tiddler's, my manager at El Bolson, told us Miss Lewis had died during the early winter in Gaiman, over in the Atlantic Colony. The women in the City of the Mill had tried to keep the school going, but none of them were teachers, and Mog, Moke, had gone across in the snow to try to find somebody, and Issylt John had come back with them.

"Issylt," Lal said, frowning. "Is the girl sixteen?"

"Not much more, I suppose, indeed," Davies said. "The wife was very worried, here. She wanted to go, but the snow was too thick. Thick till ten days ago, too. And more to come from the looks, yes."

He was right. We only stayed long enough for the asado, and by evening we were down near Epuyen, and the snow wetted our noses. We got into the forest, and gathered every stick and chopped more, ready for a week, but Tambien shook his head, and sniffed, and said it would rain before morning. It did, and we were in mud to the axle until we came on hard ground just beyond Cholila, and Lal, riding in front of the leading wagon, turned to me and waved, laughing, pointing down in the dip.

Dugald Mael MacGrannoch, Vyrnwy, and Maifron Austin were riding, split.

We were in a shout and dance for minutes there, and Vyrnwy said he brought spare teams to pull us out of mud, and Dugald came because he wanted to, and Maifron was sent by her mother because Lal might need somebody.

"Where are your peons, girl?" Lal said, looking for them.

"That old Catholic priest has got them," Maifron said. "Every man down there is working for him. Classrooms for the children. Dormitories. Goodness knows what. Vyrnwy came only to bring the teams. Dugald we met in Geza's. If not, everybody would be here to meet you."

"I had to come," Dugald said. "Another wonderful year, thanks to you. And I've a new wife. Never thought I would. But she's too good for anybody else. Would you ever guess?"

Him and his guesses I could have sent to the Devil, then, poor boy, but he was all smiles and tender with thought.

"She was helping Alys and James Smallcote with the babies, and round the house," he said, as if I was far away. "They asked me to stay a couple of nights. I did. The second afternoon I took her hand, and I asked if she'd marry. She smiled and I had the nod. So I'll get my stores and take her with me on the way back. I've plenty for a woman, now. Thanks to you. You know her. Her name's Michaye. There's none so lovely."

Ink silk.

As one remembers crossroads in going toward a place he fears, so I hold clear in mind those times I felt I must become Indio. Quick as a sneeze upon me and almost as sudden gone but the struggle was worse each time, lasting longer, and they ripped the mind and I had to turn this way and that trying to shake the memory away. No doubt Lal and the boy helped, and having to put my mind to business and the wants of the day, and calling myself a fool did a lot, though nothing took out the fear to think that one day, never mind anybody, I might go.

Looking at Dugald I knew the time was near. Never mind Lal or the baby, or anybody or anything. Nothing much was holding me, only, I suppose, that one calling me a fool inside. Three persons, at least, must be in everybody, for I had an Indio screaming to be off, and a carpenter-turned-business-man ashamed to be in witness, though idle, and another, never much help, but telling the Indio to shut his mouth, and calling the idler every fool in Christendom. But I stood there, letting it happen, listening.

Only a thought of Michaye, of the long black plaits, and Lliutro was there, warm beside me, kneeling across me while I slept, turning me in waking with Adam in pierce of wonder only a little less than flame, in fire of juice from the Tree and a drown in glory, and a softness of fingers at the nape, and sleep then, or a dream, part of the Garden and all of Heaven. A taste of blood in meat, and the heave of a galloping pony, and trees calling to me, and boughs and leaves burning scent of apples in the toldos—*ichabod!*—the vision was in and about, and no plea of mine to set against.

23

That time with Lal I suppose was the happiest of my life. The house was joy to the eye, and the garden had become a pleasure ground of bees, a place of small lawns and rock steps, roses everywhere, and in between piled boulders with spills of blossom in crevices, big beds of all the flowers we could find at the seedman's place, and more we gathered from the forest and up on the mountains. The days seemed drugged with honey. Often I went back to the house and found Lal somewhere, and leaned against her, no words, but only to lean. At the office she always came in quietly and put a hand on my shoulder and I turned only to kiss, and went back to work, and it was enough. At night we were one, and my body seemed hers, and hers mine, and the link almost unfelt because unthought. Not once can I remember thinking of Lliutro except with fondness for a lost one, though not with a want to see her and never to send a message.

Thank God we were in splendid time to see the snowdrops we had planted about the little valleys between the boulders. Snowdrops grew at Maes Corwen because Lal's grandmama planted them from the ship, but they were not to compare with ours grown in that black soil of a thousand years of autumn. Indeed, to walk in our place from the back gate was like coming into a farm from this Valley, or at any rate, what this Valley once was. There were ricks of rich hay, and chickens in hundreds, and a company of roosters in splendor of plumage, ducks and geese at the pond, turkeys by the score, cattle in the corral and horses in the stalls, and for comfort, the farm's own scent, that royal ammoniac blessing that comes of happy life and a natural folding of days. Pigs we had down at the end of the vegetable garden, and there again was a different smell, mixed with green wealth from beds of all in leaf and root, of hams and bacon, sausage and brawn, not yet made, but kept clean by water and a bit of work, for pigs will give thanks and far better meat and savor for a little care, and even more if there is something of affection. The arguments I have heard, but the facts are not to be dodged, and Lal and I on our evening walks about the place always had a word with every animal in the way, and a scratch for its ears, and every chicken, duck, and turkey followed us because they knew they would have a throw of corn at the end, and the sows in farrow came to meet us, sure of hot milk and porridge after, and they loved their necks rubbed and their bottoms smacked and to be treated not merely as friends, but part of the family.

Daffodils we had planted in clumps wherever grass grew, with narcissus of various kinds and in shadow we put the violets, in any corner honeysuckle and fuchsia, with a companionship of forsythia and plum and other shrubs, and in the cool beneath, lilies that liked gray light. Tulips by the thousand made a show for a month, there, but Lal had a special fondness for the mauve and the white, with the tall daffodil and a couple of narcissus in the plain crystal bowl on the dining table. When all of them were gone, we had the early roses, and the carnations, and delphiniums—o, the delicacy of a blue, bluest blueness!—mixed with a tiny white flower we called Bridal Veil, that grew thick in every bed and made each blossom in the garden look as if it floated on a still, white cloud. In early morning the roses could make you drunk, and at night the stocks and honeysuckle, and the sleeping breath of all our other friends would make you want to sit up beyond bedtime not to miss a moment.

Work had not slacked, for the country was growing and everything was in want, though not in quantity enough because there were not the people, yet the mileage to supply was the same for one, a dozen, or a thousand. That, as Moishe said, made the work and set the price. Good men were in charge at our depots in Port Madryn and the City of Lewis, and I had men I could trust in all our places up and down the Cordilleras. We had the Fords running between the City of Lewis and the City of the Mill, and when the first trucks came in that year, we thought it a miracle we could put in an order on any Friday, and have the goods on the dot of the following Monday night, direct from the Atlantic coast. But when Moishe wanted to retire we felt almost as if the sun no longer shone.

"Why must you go?" I asked him, the only time I dared intrude, for if we were partners, I knew little about the way he lived.

"Tired," he said. "Not tired of using time. Time, that's good. Money, it's the sister. Time and money, it's the best. But they got to be used. Here, who's using? Us? Who else? Why I should be tired, nobody else?"

"A lot of people are earning a living," I said. "We are, too."

Again that chin almost turned to meet a shoulder.

"A living, what is?" he said. "They should use time? And what? Sheep companies, you got a manager. A manager, who is? God? And how many? Two? Six? Ten? Managers, they should be kings? Of what? Dungpiles? How many Cambrians they got their own place? Add up a hundred. Two hundred? The money, they should sell sheep, wool, it's the same amount for the sheep company? Not. It's more? Never. So? We work to supply little kings, they should manage a company? With a fat wife? How many little kings? How many fat wives? They should get fat, but the Indios, they are thin? So the children, there's a school? In a school, there should be scholarships? With scholarships, you got boys and girls in the university? How many? Who? In how many years, how many? How many millions, the little kings, the fat wives? How much the percentage? How many babies they died, no doctor? Huw, a son you got. Tell him. Me, I'm tired."

"Where will you go?" I asked him.

"First, I take Merlin round the world," he said. "The harp, it makes the music. They listen? Who? Who wants music? Sheep managers? Fat wives? Patagonia? *Narish.*"

"The old boy is a bit cranky," Lal said. "We have got peace here, and everybody is doing well. What more does he want?"

"More for the brain," I said. "Sheep companies have got a few peons for how many hundred thousand sheep? But if one man owned only five thousand, it would give him and his family a good living, and employment for others in help. Two hundred thousand sheep, one manager and a few peons does very little for a country. But forty owners of five thousand sheep, that's forty good houses, and families, and children to school. Multiply by the number of companies. Think of the number of others ready to follow an example. Is a sheep company an example?"

"Well, we have got one, boy," Lal said. "And multiply five thousand, too."

"We are the owners," I said. "Not managers. And I haven't got a fat wife, either."

"Wait you a month or two," Lal said, and swinging the plait. "I believe I have got the sister of that one in by there."

Well, we had an asado that Sunday to beat everything ever seen in the valley, though nobody knew what it was for, except, I suppose, Brother Little Mountain, and there was no use trying to hide anything from that one. But I am sure Lal must have told him, though he never said a word to me. Miss Lewis' school was different again, divided for boys and girls, with dormitories and classrooms, a playing area and stables, cooking shed, bakehouse and refectory, and a garden everywhere. Each child had a job to do, even the smallest, and in the evening, before the day scholars went home, all of them went to pick up every dead leaf, or weed, twig, and the bonus buds on carnations or roses, and so the school was always a rest for the spirit to go in, and nobody more restful than Brother Little Mountain. But he had a lot of trouble with parents, to start. They were all worried about the gossip. Where it began, nobody ever found out, but where there is a dead soul, there is always a dead tongue, and a lot of people heard that he was servant of the Devil, to turn every little girl into a scarlet woman and every boy into a bondsman of Rome. In the first few weeks after he got there, only Indio children stayed, and they were looked after by Kalata and her sisters. Issylt John, brought by Mog, Moke, took day classes of girls, and the boys were lettered by Rupayan's youngest brother, Catriel, a pupil of Miss Lewis'. But when it was found that Brother Little Mountain was building classrooms and this, that, and the other, by himself, and taking notice of nobody, and having morning and evening services on his own in the shrine he built himself, and eating nothing except what he could pluck from the wild, and drinking snow-water, and coming to be thinner than his size, then Issylt, that firm one, put down a foot.

"If you are working to make a school, then be part," she said, one cold afternoon. "You are standing there, blue. Hammering and sawing about the place to drive anybody to drink. If you want to teach, then come in and be useful. But nothing about religion. Not a word about Catholics. The first sign, you will go."

Mistress Issylt, about seventeen and severe as seventy, gave the boys classes to him, and curiously, the rooms he had built by himself, without being asked, were just the right size with space for more, and the entire school was able to stretch legs for the first time, and girls were by themselves, and boys were on their own. Well, of course, after about a month, there were ten at his services, and then thirty, and children were brought by their mothers to be catechised, and at the winter close, when Issylt went up to Buenos Aires for her degree, Brother Little Mountain had a school, and if not a church, then a respectable shrine of about a hundred people, that when spring brought a thaw, were nearer two hundred, most of them our people, those strict ones, of the chapel.

"My peons are taking their families," Lal said. "I don't know what to say."

"Say nothing," I said. "Religion is their business to decide."

"They are Church of Cambria," she said. "Or they were. They are confessing, there, like Romans, would you believe it?"

"Find out where the Church of Cambria came from," I said. "Besides, what have Indios to do with Cambria? Any more than Rome? Drop it, now."

Though we were not of the Church, Brother Little Mountain knew we were friends, and when Lal invited him to join us, then on most nights he came to the house for dinner, and if we were glad of a good mind to talk to, at the same time we knew we were being called Romanizers, not to our faces, but when doors were closed and traps could clap at will.

"Because I am giving a good man something to eat, I am Romanizing?" Lal said. "Good. Let us have another. Nobody will ever bring me to Rome. But nobody, not a thousand Romans, shall go hungry from my house. Now then, for everybody."

"And push a thumb," I said.

"Ten thumbs on each hand everyone of them should have," Lal said, in charm of delicacy. "And push twenty, and I will help."

That was the year of the war, though we had the news weeks after, for if the Fords cut time between us and the Atlantic coast, still there was the sea voyage to Buenos Aires, to say nothing of delays on the way.

But at least Moishe had to come back to the office, and there was plenty to do in supply of meat and fats, for suddenly the world had come hungry, though half the ships we loaded went down with a torpedo, and sometimes it seemed insane to weigh another kilo. Many of our boys went back to join the Army, but Lal would hear not a word of my going, and Doli told Volde that if he tried to join the Russians, she would go on the streets.

"You are of Argentina," she shouted, that night. "You married me to protect me. Here. Not a lot of old Russians, God knows where. Find out where your duty is. Then do it."

Volde held out his hands.

"All I did was speak of my country, and my family and my friends," he told us. "I would love to help. So she assaults me?"

"With a pick," Doli said, still in a temper. "I know you. One day, a thought. The next, a wish. The third day? Gone. Not this time, my lad. You are staying here. With me. In our country. If your family want to come, a welcome they shall have. Why are we hearing about them now? Why not before?"

Well, when Russia collapsed, I thought Volde would commit suicide. Doli had a terrible time, there, and she had to hide the drink, for what good it did, and I had to put Barres to keep an eye on the office, because he was coming to work black-drunk day in and out, until she had to send a private message, asking me to go to Buenos Aires to see what I could do.

"This is family, not business," Lal said. "You will have to go. Poor Doli. Bring her back with you. She has had trouble enough. And poor you. A long way to go. But worth it, yes? I will be waiting. Fatter."

Up I went, and Doli was almost a lunatic, there.

"He went," she said, in the dark room, and her whisper seemed to be color of the shadows. "Went. Not a word. I've had the police. Everybody. No sign. I told them at the office to say nothing. He wasn't doing much, anyway."

"I will do what I can," I said. "Be ready to come back with me. Lal wants you down there."

"I'm glad somebody wants me," she said, in the same whisper, and not a move. "As Moishe went, once. Remember? That poor girl. I've been thinking about her, too."

Well, I knelt beside her and put an arm around her, and kissed her cheek, and eh! but she had lost weight.

"There are plenty of us," I said. "Sit you tidy, now. When I have news, I will be here."

"Stay here, Huw," she said. "I am frightened of an empty house. Don't go to that old hotel. Stay here. Please. I will be glad to know somebody is under the same roof."

Lessons I have learned in my life, but not enough I suppose. It was a big place and she had a couple of women looking after it, but their rooms were down in the coach-house.

"Very well," I said. "But I will be late, sure. So don't wait up."

Everybody I tried and I had plenty of friends, but nowhere, in shipping lists or Consulates or among the agents was there any trace of Voldemar Zhdanov. Yet once again, Von Gelsbach helped me, this time by accident. Shipping losses made deliveries by sea a matter of luck, and insurance rates were almost cent per cent. He was going to Sweden as military attaché, and he wanted to know the safest and best way for Grethe and the children. It was no trouble to us, and he got everything he needed in an envelope that afternoon and while he stood there, I was speaking to the Russian secretary from Volde's office. She was in tears for him, and Russia, and her job, but I told her not to worry, and to work with Barres, and she would soon be the new manager.

"Zhdanov," Von Gelsbach said, when I went back to my office. "I seem to have heard that name."

He took the particulars we had, and an orderly came next morning with a letter to knock breath out of me. Volde had been a student priest—well I understood his distrust of Rome!—and sent to prison as a rebel, escaped to Shanghai and entered Argentina on a Dutch ship as a seaman. His father was friend of the new Russian leader after the Czar, and he had gone back to Russia with papers issued in the London Embassy.

If that had been all, at least we would have had a stitch or two of doubt, a little hope that he would come back to us.

But underneath, Von Gelsbach wrote that in a dispatch just received, Volde was identified among the killed, with his father, in fighting with the Bolsheviks. It was the first time I saw the word and I had to ask if it was a new race on earth. But I was thinking of him in that crate of a boat with Jeff and Michaye, and hearing a mighty voice in anthem on dark mornings roaming over the song of *maté* kettles, and his laughter, and the big hands always in open-fingered tenderness to touch Doli.

What to say took blood from me, for I knew the heart would shrivel in her.

Certainly there was no excuse to stay in Buenos Aires another moment. In sudden thought I called at Dr. Kasanevich's house and found him in.

"Tell her," he said. "She is in a state of mind to accept. It will put an end to doubt, at least, and the rest is hope. Nobody stops hoping. The clock, and her family will help to heal. She has survived one deep grief. It will help to surmount this. What of your problem?"

"Not even the smallest trouble, even in the middle of Indios everyday," I said. "I believe I am well over it. Perhaps my wife and boy, and the business have filled my mind."

But at that quiet moment, God knows how, a terrible smile was somewhere near, not that I could see, but somewhere I could feel, or I knew it was there without being able to point where it was, and I was frightened only in those seconds out of speech and far beyond wits.

Perhaps he saw into my eyes, but he came to stand in front of me, looking over his glasses.

"It's been in my mind to visit Moishe," he said, and very kind. "Tell him to expect me in the warmer end of spring. You've talked enough about catching fish. I'll catch one for a change."

Direct I went to Doli's place, and to see the steady back and top hat of Benoit in and out of the lamplight, with all the other carriages, was a relief at least, and reminder that the world was not yet a madhouse, though I knew at the moment how differently others were living, and I saw Lal by the fire, and Vyrnwy in the forge, and Donato in the new shop, and Saiheque in the toldo, and I could even think of Lliutro, but I was perfectly at ease, without fear or worry, and that was the surprise. Of her, and remembering everything, I could think easily and even affectionately, and yet, not thinking of her, or Indios or anything to do with them, I had almost sprung from my hide.

A strange machine is the mind, indeed, and I had to set my face again to meet Doli.

Thankful I was when the woman told me she asked to be excused and had gone to bed, and my dinner was ready. There were letters to look at, and I read the morning's paper about the bombardment of Paris, and I remembered every instant of the day, putting aside with anger any ridiculous thought when women and children might be dying in the ruins of their houses, or perishing with fear in shelter somewhere, and the tens of thousands of men killed, multilated or blinded that day in battle. A hot bath and a comfortable bed seemed excess of luxury, and I went to sleep thankful that Lal and the boy would never know the sound of guns.

If it was memory of the day, or other times come back in a drowse, but I was uncertain if I was still in a dream, or awake and brainless, but I thought at first that Lliutro was with me, warm silk, strength and wonder together.

"Huw, I didn't mean to wake you," Doli said. "I was cold. And lonely."

She was warm, with the glorious smell of a woman, and near to tears. She had still to be told about Volde. Some, I suppose, would have flung away the bedclothes and stamped off to sleep in the coal shed, but when pity is in the heart, and Adam is firm in pulse, and Doli is the woman, then I am not the one, and I put my arms about her, and she came to me in the deep, endless shudder of one lost, home at last, at peace, and she strained, and while she cried, I slept.

Next morning I was out before she woke and I left a message for her to pack and be ready to sail that night. Benoit brought her to the quay, and I waved from the office window and she went aboard. We took on a last moment cargo of pineapple and bananas, rarities for us in that time, and sailed with the moon. Doli held to her cabin through the voyage, but on the last day, a morning of sun, sea without a ripple, when we turned to enter the bay, she came up in a striped dress, calm, smiling.

"Well," she said, and came to stand and put an arm through mine at the rail. "I have slept like one waiting for the Call. Did you miss me?"

"Of course," I said, looking at the rested eyes, sleepy still, in bluest smile. "Feel better?"

"In my life, never better," she said, and stood close. "Did I dream, or was it true? Or an angel?"

"A dream," I said. "But if angels are like you, I am in coils to be up there."

"Lal," she said.

"Between you and me," I said. "A man and woman. Nobody else."

She pressed my hand and stood straight, and walked away. Still I had to tell her about Volde, but I could see the crowd to meet us, and I knew everybody would be there, and it was not the time, so to Hell, I left it, though I had to think again that evening at Solva's place. We had the guest rooms, off the main house, and after dinner, Doli went to bed and I stayed talking with Oracio. By that time we had the telegraph, and the boy rode in with a message from Moishe in Rawson to welcome us, with a promise to be in the Andes at the end of the week. Off I went with my lamp, but all evening I had been thinking that if Doli could be brave enough to come to me, I should at least show myself not shy, so round the patio to her room I was crunching gravel not to be too much of a surprise, and three shadows sitting on the step stood up.

The three peons I had forgotten.

Caleleütral stood aside when I pointed to the door, and I knocked.

"It's me," I said. "Is it too late to talk?"

"O," she said, soft, but near. "Well. Not too late. But they are outside. I am in my own country, now. With my own people. And still I have got to tell Lal."

"Well," I said. "But there is something I have got to tell you, too."

"Let it rest till the morning, then, is it?" she said, a Mama speaking to one with a running nose. "Good night, Huw."

Like that, not even a dog with enough tail to put between his legs, I went from there, any dream of fondness a mildew.

Mog, Moke, and Idwyn worked the cars by then, and we started in the dark, and by night we were home, and the noise we made got everybody out of bed, so we had an asado with sunrise, the only one I can remember, and Lal wearing two ponchos and a guanaco cloak over a nightdress, and hair in a blow about her shoulders, and I was wondering how I could think of anybody else.

"What, with Volde?" she whispered, when we stood close in the noise.

"Tell you later," I said. "Doli doesn't know."

She frowned up at me.

"Of course she knows," she said. "He's dead, isn't he?"

"Who told her?" I said, empty with wonder.

"What need to tell?" Lal said. "She knows. If you were dead, don't you think I'd know?"

It was time to eat tender steak on crusty bread, and talk of this and that, and drink wine while the sun began to warm our backs, and speak in sorrow for Europe in twist and crunch of war.

As if it was now, I can see that first snowflake falling, floating, white, a warning.

"Early," Tampoco said, at the sky. "A hard winter. The sun looks for guanaco."

"Well, everything is ready with us," Lal said, in the house. "Plenty of everything, even if winter is a twelve-month long. Nothing to fear anywhere. The same up and down. And the school. I have seen to it."

There is no feeling like coming home. Even the smell, of bark endearing the fireplace, and late roses and cloves in the pot-pourri hidden in the cupboards, and cedar shelves, furniture polish, leather, and the pages of books all make familiar gift of welcome, but something is over, another fragrance, of the mistress in hours of sewing, or tidying, or only her pretty skirts passing through, and her gentle hand is everywhere, for the touch of a woman is plainer than print, and a house is a tomb without her.

We were both ready to sleep till next morning, and Lal came back from the bath, and I was sitting on the side of the bed while she brushed out the plaits, and telling her about the journey, and we heard screaming, thin, as if a hare was caught in a trap, but it went on too long. Lal stopped brushing, and frowned at me under a fall of hair. Before we could move, somebody was running, and hitting the front door, and men were shouting outside. Lal threw down the brush and ran in the bathrobe, and I put trousers on, boots, a jacket, and went through the back, but the noise was on the other side, and even while I turned I knew it was Doli. The crowd made way and I stepped over wailing, kneeling women, and the three peons, and Lal looked up at me. Doli lay on the floor and the right leg was dark, swollen the size of three. Oranges, bananas, and pineapples from the straw basket lay over the floor.

"A spider," Lal whispered and nodded at a crush by the wall. "O, Huw. It was in the basket. Life isn't in her."

My knife was a razor, and I ran a match flame down the edge, and slit into the vein on the inside of the thigh. Only thick drops came out, and then a fluid. The old Indio laundry-woman looked at Lal, and at me, and shook her head.

"Her mother called," she said. "She felt the wound and lay down, and woke up. Too late."

Lal came into my arms, and I lifted her with no sound, and took her into the house and put her on the bed, and kissed both hands, and ran back to Doli's room. The women had covered her, and wrapping a sheet, and the youngest was breathing long and slow into her mouth.

"No use," the old woman said. "The *paico* would have given her life. A spider stops breath and blood."

It was the first time I had heard the word. Everything went from my mind.

"What do you know of *paico?*" I asked her.

She stared at me, wide, the Indio eyes, and ran.

The peons stood in my way.

"She must be taken to Maes Corwen," Caleleütral said. "She will go beside her mother."

"Leave her," I said. "The Mistress Lal will decide."

More shouting started at the gate, and I went out to send them all to the Devil, but I saw Cerri Borth, one of our men from the City of Lewis, coming down the path on a horse in wisps of lather, and he saw me and pulled short.

"Mr. Morgan," he said, and slid off, tired. "Snow is on us just before Llangiñeu. The cars won't come through. Idwyn sent me. He wants mules. Moishe is very ill. I don't know what it is, indeed. But a doctor should go. Idwyn shook his fist to be sure to tell you."

"Get your mules," I said to Mog, Moke. "Tell Rupayan to bring out the troop. Batancal, Nüfcütun, everybody, out. Catriel, go for Brother Little Mountain. He can join us as we pass."

Doli lay as though in sleep, no line, no shadow to tell she was less than the lovely old girl she had always been, and I went to my knees and touched her hands, still warm, and sent her my love, that was nothing, and went from there in brine.

Lal lay as I had put her, staring at the ceiling, dry. In my arms she made no move. Her mouth was mutton to kiss.

"Moishe is caught in snow," I said. "He is ill. I am taking

the men and Brother Little Mountain. He is the only one knowing anything of doctoring. Have a place ready. I will be back quick as I can."

"Doli," she said. "O, Dol', my little one."

"You used to teach the children," I said. "Remember? Up there under the trees at Gaiman. 'In The Midst Of Life We Are In Death.' You taught them. Remember? Remember coming from the Singing Mountain? 'Thy Rod and Thy Staff'? When is it time to believe? Before the mist? In the whiteness, and no hope? Or after? She is with Volde. What would she have done if she had stayed here? Let them be together. And wait for me. Your boy is looking for you."

From the deepest guts I kissed her, and I went in next door to give the boy a lift and a shake and put him back to the girl all smiles. Outside I took Tamaño, Tampoco, and Tambien a few steps and looked at them.

"You will stay here," I said. "You are responsible to me. Wash all that fruit in permanganate. See nothing else crawls in it. Take care of the Mistress Lal and my son. Till later."

"Go with God," Tamaño said. "The Mistress Lal is safe."

24

Snow was light when we turned out for the City of the Mill, but clouds were black over the pampas, and Mog, Moke, driving us, shook his head.

"I will feed the mules nine months and use them for three," he said. "Nobody shall say a word to me again. They wanted me to sell them. But with them I started, and had a business. Now, you will see. Cars won't go beyond John Evans, the Mill. Mules will be in Llangiñeu tonight. See, now."

In fact, it was early in the morning, but without the mules and Rupayan and the Indios, we would never have got there, and most of us might never have got back.

We left the Fords where Brother Little Mountain and all the others waited, and snow was thick, and we rode in troops, more than two hundred altogether, for Ceri had shouted through the City of the Mill and passing the farms, and all the men dropped tools and ran for the stables. In the years, Moishe had made his place in the hearts of all of us, but none of us were sure how big until we knew he needed help.

Rupayan, Nüfcütun, Batancal, and young Catriel were guides, though how they saw, or knew where they were going, even if I was more of them than most, is still a mystery. We went over the mountains, of course, but we owed that to the horses and mules. We froze through the hours. Ice was hard in my boots, paining in my face, crinkling in the mane of my *criollo*, Huillque, and she cared nothing if I dozed, or slept or pretended to know where we were going. She followed those in front, though her pride was always to be with the leaders and there we always were. By morning we were going down to the flat, and when mist was paler, far off we saw the red points of fires and smoke blueing the snow mist, and five black blocks of the Fords with canvas roofs tenting over. They were off the track, for Idwyn had decided to cross hard ground he knew rather than tip up in a gulley. He came running through deep snow to meet us, and we would have cheered him, but the shouts stayed, and breath was louder.

We knew from the way he stood.

"I am sorry from the heart," he said. "He is gone from us. Not a word. Not even time for a prayer."

Brother Little Mountain went past on Hasdrubal, and Mihangel pointed to the only tent without a fire. We let the horses browse green bits under snow, but the mules were lined ready for packs.

Moishe seemed as if he had just fallen asleep. A guanaco rug was over him, and his little hands were very calm with him on the sheepskins. Like that I had seen him many a time having forty winks in the office.

Nothing to tell he was not going to waken.

El Pampero put a rough hand under the canvas to warn of snow.

"He must go decently," Idwyn said. "If you hadn't come, I'd have left him here with the Fords, see, and waited for a fair patch in the weather to bring him in. We can't dig. The ground is rock."

But I remembered an afternoon in the office.

"It should matter?" he said. "In the prison drain, so my mother and father. Me, I should be better? Let me face East and West. That's Moishe. It's enough. Anywhere."

A hill grew shadow behind us.

"No need to dig," I said. "Caves there are, and stones in plenty up by there, look. Find a cave facing the West. Nothing more could he want. He will rest where he was going. Where he built most and best."

While the Fords were unloaded we took floorboards from a couple of wagons and made a Star of Solomon about thirty feet between star points, and when the pieces fitted we dragged them to the top of the hill, and put in the supports and built stones about them to hold. A good soak of petrol was in the planks before they were nailed, and never mind twisted hands, but Mog, Moke, climbed up to nail them, with Batancal one side and Prosser John the other, and we sang "Jesus, lover of my soul," and I was thinking of Volde's voice, hymning somewhere.

"This man was Hebrew," Brother Little Mountain said, in Idwyn's guanaco cape blowing in a freeze, and the Book in his hands, that were almost hooks with cold, but no matter. "Some have suggested a form of service for the Unborn."

"Moishe was born," I said. "What he suffered, or his mother and father before him, none of us will know. We will put him here, in the middle of the land where he loved the people, and they loved him. Nothing of the Unborn. Let us have the Latin. If you have got a word of Hebrew, let it rest as a jewel. The best every one of us has got, that he shall have. Let this be another Gilgal. In the new world."

"Place of Joshua and the Twelve Stones," Idwyn said. "Hallelujah. You have chosen well."

Brother Little Mountain led us up to the cavern and we put Moishe to rest, head to the East, only a little way below the Star. All of us had a twig pulled from a shrub under snow, and we passed, old and young, bearded and not, and the green offerings piled in the cavern mouth, and their moisture ran as if the pampas wept with us, and snow touched, cold, a whisper to warn.

"In the beginning was the Word, and the Word was God," Brother Little Mountain sang, and the Latin echoed, and we answered.

Twelve of us had a rock at our feet to fill up the space.

"And the people came up, out of Jordan, and encamped

before Gilgal," Brother Little Mountain chanted, in the Hebrew. "And those twelve stones which they took out of Jordan, those they raised in Gilgal."

"Sion, lift up Thy voice," we sang, and went in a line with rocks to be chipped in rough size.

"And the Children of Israel hearkened, and Joshua spoke, saying, when your children shall ask in time to come what meaning have these stones, you shall tell them that Israel came over Jordan on dry land," Brother Little Mountain chanted, and signed to us to go, one by one, to fill the space with stones. "The Lord Thy God dried up the waters, and Israel passed across, even unto the smallest, humblest."

Moishe lay in there on his sheepskins, and the robe soft over him, and I set my stone over Rowland Jones' and Vyrnwy came behind, and Brother Little Mountain chanted again in the Latin, and Gilberto Bedwellty dry-walled the facing flat and fair, no room for fox or rat, and we went from there. A soaked twine stretched from the foot of the mount up to the first pile of stones, and I waited until everybody was in the saddle, and struck a match. The twine sparked and I ran to Batancal, holding Huillque. Flame under black smoke ate the length, up to the rock and over, and the Star's lowest point crackled and red leaves bloomed.

"I am the Rose of Sharon," Euros Morris sang, a lyric tenor, and we joined, and the column turned for the mountain, dark in cloud and the clothes of evening. Brightness shone behind us, though none turned, and hats and backs were red in flame, but Batancal swung golden reins to gallop over hard ground, and we followed. On the high slope before we slid down to the river bed, there we turned, and took off our hats, for the Star shone in tremendous golden blaze against snow clouds, white about, black above.

"All things come of Thee, and of Thine own have we given Thee," Idwyn called, in the Cambrian.

"Amen," we said.

"For we are strangers before Thee, and sojourners, as were all our fathers," Idwyn called, the trumpet note that puts bristles in the neck. "Our days on earth are a shadow, and there are none abiding."

"Let this place be called New Gilgal," Brother Little Mountain said, and signed in Blessing. "Rest, now, in peace. We shall think of Moishe with love, and in our prayers remember him."

"Amen," we said, and Rupayan's long Araucano scream warned of snow coming on a storm wind, and we sang Moishe's own favorite 'O, let us now to home,' turning down in slither, almost on top of one another, but if men make mistakes, horses seldom do. Huillque went, marvel she was, never a step wrong. If there are many times I have forgotten, that journey back is plain and white enough. We were passing through the City of the Mill late next afternoon, and Geza had hot rum and honey for us, and while they unloaded the mules, Brother Little Mountain had to be lifted off Hasdrubal and put in the back room with a dozen blankets, though if his voice was not in him, he still had a smile, but a bit pale, too, and I took Hasdrubal with me, and she had everything equal with Huillque.

All the way home I was thinking of Doli, that one, best of beauties, lovely old girl, and the world in grayness without her, and of Moishe, sleeping in New Gilgal, and wondering what I was to do without him.

Lal was like stone, sorry about Moishe, of course, but nothing more to feel. Doli had been buried the night before over on her place, and the garden was stripped of flowers, and with that first snow it looked as I felt.

"How will we tell Solva?" Lal said, that night. "A hundred letters I've torn in pieces."

"Wait, you," I said. "Her peons have gone."

"Gone?" Lal said, and pulled herself up on the pillows. "They would dare? No word to me?"

"They took flowers from Doli to put on your mother's grave," I said. "Who could stop them?"

"O, God, they will kill themselves," Lal whispered, and closed her eyes. "My fault. I should have thought more.

Couldn't you stop them? Offer any money for somebody to call them back."

"Twelve hours start in this weather?" I said. "Even your own three wouldn't try. You can't see a hand in front outside here."

Well, she was crying for hours, there, but it did her good, anyway, and next morning she was more herself, but quieter than I had ever seen her.

"When will you have to leave me to see to business?" she asked, looking through an iced window.

"I am not leaving here till the end of winter," I said. "Anything wanting a signature can be sent across. Anything needing a decision can be put in writing, and I shall reply. There is nothing to go wrong. When I go, you will come with me. We shall go to Europe, and back through the United States. Yes?"

She put an arm round my neck.

"Yes," she said. "You know who filled that basket for her, don't you? Me. I thought it was pretty. Pretty, mind. O, *Christ*."

"Leave it, now," I said. "We have got weary hearts. But we have got a boy, and somebody else on the way. Be thankful."

If I had known she was going over to Doli's place when I went down to Vyrnwy's, or along to the depots, there might have been something to be done. But for some reason she insisted on walking from the gate of Doli's place to the grave, about a mile, in that snow over rough ground no small matter, and so one night she was taken with pains, and when the women came out, they told me she had lost the baby.

Nothing to be done, nothing to say, for there are times when words are a noise, and an arm is not comfort, but a nuisance.

In the office was little to do after I had finished the mail, and riding a horse no longer came as exercise or novelty, and so in those days I learned to use my feet again and walked everywhere, and had the benefit of seeing so much more. The gardeners went back to work in the greenhouses and the place became a lot tidier, not that Lal was careless but she had interest only in the farm, and small matters such as seedlings and plants for next year's garden were forgotten, with the potting sheds, waterways, and drains. Once I found an overgrown wall or a fault in a stair, then day after day I looked for everything else, snow or not, and I was out of the house early and back late, but I knew the entire property foot by foot before I was much older, and anybody having pay from me did a real day's work for a change, inside when snow was too thick, outside when not. The old days of squatting through the hours in sheds to drink *maté* were over.

I have had plenty of time to wonder if Mr. Righteousness was right.

If those men had been idling in the sheds about the place, and nearer the stables, the horses, never mind the dogs, would have warned them of puma.

But they were everywhere else, and in our good fashion, working for their pay.

Snow had fallen through weeks to the knee, to the waist, thawed, and frozen again, turned to slop and into ice, and still the snow came thick from low sky, day and night, if not in flake then in mist. A strange year, everybody said, and the old ones looked in memory to find another like it, and Rupayan was sure *huenü-rey-fücha* had turned his robe inside out, and the snow would stop only when we made a gift of unborn guanaco up on the Altar of the Gods.

"O, pish," Lal said. "Where would you find guanaco in this weather? Never mind the unborn. Even if I would allow it."

"Indio he is," I said. "They have got their way. We have got ours. Leave it, now."

She looked at me across the breakfast table, candles alight although it was past nine o'clock in the morning, and tears came in huge glitter, lovely to see, but a knife in heart and soul to remember.

"We are going farther away, Huw," she said, in whispers. "Nights, weeks, you haven't kissed."

Well, I was round there in a moment and I made up for weeks and many a year, thank God, but the girl came in with eggs and bacon, and we had to behave. That morning we were sorting all the articles Rhin had sent over, piles of everything to be priced and listed. Two saddles, one for Lal and one for me, I had chosen, and Catango ran in to say a calf had been dragged from the corral and puma pads were everywhere. The forenoon was dark with mist and we could have wasted time trying to follow. In those weeks we had often seen tracks, but if in bad winters they came down from the high forest with the other animals to look for food, puma were always less trouble than the fox, and far less dangerous than wild boar.

Sometime after the midday asado we had light of the sun far behind clouds, but enough to see trees hung in white lumps and cones and rounds in crisp of ice where sheds or ricks were buried, and the river mute under dirty crystal, and the waterfall's white beard. We were stacking hides off floor level, and we heard shouts far off, and a horse in gallop beyond the timber pile, though we might not have taken notice, but groups went galloping behind, and shrieks were tiny from beyond the laundry.

Across a black oxhide, Temuco looked at me.

"That's women," he said. "A puma's sniffing over there."

A boy shouted at the door, and we ran.

The blue dress, bareback on the white mare was Lal, just going over the rise behind the house and gone in cloud. Half a dozen rode in a group behind, three, stretchneck, were her peons. Dozens more were scattered, going into mist, not one with a saddle.

We were almost half a mile from the nearest stable. We came in mule wagons, but they were gone for a load of feed, and by the time I had run to the workshop I thought I had breathed and bled every whisper of air in the world.

Not a horse was in the stalls.

In the next, near the laundry, I took one of the grays, but only wagon harness was on the pegs, and turned out to see the women, in a group, looking at me.

A smile was in every face, that smile I remembered, that I had known was near without being able to see where, each one smiling, with snow light pale in their eyes, nothing to frighten, and yet terrible with knowledge not yet in me, gentle with a truth I had still to know.

"Why is the Mistress Lal riding?" I asked them, without voice.

"Your son," the older woman said. "He was not in his cradle. She followed blood."

"Puma," I said.

She nodded with the butt of her right hand cutting the air toward the mountain.

"She feeds cubs," she said, and smiled.

I turned and kicked into a gallop, and they were all fists on knees, screaming laughter behind there.

God knows what I thought I was going to do, or where I believed I was going. Everybody was minutes in front and better mounted, but the rest of the men were coming up, and Temuco led, following the tracks, and cut across where they had doubled, and went for the crest to look about. On the high rock we waited, hearing shouts, but uncertain which way to go until the pale blue dress came from the trees far over, and we went down, direct, into the river bed and across, through thick timber, dodging branches, kicking through briar, and all the time I was praying, but without words, seeing my boy, not believing, not wanting to believe, and yet Lal had gone from the house in that thin dress, without boots, bareback in that weather, and knowing her, I knew.

The boy had been in his cradle out on the porch, quiet, nobody near.

In the saddle I sat, spurring without spurs, flogging with an empty hand, shouting without a voice.

We came up where mist blew, just behind the house, high above the river, but held there by the chasm where the waterfall ran, and the pale blue dress I could see jumping through stirrup-high brush, and the others came from the forest and spread in half-moon, and we heard their shouts, trying to keep the puma moving not to crouch and maul.

But then the smile I knew, that frightened me, came into my spine as a molten spear, and I felt the heat stitching a grin in my face, and I turned the horse up the incline, and came round on hinds, and sent him for the edge. Temuco tried to cross me, but I was past, and jumping over that icy space where the waterfall lay frozen, and the horse got fores on the farther side and kicked, and we were up, and riding hard toward Lal.

In that smile I knew I had become Indio. No doubt was in me, and the horse seemed to know. We jumped, climbed, slid, galloped, and I must have closed within half a mile, and Lal pulled up on hinds and turned for the cliff edge. Over there I went, riding on the lip of the long curve, with another ledge about twenty feet down, and the forest dark, under mist, a thousand feet below.

Perhaps she saw the puma on that lower ledge, but I could see only the boy's blanket down there, with a corner hanging, and a fold blowing, slow.

Lal, O Lal, *galôn fach-i!* sweet heartsblood of mine, no look, no sign, nothing to remember, but only a gathering of reins, and riding along the neck as if to finish a race. Not her peons nearing and screaming, not I, nor any soul on earth could know, but without look or pause she sat up, and back, into a jump, out, over the edge.

The white mare stretched hinds and kicked wide once, and went in a fall fores first, mouth open, head twisting to the side, and Lal came from the saddle, gently, hair blowing, dress clinging, and fell as a dancing angel into the mist.

Tambien looked over and held up his arms as if in beseech of the High God, turned the palomino's golden mane to circle, howled as a fox in mourn, dug heels for the cliff, and jumped. Tamaño on the black with the white mane and tail rode a neck in front of Tampoco on the white with black mane, and they jumped almost together, turning, tears in flash, holding out hands to each other, falling, gone.

No sound, no breath, and down in the dark timber, no sign, only the mist blowing, white, white.

Snow stuck to my face, froze my eyes, blinded.

The horse cropped.

Two came without sound, gray shapes, both with the smile I remembered, and one took the horse by the ear, and the other vaulted up behind, and put her arms about me, and rested her chin.

"*Mari-mari, huarancá,*" Lliutro said. "Now, it is our time."

Moyamachi smiled up at us, and children came quietly from the snow, shapes of breath, and we walked.

25

Sitting here now, I am sure that in those years my mind was very near an Indio's except that he had early training and free will, whereas I had neither. Useful ideas of any sort were not in them. Thinking as a child, I knew they were children of another kind. Nobody was ever cruel to anybody else, and if man or woman was unhappy everybody was unhappy with them. A spirit of being a smile in the same body was in all of them. Quarrels could begin among the young men over the girls, but everybody knew why, and the mothers stood between the squabblers, each trying to shout louder than the next to prove herself the better guardian, more deserving of respect for devotion to the rule of the toldo, that was strict enough, though young men broke any rule to take the girl they wanted.

Perhaps, but I am unsure, I lived my days in the doorway of the toldo, or on horseback with Lliutro and Moyamachi when they went to gather berries, leaves, roots for the waters and medicines. Certainly my skin is burned with the open air, and probably I shall never be really white again, though since I always thought a white skin looked unhealthy, except a woman's, I am far from worried. All I can remember is either sitting somewhere and watching, or riding, and listening to the voices of trees, lakes, rivers, and learning the language of the grass and flowers and stones. Moyamachi spoke for hours, and I know I listened because I remember the drone, but what she said is gone. If I think now, I can remember only her smile, and if I think of Lliutro then I smell the apple-scent of the toldo, and her warmth is with me, and faint, a wist of wildflowers.

Our toldo was largest, on the crest of a rise, and Lliutro always put my saddle inside the door. Moyamachi and three or four other girls slept there, and kept the fire burning, brought food, or cooked, or made drink, or perfumes from plants and berries. The perfume was most for Lliutro, after bathing, and others for the beds, robes and clothing. They all bathed twice a day at least, and the toldo was always swept morning and night. In summer they swam in every river we crossed and combed their hair. In winter they bathed in hollow tree trunks, rubbed each other with snow, and dried themselves on rugs about the fire. All of them were small, barely higher than my elbow, without a hair on their bodies. Their legs were far thicker than mine, at thigh, knee and calf out of all proportion to a doll's waist, and their skin was in high polish from a lifetime of wearing guanaco pelts, but with more muscle beneath than many of us twice their size. Moyamachi seemed an old woman, but only when she wanted to be. At times, she smothered herself in a gray clay and let it harden, and went in the river for a few moments and came out almost white, with black hair to the ankles, and beautiful even to me, and young as any, not a wrinkle.

I am still not sure how I thought about women in that time. Lliutro was always with me, and I could take any of the other girls at will, but I remember nothing of any feeling, any more than recall the taste of a meal. There was no jealousy, because the toldo and all in it belonged to Lliutro, as a princess, and her word was enough even for the oldest men. She ruled because of her mother, though I never saw her or anyone she would bow to, but everybody bowed to her except Moyamachi.

Perhaps I always trusted them, I am not sure, but certain it is that I was fond of them in some way though I suppose

I should have hated. Nothing is clear about that time. No thought of love or hate came near. I was never hungry or thirsty or too hot or cold. I was not a prisoner, except in mind, and that was effect of the *paico*.

I know it now, but it was less than a thought at that time.

I lived, and I moved, and I had feeling and sense for light and dark, eating and drinking, looking and listening, and sometimes I could use reason, but I was never sure of it then, and any memory now is like a forgotten tune, known perhaps, but not to sing, except for a note or two, and then the cloud, the scarves of light across the eyes, and the whispers of Lliutro and Moyamachi.

We never went farther north than the Bio-Bio, the only time we were going to Santiago. Through the lakes by canoe we went for days, and put up hide tents at night. The hours of sun on calm green water among the mountains, and the forest bathing in the stillness, every leaf clear enough to pick off, and fish in shoals under us, and Lliutro using a paddle easily as she rode a pony, no effort and all mastery, and Moyamachi in the bow, and the girls in the canoe behind, all come as in small songs, nothing linked. Bio-Bio I remember, for the river seemed like the sea, and the little islands felt over the water toward us, touching us with their treetops in welcome. There we lived with the *aillarehue* of Lliutro's family, all the members in hundreds with their families, each in their own toldo, and it was then I saw what power Lliutro had, and what respect was hers as one of the tree of *Queupoliquen*. Her toldo was largest, with silks and embroidered ponchos, and new pelts on the floor. Dozens of girls waited to run any smallest service, and day after day, hour after hour, she sat outside touching children's heads to protect them lifelong from the eye of *Huichancüllín* and the *huecufü*.

At those times I hid my face, for she smiled, brows up, eyes wide without a blink, mouth in a line, with the terror of truth in the palm of a small hand and the horror of all knowledge in the sweat of her forehead. Moyamachi stood beside her and took the sick and deformed children, and the mothers unable to walk, or with broken bones, or faults in the womb. If she cured them all or not, I never knew, but I often saw her put a child to sleep, break a bone and reset it, bandage it in hot bark and give it, sleeping, to the mother. Many a woman in shrieking labor had a child in perfect ease and walked away after Moyamachi had given her a bowl to drink, and every day gifts piled against the walls to the roof, from men, women and children freed of fevers, torn muscles, aching jaws, and open wounds.

But I knew nothing in detail, and I remember only because I saw and heard, and the mind holds part, though if I try to think, then I freeze in a white cloud again, seeing Lal and the three peons jumping out, forever in a kick and stretch of fores, and the white mare screaming from an open mouth.

For the third or fourth time, *coyaique*, the meeting of caciques voted against sending me to represent them, and Lliutro came back and tore off the silks and embroidered ponchos and ripped them in strips over the fire, and flung the necklaces and bracelets in, and knelt weeping, but quietly, and Moyamachi gave me the pot to make a rare coffee. Perhaps I remember it because that overpowering aroma seemed part of Lliutro's anger, without words or any sound, and the tears dropping silver from her cheeks ran down her breasts, and the feeling which came from her, a pulse that seemed to move and burn the air though she knelt naked, still.

If I loved her as I loved Lal I am not sure, but there were children, though I had no interest in them and I can never remember seeing them. During those times I took the other girls, but I remember little, except that they laughed with me as a child, and Moyamachi sat braiding their hair.

No doubt I behaved as a halfwit, though I dressed as a cacique, with a face plucked clean up beyond the temples, and condor feathers in a small tuft on top of my head, and I wore the apron, sometimes a poncho, and a cloak, and guanaco sandals for I could never walk barefoot as most of them.

But I was halfwit of special sort, and I was treated as a

being half out of the world and in touch with the *pillanes*, souls of the dead, and able to ride at will in the *huenu-leufü*, the sea of stars always above us which we call the Milky Way.

What I said, or what I was told or made to say while I slept, I have no memory, but I was treated always with a respect only slightly less than that given to Moyamachi, which was a little less than that shown to Lliutro. It was known that I had been *Ulmain* among my own people, with power even over soldiers, and that I was so easily put in control by Lliutro and Moyamachi brought them even greater devotion, especially from the older men with memories of fifty years of battle, and the tales of their fathers and grandfathers before them. There was no writing anywhere among the people. Everything was in the mind, and the system of learning, recording messages, or memorizing in sleep seemed general, and the women were always in the space beyond the door, asking for *paico*, a common name for any tea made with herbs or roots. What kind of *paico* I was given I shall never know, but the effect of two or three mouthfuls lasted all day. Mouthfuls I am sure, because I can see the size of the first bowl, even if, after that, I never remember seeing another.

But though I was refused as spokesman, I must have been of some use, because I seem to have gone on living with Lliutro in the same fashion, and clearly they never stopped giving me *paico*, if in smaller doses. Never can I remember speaking, except once, to Lliutro, after the *coyaique* had decided for the last time not to let her take me to Santiago. It seems silly now, but never at that time was it in my mind to refuse to do anything. I was led, and told, and did.

"*Kintú*," she called me. "We shall ride together."

"Together," I said.

"You will speak without halt," she said. "Every word as I say. Now, you speak and understand."

"Understand," I said.

So clearly I remember it. The last word of all she said, I repeated as a child.

"Listen to me," she said, and laughed, and shook me, but gently, for she was never else. "We shall go through the valley to Santiago. We will speak and we shall have letters. With the letters we shall go to Buenos Aires. You will speak for us. Our lands will come back to us. We shall waken in the morning sun. El Pampero will eat our smoke. Then you will go back to your people, and I will join you."

But she had made one mistake, and because of it, there was error in my memory but not in myself.

My own language had been a form of Cambrian, given by my mother and father, spoken from infancy, and almost forgotten in youth, and over it I had learned English.

Lliutro and Moyamachi had taught me Arauco while I slept, using the Castellano I had learned as basis. But in time, they had to remind me of words because I was forgetting the Castellano, and then, I suppose, they either stopped giving me *paico* for a day or so, or gave me less.

It was at that time I began to remember far back in my childhood, to the last detail, and I am in wonder how the human mind could stretch so far. Often I woke crying for my mother, and for a toy, something with wheels, I think, in color blue and red, but I could never remember size or shape, and for that I cried the harder, and Lliutro whispered more, held tighter.

Except for the sun and moon, and the cool toldos of summer and the high coal and log fires of winter, and the spring hunting of guanaco and the slaughter of wild cattle for winter, I was never concerned with a notion of time, and in surety I never missed a clock. What news we had came from old women padding about the roads, sure of a good meal if they had a cropful of chat about births, deaths, and visitations of spirits. If any were curious about the world outside I never heard a question and I never heard anyone speak of a country, but only of *mapuche*, the people.

More than an Army would have been needed to find us.

Now, of course, I know how the General tried with the southern Army, through spring and summer to find a trace. Everybody thought I had gone with Lal. But it tells how closely Lliutro's people held the secret, that Rhin went everywhere with Saiheque, but they never found out until it was too late.

If sight and mind cleared in that time I thought always of Lal. First thought, first clarity came in the cold claws of grief, a helplessness, the rock, silence, gray clouds, the whine of winter's avarice, that distance to gallop, to reach out a hand, to call, to put an arm about her, and knead her beautiful teat as I so often did to make her stand still and listen. But then I could see her dancing, head down, laughing in a golden sky, hair blowing scarlet clouds among troops of white mares in stretch gallop, fores and hinds kicked wide in endless leap, heads twisted, mouths in gape of windscream laughter. But scarves of light across the eyes, a float of cloud, and in darkness always a whisper, perhaps Lliutro's or Moyamachi's, and if I had seen, or if the dream came and passed, I never cared. Nothing seemed in me. The only reason I remember anything, I suppose, is because I was living and my eyes were open and I could hear. But a stone would have as much interest.

Perhaps after the *coyaique* had voted, Lliutro either gave me less *paico* or none for days, and so I was sometimes more myself, with clearer thoughts about everything and then, probably, they saw risk of losing me because I knew the country well as anybody, and horses were always outside the toldo, and the dose went to normal again. It was in those spaces, possibly, that the time slipped by without memory.

Months go day by forgotten day into the years.

First true memory was the morning I woke with water washing over the guanaco sleeping rugs and getting a nose full and sneezing—and I know, now, that they gave me *paico* before I was really awake—and the toldo fell on the side near the cooking fire and the ground lifted under me and I was flung on a pile of broken timber and lay there, looking at darkness, hearing the wailing night. The toldo roofhides burned in a sudden blaze and the earth lifted again, women screamed, trees fell in a crack to sting the ears and ponies ran, jumping and kicking, in flame and out, and earth sprang as water, falling to bury voices, carrying fire, ponies, trees down in smooth path to darkness.

I stood, and saw the ground ripple as a shaken blanket.

Lliutro and Moyamachi put their arms about me and we stood a long time on the rock, feeling it tremble sometimes, though the earth and trees about us moved, fell, slid, and the sun tried to see through gray dust falling from the volcano. There was nowhere to go. We were swaying with the movement under us, but the ground downhill was split, and each moment the split widened, or shut, or filled with savage water, and everywhere people screamed and died. The toldos near us, with all the families, goats and ponies, and the stands of trees, patches of gardens and hides hanging to dry were gone in the ragged split filling with waves from the lake.

Lliutro called out for her people and I felt the voice tearing her body, but the sound was only a whisper in a noise of blowing volcanoes and the rocks and ash falling with the roar of steam. I picked her up, and walked to the top of the crest, and Moyamachi and a couple of girls brought what they could. Up there we saw the new volcanoes, spitting yellow fire to the dark sky, but nothing below, except the gray rain of cinders. On the other side below us, the horses and ponies waited in falling ash, heads bowed, as if praying. We climbed down, and Lliutro mounted and went at gallop, calling her people. Moyamachi packed everything on the horses, and we waited through the day, and Lliutro came back with dozens of women and children, but they were shocked beyond speech, and they had to be led to a pony and shown how to mount. The forest to the south seemed untouched, and we went through the darkness of leaves, clear of ash, able to breathe air without sulphur, though we climbed always up, for the mountain falls only in places, but the ground shakes and opens everywhere. We came out high under a peak, with another forest above, and there made camp. The children were washed in the cascade, and the women bathed after, and we shared rugs around big fires, and ate an asado of horseflesh. Night after night, day after day, the ground moved, and though the women screamed, soon they were quiet after Lliutro had torn the clothes from a loud voice and thrashed her bloody with a bridle. But in that time Moyamachi had space to gather more plants and *paico* soothed nerves and gave quiet.

In a late afternoon the hunters found us, and the women stripped the carcasses of bone, and Lliutro went down to see if any more women and children were alive. She came back days later with dozens, and flocks of sheep and goats and hundreds of ponies. Many husbands had lost wives and children, but not so many as she had thought and not nearly so many as in other *rehue* of her family. But ash still fell, and the ground still shifted, and day and night the white-hot rocks hissed from the sky, and darkness was lit with burning paths and the red flame of new volcanoes, and when the breeze shifted we sniffed the stench of the earth's entrails.

From the south, a *coyaique* came in twos and threes, until almost a hundred cacique were with us. None came from the north or from the west. They said the sea was over the land, rivers ran salt water, islands had gone, and there were no more *rehue* or any single toldo on the coast. Some shouted that I was cause of bringing the anger of *Huichancüllín* on the people, as a stranger granted the favors of a *toqui*. Others shouted that too much time had passed since sacrifice had been made to *Ranginhüenüchaü*, the father, and *Ranginhuenue Nuque*, the mother, and they were angry, and it was time to gather in *nguillatún* to ask for pardon, and peace. *Nguillatún* was not a church or a ceremony, but a place where all the men and women called on their ancestors to join them in spirit, and on all those not yet born but ready to take their places, and to advise what was best to be done. Moyamachi lit fires, and women went stiff in trance, and men fell and lay still through a day and night, and Lliutro sat in darkness of a tent, staring, sleepless, without food or drink, and I never saw her move.

But the ground still shook and the volcanoes seemed to throw thicker flame higher, and there were seven instead of five, though none had been before.

Lliutro fell asleep in the early morning of the third day and I carried her to Moyamachi, and there she was washed and put to bed on a pile of green branches with a mattress of flowers gathered in the forest. Just before noon, the *ngenpin* called all the women and told them to burn everything not made in their own *rehue*, and to destroy all in use not made by their husbands. The women bowed their heads to the ground, and stayed for moments and went away to light fires.

He called the men, and told them to put on the white garment, and burn the pelts they had worn in the past, and then to choose five among themselves with a first-born son not older than a moon. Because hunters go out at regular times, nearly always a crop of children are born in about the same month and more than five first-born sons were found and the fathers had to toss knives to see which should be taken.

Two trees were cut from the forest, peeled and greased with mare's fat, set on both sides of an altar, and burned. The flames went to ash next morning, and five fathers took their sons, white bundles, one to the highest peak of the mountain we were on, one to the bank of the nearest river we could see, one to the lake below us, one to the ocean not far away, and one to the edge of the forest. All the women lay in the dust and wept. Lliutro never moved. Her eyes were shut, and she seemed not to breathe. Moyamachi took notice of none. She and her girls and the older women made *múdai,* a drink of maize, and *pulco,* a heavier spirit, and boiled and stirred and strained through white cloth all twelve of the pots filled with the mix of *mari-epú-ilahuen,* the waters of blessing, that cleanse and sanctify.

Late at night we saw the fire near the peak, and another down at the lake, on the river, and at the edge of the forest, though if the ocean was still in cloud, we were sure the fire on the peak would be seen. Before dawn, sheep, goats, and mares were tied near the altar, and a signal fire was lit. By light, we saw smoke from the peak, from the lake and the river, from the forest, and through clouds the ocean shone and the smoke was blue. Wet leaves raised a thick column of smoke five times. The *ngen-pin* cut a mare's throat, and dipped branches in the blood and splashed all the men, and women, and children. Sheep and goats were slaughtered and the blood went into vessels of hide.

A mother came with a first-born infant daughter, and the father cut the throat and the blood filled a stone bowl, and the women stood in lines to sip, and dab the children's foreheads.

All day people lay in the dust, and the *ngen-pin* waited for the sun to reach a shadow, and dipped the branch in blood from the hide vessels, and splashed men, women and children, the animals, the sleeping places, and to the north, south, east, and west.

At night, the five men came back, each with a skin pouch of blood, and the *ngen-pin* daubed everyone on the forehead, and the animals, and gave to each father to drink, and Moyamachi and some of her women, and woke Lliutro to spread blood over her body, on her face, in the palms of both hands, and gave her to drink, and emptied the bowl himself.

Lliutro stretched, kicked flowers, and called for me, and I carried her to the cascade to bathe, and helped her back for the *mari-epú-ilahuen*, splashed on all of us with twigs, sweet-smelling, healing, sign that *Ranginhüenüchaü* nodded thanks, and *Ranginhuenue Nuque* sat again to weave the guanaco poncho that covers the sky.

We had grown used to noise, to movement of the earth, blowing ash and spouts of flame, and I believe nobody noticed when it all stopped.

At some moment that night the earth became still.

Volcanoes died. No more rocks fell. Ash was less, blown in drifts to the sea.

We woke next morning to a gray land, clear, quiet in depth of cinder.

That night we had the great asado, *conchotún*, of horseflesh, and Moyamachi's *pulco* and *múdai* went round in goatskins, and everybody and their children were drunk, and families in feud made friends once more, widowers found new wives, orphans new parents, and mothers of sacrificed children conceived again.

South we rode for days, always on the mountain slopes because the sea had come in, land had fallen, rivers ran in other ways, guides had to learn new paths, and all the animals had gone to the higher forests and we had to ration scarce horseflesh. Hunters sent messages to say we would have to leave the Bio-Bio and cross the mountains to find winter food. Trees were red in autumn, and time was against us, snow was near, and we had to find fuel and water, build toldos, smoke meat. But in that time, possibly, it was seen that I had wakened and they feared what I might do. No real memory is clear afterward, only of riding, or eating or sitting at a hot fire, or listening to Lliutro whispering.

That last morning, I woke in sunshine out in silent pasture yellow in sway of *amancay* in bluest shadow of the Cordilleras, and condors, eagles and the kites flew in circles to make a moving shadow, and darkness was over me.

Lliutro lay out of the guanaco pelts, knees drawn up, fingers clawed in the earth, head turned the other way, staring wide at the sky. Moyamachi looked into the ground, and the girls had crawled about her, some with their hands out in appeal, others to Lliutro. Beyond, the bodies lay in rings about dead fires.

Nothing moved except the circling birds. Wings made the only sound.

If I felt weak it was because I was hungry. The greatest real luxury I have ever known was to move my legs, stretch my toes, and sit up, feeling myself as I had been, once again knowing my name. The rugs were dusty with at least three or four days of El Pampero. Perhaps we had camped a week before, and then the sickness struck and lasted a day or two. Under shade of my hand I saw the patches on the bodies and swollen eyes, and I could almost hear Idwyn warning of measles that kill in a night, man, woman or child without hope or defence, and Indios die easily, knowing they run at the end of their skiens, laughing, up to *Ranginhüenüchaü* winding in, and families waiting to welcome them with the *curantó* that lasts forever.

Lliutro, I knew, in those last moments had clawed her fingers in the ground to find strength to turn from me, to be the first to run, wonderful girl, and so be beautiful without a mark when she helped me in.

My shadow moved, a strange shape, and I reached up to tear the feathers from the fillet of leather about my head. I was thin, but strong enough. Everything I left as it was, and I wore only the apron and the sandals.

My friends lay in circles about the fires, hundreds of men, women, and children, and the birds were waiting for me to go.

Without goodbye, or a word, or other look, I turned and walked to the south.

Home, I knew, was that way and I was hungry.

But tears burned and blinded for Lliutro, of the small hands, and the whispers, and the smile, and the apple-scent of a lovely girl.

26

All that day I rode south, every moment remembering more about myself, though the more memories that came in pain to me, the more frightened I was of being seen. Many times I saw smoke and turned away. In the afternoon a Gaucho called from a river crossing, but I went in panic, I am not sure why, and then, in the early evening I saw the lake's blue smile, and knew that Little Looking Glass was on the other side. We went over the fence, through the river, and two forests between pasture, and across the home fields to the corral behind the house. The pony went with a pat, and I took time to go from shadow to shadow, wondering if Angharad was there, and what to say when we met.

Every word of Cambrian, English, and Castellano had gone.

Not a syllable of any was in my head, and I rummaged, there, for minutes, but no use.

The house was dark in evening and the shutters were up, but light was in the laundry shed, a fire, and there I moved, and a woman stood at the table, ironing.

No doubt about those piled black and white braids, the straight back in a white overall.

Kalata.

Softly, in whispers, each louder than the other, I called until she heard, and she stood, fist to mouth, staring at the wall, and the iron hit the holder, and she untied the apron, and turned to me and came, arms wide, as a familiar. We stood for moments, silent, and still silent she led me through the shining kitchen, and the dining room with furniture I had made, and upstairs, along the corridor to the bathroom. Hot water she poured in the bath, and went to get towels, and brought them back with clothes and a lamp.

Never again will I know the shock I had when I saw myself in the mirror. My face was thin, almost without a line, and black, smooth in cheeks and chin, with a cap of hair cut short above the ears and a deep wave where the fillet had cut. But the eyes had a wildness, with a stare that seemed not to see what was in front, but to look through and past.

Indio, pure.

Even to me, I was of the Race.

The soap I shall always remember, and I realized then why Indios were always so ticklish in the nose. That smell was enough to make me giddy, yet I knew it was an ordinary toilet soap, though to me, then, a thunderclap inside the head that might have frightened, and I used it with care for days till senses were less keen.

Never again will anyone know so much joy in putting on a clean shirt and a pair of trousers, socks, slippers. They were Mr. Gruffydd's, of course, but velvet and ermine have never been worn with greater sense of dignity, or with more humble thanks, and I went downstairs with a feeling I was back home.

I was in a good way to be myself again.

The dining table had been laid with a cloth and silver, and candles were alight.

Lal was with me in a moment, and I clapped hands to ears, and Kalata must have known because she gave me a glass, and I drank three gulps of whisky, and woke next morning in the big bed, and lay there in wonder.

Those times of wonder are still strange to me, and I know how Indios feel, though I had advantage of experience and memory, and they none. In truth it was another world, of other creatures, sounds, smells, fearful thoughts. Enemies were behind doors that creaked, under squeaking floorboards, in wait beyond a moving curtain, trying to open a rattling shutter, inside a wardrobe on a loose latch, under a bed with rusty springs. Ears flicked as a dog's at any sound, and the nose was just as lively, and I knew why they had stood to sniff coffee. At night I had no need of a lamp. I seemed to feel with my skin. No need to tell me how to get to anywhere. I knew.

Kalata had told me by the hour most of what I wanted to know, and often left me helpless, trying to arrange my mind. Vyrnwy and Teg, with six children, had gone, she thought, to the City of Lewis, because there were so few horses to be shod, and there were more cars and trucks than teams and wagons. The Army had gone, and police and gendarmes were in posts along the border. The school had been taken by the Government, but Brother Little Mountain opened a place of his own and the scholars came from all over Patagonia to be taught handcrafts.

In my workshop.

Rhinberry was in Chile with his Indios, Saiheque and his people were in the South, and Donato had sold his business and he and Gwenonwy lived in the Territory. Solva took Doli back to Maes Corwen. Months they searched in parties of dozens for Lal, but they never found trace of her or the peons or me. Temuco had shown where I jumped the waterfall but nobody believed him. The others in the chase were blind with snow, and after more than a week of blizzard, not even the best dogs could nose a track. So many thoughts and memories, but too much in one lump, and one morning, after I had read Angharad's letter, heartbroken to tell of Mr. Gruffydd's death, Kalata ruled no more, and I must sleep and have a firm mind to go back. But any notion of going to the house put a blade in an artery. When any of the peons working on the place came to the door I was always gone, and Kalata never told anyone I was there. Solva had put her in charge on instruction from Angharad, and she had her money by the month from a lawyer in the new town of Bariloche that once had been Vuriloche.

But without telling me she sent a boy to Saiheque, and to Rhin. It took weeks to find them, and by that time I was far stronger in mind, and Kalata showed a wisdom there, and in the kitchen, for she fed me the simplest plates, of meat at first, and then vegetables, but little at a time, never bread or sugar, though plenty of raw liver. She said she had known the strongest Indios die in weeks from eating *huinca* food.

In those days the Castellano was coming back to me with Kalata's help, a few words, a sentence at a time, but not a notion of Cambrian or English. The library in the house I passed as guanaco trackers pass the unwanted fox or ostrich, seen but ignored. A clock simply made a noise. Time or dates meant no more than the sun in the window, or the moon. But when I held the envelope with Kalata's pay, I might have dropped to see the date, and I asked her if it were true, and she looked away and nodded. After that she got me some newspapers from the next farm. *La Prensa* came as an old friend, but the news I could read I hardly believed.

Even more, then, I wanted to keep away, to hide, to live my days in quietness among the lakes and forests.

One morning I awoke and Rhin was standing at the foot of the bed, hands in prayer, whiter, but not much changed, and happier, because light came from him and the smile was always in his eyes.

"Well," he said. "A fine one, you are. Everywhere I have wasted time looking for you, boy. Where were you?"

Well, I started to speak in Arauco, but fast as I spoke he translated in Cambrian, and I suppose it was only a day or so that the words came back, but the moment I tried to speak I fell asleep. Kalata had the remedy. She sent Rhin away, and I had to stay in bed with the curtains drawn, and she gave me drinks of some kind four or five times a day, and I slept dead. But one morning I woke up, and I could speak Cambrian, English, and Castellano without fault, and such relief of the mind I have never known. Saiheque came then, but he stood and laughed, holding up his cut palm, and we went out day after day, hunting, but we never said a word about where I had been.

Rhin came in one night with all his people, and called up to the window to say they had buried the bones of all at the *aillarehue*, and Lliutro had been taken back to her people at Bio-Bio, with Moyamachi and all the *toquis*.

"It was an *ahuin* to welcome the party they sent to Buenos Aires," Rhin said. "A feast, with all the lawgivers and the best of the peoples, *Huilliche, Puelche, Tehuelche, Nguluche, Picunche, Moluche, Pehuenche,* not one survivor. Perhaps some of the young men got drunk and slept where there was measles. Or somebody in the party brought it. All it needs is a breath. They die in hours. A day or two, the strongest. There were a lot of children. That's why I wouldn't let Saiheque come with me. We all bathed in the lake and we burned our clothes, saddlery, everything. I shan't come in the house for a few days. Nobody knows what the Government allowed them to have. Not a soul is alive of the hundreds. Will you be ready to look for Lal at the end of this week?"

"Yes," I said.

"God give a Father's Kiss to everything here," he said. "As you did once for me, so I will do for you."

It was all I could do to stop Kalata coming with us, but I promised to be back, and we went off one evening and rode during the night and slept in the forest by day. That way we met none, and our party rode in small groups with plenty of space, so that if the disease still held it would have less chance to reach all of us. But we went south for a week without sign of sickness, and reached the City of the Mill just after daylight. There were more buildings of wood, the main street was wider, but the greatest change was not to see our names over the corner shop. Geza and Tina got tired and left, Rhin said, for Buenos Aires. John Evans, the Mill, had joined his mare, Malacara, and many more of the oldest pioneers were gone to their fathers, though the very air seemed to breathe their names.

I kept my face to the mountains blue at the end of the valley, hearing chords of an unfinished hymn, a grieving yearn at the end of a dream. The people I could see were not of us, but only the mix, not Indio, not anything, except what came from a pile of sheepskins in shelter far less sanitary than a toldo. They sat about the street with a bottle, or they waited outside a wine shop, and scratched.

"I see you have noticed," Rhin said, beside me. "You won't find much to give heart. Everything is going in idleness. Work, today? A favor, and you must pay tenfold."

"When we came from the Singing Mountain, this is the way we drove the wagons and cattle," I said. "Lal was with me. There were two houses, John Evans and Robert Roberts. The others were over there, behind the trees. Others near the river. But everybody was out to meet us. We had an asado and we sang in the willow grove. There were never finer people, better hearts, stronger souls. Where did they go?"

"To the grave, and many with not a living voice to sing them in," Rhin said. "As most of us. Our sweat and our bones will be here. With the Indios. But they never sweated. They lived. We worked. We are still working, a few of us. These idlers are living. God allows? Very well. There will be few Indios of worth after Saiheque. These are the wine-breed. No law except Want. No god except Money. Money buys a bottle. Find a woman thinking the same, and take her to bed. The result will live by chance, and most by charity. If it works, it will be the least. These with me are of another kind. Some of the boys I am leaving with Brother Little Mountain. The rest will come with me and go back to proper work."

"Well, Rhin," I said. "Surely, now. Supposing any of them don't do as you want? What, then?"

"They get what my father gave me," Rhin said. "It altered my ideas. It alters theirs."

"What does Brother Little Mountain think?" I asked him.

"No discussion," he said. "Talk to him, and see."

I turned off the track and went down Our Way, and the moment I saw the hydrangea's blue blossom, Lal was with me and I expected her to take my hand. The trees had grown tall, and flowers in all the spaces laughed and blessed the air, but they were chocked in weeds, and the beds had been chewed and trampled by cattle loose from the corral. Trees had been lopped of branches, and some had died, and many were cut to the stump and left. I got off beyond what had been the laundry, that had no roof, and walked past the girls' house that had sheltered ten in cleanly comfort, and had only one wall of half-burned planks in waist-high weeds, past the stables, with neither walls nor roof, through the kitchen garden that flourished a planting of potatoes long gone to seed, and into the garden, once a glory, become a writhe in strangle of rotten fiber.

The kitchen yard I saw from the corner of an eye, the bones, paper, rusted wheels, tins, bottles, and walked around walls of dying and dead rambler roses to the porch, and went up steps and crossed a floor of dried mud, opened the door on one hinge, and walked into a room I had never known. The cypress paneling was black with the soot of years, and some of the boards were gone. The floor was even worse than the porch, with helpings of grease from the grill in the fireplace. None of our furniture was in that room, or the next. A rough table, two benches, four cane chairs, a calendar on the wall, artificial flowers on a chest of drawers, and saddlery in a corner was all, but enough. The dining room was store for hides. The kitchen got one look. My office beyond was a grain store. Hay bales were in Lal's. The bathroom stank. The plunger was broken. If the bath had been used, it must have been by animals, and many a dry day before.

Two snored on the bed in our bedroom. Window glass had broken, and a blanket was tacked except for a corner to let in light. Again, none of our furniture was in there, and then I remembered that Solva had taken everything, and I blessed the girl. That floor, which many a time had shimmered the long beauty of Lal's whiteness, was become a gritty mat. Man and woman were strangers to me, and I walked out, knowing from the rubbish on the kitchen table and the demijohn of wine, that they had eaten and were sleeping a tipsy siesta.

There was nobody else about the place.

"Only once more will I set foot in here," I said to Rhin. "After that, never."

We went over to the workshop, but instead of one long shed and the stores I had known, two other huts were joined at right angles with a solid fence of six wires, and a peeled-log gate, and the grass was cut, and flowers grew as they should, and the roses were a marvel everywhere. We walked through the shop that had been mine, with about twenty boys working on doors and shelves, and down to the opening into the timber yard. Brother Little Mountain's voice explained a formula on the foundation of cement structures, and he turned from writing on the blackboard and saw us.

He knew Rhin, and the big smile broke immediately to make the class turn. He was about to put down the book, but then he looked again at me, and stared, with light coming into his eyes, and suddenly he threw up his arms, half-turning away as though the vision were unbearable, and swiftly he jumped the steps.

"Ah, but you see, we have answer to our prayers," he said, and waved to the class. "Dismiss for ten minutes. But if you knew how we've missed you, my dear sir."

He embraced as a brother, Rhin and me, and took us to his room. The small bed looked to be not much more comfortable than boards, and it was covered with books and files. Shelves were nailed about the walls, with pictures of churches, a few saints, and a crucifix hung over the bed. A window showed grass and the roses, and the mountains' blue. The floor had been scrubbed that morning.

Rhin gave him the bones while he stood with his back

to us making tea. He asked no questions, and I was glad. Instead he spoke of the school, and Solva's interest, and the number of students and the success of the graduates.

"Unfortunately, they're so good they go away," he said. "There is nothing for them to do here. We are still in the era of the village. No real work. No reward. Nothing to tempt them. Shopfronts. Little houses. But we shall grow. There's a new spirit abroad. It's sinking in that foreigners have always been the mainstay of the country. If we wanted anything done we asked a German or a Frenchman. Or an Italian. English. Now, I believe we're starting to do things ourselves. It's healthy. When this class graduates, perhaps Patagonia will not be the political stepchild it's always been. A few dams along the river, a network of canals. That's what these boys need. Ideas, like lights in front of them. Then the new towns. Cities. Schools, parks, buildings. They must dream while they learn. While they work. They must be sure that what they work at now will one day come to pass. I shan't be here to see it, but have no fear. In some quiet corner, I'll be looking on. If only from a pupil's heart."

"You have Faith," Rhin said, and took the cup. "You have done wonders, here. But your tea is terrible, with you. Why don't you heat the pot, first, boy? You're at least a couple of teaspoonfuls of tea short in the measure. And you boiled the water too long. Your milk is the blink of an eye from going sour. But for an old Popisher's cup of tea, not bad. Not good, mind. But not bad."

The smile I had always remembered warmed the air in wonder above us.

"Perhaps you might spare the time to teach an imprudent illiterate," Brother Little Mountain said. "I was taught to make tea by an English engineer. Surely, they are the only authority?"

"In things English, certainly," Rhin said, quick. "In the matter of tea, they have room to learn. Your coffee's no good, either. English again, is it?"

"Italian," Brother Little Mountain said, with sufferance of a martyr.

"Ah, well," Rhin said, as if it explained everything. "Come over to me, one day, and I will put you in the right. Tea and coffee, two good friends, and no two were ever so mistreated. Because they are made with water, and water is cheap. It is only water. Like the Indios. They're only Indios. Anything will do."

"Not here," Brother Little Mountain said, still with the smile. "Elsewhere, perhaps."

"But that's the only reason I'm here," Rhin said, and held up his cup. "Another, please. Less milk, less sugar. I would like to taste the tea, if you please. If it is tea, mind? There's a bit of a doubt, somewhere, yes?"

Brother Little Mountain made a move with the tea pot as if to pour it over him, but a couple of boys ran after a ball and shook petals from a rosetree outside, and he reached to rap the pane, shaking his forefinger crossways, pulling a face to murder, and the boys flew.

"Little vandals," he said. "Four hours extra work for that."

"Only playing with a ball, and four hours extra?" Rhin said, straight-faced. "Well, there is cruel, you are. No wonder you can't make a cup of tea."

Brother Little Mountain turned, and gripped him by the coat and pummelled him on the shoulders, and Rhin fell across the papers on the bed, laughing.

"If I had you in class for a week, I'd give you cruel," Brother Little Mountain said, breathless. "Discipline is what they need. Most of them grow up without it. Then? How do you expect any standard of work? Or anything except a rascal? Good for nothing. Discourteous to women. Insulting their teachers. How do you cure it? With words? They laugh. But, you notice, none of these laugh at me?"

"Why don't you get them to build some shelves for all these books and papers?" Rhin asked, making a place for himself. "Much more comfortable, yes?"

"My scholars are not here to study my comfort," Brother

Little Mountain said. "That stuff is piled to reduce the temptation of a little sleep after the midday meal."

Rhin looked away, through the window.

"You are a good man, you know," he said, as if he had just thought of it. "I was always told you Catholics were the wickedest people beyond Hell. You've changed my opinion. Remember, if there's something I can do, only say."

Brother Little Mountain washed the tea pot in a bucket, and I was sure to have a good sink and pipes of running hot and cold water in there before another day was out.

"One thing," he said, without turning round. "Bring me the children. Infants. That would die without attention. Those left to die. Tell the women to bring them to me. There are so many."

"Who will look after them?" Rhin asked him.

"Bring them, first," he said. "When they are here, then we shall know."

"A pity you can't deal with the rest," Rhin said. "The ones too far grown. I have only got Indios. Of the blood. But they are coming fewer. The young go off. Most to Buenos Aires. Where the wages are. And the lights. The girls follow. I have tried hard. They all leave me with a good trade next to their fingers. But there aren't enough. The race is gone. There are no more. A few in the Bio-Bio, perhaps. Finished, a nation. What can we do? What?"

Brother Little Mountain clapped the dried, knuckly hands of a workman under his chin, and looked out at the roses.

"I would build towns," he said, a long way from us. "Houses, streets, lights, cinemas, football fields. And a theatre. It is important that we should see and hear ourselves. Condemn our stupidities. Relish our idiosyncrasies. I'd put all of them walking about without work into those towns. Free. The seasonal hands, thieves, beggars. Those who work for enough to buy a liter of wine and disappear. The can't-works. Won't-works. Don't-works. Shan't-works. Those and their womenkind. As obnoxious. As worthless. Nobody could visit. Once in, a man or a woman could leave only with a certificate that a certain trade had been learned, and they had a job to go to. The vast majority would never wish to leave that comfort. They would more than pay for themselves with the produce. The great advantage would be that the children would grow up with proper schooling, and all the decencies of a civilized life. The children. They're important. They are the future. They wouldn't need walls."

"And you would use the whip," Rhin said, still looking through the window.

"For the recalcitrants, there is no other medicine," Brother Little Mountain said. "We perish of idleness and sentimentality. We condemn ourselves in the indulgency of idiots. They require draconian measures. We pat their heads."

"I would like to help, indeed," Rhin said. "Who will build the towns?"

"The Government will have to move," Brother Little Mountain said. "With police to round them up, and guard the gates."

Rhin held up his hands and stood.

"It will be long after my time," he said. "Be quite sure there will be none of us left. Not one. Or anything of what we stand for. Except in a few places where the blood is obstinate."

"Why shouldn't all the blood have been obstinate?" Brother Little Mountain asked, bending a little to see Rhin's face. "What was it that swept you Cambrians away? Your strength. Your influence. It was a power. Suddenly? Gone. Why?"

"Not enough love," Rhin said, without hesitation. "No love for anybody, or anything. In the end, none for ourselves. Everything grows only in love. It is the truest food of the soul. We had none. We died."

Brother Little Mountain looked at me with wrinkled eyes to have the answer, brown eyes, in that light, pale, the color of brandy.

"What do you think?" he said.

"He's not capable of thinking much," Rhin said. "We are

going now to the other valley. We will find the best in his life. When I said not enough love, I meant we didn't love the Indios enough, or ourselves enough. We were contemptuous. Or we hated. We didn't really treat them or ourselves as people. They were only here-and-there our friends. If it suited us. If they had money, or power. Caciques or *toquis*. Those who could show us favor. As the English once treated us, so we treated the Indio. At last we had a people lower than us. So we spat, and passed on. Or used the women. But the Indio knew. He drank himself to death because he knew. Glad to be away from our eyes. That had no love."

"Love," Brother Little Mountain said. "Now, I wonder."

"Too late," Rhin said. "Wonder is part of innocence. With the little ones you can use love, and wonder. With those older and spoilt, the whip. Teach them in their flesh. Love and wonder is beyond them. They are in Hell before their time. Or perhaps this is really Hell. Who knows? I have never had proof, not."

"*Ora pro nobis*," Brother Little Mountain chanted, hands together, and walked out, and the class chanted with him from beyond, and I was gripped by the throat, for the voices were boys' in choir, and I could hear us, here, in the Valley, when we were singing "Come, Let Us Sing Unto the Lord."

We went out to find the horses, and sent the troop on. Saiheque had the lead, but I went forward to tell him which way. We climbed to the top of the mountain and I found the place over the waterfall where I had gone across, though I could barely believe it, and I knew why Temuco had been laughed at. Miles down, we found a tree-trunk bridge, and we rode the miles to the edge of the precipice. We had left a man to light a smoke fire where my pony had taken me over, so that we had a straight line to the place where Lal had jumped. We rode a long way until I knew I was where I had watched, and I could see below, where that blue blanket had lifted a slow fold in the breeze. Up to the lip we went, a long way, and there was a piece cut out in the ledge down there, clean as if dug, and beyond, the treetops dark in shadow below.

"She saw the puma and jumped for it," Rhin said, looking down. "The rock gave way."

"If it was a puma," I said. "Lliutro and Moyamachi found me soon enough after."

"I buried their bones," Rhin said. "Let us leave it, now, and go down to the other valley."

We left men on the cliff top to light smoke fires to show us from below where we should search. Three days it took us to ride down and round, and late one afternoon we came out of a forest into the farther valley, and saw the smoke on top of the cliff.

"I'll stay here," I said. "Find her. Bring them all. And the horses. They shall go to Maes Corwen."

"You told me she wanted to be at the waterfall," Rhin said.

"Her mother and Doli are at Maes Corwen," I said. "Solva will be there. I shall go there. Doli's peons cut their throats on the mother's grave. Where would Lal choose for her peons and herself? I doubt you will find my son. Him, I would take back to the Valley. But I am denied."

The scream, as if from between the eyes, of an Indio tracker, I knew was sign that Lal had been found. They were away hours, and they came back with bundles, and Rhin put them in order, and we rode back, across eleven rivers I counted, and eight mountains, and all the forests, and into the valley.

Without sleep, to the house I went with Saiheque, and with no word we ripped the cypress and alerces from the floors and walls until not a plank remained. The man came out in his shirt, and scratched himself, and I told him to get back to his bitch and he went. They were in their sheepskins when we tore out paneling and floors about them, but they said not a word, and right, for Saiheque would have killed them.

Up until noon we worked with spokeshaves and planes, and we made four coffins, and four coffers for the horses, those of Lal's and her peons' in soft red alerces, for the horses in gold cypress.

Brother Little Mountain and Rhin settled the bones and saddlery in each and we waited for the horse teams. We could have gone easier by truck, but I knew Lal would have wanted the horses. Ieuan Bedwellty, and Tom, Tot's, eldest boy brought two teams of six pair, and Mog, Moke, brought the only other Shire team in the valley.

"I kept these," he said. "I knew they would be wanted. I am glad for the day."

"Thank you, Mog," I said.

"Nothing, Sir," he said. "I told you long ago I would remember."

27

Without a woman there is nothing in life to love, nothing to taste, and no reason To Be. A warm hand to hold, a waist to slip an arm around, a neck with little loose silks to kiss, hair to run the fingers through, a beautiful girl in scent from the bath, there is all of life with, but nothing without her. Night is only hours awake. Day is hours waiting for night. No makeshift will do, or anything bought, or something for a time.

There was nobody to put a hand on my shoulder, or kiss my chin, or throw herself tight against me, or whisper, or squeeze me with her knees.

Love had left me, and I stood in black night, with grief for stanch companion.

Selfish I have been, but sometimes I was so empty, there seemed no room even for selfishness.

Finishing the garden, we were, that afternoon, and I saw Solva's poor, frozen face, set-stone with her, and I threw down the spade and went to her and took her in my arms. But she was colder than stone, not a tear, and she went from there, no word.

She and Rupert von Gelsbach had done well between them, I found out later. Moishe's property and mine had been sold. The properties in the Andes went in shares to Solva and me, though she had given her share of Lal's estate to Brother Little

Mountain. The two I found in my house were a shepherd and his wife put there by the company, so I no longer had any right in what I thought was my own house. But I had shaken the dust, and a riddance from the heart. But that was all. The moment the last plants were in, and the paths were flat, I took a fistful of earth from Lal's plot, so silly I was, and rode straight for Port Madryn, no message to Solva and Oracio, though they knew.

A year, a couple of years, it mattered nothing. Angharad wanted me to go to the Cape, but there was nothing in me. She had no idea of going back to the Argentine, and hoped I would look after Little Looking Glass. But there was nothing in me to look after anything.

Hungry for the love I had lost, I was, and numb, with nothing.

No wish to work, no want for living.

Perhaps those years of idleness with Lliutro had pulled out the spine from my will. The whispers of Moyamachi might still have been at nag. No man can be idle, and a plaything of women for year after year, and then become himself. There was nothing I wanted to do, and I did nothing. Only go from place to place, though I have no memory of being anywhere. I know how an Indio feels.

Back to the Valley I came, that time, and saw a few people, and walked the gray streets, small streets, ugly with sameness, and much more of the dead than that little plot never far from my mind. Earthquakes I had seen, and the drape of ash, but in this Valley and the others had been an earthquake of the spirit, and the cinders were underfoot, in closed doors, and roads in ruts, and gardens in weeds, and pitwheels idle, and nobody singing.

To Oxford I went, but I only telephoned to Olwen, and I knew from her voice that she was sorry, though not enough to drop everything and come for a holiday and just talk, if that would do any good.

"Oh, no, Huw, it's simply not on," she said, and it stuck

in my brain. "Come for a drink, sixish, my dear, and let's see what we can do."

Off I went, to London and other places, but hours of sitting outside a toldo and caring nothing for time have an effect, and I suppose I might have gone on for more years, except that chance took me to Hamburg, and in the business part close to the port, I saw our names Levy, Morgan over an office. They knew Rupert, but nobody knew me, and I needed some money. They telegraphed Buenos Aires, and by return cable Rupert authorized the draft and begged me to give him an address. The office had nothing to do with me at that time, for they had bought the name with the business, and I suppose they sent Rupert my address, because that night I had an eight-page cable to say that Saiheque was being put off his land for lack of title, and Rhinberry Wynn had been trying to find me, and cable instruction.

Blood brother though he might be, and a cut palm for reminder, still I tried to find excuse to do nothing. Saiheque and his people had the wild country at beck. They could go where they wanted, stay where they would. A grant of land was a prison, a *huinca* trap, a place of penal work where men and women had to sweat the months to clear ground and plant what was to them no more use than weeds, for they never used cereals or any root. It went against the sense, mocked the belief of the *mapuche*, because *Ranginhüenüchaü* provided all, and asked the hunter only to find what his family needed, and the woman to care for him and their children wherever they had to go.

How long I might have dawdled, or if I would have cast out any thought of help and gone on in disgrace of idleness, I have no notion. It was midday when I went downstairs in my hotel, a big place, and busy with people, and I was finding a way through the crowd and if I was careless, not looking where I was going, but I bumped into a young woman and she almost fell but I grabbed her in time and held her those seconds by the waist.

To hold a woman close again, to know her tenderness, that

glory, that wordless joy. I saw the soft pink rumple of her mouth, without kiss for me, and felt her breasts against me without hope of taste, and saw the fright and glint of tears in her eyes at sudden shock of roughness.

Instantly my mother's voice called out high above the talk and traffic.

"Going from the house again, now then, to push little girls down and make them cry, is it?" she said, plain, and every single word a knife thrust. "The brave Master Huw Morgan. Push, you. Make them fall with a bump. There is a credit. Credit, indeed, *ach-y-fi*. Making little girls hurt with them."

She was limp, soft under my hands, head back, looking, and I put her firm on her feet.

"Madame," I said. "I speak no German."

"I speak English," the man said, from the other side, with attack in his eyes.

"Then, sir, please tell this lady how deeply I regret my carelessness," I said. "If you dug twenty yards down under my feet, you would still find the stain of disgrace."

"Very well, my dear sir," he said, and smiled, and offered his arm. "Mistakes are not unforgivable, I think?"

She must have understood because she turned, going away, and smiled, and I might have smiled in answer but I was sideways to a full-length mirror and I saw myself. The voice of my mother brought clear as the day the bath house outside here, and I could see her and Angharad with brooms, and Ceridwen with buckets of water swilling away soap foam and coal dust after my father and brothers had bathed, and I heard the bristles shriek at stone and the *plash!* of a bucketful, and water in the gutters ran clean in sun.

"Ready for another day," Mama said, and propped the broom head up in its place. "Ceridwen, lay the table."

"O, Mama," Ceridwen said. "Always the old table. I've got a meeting for the lace class, look."

"Table," Mama said, plain faced. "Angharad, look at the potatoes, with you."

"Well, *tŵt-a-bŵ*, girl," Angharad whispered to Ceridwen. "Don't cry, then. I'll lay the old table, no odds, see."

"You will both do as you are told, and now, just," Mama said. "Huw, you are standing like a goose, one leg. Inside, knives and forks. Knives on the right hand, remember. No left-handed johnnies here, if you please. Ceridwen, you should see yourself. Like an old frimp, with you."

"Frump, Mama," I said. "English is frump."

"When I need correction, I will apply," Mama said, and made a move, but I was quicker. "*Anwyl mawr*, listen to it. And wash, and put a comb in that hair, and clean those boots before you dare to leave this house. *Ty'n cofio?*"

"Yes, Mama," I said.

"A bath to remember you shall have tonight," Mama said, and in fair temper, too. "English are frumps, indeed. What are we coming to, here? A disgrace to the house, and daring to do a bit of interrupting? Go, you, and wash after, is it? And basket to Mrs. Rowlands. Eggs."

My hair was over my coat collar and uncombed, and I had a beard untrimmed, and my clothes were anybody's from the gutter, and my shoes I can still see, and turn from.

A disgrace to the house, indeed. How they let me into the place I cannot think.

Those buckets of water and the brooms seemed at work in my very soul, and I could feel my mother looking at me and every word she spoke was scraping the wound. But I saw the soap foam and coal dust being driven and the clean stone shining under.

To the desk I went, and asked the man to find the quickest way to Buenos Aires, and which was the best place to buy clothes. Out I went with the card and came back with parcels, and straight to the barber's shop for a steam bath to boil, and a clean shave and short hair, and upstairs, then, to dress.

A difference indeed, and I took out the little silver box with that sacred earth in it, and kissed in memory, and vowed in her name to be what she would expect.

Tickets were ready that evening down at the desk, and late

one night I flew in the Zeppelin to New York, the first time I had ever been off the ground, and a dream every moment, and a marvel. If it was a cure I was looking for, then it was that I had full benefit, for I never finished admiring those engineers, or reviling myself for squatting before a toldo I had built for myself in the mope of my mind, while others were using themselves as men, creating wonders and doing their decent duty. We landed in New York long before I was ready, and came down in the lift, and straight to the docks, and on board a mailboat for Buenos Aires. All through the voyage I wrote letters to everybody until my hand was in cramps with me, but I got a lot of soap foam and coal dust out of my system, and nobody was left in any doubt what I was going to do.

Rupert von Gelsbach met me, and that night he showed me how everything of Moishe's, Lal's, Doli's, and mine had been arranged by agreement with Solva, acting in my name.

"Did she believe I was alive?" I asked him.

"She told me she'd believe you were all dead when she saw the bodies," he said. "A rock of a woman."

"Her beautiful sisters, the same," I said. "In other words, the capital has been gathering interest all this time, and nothing else. Nothing useful."

"My advice is, send it out of the country," he said. "Times are becoming unsettled."

"It was earned here, and it will be used here," I said. "I will tell you how, and soon."

"I can't allow you to go down there alone," he said. "You won't come back. I'm going to get you a few bodyguards. That grant of Saiheque's is worth millions. Men have been killed for far less."

I laughed at him.

"I am going to Solva's place for a few Tehuelche," I said. "In the Andes, Saiheque will see to everything."

I was wrong.

Not one Tehuelche was left with Solva. Her own peons were long pensioned and their children were all in good work, not one of them bred to the horse, or animals, or the land.

"We've schooled them away from what they did best," Oracio said. "They've all had what's called an education, and they passed examinations, and they've got good jobs, and they earn steady wages, and they live in the lamplight with a cinema along the street, and a bar on every corner. That's the life they wanted. And? Nothing."

But the City of Lewis had changed, well, to take the words from me. When I went there first, even the air itself had a taste of Cambria, and the voices were Cambrian and any want had to be asked for in Cambrian, if in a few places English might be tolerated though not everywhere, and Castellano was barely known. Streets were in dust with the best horses I ever saw and the traps and wagons shone with enamel and elbow grease. Nearly everybody drove a Studebaker two- or four-wheeler from the United States, or slenderly sprung marvels from Britain, or those Donato and I made, or else they rode champions groomed to shine. Over almost all the shops were Cambrian names, and the goods for sale had a Cambrian quality, for the best had always been just good enough. Second rate had no market. In those days, of course, they used gold pesos, and paper was something to read from, or wrap things in, or cut up to put in the little house outside. Women dressed well to come in from the farms, and the men dressed to come in later when their work was done, and meet, then, for a good cup of tea, and bread and butter and all sorts of jams, muffins, pastries, cakes, and indeed to God, sitting here, my mouth is in rivers to think of the goodness.

Gone.

Not a good cup of tea in the place.

Bars in plenty, and shelves of bottles, very pretty in the label, not one worth a sip. In the early time, the whiskies, brandies, ports, sherries and wines were all imported, or brought over from Chile and Mendoza, of the best, and beer came by cask, none better. Poor old Damaglou had long gone. His hotel was a place for petrol with a drinking den on the end. Dalar Roberts' stables had become a garage for trucks, an inch in grease everywhere, and no longer the healthy smells of horses, hay, and clover, but the stink of humans from a pit in the ground.

The shops were stocked with cheapness at highest price. The poor Cooperative had failed because of no brains at the top, and shareholders lending themselves their own money sold everything, without a word, to clear their debts, and many a crawling thief went unpunished, if the biggest thieves bought properties at laughable cost and made more millions later on.

That morning I remember well. The street was without a move except for a white cat on the only red corrugated iron roof. The street had never been in anything but a bustle and shout since I had known it.

"What in God's name has happened here?" I asked Oracio.

"The second flood," he said. "That was the end of everything. A second house, and furniture, and cattle, sheep, crops, even the topsoil, carried out once more to the Atlantic? No preacher could explain to people living a decent life, why they were cursed for a second time. Everything out to sea. Why?"

"A dam, a few miles up the river," I said. "Moishe told them, years ago."

Oracio shut his eyes.

"Talk," he said. "Before, they trusted God. God washed them away with His natural forces. Now, they trust the politicians. A dam is being built. In the wrong place, for the wrong reasons. Who believes anything? Why should they? The boys are being paid. That's all."

"Rotten as that," I said.

"Rotten down the middle," Oracio said.

"Except the engineers," I said.

"Always except," Oracio said. "Every man has to make a living. There are plenty of good ones everywhere. They have nothing to say. No power. And what?"

And what, indeed.

More than everything, I missed the men, and women, and the families of children. Families came in to shop, women drove in, men would gallop miles to buy something. All day the streets were noisy with voices and hoofbeat, and happy people shouting to each other, or a lot of people singing.

Silence.

Flat, everywhere and everybody, in a way to amaze, just as in this Valley outside here, to make anybody wonder if all of us, wherever we were, had caught some silent disease of the spirit.

"There's nothing of your people any more," Oracio said. "It's all over. Now you have the city-bred from Buenos Aires coming down here to make some money, or show off for country cousins. They couldn't sing to save their lives. If they didn't have a radio, they'd go mad."

Radio was a new wonder to me. To turn something and hear a voice from far away, or music, was strange. Radios were grating and bawling everywhere. It was mark of privilege to have a radio, and so every fool had one, each overlaying the other and the place was horror to the ears, especially from the horns hung in the streets, asking people to buy rubbish from this one or that.

We went from there before the sun, and thankful, down to Rawson, where the pioneers settled first, but the little boxes of houses had gone, those castles of Faith, where they had eked those first years to thumb a nose at Jeremiahs, turn desert into gardens and reap corn by the flowing mile where only pampas was before.

The Registry was in an old, well-used house, with the books and records on the other side of a long counter. Both the clerks were helpful, but though we had all the registers down, and five of us searched for hours, there, nobody found Saiheque's certificate, or Rupayan's, Nüfcütun's, Batancal's, or any other Indio's with rights given by the General, and filed by Lal, or Moishe, or me, and neither could we find Rhinberry Wynn's.

"Somebody's been here," Oracio said. "Wouldn't be difficult to search the records and destroy or steal anything they wanted. Down to the last detail."

The Registrar shrugged when we asked.

"Before my time," he said. "I'm not responsible for anything before. There's been a lot of falsification. We know that. But it's got to be proved. How?"

"Their titles were as good as ours," I said. "Where are they?"

"The lands were gift of the Government on covenant, and the Indios weren't there when the Commission inspected," he said. "That's about what happened. So somebody else claimed it as derelict. Are there any buildings on any of them?"

"A village for at least two hundred people," I said. "Built strong, with wells and sewage. How can those rights disappear?"

He turned down his mouth.

"The claimant hasn't been here or made a complaint," he said. "What can I do?"

"You can find out where all those titles went," I said.

"Something else to do besides bother about Indios," he said.

We walked out to the car and I looked at the sun in stained glass panels in the porch of the Governor's house, and in light and shadow on the windows of the Legislature farther down, and felt more an Indio than at any time in my life. Oracio saw it and put an arm on my shoulder.

"Come, now, Huw," he said, as a brother. "You know as much of politics as any of us. When you get to the Andes, you'll find out who the owners are. They'll be some of the Governor's own party. What can you do? Complain to the judges? Political appointments. To the President? He needs the Governor's help. Who else? God?"

He looked up at the sky, a clear, Patagonian blue, the pure breath that gives hope of the truth of Heaven.

"Not a word," he said. "Indios have no friends."

But coming up the hill on the other side, I saw Dugald Mael MacGrannoch and Michaye and the children, and he saw me in the same moment, and it was minutes before we had any sense, though when I told him about the titles his eyes came sharp enough.

"Michaye's father, the same," he said. "You're wasting good time. His name's not there. Or her mother's. Or her brother's, or her own or her sister's. The titles have gone. Indios don't read or write. How do they know? They're paying ten pesos gold for Indio ears, down there in the South. They're shooting them out. Sheepland. Oil land. Men, women and children. They've all got ears. They'll pay ten pesos for every pair."

"Not true," Oracio said. "I swear it cannot be true."

"Go down," Dugald said, and gray eyes cold as El Pampero. "Go down and see. They'll show you strings of ears. Have you seen a child's ears on a string? They dry small. But perfect. My mother had a cameo brooch. I remember the carving of the ears of the woman. I was reminded. I saw the lives of more than fifty men, women and children on a piece of string. Think of Michaye and me and these little ones. Is there any difference? Except we're alive. As they were."

"Who permits this?" Oracio said.

Dugald laughed at Michaye, still small, beautiful, barely older through the years and still with the ink silk in two thick plaits below the waist. All the little girls had long plaits, though not one had her Mama's eyes. Two boys were their father, in the piece. One was his mother, and she never took the hand from his shoulder. She knew where the weakness might show.

"There's money in sheep and oil," he said, as if wonders were about us. "The Government takes the oil. Who takes the sheep? Who's got the pocket to pay for ears? Who brings in the professional murderers?"

"It's enough," Oracio said. "This is hearsay. It's criminal."

"Do me the great pleasure," Dugald said. "You're a friend of Huw's, or I'd give you other answer. Go down, not fifty miles, for your enlightenment. Then keep on going down. Ask where the Indios are. They'll think you're out to earn a little easy pay. If you find a couple of families, remember, let's say, ten or twelve in number, that's twelve bullets. Little enough capital investment for a hundred and twenty pesos, gold or paper, would you say? Go on down. Find out. Stand there denying, you're like everyone else's self. But the Indios die. They are not there any more. And they've no land. Did you know that children's ears crackle together like seashells?"

That night we went to sleep in the echo of Dugald's pipes, and the children singing "I'm awae through the brae to haver with my laddie-O!" in the accent of their father, and I never heard a prettier lullaby. The wild, male lyric of the pipes brought a crowd of Gauchos about us, silent during, roaring after, and certain it is, the best guitar sounded very tame by compare.

We went together as far as their new home, of bricks, and tiled floors and plenty of windows, and it was plain enough that Michaye kept a strict household. Yet wherever I went, in any house, or any room, I missed the touch of Lal. In the back of my head I always saw the colors of our rooms when she was there, silver and crystal in shine, everything in polish, and little flowers in bowls for only me to enjoy.

Four peons Dugald sent with me to buy stores, so that I had all the protection I needed, though any thought of danger was laughable, since I had always been alone through the years.

But I was wrong, again.

We passed through New Gilgal and I went up to lay a hand on the rock face of Moishe's tomb and say a word, and with my eyes closed I am sure I heard his voice, and the voice of Lal, and though I shall never know what they said to me, still the best idea that ever came in my head was born then, and I went back to the car happy, sure I was right, and for the first time in all those years, of steady, settled purpose.

They told me drought had been with them for three years past, and going into the fenced land we saw the humps of dead sheep and cattle even if we were only a few miles from the lakes, though water could be had nearly everywhere by digging down and putting in a pump. The nearer we got to the City of the Mill, the more I wanted to turn back, and I was devout in thanks that I had my idea to send me on. It seemed I was two people, one wanting to go, and the other sure to stay. Drought was bad farther in. Lands that had always been green were brown. Cattle and sheep were not to to seen. Horses fed at the ricks, but there were not many, and not much hay was left in any of the barns.

"Rain by next month, or we finish," one of the peons said. "The only pool we've got will be dry in a week or so. We'll have to slaughter to keep the best."

The City of the Mill had never looked so poor in spirit. Only three shops were open, and empty, and two bars, with a few peons in each. Dugald's peons got down at the farthest, and we said goodbye. To the school I went, but it was in quiet of locked doors, and a woman told me Brother Little Mountain was taking his pupils home after the summer term. There was no heart in me to go down to see any of our places, and no wish to meet anybody I might have to talk to about Lal. Instead I turned back, across the river to the land that had been Saiheque's. A hut of planks with a tin roof was new, but the bones and tins strewn about were of the years.

"Whose land is this?" I asked the man at the door.

"Private property," he said. "I'm the overseer. Want anything?"

"I would like to know what happened to Saiheque," I said. "This was his land. The next league was Rupayan's."

"Not now," he said, and rolled the toothpick to the other side of his chops. "Belongs to Urtiaga and Barramendiz. They're partners."

No need to say another word. The moment I heard the name, I was certain it was that shyster lawyer put into a timber prison by Oracio those years before. Without waiting to ask, I went to the car, and backed out, on to the road, though while I was turning in deep dust, I saw him mount a pony and go at a gallop, but I thought little of it. It took time to drive along the track in dusty ruts, and cross the river's stones that once had been in deep green run. Turning down for the City, I saw the logs across the way and slowed, thinking that a timber wagon had tipped. But when I stopped, half a dozen men came from the bushes, knives out, no doubt in any face what they would do. Why, that day, I should wear the knife Moishe had once given me as a joke, a real Gaucho blade, twenty-two inches long, in a graven silver sheath, I am not sure even now, but it saved my life. There was time to slip off my jacket and bind it about my left arm to ward off a slash or blunt a stab, and then face them with a point a good ten inches longer than any of theirs, and knowing something, a little more than any of them, perhaps, of knife-fighting. Three of them I cut to the bone and they went. One of them cut me in the shoulder from behind, but I got him in the neck. One of them cut me in the scalp but he went down, sliced deep, and the other ran.

"You were lucky," the doctor said, stitching me later that afternoon, in Skeleton. "Tomorrow I wouldn't have been here. A thousand to one it's Barramendiz. They burnt the villages and chased the Indios out. Nobody knows where they went. They were working at a timber mill, down there. Then that burned. We haven't seen an Indio for months. It's a nuisance to us, too. We can't get a maid. There's nobody here to do any work."

Then, it was, in the chair, that I knew I must go to Little Looking Glass, and Kalata. Only she knew how to find anyone.

And I was hungry for a smile, and the touch of a hand, and the warmth of a woman's dearness.

28

Going back to Little Looking Glass I suppose was the best and wisest I could have done. There was nowhere to stay down in the Colony and the last I wanted was to be with friends and have to talk to them and their visitors. There were plans to be drawn and quantities to reckon for my idea, and I needed silence.

Though I never saw them, sure it is that Kalata had lookouts everywhere, for the house was in miles of forest, yet she was ready when I came from the last stand of timber that afternoon, and a meal was on the table in minutes, flowers everywhere, and my clothes laid out as if I had never been away.

It was very hard to tell her I must go, again. For news that might break their spirits, Araucano women never cry. Their faces seem to go smaller, as if their hearts were in a pincer and no more pain in the world to be felt. But no tears, and no move.

"Take me with you," she said, soft, looking out at the lake, a mile of pale blue through the window, and green mountains beyond. "What is a house? A place for a man. Put your saddle inside my door. Shall I live only to see the leaves change color? Or the *kalafáte* dress in blue berries again? I am a woman. Treat me as a *Chena*. But take me with you."

That word was given to servants of not much worth.

There was nothing more to do, and I put my arms about her, and she rested, sudden, heavy.

"You will come with me," I said. "Choose the saddle. It is yours."

But she never came near because I never asked, and Kalata's pride, her tenderness, knew.

How many messengers she sent I never found out, but not a month, and Saiheque and all his clan came in from far south with their pack animals loaded with guanaco meat, ready for winter, but readier to help me. Rhinberry, he said, was over the Cordilleras with his people, and it would be easier for us to go there, on, and direct south to New Gilgal, than for him to come up to us, and then go down. For them, of course, I was always *pichamanque* and brother-in-blood to their *toqui*, and all the older men remembered cutting stone and helping Vyrnwy, and their sons were not less ready, so that when they heard I was going to build again, we were in uproars there. Saiheque's five boys had just left Brother Little Mountain's school, and when I saw them do a few small jobs in the shed I knew they had been taught how to use a tool chest.

Saiheque sat for hours, watching me drawing the plans, copying details from the books in the library, and I thanked God many a time that Mr. Gruffydd and Angharad loved books, and bought plenty. From them I made the model, though the idea was Lal's, and nobody else's.

"Why haven't the Indios got a church of their own?" she said that night, sitting in a nightdress I saw everything through. "We've got chapels, and the Catholics have got shrines. But where do you see Indios? Would they be allowed to build one?"

"Well, yes, girl," I said. "If they wanted."

"You know perfectly well they would never want," she said, brushing long plaits, that crackled with her vital wonder. "I would like to build a church only for Indios. They have a God. They should be able to go to Him."

At that time I knew very little, and any notion of Indios in a church was silly.

"I suppose you could get a few to pay for it," I said.

"Pay for what?" she said, tugging at the brush. "I could afford it. But who would build? We need an architect. I'd like a church in the form of a cross. White. With the altar in the crisscross. Then everybody could see and hear. Our churches, the Indios have to squeeze in the back. The richest of us are in front with pews and hassocks. In my church, everybody the same. Indio or me, the same."

That was my idea, but only Kalata knew, and she was in glories, looking at the drawings as they grew, always touching the paper, putting the hand to her forehead and taking a deep, deep breath.

"Why don't the Araucano build a church for themselves?" I asked her, one evening.

"*Ranginhüenüchaü* has no need," she said, instantly. "Here is the church. It is built. We use it."

"Then why do you touch these drawings and breathe them into your head?" I asked her. "You have a church. Why do you need another?"

"If you dream, and you build, it is because you are nearer *Ranginhüenüchaü*," she said, in stare. "We shall also be nearer. You are *Ulmain*. Who is in your place? You speak, and it is."

Before light that morning we left Little Looking Glass, a wonder of still green water that later would be blue, always holding the mountains close in love. Days we went climbing, up and down, seeing not a soul until smoke signals on all the southern peaks warned us.

"*Camarúco*," Saiheque said. "They ask for rain. The forests are on fire."

Dust from blown soil blinded but we dare not go through timber, and even in rough bush there was danger of flash fire. Our animals were unshod, so we were able to take risks and short-cut between pools, most of drying mud, and rivers barely trickling that before were in torrent. We had water bags, but the animals were thirsty, and we wiped their nostrils with our ponchos, dipped when we drank, and they did well and whickered thanks. Never yet have I ridden a horse unable to say Thank You plain as the next, but only if you are fond. They are like Indios, or any of us, for they will do anything if there is a touch of love, but without it, they are Indios, or us, or horses, and nothing.

We crossed into Chile at Millaquen, but little on that side to tell the difference between two countries except for the place of the sun, and the size of the lakes, but haze hid all else and we could smell fire from the south. That night the scouts came in late, and said the *camarúco* was to be held near the Devil's Pelt, about two days ride away, and there was water in a cascade near the Lake of All Saints, and enough in the rivers and lakes from then on. Well, they were right, but I am not sure I would ask to do the journey again. We were in the mountains most of the time, and on the slope, crossing rock and scree, and nothing much to hold us except animal strength and instinct. That first taste of clear, cold water I will never forget, or the delight of the horses, that once we were off, galloped in, saddles and everything and swam and rolled, and came out to kick and jump, and stand steady for us to mount, and off, then, quiet and happy as the next. Toward evening we saw the signal fires higher up, beyond the dry, lower timber, and we climbed with the moon, around peaks and crags I would never dream of going near, along ledges with a fall of thousands of feet sheer, down paths almost vertical, jumping chasms without being able to see the other side, though if the horse in front went over, then so did the rest, and I was among them, and thankful, and I would much rather be sitting here.

We were outside the forest just before the sun came above the peak, and a village of women met us in white garments and served an asado of guanaco meat. We left the horses with them, and splashed in the waterfall and put on the clean fluffy woollen robe with a smell of apples that brought Lliutro almost to stand beside me, and in we went, to the forest. Dark, because the branches had been cut years before at a height of about twenty feet, and rising, thick, and no light of the sky, or sound except leaf whisper, and no birds, and only the deep loam underfoot. A long way we walked, down, and round, and up, always in darkness lit by the white shapes of those walking in front, and we came to a space where odd trees had been cut down, and the stumps taken out, perhaps a hundred yards all round, though even then branches were interlaced to make darkness, all in thin blue mist of smoke and reddened by flame of a hundred firepits.

Countless scores of men in white robes walked slowly, head down, hands behind, from fire to fire, lit in rings inside the circle, and at each fire a *ngen-pin* made prayer to *Ranginhüenüchaü*. None of them asked for rain, or for more food, or to save the herds or the women and children. None of them asked for anything. They all told stories of better times, and gave thanks, and wished for more. Men in the crowd whispered homage for a first-born son, or a good wife, or a troop of horses, or a herd of cattle or a gallop of guanaco.

Nobody asked for rain, but only for the life they had known, that till then was blessing.

Out at the side, where the trees were thick, I found a place to sleep, and Foyel came with blankets to make me comfortable, and said he would bring food and drink twice a day until the *camarúco* was over, and his father was at the big fire in the middle. If he was or not, I never found him, and I never saw anybody I knew. Time seemed never to have been. Men walked, murmured, or went to the side and lay in darkness to sleep. The murmur, the constant passing of white robes and the fire's flame in the branches above made the mind drowsy, and I slept often, and walked the circle, from fire to fire, looking for somebody I might know, but I never saw one. Several times I woke, and made up my mind to find Saiheque, and walked for perhaps hours, going from one fire to another, looking at any face I could see, but I never saw anybody to greet. Often I went back to the sleeping place to find food and drink waiting, though after the first time I never saw Foyel come near again. Sleeping, and waking to the same round of white robes, all walking in one way, all at the same pace, and hearing that deep murmur of men speaking in the throat, all in prayer to *Ranginhüenüchaü*, all praising for remembered moments, all searching their lives for times when they had laughed, back to childhood memories of play with brothers and sisters, or a father coming home with a saddle-load of meat, or a bowl of warm milk from their mother, or a comb of honey, or the marvel of a girl's eyes in love, or the birth of children, or a fine colt, or only a few minutes of laughter with a friend, all, in those hours of walking were remembered, and told again, and offered in grateful thanks on the mind's altar, and the *ngen-pin* at a hundred fires took the thoughts and made prayers, asking nothing, telling only of sons and daughters in praise for a happy life.

How long we were there I never knew, but I was on the far side, near the lane to go out, and all the women and children came, a quiet, white cloud, all carrying an asado of horseflesh on skewers, and the winebags, and we went to them and they served us, and we passed the wine, but the *ngen-pin* still sat beside their fires in prayer. The women and children cleared the space of bones and stood to the side.

For the first time since I had become myself again, I heard the deep blare of the *trutruca*, war trumpet of the Araucano, and men, women, and children slowly went to their knees and bowed their heads to the ground. For a long time, until my legs were asleep, we knelt, without sound even from the children. Behind, the *ngen-pin* prayed in louder voices. Above, the branches whispered. Flame put red light in white robes. Children cried and women murmured. Beyond the trees, and in the lane to the open, only darkness, and silence.

Numb though my knees were, I felt the gallop of horses long before they turned into the end of the lane, and a dozen men got up to block the way with swung lassos to bring the troop to a trot, and then to stand. All of them were white, without blemish, stallions, mares, colts, and foals, and the best I ever saw, picked from up and down the country. The *ngen-toqui* led his priests, still praying, in a ring, and the horses were sent in one by one to be judged. A mare was chosen, a wonderful animal, and the *ngen-toqui* shouted once, and the priests answered in a long scream, and the *trutruca* blasted a deep sound that seemed to shake the skin away from my bones. Slowly in paces, the *ngen-toqui* went toward the mare, and ran his hands over her as he might if he were starting to tame, for Indios never use whip or shackle, but only the hands and a whisper, smoothing both sides, down each leg, and under the belly, until the animal will put its muzzle in the small of the back and follow anywhere, into the house as well. More hours we knelt in silence, watching the mare slowly becoming used to hands and voice, losing her fear, standing without nerves, no rearing, no stamp, no longer the roll of eyes here to there, but first calmed and then gentled, until she trusted. Hours passed again while the *ngen-toqui* knelt with all the others, and I suppose I slept, because I was wakened by the *trutruca* in higher blasts, and everybody was standing, and the *ngen-toqui* stood with a long, heavy stone knife at the mare's head, with a *ngen-pin* on either side.

Everybody shouted, and the *trutruca* might have broken our eardrums, but in a sudden move, the *ngen-toqui* thrust the knife deep and high between the forelegs, where the neck joins the body, and pulled out the knife, levering up and down to cut a wider wound. He gave the knife to his second man, and watched him bury it in the nearest fire's ashes, and held up the right hand and the robe slid to the bloodied elbow. Everybody raised the right hand, and screamed long, and the *ngen-toqui* pushed the right fist into the wound, and reached deep, and wrenched, and pulled out the heart, still beating in small veil of mist, and settled it into the palm of the left hand, and brought down the right hand *slap!* on to it, and the mare went down, foreknees bent, slowly, to the near side, and lay still.

Instantly, the scream burst and held from every open

mouth, and the *ngen-toqui* led the dance, down the lane toward the entrance. Want or not, but the crowd pushed in a run, and children were held up not to be trampled, and women were strong as anyone else with shoulders and elbows, and only the tree trunks and thick growth on both sides held everyone to the path.

But as we got nearer the opening I felt a drop on my face, and another, and everybody screamed higher and women trilled in a din to bring a headache, and suddenly we were in daylight, beyond the trees, in a roaring froth of rain, and nothing to be seen beyond a few yards except the fog of cloudburst.

"All right," Rhinberry shouted, just behind me. "The horses are over here. Come, you."

Saiheque and his people were all there, and we rode down the slope to the lower forest, and in shelter of the trees an asado was ready, and we drank a cup of tea, perhaps the best I ever had.

"I didn't like killing that beautiful mare," I said. "They've got no conscience about killing anything."

"How many chickens and ducks and turkeys have you eaten in your time?" Rhin asked me. "How much beef, mutton, pork? Sucking pig? Veal? Lamb? Bacon? Did you ever care who twisted a neck or stuck a knife in a throat? Everything very good on the plate. But killing is wrong, is it? Leave it, now. They have got their way to do what they want. And from the look of everything, it works."

"Do you believe it?" I asked him.

"Believe it?" he said, with his teeth in a cut of horse meat. "Well, use your eyes, boy. A few minutes ago we were dying for a drop of rain, here. Not a cloud anywhere. No sign. Now you could be drowned, and no trouble. Believe what?"

"You believe the *camarúco* made the rain?" I said.

"Huw, it's not the first time it's happened, and not the first time I've seen it happen in front of me," he said, and in care to cut a thin strip from the fillet. "*Camarúco* or not, the rain falls by the ton where not a drop, or any hope of a drop was before. And depend, now, it will fall for weeks. But I have got far better news, and glad I am, and thankful to the heart."

He was looking at me from the side, and smiling, bread and meat in one hand, knife in the other, but no move to eat.

"Well?" I said.

"If you were not in thorough health and your own self again, you would never have asked such a question," he said. "Brother Little Mountain's prayers have not been for nothing, then? You have stopped even to think as an Indio."

True, and I knew it, and I could have hymned for joy of deep relief, and devoutest thanks.

Well, rain fell, fell, and fell, as only it can fall in the Andes.

Then it was that I was made to learn again why the Indio pony's hoofs were called nails. The three I rode in turn saved my life many a time. Crossing a deep scree of pebbles on a steep slope, they put fores and hinds together and stayed in moving ground as if nailed, and waited, while the entire ramp shifted, with stones often piling against my left shoulder and my right-hand boot free and pointing down at a drop of thousands of feet, but in some moment, they sensed a loosing of the slide in front, and heaved their fores free, and leaped, a backbreaker for any rider, but I only had to stay in the saddle and I was safe for the next nailing, and the wait, and heave, and leap, and so to firm ground. None of us were lost, and only two packhorses, but as Rhin said, we were lucky to be able to blow them a kiss of thanks, and farewell.

We crossed the pass into Argentina without seeing anybody, and rode to the sunrise, and sometime that late evening we were in New Gilgal, and a barer place, of less pleasure to the eye would be hard to find, and I was cut in the spirit to think of Moishe left there, lonely, in rock and dust.

"Water is all we want," Rhin said. "As we argued all the years, here. Water. And make it a garden."

"Water there shall be," I said. "We will deal with a garden after."

Saiheque found where to dig, but the wells were deep and

we needed pumps, and Australian tanks, piping, and how many other items, and though I wanted what we were doing to be kept secret, an order for that amount of material could only bring the curious to sniff. It was all done by sending a note to Solva and Oracio, and asking Mog, Moke, to bring it without telling anyone what or where.

All day Saiheque's people chipped rock or helped Rhin with timber, and I had the rest putting in the foundations and squaring off ground for the garden. Mog's first loads of corrugated sheets and the pumps and piping came at just the right time, and we had the pumps working, and water running in the little canals within the week, and I was sure the Indios would go mad with wonder. They had never seen a pump. When we started building the tanks they thought it was a row of houses, and Foyel had the courage to ask if such a toldo, of metal, would not be too hot. The sheets we bolted in rings forty foot in diameter, the width of six sheets, banked and floored with cement, and everybody was in a crowd, waiting to see me put on a roof. Instead I got the pumps going and when the first tank began filling they were looking at me as if I had gone mad at last, but I said nothing, and went on to the next, until they were all in work and taking a strong gush of excellent water, and I was thankful to God for no more worries.

"In such a toldo, how do women cook in winter?" Perqueñ, third of Saiheque's boys, asked me.

"They stand in water to the neck," I said. "The children hang on to their skirts. The cooking fire, of course, warms the water. When the hunters come home, there is good soup ready."

Foyel slowly squatted down and held his ankles and began to laugh, and soon they were all in stitches, there, lying about, shaking their heads, laughing, not at a silly joke but at each other for being bitten. It took a long time to get over, too, and when they were calm again, any word anywhere would set them off. They helped to plait roofs for the tanks to save evaporation, and then we dug waterways to the farthest points of the garden, and crisscrossed with canals, and put down piping for the fountains and for the school's water tank.

One night, Mog's column came in and he gave me a letter from Oracio to say that the lawyers had prepared the case for restoration of titles, and Rhinberry and Saiheque, and all the others must present themselves at the Governor's office to file a claim and show proof.

"I am not moving one foot from by here," Rhin said. "They can keep it. It wasn't theirs to give, to begin. Fifty years and more ago, my father was here. My wife's people were here for thousands. Should I ask a thief to share the pillage?"

"Well, Rhin, boy, look," I said. "The lawyers have gone to the trouble of making a case."

"No trouble to them," he said. "The biggest thieves of the lot."

"But haven't you got the heart to defend what is your property?" I said. "As guardian of the Indios, isn't it your duty?"

"Soon I will be at the waterfall with my little one," he said. "Property is nothing to me. She never had any, except a strong, beautiful spirit and the days and nights of her time, and the land to ride in. Her father's land. His father's land, and how many before? Property? What good is it to me, or to any of these? They will be cheated from it soon enough."

"Not if the Governor signs title," I said. "The General was good enough to give it to you. You should protect his gift at least. After all, you could sell it, all of you, and use the money to build a school for the children. Or live here, and be of use to the community."

"First, I don't want to live here," Rhin said. "Second, I want nothing to do with any community here. If we get our land back, how long would we last? Saiheque's village was burned down. They blamed drunken Indios. A lie. The timber mill burned. Again, drunken Indios. Another lie. But the families had no homes. And no work. They had to move.

Where to? Chile, of course. There, they don't get killed. Leave your house for years. It will be there when you go back."

"But put up a fight, boy," I said. "Don't be treated like this. Don't let the Indios suffer because they can't read or write, or understand a word of law. Go and represent them. Get back all they are entitled to. At least, you are a pioneer. You speak Castellano. You will be listened to. And you have plenty of friends."

"Vote on it," Rhin said. "Ask Saiheque and his people if they want to stay here. If they want land."

Saiheque looked at me with the dead, black, eternally dead, black stare of the Indio.

It was enough.

Nothing I could say would budge either of them, and until night and a rising moon, I wasted time in arguing.

"Very well," I said. "To Hell. I won't sit fat by here and see it go by default. I will represent everybody."

"Go, you," Rhin said, short, the first time he had spoken for an hour. "Take everything for yourself. It's yours. None of us have got anything more on this side. We are here because you asked. After, we shall go. You will have a journey of regret."

Right, too.

The way across with Mog, Moke, was very comfortable in his big truck, remembering other times, and soreness often in my throat to remember our first men and women in those wagons, and the hymns at night and in early morning, three weeks, a month or more, and every mile, every breath in Faith, if not to move mountains, then to bring them nearer. But without any hymns, and with little enough Faith in anything, we were in Rawson the same night, and I saw the Governor in his office in light of candles because bare bulbs hurt his eyes, and he liked older ways far better. Laurel burned in the fireplace, and we had *empanadas* and wine and a good talk before we began business. We had known each other for years, when he drew all Moishe's marine contracts, so that we had no need for preamble.

"This is pure politics," he said, tapping the files. "All the land near the Cordilleras will become a National Park, north to south. Nobody can build or live there except the people already homesteading. When they die, their families will be moved out. It will revert to wild country."

"Francisco Moreno's dream," I said, and raised the glass. "To all the Franciscos, cursed or mocked in their time. Their dreams are seed of reality."

"Amen," he said, and drank. "Apart from that, there's been a murderous fight to claim the land immediately adjacent. Most of it belonged to Indios. Cambrians took the flatter land farther out. Except you, and about a dozen others. But it's valuable. That's why there's been this continuous violation. But there wasn't anybody living on the places, not even a few old Indios left there to die."

"Saiheque's village was burned to the ground," I said. "The mill burned."

The Governor's shrug almost matched Moishe's.

"Indios are careless with fire," he said. "They get drunk."

"I have had years with Indios," I said. "I never saw a toldo burn. I never saw a woman careless of fire. They are the guardians of fire. From little girls, they are taught. And Saiheque and his people drink sometimes, yes. But never in those villages. That was a rule."

"The village burned, and so did the mill," the Governor said, and drank as if the case was proven. "There were no witnesses. No proof of incendiarism. Nobody there to talk to. I have the report."

"Written by frightened women?" I said. "They took the children away. The men followed. Did you know that Indios are being hunted by murderers? A few pesos for each pair of ears? Proof of death?"

"No evidence," he said, and opened a file. "None at all."

"Supposing I lay a string in front of you," I said. "What, then?"

"Ears keep," he said, still looking at the file. "They could be a hundred years old."

"Yes," I said, remembering. "They rattle like seashells. Especially babies' ears."

He looked at me, tired, across the polish of the wide desk a little dulled with the day's dust.

"Politics, I warned you," he said. "I have to be careful. Land has value. Sheep, cattle, that's money. Money has become politics. The home of politics is Buenos Aires. I hope we understand each other? The people who took this land are directed from Buenos Aires. They have a hold north to south. Powerful. If I want this or that, I must give that or this. That also is politics."

"Well," I said.

"Patience," he said. "I'm going to restore all these titles granted by the Army. I'm telling you plainly, because I know that if you go to the Minister, there'll be the Devil to pay. The Army won't permit any nibbling. Their authority is preeminent. Therefore, I restore all titles. But when the Commission inspects, who'll be there? Who'll pay the taxes?"

"Give me the titles, and I shall be responsible for everything," I said. "Every league will be worked either in stock or cereals. I'd like to get the younger generation of Indios settled and making something of themselves."

He sat back, laughing tiredly, rubbing his eyes.

"I thought I heard the voice of Moishe," he said. "Wonderful man. Long before his time. So are you. You'll never get them to settle. Any of them. They were born to gallop."

"There's many a good gallop on a square league," I said. "Don't forget there's Brother Little Mountain teaching over there. He'll wrestle with any terror of Hell for dominance over what he believes is his. I will put everything in his charge."

"Including your own league, and your late wife's, and her sister's," he said, turning the pages of the files.

"Everything," I said. "Everything worked will go to the school."

"Including the league of your wife's daughter?" he said, looking at a page.

"My wife?" I said, and sat, feeling as if he had struck me through the head. "Wrong. Mistake. She never had a daughter."

"This is the birth certificate, and here is the claim, for the league opposite yours, between Rhinberry Wynn's and Rupayan's," he said. "The daughter is now of age to take control. Where is she?"

29

If I imagined I was going to explode a keg or two, well, Solva poured enough cold water.

"O, deuce, come on now, boy," she said, and laughing. "We had her at Maes Corwen when we came home from school. After Ithel brought her. His daughter she is, with a girl of Clais'. Beautiful little thing, too. But the mother wanted her back, so pull one, push the other, she had to go. Pity. She was doing lovely with us."

"But why's Lal down as the mother?" I asked her, easier in mind, a great deal, but far from satisfied. "Why didn't the parents register?"

"Well, to begin, they aren't registered themselves," Solva said. "They can't read or write. They were frightened to go near the Justice. Lal simply did the sensible thing. Put the child on her saddle, rode her in, and signed. She had a piece of my mother's property from each of us, as well. The league was an extra gift."

"But why put herself down as the mother?" I said. "Why not take the real mother?"

"Would she be made to go?" Solva said, eyes wider, paler gray, much more serious. "You don't dare to think Lal was the mother, do you? Those things were done when she was with us. One of the family. To protect."

"That league was put in her name years afterward," I said. "Long after she'd been taken away."

"There are five leagues in her name in the Territory," Solva said, and went to look from the doorway, across the lawn to the ridge where the pampas began. "They tried to get her to school. Sent her clothes. Did all they could, I suppose. But her mother, and that old Indio grandmother, they wouldn't allow anything. I haven't seen Ithel for years. Find him. He'll tell you. I'd like to see her again, mind. Spoiled for everything, I'll bet. And no doubt married. Brood, as well."

"Couldn't you have applied to adopt?" I asked her.

"Not if the mother disagreed," Solva said, and saw the trap too late. "Look, Huw. There was trouble enough with Vrann. They didn't want a tribe about the house all shouting for the little thing. Could Lal go to old Justice Dab and Blow, and tell him she had sworn a false document? The other could prove she was the mother. How could Lal? And if that mother had registered as a daughter of Clais, with Ithel as the father, then all of them would have had a chance to register. We'd have had how many half-brothers and -sisters, all half-Indio?"

"But Ithel is down here as the father," I said. "Orkiki is here as a witness. So two statements are false."

"Perhaps they didn't know," Solva said, still looking out. "How could they know, if they couldn't read or write? No doubt if you ask Orkiki he could tell you more. Lal couldn't have used him as witness without telling him. He's still in the City of Lewis, somewhere."

"It wasn't like Lal to swear false testimony," I said. "How could such a sensible girl do such a thing? This is her writing. Mother and father couldn't read or write? What matter to them, or anybody else, if their names are here? Who will question?"

"I have told you, Huw," Solva said, as near to being angry with me as I ever saw her. "If two Indios are registered, with Vrann as one father and Clais as the other, then a male and female half-Indio are in the civic records as son and daughter of two Corwens. It is a step from there to registering all of them. All of them would have a claim on Corwen property."

"But they have a rightful claim, girl," I said. "If they are children of Vrann and Clais, of course they could claim. Every one of them. And the Law would support them."

"That's not the way we think," Solva said, and far from sweet. "If one of them had lifted a hand to help us all these years, we might think differently. See Orkiki. He ought to be able to tell you more."

In the way the words ripped in that little voice, I knew we were near a quarrel.

"Solva, my little one," I whispered behind her. "You know I would never draw one breath against Lal."

She turned to me in a moment and put her arms about me.

"I know, I know," she said. "I hate to talk one moment. I didn't even think of it, all these years. Do you want to find the girl? Why?"

"Anything Lal has touched, or even thought about, is dearer than all the world to me," I said. "Dear as herself in beauty would be a girl she tried to protect. I will protect, instead. I will find the girl. If she has got a family, I will take care of them. And I will thank God on the knees that He allowed me."

Solva's kiss was like a little blessing, small echo of another's, and I was sure I could see Doli, with pink ribbons in thread through lace in her nightdress smiling at me that last morning.

It took time to find Orkiki, and I had to drive from Port Madryn to a small fish-salting factory near Rawson. Those years before I remembered him, a fine big man, with the size and strength of the Tehuelche, born to the horse and able to do anything with them. But in the factory yard I saw a little old bent thing, sitting in the watchman's hut and mending a net. A stink of fish was heavy, broken boxes and rope ends lay about, the sheds were shut, and nothing moved anywhere except the flies, and they made the only noise.

First I had to explain who I was, but I think he remembered Moishe better, though when I spoke Arauco instead of Castellano there was instant wide-eyed change. Tehuelche speak only another kind of the language, and Orkiki almost burst his lungs to tell me all he knew, for when Indios have anything to say about themselves they shout at pitch of their voices to tell all the listening spirits, and start by warning those to be talked about, so that the guardians, those gone and others waiting to take their places on earth, may hear any untruth and punish there and then.

Orkiki bellowed, raising the bones of his arms, and I had to listen for minutes about past ones, until he came to his own day, and he told me Ithel was not Vrann's son, but Tanfi Corwen's, and the mother was daughter of Tynant Lewis, and Lal had given him a troop of horses to make a thumb print signature in front of the Justice.

"But how could you deny your own people?" I said, still dense. "Children of Indio and *huinca* parents are still your people."

"Not my people, not Tehuelche, those," he shouted, wide in the eye, with spittle at the corners of his mouth, still with no gap in those broad teeth. "Which people are they? Cambrian? A *diâwl*. Tehuelche? Which father? They are of no people, of no blood and no worth."

He cursed in Cambrian that he spoke well, and looking at him, in rags of shirt and *bombachos*, with a bit of leather bound about thin white hair, I wondered what he meant by worth, standing in a stink of rotting fish, with broken net coiling about him, and the planks of the hut needing only a little push to fall flat.

"My blood will go back, clean as it was given, to *Ranginhüenüchaü*," he shouted at the clouds. "I was not touched by another. No other except of my blood touched me. I kept my blood and my promise. The guanaco are all gone. My women have gone. My children are with El Pampero. My horses wait for me. The day is known. I shall run, and laugh."

He pushed aside the money I offered.

"I have enough," he said. "I am here to be away from *tabolongo*."

The word was given to beetles with a horrible smell, and I wondered again that he could think of it, and yet stay day and night in a real stink of rotting fish.

"If you want to leave this, and work among horses, I can find you a place," I said. "Not far."

"I shall be here until I run," he said. "Here, the fish come to die. Who will be here to welcome them if I go? They have their time. I have mine."

He sat to mend the net and I left him without the heart to turn round.

All the way back I was thinking of him, knowing he had become witless. Everybody knew he was half-brother to Vrann and Clais, a son of Tanfi, the pioneer Corwen, and no purer in blood than any of those he cursed. But even the half-Tehuelche is friend among friends, and their word given is a word kept. Whether he believed what he said, or if he said it to protect Lal, I shall never be sure, but I was doubly sure I would find all the Corwen family, and see what I could do to make them happy. The patience of angels could chafe in those weeks, of trying to find a trace of any of them. Rupert von Gelsbach sent down a list from Court records of the children Vrann had registered, and I asked the gendarmes and police to publish the names all through the country, with a reward.

Not one was found. Many reports came in of those dead. Whispers were here and there, but they were only that. A pensioned Inspector of Police, José Olivos de Garcia, went for weeks everywhere, but he came back to New Gilgal one night, and had to report not a trace of any of the dozens.

"You know, sir, I have a theory," he said, over the fire, after a long silence. "You must please bear with me for a moment. After all, I have fifty-five years of service. I know Patagonia from Rio Gallegos to Port Madryn, Vuriloche to Puma Canyon. I believe I know every settler in the country. I've been considering all the stories about Indios being murdered. Of course, they were. Thousands. These you look for could have been among them. With reason."

"My wife would never have given it a moment's thought," I said. "Put it beyond discussion."

"Your wife, you must permit me, sir, was a woman of strong character," Inspector Garcia said, handing the *maté* to Kalata for refill. "She is known to have used pistol and rifle more than once."

"Never to kill," I said. "She knocked their hats off or stung their ears. I know. I was once a witness. The day we met."

"I regret I must disagree, sir," he said. "She often shot to protect."

"My wife was never a murderess," I said.

"Self-defence is never murder," he said. "She defended her property. She had reason."

"Look here," I said. "I'm employing you to find a number of people. I am not interested in theories. Consider yourself on full pay for the next three months. By that time, bring me news. Stories have no interest."

He stood, and bowed, and went.

Kalata sat.

"I heard," she said. "I know where the *Domomalén* lives."

Young virgin, she called her, and I could have shouted for joy, and I took her by the shoulders.

"You should have asked me," she said. "Why didn't you?"

"You are of the Andes," I said. "What would you know of the other side?"

"I know every family of every *rehue*, and every child born of our women by the *huinca*," she said.

"Where is she?" I asked. "I shall ride in the moment these walls are dry."

"She is with the families of the peons," Kalata said. "They are near the Hidden Water. But I can bring her. You would never take her. Or see her. Let me go."

"We will go together, and I will stay at the fire, half a day's ride behind you," I said.

The families of Lal's and Doli's and Solva's peons had not

been in my mind, though, of course, they could have told far more than anybody. Solva must have known that her peons would have plenty to say, but she never mentioned them.

Doubt began to eat as rust, till I was not even able to look at the little gold box, so dull I was.

In the early days I remembered that Ithel had always been somewhere near Lal, though she was never in good comfort to speak of him. That afternoon we were together, and somebody shot at me, she seemed to want me to believe it was Vrann. But if I had thought for a moment, I might have wondered how Vrann, that marksman, could have missed. The night Matti Mumpo died, no doubt Ithel brought in the Indios, and less doubt somebody told them what to do.

Over to Rhin's shed I went, and found him at the fire polishing silver ornaments for the altar.

"You have got everything hinds first, as per usual," he said, without stopping work. "If Lal had a baby, will you tell me how she would hide it? Months of work at the dam? The farm? The cattle? Sheep in the Territory? And women all round her? It's unjust to think in such a way. Ithel was a good man. Perhaps he told the Indios he wanted Matti put from there. As a service to Lal. But remember who was also getting married. Mr. Elias, Snuff, and Nelya Penninah. If old Matti was out of the way, she would inherit everything. Elias knew nothing of the marriage contract with Lal. I don't suppose he would have looked at Nelya if he had. And who gave the Indios all that drink? Lal? Was she that sort? Would she dream of it? Elias, yes. Those tents were only a spit from Damaglou's. That's where the wedding party and the drink was."

"Well," I said. "Wait till we have found this girl. Then we'll see."

"You will never see, even to the end of your nose," he said. "Leave the girl where she is. Her life is there. What can you do for a girl that age? She is long past school, or even what we could call decent habits. It's like pulling up a flower by the roots to have thick blossom next week."

"I thought you wanted to help Indios," I said. "This is half an Indio. Half a Corwen. I shall do all I can. If I fail, very well. You were right. But remember. I have got Kalata to help."

He nodded, still polishing.

"Go, you," he said. "I know Lal is watching, mind. Somebody else, too."

"Who?" I said.

"My little one," he said. "She was nurse to Lal from when she was born. Hurt to Lal is hurt to her. So, careful, now."

Doubt was in me, not so much a spreading rust, but a paralysis, and sleep became a stranger, and waking was hateful return to anxiety that I felt almost as another skin. The only two physicians of that time were dead, and nobody knew where their books had gone. Inspector Garcia made inquiries about the midwives, but without a word of help. It was no use going about and asking questions of neighbors and raising a dust of gossip. But he found Mrs. Justice Dab and Blow living with a son and his family outside Commodoro Rivadavia, in the new oilfield. Down there I went, one Sunday, and met her in a little house in the desert, with a few trees about, and the strange shapes of oil derricks making long crisscross shadows in sand and low hills, and the sun like an open firebox. She put her arms about me as one of the family, and we talked about everybody, with some tears here and there, but plenty of laughter. We had a splendid cup of tea from a big Cambrian tea pot she had brought from the Colony, and tea-cakes with currants, and apple tart good as I have tasted anywhere, so I was almost home.

But the moment I spoke about the certificate, she became the wife of a Justice.

"Absolutely not, and be certain, because I had forty-six marvelous, marvelous years with my husband, and I believe I have the right to know what I say," she said, and sat straight in the wooden chair, and tied the lace a little tighter under her second chin and so covered the other two. "He would never have accepted what he knew to be false. If she was put down as mother, he would require the physician or midwife as witness. The father would have to be present. Resolve any question in your mind, sir."

There was no age in the big black eyes, but only stern spirit to defend love, and I went to her, and knelt to take her hand, and kiss, feeling the rough palm of housework.

"It was not my intention," I said. "I wanted the facts. How could Lal put herself as mother, and how could Mr. Justice allow it, if it was untrue?"

Her eyes opened wider, with a smile that began far away and she unfolded the certificate again.

"But, sir," she said. "Look at these names. Lal's name was the same as her mother's. Milalai Sabel. Her father's name was Ithel, too. Ithel Vrann Cadwallader. His father called him Vrann. Everybody else did. I remember it very well. This certificate is for a sister of Lal's. Look at the date, and look at the death certificate of the mother. She died after childbirth. Isn't it clear?"

Well.

Back I went to the Registry, and sure enough Mrs. Justice Dab and Blow was right, for the date of death was ten days later, and the names were the same, and a physician had signed.

To burn the road I went back to Solva, and found her in the garden house, and put the certificate on the table, and I knew she was frightened and not wanting to show it.

"What is the mystery about this?" I asked her, not a word of greeting. "Come you, now then. This isn't my Lal. It's your own mother and father. This Ithel isn't the Indio. How could you let me believe or doubt, or be in such a state? You knew I would find out, didn't you?"

Her hands were trembling so much that the certificate made a noise almost louder than her voice.

"Will you believe me if I tell you the truth?" she said. "This is the first time I've ever seen this. Mama died eleven years after I was born. I believe she had one or two stillborn. Vrann wanted a son. Only Lal could tell you anything of this.

Doli and I were at school. The little one was at Maes Corwen once, when we came home for holidays. After that we never saw her. Children forget soon enough. If we talked about her, it was only to wonder what she was doing, or where. But I can never remember thinking of her as a sister."

She put trembling hands to her face, and tears ran jewels through fingers.

"O, Huw," she moaned. "But she is. She must be my sister. My sister? Good God, I'll have her from wherever she is, and quick. Do you know? Can you believe I don't even remember the girl's name? Sûs, we called her."

Kiss, in Cambrian, and Solva's eyes in drown of tears, and her whisper were with me on the road back that night, and I was in New Gilgal with the sun, and Rhin was just making the tea.

"Look here," I said. "You knew damn' well I would have this right. Why didn't you tell me the truth?"

"I told you," he said, and very calm. "Have a cup, now, and hold your temper and your language. I don't know everybody's business. I knew there was a little girl. Whose, I didn't know. I knew she was out in the Territory. Why, I didn't know. But if she has been there all these years, it is cruel to pull her away. Let sleeping dogs. Will you ask for trouble?"

"Yes," I said. "She is sister of Lal's. I am off, now, to find her."

The strongest truck would have been useless across that ground, so off, with a troop, Kalata and I went, and that night we were in the hills' silence, and the stars seemed to blaze brighter for me, and I think I started to be happy then because I was sure I was right, surer still that Lal's voice hummed lullaby in the pampas sough, that was barely part of any sound but dearest half of silence.

In the afternoon of the third day, Kalata lifted a hand and I reined, and she rode over the skyline, and I found a place to make camp, ready to stay a week or longer if necessary, for we knew she might have days of argument. Nobody on earth can argue, word by word, and even syllable by syllable, to come near an Indio.

About an hour later I walked up to the ridge and looked across a dry, sloping plain to another range of bare hills. Kalata was a moving puff of dust going up the rise to a group of red roofs below a little waterfall, with a spread of green about, and poplars in tall plume round the corral. That sort of house I knew well, of mud walls and tin roofing painted red to hold off the sun's heat, a ring of stones for a fireplace, a kettle and a couple of pots, and a chair or two, or crates on end, and sheepskins for beds. A girl used to such a hovel takes time to adjust to a good house, but once out, I have never known one go back, so I had reason to feel I was doing her no harm.

But I never understood, even to this day, why Lal had never said a word about her. Solva told me afterward that Vrann had gone twice to get her, and always came back without, and drunk, and she was sure Lal went several times, but never brought her back, and never told why. In that way the years went, and the girl was left to live as she wanted, and forgotten.

The reason, of course, was simple and tragic enough, but I only wish I knew why Lal never once spoke of a younger sister to me.

Shame is greatest of all slavemasters.

Next morning, just before midday, two riders left the corral and galloped down to the plain. One stayed on the track that came in long curves up to a pass on my right, and the other climbed direct to me. A group of women stood to wave under the poplars, and went in. The rider coming to me was hidden by ridges most of the time, but when she was near enough, I knew Kalata had chosen to ride the longer way, and I blessed the soul of a dear woman.

But my heart seemed to stop beating at thought of meeting Sûs, and I turned quick and went back to the camp, and shouted to the peons to go for the horses to be out of the way.

At the fire I waited, and I heard the pony picking his way down, and turned.

She was still on the skyline, and she reined, looking at me, and for moments I stood.

Lal.

With two plaits, dark, a little darker than Lal's, below the knees, but Lal.

Gray eyes, not the royal, golden-deep red wallflower velvet, but gray, not so pale as Solva's, but shining in the sun, and a smile that could only be of a Corwen, Lal's, that came from a heart and meant to rest in one. The Cambrian smile, secret of the Cambrian woman.

She was off the pony as an Indio, with no move the eye might see, and walking toward me.

"*Mari-mari*," she said, loud, but in the same depth of voice as her sisters.

My arms were out wide, and she opened the cloak as an Araucana, and I put my hands on the warmth of her waist and her arms were strengthy about me, and I knew she was mine till the last breath.

30

Teaching a child A.B.C. is a matter of patience, but how to teach a young woman to live through a different kind of day after using her time on earth in learning another, almost purely Indio and not far from the animal, put our heads in our hands round the table that night, and we agreed that Solva would keep her there for a couple of months till after the shearing, and then take her to Buenos Aires to give her a notion of grace and beauty in other women.

She was like a little girl still with dolls, not a word of Castellano or Cambrian, not a moment of school in any subject, but she could cure hides, make a robe or cloak, or weave a rug with the best. In the few days I stayed there, she had learned to make butter and three sorts of cheese good as Solva, and her bread was even better, and after a bit of practice her pies, tarts, and cakes were far in front of anybody's, because she had the Indio way, with honey instead of sugar.

"There is nothing, nothing wrong with the girl," Solva said. "We have got to teach her Castellano, first. She's got a small memory of Cambrian, so she'll pick that up with the children. I'll have a governess here for the three R's. No use to think of anything more, and if she doesn't learn easily, I'll stop it. I won't have the girl humbugged for a moment. After all, there are plenty of ladies without even one R, never mind three, and they are doing lovely, indeed. So will she."

"Then I will leave Kalata here to translate," I said.

"You will do nothing of the sort," Solva said, and the flat of a small hand firm on the table. "Sûs has got to learn from the beginning, from me, direct. I will have her to the doctor tomorrow. Vaccination, and complete examination. Most of them suffer from worms. But she is very clean, nothing like an Indio. Her hair is beautiful, with her. But those hands and feet? Well, I could have cried pints, again. Poor girl, she couldn't understand."

Those hands were used to hard work but not to soap and water, and the feet had been brutalized by walking barefoot through her years. Strange it is to see a girl lovely in face and form with ugly hands and feet, at any rate to our eyes. And I have often wondered who the Hell we are, any of us.

"Indios are very clean in themselves," I said. "Clean hair and skin, to them is duty. Hands and feet are tools. She was lucky to be with that old woman. At least, she was strict."

That was the reason why Vrann and Lal had never been able to find her. Every time they came, Sûs was taken from the house and out to the pampas and kept there until they were gone.

"Fifty men couldn't have found her," Solva said. "Police? In those days? What could they have done if the old woman denied having her? What could Vrann say? Everybody knew he as good as killed poor Mama. He lived on wine and false hope. Anyway she is here now, and thank God."

The old woman had been maid lifelong to Lal's mother, and pensioned, and when Vrann, screaming-drunk kicked over the cradle because Sûs was a girl instead of the boy he wanted, she was taken to Hidden Water by the old one for safety, and she never came back because Lal's mother died, and as Indios believe, the old one was guardian to the grave, and her daughters, widows of Lal's peons, kept her promise. Kalata, nobody else, could have talked sense into them, and because they trusted her as one of themselves, and they knew who I was, Sûs was allowed to saddle her pony but only on oath that if she wanted to go back, we would have nothing to say.

She put that saddle inside my door on the night we got to Solva's and never used it again, and I went to the City next morning and bought her the best Australian saddle I could find, and put it outside her door, and she came to find me in breathless skirts, and pulled me in a run to stand in the doorway, and point with two fingers together.

The saddle was at the foot of her bed.

"I am old for her," I said to Solva. "If she finds a younger man, I will go."

"Look, boy," she said. "You have got many a good year. You have got a family in front of you. She is not the sort to change her mind. Be tidy, now, and wait till we come from Buenos Aires. Then we will have a wedding here for a monument in the memory."

"Not here," I said. "On the other side."

Solva held up the flat of her hands.

"Wherever," she said. "Oracio and I will be there. I wish he would come home. That old waterworks will drive us all mad. And we shall have nothing in the end, either."

Oracio was helping our Canal and Waterworks shareholders to make the Government pay after the Supreme Court allowed their claim for some millions of pesos, but a Court order is one thing, and a banker's draft is another, and he had been up at La Plata and Buenos Aires for weeks, trying to get justice, and the money. The canal system and waterworks had been paid for in sweat and gold pesos through two generations of Cambrians, without help of State or Government, and miles of canals dug by men and women, and the children, too, brought the desert to green wealth, and over the years they formed a company of those using the water, and a few men were employed to keep the canals clean and maintain the pumps. But when the State took control, dozens of idlers were put on pay only to make work, yet the canals were always choked and water came in dribbles, if at all, and outsiders were able to use the flow without right or payment.

The Maes Corwen estate was one of the heaviest losers, not only in bonds and cash, but the farm's canals were dry, and one morning I took the peons out there to clear the block. Miles away we found tons of earth and stone dumped to divert the main canal out to a farm owned, we were told, by the zone's Military Interventor. We dug out the tamp, restored the flow, and filled the diversion with help of a few sticks of dynamite that meant weeks of real work to have it free, and off we went home.

Next morning, when I was getting ready to leave, three cars came to the door, and soldiers came in with guns, very fierce, and a few officers, and a fattish one, with more braid, stood alone.

"Don't move, anybody," one of them said. "Military Interventor."

"Which is Morgan?" the fattish one asked the air.

"I am," I said.

"A moment," Solva said, ice. "This is my house. Who are you?"

"You blew up a canal on my property yesterday," he said to me, taking no notice. "You are under arrest. Get in the second car."

"Good," I said, and turned to Solva. "Tell Oracio to get in touch with General Von Gelsbach at the Ministry. He will settle this."

The Interventor's face could have belonged to several other men in as many moments, because at that time, Von Gelsbach was Chief of Staff.

"How are you acquainted with the General?" he said, not nearly so sure.

"I was an Army contractor," I said. "I am also acquainted with Army law. Have you spoken to the Governor?"

He shook his head, and looked at Solva, a movement of eyes, and at me, and nothing lamer ever hobbled.

"My husband is Brigadier General of Second Gaucho Cavalry, on the Reserve," Solva said, with sugar in the crystal.

"Won't you please have a little something to sustain you for that long ride back to the City?"

But the Interventor was not to be made a fool of in front of his men, and at a nod from him, I went between two holding my arms and nothing courteous about them, either.

We had not gone far, and Solva passed us in dust, and when we reached the barracks, she was waiting with her lawyers and the Justice. Whatever they had to say made no difference, and I was put in a cell for the second time in my life. The sun's evening breath made a pretty pink picture through the bars on the wall a yard above me, and the door opened and a sergeant called me out very civil, and took me to the office.

The Governor was there with Solva and a crowd, and the fattish one stood pale, in black stare, behind a General and others with braid.

"You are free, Mr. Morgan," the General said. "Any further move must be at Civil Law. Your Excellency, permit me to apologize for needless trouble."

Everybody shook hands and out we went, and I remember that other time, of breathing fresh cold night air as if I would never have enough. Solva had telegraphed Oracio and he must have galloped to the Ministry, and Von Gelsbach lost no time. Oracio was of the Governor's political party and the next election's choice for Mayor, so plenty of guns were firing for me. As to civil action, I never heard of any, and the lawyers told me to sleep well, for the property was not the fat one's, but a friend's, and permission of the State to divert water had not been got. What happened to him after I am not sure, though of course I had to run into him again. Soldiers, I have found, are not good or bad, but human or inhumane, sportsmen or spoil-sports, straight in the eye or crookedly anywhere, honest unto God or a knife in the back. But the Army had changed since I had known it. They wore khaki or sandy clothing instead of the blue, and where before they were the servants, now they pretended to be masters, with any smallest word a law. Ordinary people were afraid of them, and knuckled.

"They control everything," Solva said. "A General is the head of the Government. How long would he last without their help?"

History, in a few words.

Sûs' face was pinched, and smaller, and her eyes dull as any Indio's when I said goodbye that morning, and she stood as a baulk of timber. She had wanted to wear the cloak because the Araucana opens it for her own man, with nothing under, but she had to learn, and I said I liked most to see the dresses she had chosen with Solva. Her feet were too wide for shop shoes, and Solva said she must have them made to measure in Buenos Aires, so she wore sandals with a strap between the big and next toe, and I could have started to kiss from there, as I have done many a time since, thank God, and no man on this earth tidier, but then I had to speak sensibly, and she listened.

What is in the heart of a man when he looks into a girl's eyes, big, brilliant gray, and tries to tell her something, and she is looking at him as if it was the least she wanted to know, and he can feel from the way she holds her body that bed is the only place to be, well, God knows, the best time is not up and dressed in the morning. But the mind's daze is what he feels and a hymning shout in the spirit. By the arms I put her away, and told her what she had misunderstood from Solva's Castellano, and that when she came from Buenos Aires I would be waiting with her saddle on pegs over my door, inside, where only a wife can rule.

Her hand was on my shoulder when I turned, and her finger tips were sparks in my nape, and she knelt, and Solva stood between us, and the car went off in sharp spurt of Patagonian dust that blinds, and yet preserves bright in memory any face lit by love's eyes, or held in charm of love's regret.

Back to the City I went, and made my orders for stores

with Mog, Moke, and at the end, he put the pencil behind his ear.

"Mr. Morgan, I don't think anybody except me and my drivers know what you are doing in New Gilgal," he said. "You can be sure we will suffer before to tell. Would you do something for us?"

"Of course, boy," I said. "What?"

"Well, only a few of us have got trucks for long distance work and we're finding it hard to get spares, especially tires," he said. "Because we've got the trucks, they want us for a bit of smuggling over the Parallel. I'm not going to. But if I don't, I won't get the tires or anything else even by paying a fortune. Only one man has got them. It's blackmail, do you see? We are going to Hell, here. And nobody to help us."

We lived south, far from anybody, and we had been allowed to import below the 42nd Parallel everything worldwide without tax. But in late years, roads had scratched the desert north to the Province of Buenos Aires, and anything could be taken across an unmarked, unguarded line and sold for five times as much because up there was politician's country, and imports were prohibited, but people needed them.

"If I let them use my trucks to run the stuff up, I would have no trouble," Mog said. "Any of us could get what we want. But if I say no, I get nothing. I'm finished. I have got two weeks of life in my tires, if that."

"Who are 'they'?" I asked.

"The boys on top," he said. "The things that are short up in Buenos Aires, they take up there. The Navy does more than anybody else. We can't say anything. But it's good business. As much as a thousand percent profit."

"You don't like a thousand percent profit?" I asked.

"My mother is of the chapel," he said. "She is old. God has been good to us. Shall I go against what I know to be right? Shall I make so much money out of my own people? I would rather put my trucks on good tires, and have a good business, and work, and know my mother was happy, than have a million percent. Am I a fool? Very well. To Hell with the boys and Buenos Aires."

Back I went to the Governor, and he looked at me across the desk with that sad smile between fright and disgust, that tells of a man aware, and helpless, and on guard.

"Listen to me, Mr. Morgan," he said. "You may have known this country some time ago. It's changed. Get used to it. Tell your friend to find the tires, and pay any price for them. And be thankful. And keep his mouth shut. You do yourself no good by interfering like this. Your brother-in-law could be harmed. Everything these days is money. He's got to sell a wool-clip. Something could happen to it. Understand? He and his wife have certain properties. They could be expropriated by the State. I don't say it will happen. It could. He could lose all chance of election. His bank account could be sealed. And his wife's. And yours. You've got yourself into the Military's bad books. For the love of all the Martyred Saints, don't get on the rough side of the Navy. We know they smuggle. Who's going to stop it? Why should we? At least we're getting new money into this economy. We need it."

He wrote a note and passed it over the desk.

"That's the address of a friend of mine with tires, and spares of most kinds," he said, and leaned back, tired. "Tell him I sent you. And please, for God's sake, keep in mind what I've told you. We're in a dictatorship. I love Perón. He's done a tremendous lot for the country. Advanced us fifty years almost overnight. But the little jacks-in-office can do what they like. Nobody to stop them. They've come in here and told me what to do. I do it. I can be pushed aside like a bale of hay. How many are in prison merely for asking 'why'? Any idea? You could be among them. Tonight. All I have to do is touch that bell. Your crime? An uncomplimentary remark about the General, or his Government. That could mean two or three years in prison. Without trial. Have I taught any lessons? Oracio is a friend of mine. But if anything happened to him, I'd be helpless."

Round to the address I went, and sure enough, it was our old place enlarged, and the street had a new name. Tires and spares I bought for Mog, and had them sent round, and left him a credit account, and the owner saw me to the door, perhaps to see if I fell dead with shock at the prices.

"Very happy to have you back with us, Mr. Morgan," he said. "Is there any chance of you entering into business? Perhaps I could show you an excellent opportunity here for further capital."

"Sell enough, and you won't need capital," I said. "How can people afford it?"

"They get it from other people," he said, in a cackle, there.

Remembering what the Governor had told me, I kept my mouth shut, but a group of peons from the Territory, in best clothes, were looking at the window, and I nodded.

"How about them?" I said. "Will their money buy much of this?"

He put his lower lip over the top, and shook his head, a little quiver that made his gray whiskers into a silvery mask.

"Trying to put wages up, now," he said. "But if wages go up, wool goes up, freight goes up, everything else goes up, and we're back in the bucket. Thank God, they don't want much more than to buy meat and bread for the family, and enough wine to get drunk. Take the day as it comes. Turn your back on tomorrow. Nothing else. That's us."

Well, who was coming up the road on the other side but Vyrnwy, and I shouted like a fool, and he turned, and stood shot with lightning for a moment and ran, and we met like a couple of girls, there, dancing rings. The boy was fatter, and a little white to bless the hair above his ears, but still the same granite, and we went in the hotel for a drink. Tegwyn was in Buenos Aires with the children at school, six of them, and he was back, looking for a ranch.

"We are sick of the City, boy," he said, and raised a hand in oath. "The only life for us is down here. Air. Beautiful fresh air. You don't miss it till you haven't got. So I sold the business, ironworks, it was, and here I am."

Well, that afternoon he was on the road with me, and that night we were climbing over the stonework of the school and church in New Gilgal and he could only look wonder.

"Gates, doors, and chancel rails in iron scroll," I said. "I can see it. We were missing you, here."

He wiped his eyes and drew in a long, long breath.

"Happy the day, boy," he said. "I will go on my knees in by here, now. A beautiful place to say a word for Teg and the children. I wish the girl was here. Lonely I am, without her, see. A beautiful old girl, she is, aye. Now I do know it, indeed."

His face looked as I felt, but I think I never felt such pain of the spirit as the morning he started the forge. The sweet, half-tone belling of hammers on anvils I had never heard in the years, and I could hear Volde singing to the risen sun beyond the trees, and I was torn in blood again to think of Lal, and Doli, old beauty, and in sad longing for Sûs, so I was having a wonderful time, there, and asking if there was anybody on earth more miserable with so much to be thankful for, and Cadfan Rhys drove in the first of Mog's truck column, and jumped down and came running.

"Mr. Morgan," he shouted. "They are pulling up the cemetery at Gaiman. Ours. They want the land for a school. Some of the families have taken the bodies. Will you let me go to the City of the Mill, now, and tell the families, there? In case they want to bury them somewhere else?"

"Go, you," I said. "Unload the truck, first. If any of them want a lift in, take them. Bring the bodies back wherever they want."

Vyrnwy put the hammer in the rack, and took off his apron.

"Teg has got family in by there," he said. "I have got six, at least. Are we off?"

We had two punctures that night, and in the morning we were beyond The Feathers, and we stopped, quiet, out of petrol, and we sat for a couple of hours because of course I had forgotten the spare can. We were lucky. Many had sat for a day or more, waiting for somebody to pass, but Idris

John came up, and we filled from him, and got to Gaiman just before midday. A small crowd waited at the cemetery, about halfway through the main street, up some steps to a rise so that nothing could be seen from below. The Evans' sons came down, carrying bodies wrapped in soft hides, and the youngest, Plethyn, had a little bunch of brown flowers held close, with a hand about them to protect, but the petals were dropping with his tears.

Vyrnwy put a hand on his shoulder.

"Where will you take them, my little one?" he asked him.

"O, I'm not sure, yet, see," Plethyn said. "To the farm, first. But if we have a flood, she will have to move, again. They've got a new cemetery, along here. But a couple of years, they will do the same. Poor little Mama. Will they ever let you have your rest, then? I will pray the bastards die in filth and blindness. And I never hated before."

Vyrnwy went in, and I took the truck up the street to get a fill. The garage owner was German, the best machinist in the area, and a good man. While he pumped he swore, and if he was serious, it was still funny to hear a German swearing in Cambrian.

"Remember my words," he said, while I paid. "They have ruined this country. People used to be honest. Courteous. Hard-working. And now? In just the years of this Government, they are rotten. They can get money for no work. Who pays? We. We work. So to be idle, you are paid? To work, you pay tax? So who works? I shall sell, and go to my ranch. Let the sheep work, and pay tax to me."

Back to the cemetery, and up the steps, and on top I stood.

Most of the graves all the way back had been dug up, and families had taken some of the bodies away. Rotted coffins, faced rock, bricks, headstones carved with all the most illustrious pioneer names were in piles, with tomb railings and crosses, angels with cracked wings, cherubs without arms or legs and wax flowers under broken glass. Groups of peons were digging over in a corner, and Vyrnwy walked along a row of broken coffins tipped anyhow on the piles of earth.

"Ignorant swine," he said, no man in deeper despair. "They broke the copings and threw all the stones over by there. There isn't a name to be seen. How are we to tell?"

"Knock the earth off the lids and see if there is a label," I said. "Not many go in without."

Sad little journeys, they were, up and down, praying a smile to many an old friend, and I found Sarah, Buckets, and made sure of her, and Paco, the old stableboy at Dalar Roberts' and Damaglou's daughter, a good girl, and I was more than happy to find Mrs. Betti Bont, for none of them had any family to look after them, so I took them with us. Vyrnwy found his mother and father, and his mother's mother, but not his father's, and we looked for a long time there, while the cemetery peons had an asado, with a soak of wine, and showed respect by singing songs of many verses about women without soap or joy. In twank of strings and bawled spittle, Vyrnwy found old Tibbald, him of the best shop for many a long year, and just after, I found Galardier the French barber, a companion of the imposter Emperor of Patagonia, once preening himself as the Viscount Drotingolle de la Fouchise, written in gold on parchment behind the chair we all sat in while he talked and clipped, and now black and warped on his box, and I was glad to find Emrys ap Talfan, that friend beside the canal beyond the town, with a pot of cold water for you and your horse, and how many had blessed him in a dripping muzzle, and Katie Prings, always of the white apron, and sandwiches of cold lamb and home-baked bread, and beer made in the cellar, with a pocket of coins under the starch that jingled when she walked, and some said, when she slept. Vyrnwy shouted to find Eos, Fog, his first striker at the forge, and I can see the muscle piling
Roberts' and Damaglou's daughter, a good girl, and I was
now, gilded with sweat, hammer up, ready to hit, a poet of only the first line, and a little voice, and so excited he had found that first line that he never had his wits to find the second. So he flattened iron, that was soft, and hot, and had to stay on the anvil to be hit in any shape he wanted, not like

that second line, that he knew was somewhere in his mind though he could never find it.

Our own peons took them out, and we went on knocking earth off coffins, if rough boxes most of them were, many heartless to say, with no name, as if the years were danced, and not even a bit of tagged clay to go back to the Potter.

Well, on them we laid hands and thought of them with God in love, those little ones known well in life, and unknown now, whose hearts and willingness gave the rest of us a comfort of green goodness to live in.

Vyrnwy clapped his hands of dust and looked at me over a space of about fifty yards of open graves.

"Finished, boy," he called. "I would like to take them all. But somebody might be coming for some of them, see."

"Speak a language," a voice said. "The language of the country. Learn it."

Very slow I turned.

That fattish one, of the black stare and braid, the Military Interventor.

But as Vyrnwy came toward him, the cemetery peons started a shout and a tune, and one of them had taken a woman's corpse from a coffin and he was wheeling and pacing the steps of a tango, and the black silk dress had rotted and pieces flew as leaves, and the bones of her legs showed, and her teeth were in a grin and the sockets of her eyes glared horror as if she knew.

A terrible feeling is always with me that she was Miss Lewis, but I shall never be sure.

The man saw us coming and dropped her, and the head broke away. We put her back in the coffin, without looking, and closed the lid and our peons took her out, and the Interventor came to stand and smirk.

The cemetery peons had gone, and except for ours going down the steps, we had the place to ourselves.

"What do you intend to do with so many bodies?" the Interventor asked Vyrnwy. "Sell them? Or are you collectors of necrophilia?"

"They are friends, and we shall have them where they shall not be disturbed," Vyrnwy said, and fury's water red in his eyes. "And while we are about it, the language I spoke just now was the only one spoken here, before you were born, before you and your filthy kind came to infest us. It was the language of the country. Except for the Tehuelche."

"I do not permit lessons from you or anyone like you," the Interventor shouted, and lifted the riding crop. "Get out before I call my soldiers. They'll stamp you in the ground, you ignorant ruffian. Outside, the pair of you."

He stepped across a pile of earth with the whip raised, but Vyrnwy went to meet him, and his fist went up high in that blacksmith's strike and came down on top of the braided cap, and the Interventor's eyes went under the lids, and he dropped in the grave in a shower of earth, and the last we saw were leathers and boot-soles, and Vyrnwy kicked more earth on top, and so did I, and we went.

"In case there is something more about this, you go to New Gilgal, and I will go to Solva's," I said. "Say nothing, know nothing. I'll be with you in three days."

It was surprise to me not to be arrested that night, but nobody heard a word during two days, and Solva came back from shopping and said the Interventor was in hospital and nothing else known.

"Good," I said. "Now, then. Make up your mind. Supposing, only supposing Maes Corwen is expropriated for any reason. Or a part. They might put a road through. Anything. What of the cemetery? Would you be willing for the family there to be taken to New Gilgal? A church, it is. It will never be violated."

Solva put her beautiful head on my shoulder and cried quietly.

"There will never be peace on earth," she whispered. "Even for them gone."

"Until the Coming," I said. "Then there will be peace."

She turned away, and went to the window, hands in prayer under her chin.

"I used to believe that," she said, out, to the pampas. "I don't now. O, Lal, *merch i.* Doli, my little one. Why was I left? The most useless of the three."

"Oracio doesn't think so," I said. "Your children don't. Answer me. Shall I take them at Maes Corwen out to New Gilgal? And have a peaceful heart for the rest of my time? Or think of some peon dancing with your Mama?"

"Huw, don't say such things for Christ's sake," she almost screamed, and twisted her body. "Poor, dear little soul, no help anywhere. Yes. Take them. Then I shall know. But will they be Roman Catholics? Will the priest have them?"

"They will be in a garden," I said. "Not a single Catholic, or Baptist, or Methodist, or Congregationalist, or Presbyterian, and what else, to be seen. Flowers, yes, and names cut in stone, yes, and at least one will be Hebrew, and a lot of Indios. They will be together. As they lived."

In only that short time, the change in Sûs was a startler, and though she still spoke little Castellano, she was not slow in learning, and when it came to appearance even Solva had nothing to teach her.

The young men in the zone had found out there was a younger Corwen sister, and they called, by accident of course, always at about asado time, or in early evening, and indeed, Sûs was well worth calling on. She was taller than I had remembered, with a white, white skin under the palest gold tan, gray eyes of a brilliance and yet as if she looked at you through clear bluish smoke of a woodfire, and plaits of deep chestnut hair below her knees, or bound in a richlit mass with two small pale blue velvet bows behind.

A smile in those eyes, and she sat, and looked, and said nothing, or when she did, it was in the rudest Arauco that only I understood, and she often had me in torture of laughter, and the more I laughed the more she would find to say, and always flat-faced as any Indio.

A lovely girl speaking another language, never with the smallest expression, and her eyes in dance of lights on the heels of small devils inside there can be a maddener, indeed. Poor boys, too. I was lucky to be sorry for them.

Kalata I had missed, but I thought she was living as she did at Little Looking Glass, when I saw her once in three or four days, so close she kept herself, and nothing to tell she was there except that meals were always on the minute, and the house like a pin, and laundry held breath of sun and air and the little sprigs of lavender she put in the wardrobes.

"I'm sorry, she's gone," Solva said. "A pony, and a pack-horse, and off. Nobody knows where."

But I knew where, and why. Nothing is sadder in this world than to be in love with one woman, and yet to feel pain of sorrow for another that almost could be magic hurt of love, but without that want to kiss dry lips, or put a hand under the skirt to roam in fields of silk.

Plain as Solva spoke I saw Kalata riding off, leading the packhorse, leather-strung plaits skipping in pony jog, and an Indio face toward the Andes, Indio, with no line or wrinkle, showing nothing, nothing, and volcanoes in spout of flame inside.

Ah, Kalata, if I could put my arms about you, dearest, sweet, sweet woman, so alone, so proud.

Indio.

Araucana.

31

A shock there was that morning, too, when Angharad's letter came enclosing one of mine to Dai Bando and Cyfartha, sent on by their accountants. It was like Dai, at his age, to try lifting a barrel, and when he fell, I could see Cyfartha, only a couple of years younger, picking him up and whispering to him all the way down to the doctor in the next valley, and both of them breathing in the oxygen tent and dying within minutes of each other. A verdict of Natural Causes, and the coroner's remark that Cyfartha as good as broke his heart for his friend and Greater Love Hath No Man seemed to roof the friendship of a couple of men good as ever born. If they were not good Christians, then many a Christian could have learned from them, for they lived the humble life, knowing only what was in reach of their fists, with little of brain, perhaps, but all goodwill, and of harm to none except those deserving, and not a thread of shoddiness between them.

They left me the Six Bells and two farms, and the property left to them by Hwfa and Old Twm, and the accountant was worried about taxes and other business.

"To them that hath shall be given," Solva said. "When will you go?"

"When you are back from Buenos Aires," I said. "A wedding is the best excuse for travel. When the place is ready, we will fly."

That night, when we turned off for Llangiñeu I saw there was something very wrong. We should have seen the lights of fifty fires over at the water tanks, but there were only two, one at the forge and the other at the carpenter's shop beyond the store sheds.

Vyrnwy came from the church to meet us, and not very happy.

"Not an Indio here," he said. "Rhin had gone the day before I got here. Not a word of message. Would it be measles again?"

"If it was, he wouldn't be fool enough to take healthy men back to sick women and children," I said. "If it was measles here, he'd have burned everything. But their spare blankets and saddles are still in the toldos. We'll hear soon enough."

That night, after we had reburied everybody in spaced lines, and marked their names along the wall where the garden would be, we heard the gallop, and Cheuquen came in with a stick and a piece of bark. Without a word we saddled and rode through the night, south of the City of the Mill, direct for Rhin's league. Cheuquen, ostrich hunter, was crippled from birth, and I knew he had been sent because all the others were needed, so it was an anxious ride, and nobody about when we got there.

Vyrnwy turned for the old forge, and sent a man over to our place and I went along to Corianth Austin's house, bigger and more comfortable, with many barns and fields to distance in good order. All the children were married and gone, and Corianth had a few Chileans working in the fields and a couple of girls in the dairy, and life was good except for the price of everything. He knew nothing of Rhin, and no Indios had been near for years, but there had been some trouble about fenced and unfenced land, though nobody had worried him.

"A lot of Chilotes have taken land without right," he said.

"A few might have been Indios, I suppose. But you can't tell a real Indio from a mix these days. They all dress the same, see. I believe they rounded a lot up and sent them off."

"You didn't hear where?" I said.

"O, well, no," he said. "No interest. Better off without them. Lazy, dirty lot, they are."

Well.

Off I went, down to Brother Little Mountain's school, riding round my old place that I simply could not bear to see, and went in to silence of locked doors. Two men worked in the kitchen garden, and everything in a glow there, but neither knew when the Brother would be back. Over to Rhin's league I went, and noticed the pieces of red cloth that surveyors hang to show a point, seeing them on poles for miles across the flat. Somebody had been mapping, perhaps ready to fence and enclose.

Vyrnwy had started an asado, and he told me that all the Indio women and children were in the mountains, somewhere, on the way to Chile with a guard of police, so the wife of one of his peons had told him.

"I suppose Rhin heard from somebody, and went after them," he said. "I doubt we shall see him again. What will we do without him? Where shall we have men as good? Or as many?"

"Something is wrong, here," I said. "A couple of hours sleep, and I am going down to the police."

Well, luck, for the Captain was son of my old district superintendent, Davies, Tom Tiddler's, a title that came from land claimed by this one and that, though meantime Davies went in and made a fine big farm, and when claimants came they were turned away, because the Law upheld the work, and gave the land to the workman, and hence, Davies, of Tom Tiddler's Ground.

"You've been misinformed, sir," he said, and not pleased. "Even the Military would have to get a warrant from the Justice. There's been no unusual movement of that sort. No report of disease. We'd get it first, here. I don't know what to say to help you."

He telephoned to military headquarters to ask, but nothing was known, and he sent a sergeant down to the town's worst quarter to ask questions, and I went to Rhin's league for some sleep.

Two days later, and we were thinking of going back, and a gendarme sergeant came in riding hard.

"The police passed on your enquiry, sir," he said. "We have a patrol going after these people. They're making for the pass above Apple Lake. But it's a mystery."

"Why, mystery?" I asked him.

He shrugged.

"Why not an easier way?" he said. "A bad road, a high pass, many women and children? Why? Where are they going?"

"Let us find out," I said, and we saddled, and followed him, and again the days of climbing through dark forest, jumping trunks, kicking over brush and briar, sleeping toes to a pile of logs, and waking to ice in the air, and the sun tipping points of lilac on the peaks and the sky behind deep green. Late afternoon, it was, and we saw a gendarme high above us coming down and we waited.

"I'm going for the squadron," he shouted. "They're fighting up there. We warned them. But we haven't got the arms."

"Who are they?" the sergeant asked.

"Not sure," he shouted. "We thought they were Carabiniers from the other side. They're not. We've seen a couple of bodies. The Indios are killing them with the Lost One. They'll murder the pack, whoever they are. You'll find a camp of women and children about two hours up. Keep your heads down. There's a lot of shooting. See you later."

We passed the camp higher up, and the women waved to us, but we went on. Scattered cracks of rifle and revolver fire made small echoes, and soon we heard the first Indio scream, that seemed to burst as a flower from the top of the nose and hang in the air as a splash of blood, and we knew that the

Lost One had left another body warm for the carrion flying in black circles just below the peaks. That fist-size ball wrapped in leather on a two-foot thong, swung round the head to stun an animal or crack a human skull was thrown with rarely a miss at fifty yards, almost never looked for, and so, Lost.

We were out, crossing the rocks, and we could see the lakes, blue and green jewels among miles of forest over to Lake Mascardi, and a bullet snapped the air between me and the sergeant, and he pulled a funny face and spurred to a gallop for cover of the trees, and so did we. Not a sound, not a bird called, not a leaf seemed to be falling in the forest. We made enough noise for a town, and without a moment's warning, an Indio was in front of us, stripped to the apron, painted white and blue for the kill, and he pointed, and in shadow of a clearing Rhin held out his arms, and beyond him were Indios bandaged white in head and body lying about a fire.

"Thank God Cheuquen found you," he said. "He would never have gone to the police. For days here, we couldn't find a track. But the families are safe, anyway. What do you think you can do, Sergeant?"

"Where are the rest of us?" the sergeant asked.

"One has gone back," Rhin said. "One is up there. They came up yesterday. Nothing much to be done. I believe the families were used as bait."

"Bait?" the sergeant said.

"To get the men up here and kill them out, like guanaco," Rhin said. "A sad mistake. Silly to fight Indios in their own country. I curse the day I ever heard of land. Gold it is, to some. Every one of these men has a league, or a half. How many leagues altogether I don't know. But worth a fortune, no doubt. They drove the families up here, knowing the men would follow. A quiet place, it is, and far from anywhere. So now, kill the men, put the families over the border, take your money, and go where you want. And down below, Mr. Barramendiz and his partners make a claim to how many leagues, and not a word to be said, and not one peso to be paid? A splendid fortune for a few centavos, some wine, and new rags. Every single one dressed the same looks like a uniform, isn't it?"

"Barramendiz," I said. "I remember him from years ago."

"Careful, here," the sergeant said. "He plays a big flute. He's a live 'un. Got a line right through to the top. Is he up here?"

"I don't know who is up there, except that my boys will kill anything they find," Rhin said. "Nobody to say a word to them. I've got to look after these, here. The women can't come up till everything's quiet. It can't last long. Night is coming. They can't light fires. They've lost their horses and stores. They'll be dead before morning. You'll never see a body. That's the end of us in this country."

"Why?" the sergeant said. "Who's going to interfere? The squadron can't fly here. Take at least three days."

"It will long be over," Rhin said, and looked up to the peaks at more shots, and echoing screams, and the fainter trilling of the women from below us, sending strength to their men. "They are climbing to find enough loose rock to send it down on top. Go up if you want. You will be a nuisance."

Almost into evening, and Saiheque and about thirty of his men got a thick sapling into the crevice of a peak and sent it down the mountainside. The ground shifted and treetops bent as if in a storm not far from us, and dust went up in yellow moil, and rocks burst from clouds and fell, slow, turning, falling, and entire trees spouted out, as if flung roots first, and for moments, there, we heard no sound except the leaves about us, but then a rumble of tons in slide blasted up from the mass slipping down to the river more than a thousand meters below.

"You will find very little there," Rhin said, to the sergeant. "I am not sorry, one bit. Now. Give me some advice. Shall I take the women and children over the border? Or could we go back, and no trouble?"

The sergeant looked up at the dust, blown high, and away, to cover the peaks and the carrion birds.

"If you take them down and go about your business, I don't see what anybody can do," he said. "This was only self-defence. If somebody took my wife and children, what would I do? My mother was *Pecunche.*"

A smile came into Rhin's eyes.

"You have told me, and I am thankful," he said.

Saiheque came with a crowd of his men, all bathed clean of paint, dripping and spitting, and pulling a *huinca,* sobbing, whiskery, on a rawhide.

"The only one we found," he said. "He slept in wine."

The sergeant took the loop and pulled the man closer. He wore a stained shirt and *bombachos* with the newness still in shine.

"Answer me or you go back to them," he said, and the man groveled, without a sensible word. "How much did Barramendiz pay you for this?"

The man talked in slaver of fear, knowing what could happen to him at an Indio fire. Vyrnwy, Rhin and I went over to the camp for a cup of tea. Rhin was too thin, bruised blue under the eyes, in patches of clothes and cloth slippers, and barely a voice from tiredness.

"We have got a friend in this sergeant," he said. "But he knows as well as I do, Saiheque will kill Barramendiz and every man in that office when he finds out. No need to say a word. We have got trouble to come, and nothing to be done."

"But you asked the sergeant what to do to save trouble, didn't you?" Vyrnwy said, in a stare.

"I put the weight with him," Rhin said, while the sergeant slipped the loop off the *huinca's* neck and shoved him toward the stand of ponies. "His Mama was *Picunche.* It's enough. He is with us. And many another."

"I give you thirty minutes," the sergeant shouted at the *huinca* in a weak trot. "Ride for your life."

"Hard on the poor pony," Vyrnwy said.

"He's got just enough in him to sit there," Rhin said. "The pony will pick his own way down, and the Devil himself couldn't send him one step faster. A pony is a stubborn old thing, you know."

Well, we were a happy lot going back to Llangiñeu, and we started work without a word, there. The school building was up, and the church's barrel roof almost finished, everything plastered white and drying out. Floors were down, altar up in three levels of alerces timber in the form of a squared cross, rails, gates, and window scrolls in iron ready to go in, garden pathed in stone and planted, five fountains working, and every day another joy. Mog, Moke, came in with truckloads of young trees and plants, and glass for the greenhouse, and gave me a note from Solva, asking me to come in, and I was there that night.

Shearing was over and the wool-clip was loading at the port, and she wanted to take Sûs by ship to Buenos Aires.

"She will have enough of roads and railways," she said. "Give her three months with me. I promise you something to marry. There's another Lal, there. But something more. I don't know what it is."

I knew.

A lot of Lliutro.

Indio.

More tender than light in dew, dearer than desire, stone-hard beyond her want of one, blind to any except the heart's own, happy with nothing else, richest then.

Sûs.

They were leaving next day, and all the families came up for an asado to see them to the ship. I suppose it was the last real, Cambrian party with everybody in National dress though I was surprised that most of the girls had no notion how to wear the hat. My mother and all the women in this Valley wore theirs on the front of the forehead, over the lace cap with cherries and forget-me-nots and roses, but most of those at Solva's party wore it on the back of the head.

Not Solva, and not Sûs.

Both their hats were of beaver fur in polish, small, hard in brim, tall, narrow in crown, but most of the others were made of cloth on clumsy shapes, and some pulled down to the ears, and others beyond, to strangle.

Sûs, I am sure, wore Lal's hat, small brim, narrow crown, big silver buckle and wide silk bow in front, with the edge a little worn from brushing and the nap sitting flat in glisten.

The Governor came in for tea with the Minister for Education and the Chief of Police and other friends of Oracio's and we stood talking in sweet sniffs of hot red currant tart cooling on the window sill, and a batch of tea-cake with blackberry jam, and the girls were all in the kitchen singing "Hob-a-Derry-Dando!", tipping out saffron or fruit cakes, waiting for scones from the oven, buttering toast and muffins, cutting strawberry roll, and Sûs was in the thick, with a pan of her own, of ground meal, honey, apple chips and the blue berries of the *kalafaté*, favorite of the *mapuche*. All the girls were putting their hands round her to steal little bits, and she was stamping in temper and laughing gray crystals and cursing in Arauco, and very rude, and I could have gone in there and picked her up and eaten her down to the sandals.

Solva's house was in one story, red-tiled, with rooms all round a patio garden and lily pond, with plenty of trees outside so that everybody had space to walk about in the shade.

The Minister of Education came to stand, hands in pockets, looking at the tables being laid, and up at me.

"The more I see of this, the more I regret there aren't a great many more of you," he said. "I've often wondered what this country would be like now without the moral strength of your people all these years. But you're going into the marsh. Your children prefer jazz. It's not often the girls sing like this. We can't get it in the schools. It's a pity. I hear you're building a school?"

Impossible to keep anything quiet where villagers will shout any snip of news only to show they know more than the next.

"And a church," I said. "For about a couple of hundred."

"Protestant or some other non-conformist assembly?" he asked. "And why in such a lonely place?"

"It's for Indios, and Llangiñeu is far enough from everybody for them to have some peace," I said. "I'm quite willing to build a larger school. If you'll provide the teachers."

"Show me the plans and give me a date," he said. "Let me give you a word of warning. Do you know a lawyer called Barramendiz? Very few scruples. Powerful friends. If your Indios can be half-proved as Chilenos, they'll be rounded up and sent across the border as undesirables. Any land they may be entitled to here automatically becomes available to the first claimant. He's in Buenos Aires. He's already put in the claims. With the friends he has, he can't fail. Why not talk to the Governor?"

Solva put an arm in mine and we strolled across.

"You and your old Indios," she said. "You are coming more like Rhinberry every day, boy."

"Lal's idea," I said. "For me, it is mandatory."

She gave my arm a good squeeze.

"I know," she said. "I will give every bit of help I can. I've written to Oracio, too."

But even with red currant syrup making him close his eyes with goodness, the Governor had little hope.

"If the gendarmes are given an order to clear them out as undesirables, there's nothing I can do," he said. "That's federal business. It affects the nation's well-being, citizenship, and the border. Delicate, all three."

"If those Indios had been killed off a few weeks ago, nobody would have been the wiser or cared a curse," I said. "It was the one survivor allowed to warn Barramendiz that sent him off to Buenos Aires."

"Whether or not," the Governor said, and spooned butter pastry and red currants and thick cream. "I warned you. He's got powerful friends. That land is worth millions. It'll feed at least a couple of hundred thousand sheep, besides cattle. That's money. Annually. The Indios did nothing with it. If they disappear, who's going to cry?"

"Supposing I apply," I said.

"You have very few friends in the ruling party, Mr. Morgan," he said. "His claims are already in. With pressure from the top. He's extremely generous to party funds."

Watching pastry, red currants and cream dancing with a spoon, and the tears in Solva's eyes, an idea tickled to put crinkles in the bone of my spine.

"I won't come to the ship," I said to Solva, and kissed her. "I am off, now, to the Cordilleras. No time to waste. Give Oracio a good hug for me. The moment we are finished, I will be with you."

Under the brim of the hat, Sûs looked at me, and her face went smaller, and the crystals dulled, and she stood as an Indio, hands beside, stone. Her dress was pale blue dotted in little lilac flowers, with pannier and bustle, one of her grandmother's, with lace at the half-sleeve and throat and a lace apron and how many petticoats.

"I have taken my saddle," I said, in Arauco. "My love is in your eyes. Our sister will ride first to show the way. You will follow. In a month the hunter will bring guanaco. He will be hungry."

She turned from me and went head bent, so slowly, into the house and never once looked back.

Sûs mine, my wonder, my beauty, my love.

The Police Chief hurried over to the truck as if he had been looking for me.

"Let me give you a word of advice," he said. "Oracio's a good friend of mine. I want no trouble with him, or your friends in the Army. I just had a talk to the Governor. He's worried. I'm getting through to my captain over there to send a couple of men out. Just for safety's sake. The sight of a uniform, that's all. But don't go anywhere alone. Till it gets round that we're interested. Clear?"

"Very clear," I said, and looked him in the eye. "Thank you. Is this because of the Indios?"

"No," he said. "It's because of money. Have a good journey."

There was a lot to think about on the way back, and a little more a couple of hours later, passing the cemetery, because all the headstones and crosses, angels and cherubim had been piled in a space used for refuse opposite the road, and Mari Rhys, and Gwladys Jenkin, Milton Griffiths, Rhos Hughes, Ieuan ap Endry, and Rhian Jones were among them to be seen flung together as they never were in life, and I thought I saw all of us, a Nation, in the same place, whole in name and being for the few, so few, years on this earth, lodgers, not much more, in our own or any other country, giving our time usefully to hidden masters, all of us hymned in dying, and in death, heaped.

We had to stop for a crowd at the bend in the road along the river, and in deep shadow of the trees I thought it might be a drove of sheep with peons behind, but nearer I heard the singing, and a shape in hides was being carried among a crowd of girls and young women, though the men were all in work clothes as if they had just come from the fields. They were turning into the Bryn Gilfa place, and Idris looked back and saw me, and came over while they were singing There's A Friend For Little Children, yes, Above The Bright Blue Sky, indeed, and hope is eternal, so they say. While I listened, hearing Lal's contralto, I could almost believe it.

"Miss Lewis's brother came up from the Senguer to find her," he said. "They'd closed the cemetery to the families, and they wouldn't let him go in. So a few of us went down there with him, now just. And we had her out, and God help the one to stop us. A herd of dirty animals has been loosed, here. Life isn't worth the work, indeed to God. Well, he had nowhere to put her, so I said bring her here. Peace she shall have, see."

"They will always have peace and a garden about them where I am going," I said. "Where all the others have gone. Ask her brother. She shall have violets and forget-me-nots and heartsease with all the other girls, and roses everywhere. She was a kind, good friend to me and Lal, and they both loved little children, and they will be close again. Come, you, bring the little one here."

32

That noon I turned off on the south bank of the river to the property the girls had given me for a wedding present, that Lal had christened Down Where The Moon Is Small those years ago, though the little cabin had gone long since, and Oracio's men had built a bunkhouse beside the lake, a cool place for the midday asado and always a pleasant break in the journey. The other idea came to me then, while I sat there, and I barely had the patience to wait till Rinzetti, the supervisor, came back.

"Two parties of men have been looking about the place these past few days," he said. "Another lot this morning. But they always cross the river before I can find out who they are."

Expropriation came before my eyes, because just as Indio titles had been filched because they were never on the land, so, and easily, could my title go because I had never lived there.

"I'll send you more men, and in a couple of weeks the builders will be here," I said. "If anybody wants to know, I shall be in and out for the next few months. Go armed, and don't hesitate to shoot. Were they Indios?"

He shook his head.

"I wouldn't bother about them," he said. "They camp, hunt, and move on. Too few to notice. But we've seen a lot of peons moving west these days. I don't know where they're all going. Some sort of fiesta? Where?"

It went out of my mind because the other idea, of a fine new house at the end of an avenue of poplars, with the lake in front and a garden going to the water's edge, well, I could see Sûs pouring the tea, there.

Off I went then for the City of the Mill, and I found Brother Little Mountain in the garden mounding potatoes, the only time I ever saw him out of soutane or cassock, and dripping, with an old shirt stuck to his back that was mended and raggedy as any of Rhin's.

But his smile was gone and he shook his head before I was finished.

"That would be a matter for the highest authority," he said. "I could never take it upon myself. I'm a parish priest, and no more. If the Indios want to give me the titles, then my Bishop would take charge. But it might be a long time before there could be a decision. And that sort of matter doesn't wait. Our interest isn't in property, but people, you see."

"But you were given this property by Solva," I said.

He laughed and put a hand on my shoulder.

"Given, yes," he said. "For a time. Only until a site has been chosen for the new school. Then what was 'given' will go back to you. And remember, your sister-in-law and her family, and you, are in our prayers every day. If ever you need me, I am here."

Well, that was the end of that. Sorry I was, for I thought that if he took the land, he would have plenty to look after the Indio children. It was surprise to me that the Church was so careful, and then I wondered if he would refuse New Gilgal, but I said nothing, and we had a cup of good tea, there, because he had learned from Rhin, and off I went.

Lights were on when I got back that night. Elvet Martin, one of Vyrnwy's workmen from Buenos Aires, was finishing the altar rails, and the others were setting the stained-glass panels under the windows, ready to be put in. They were only shapes of different colored glass, leaded by Elvet with some help from Vyrnwy, but indeed the boy had done well, and when they were all in, and the sun shone, and the colors patched the flagstone floor and splashed the white, half-circle roof all the way down past the altar to the south door's iron grille, well, even the Indios stood with their mouths open.

None of them had known the beauty in the mind of man that comes in grace from the work of his hands.

But when we pulled the big bell up to the tower, and bolted it, waiting till Rhin pointed his finger at the watch, closing his fist on six o'clock, and Foyel jumped up the rope as Vyrnwy had shown him, and the bell tolled a bronze prayer that echoed for moments, all of them scattered as though Heaven had broken in pieces, and poor Foyel lay on the ground holding his ears, turning his head in staring fright at what he had done. Vyrnwy jumped and jumped, and the call from a swinging mouth reached across the pampas and set the wild horses in a kick, and ostrich stamped with their little wings out, and the foxes come to eat our scraps skulked green-eyed in shadow, but the Indios looked up as to the Voice of God, and O, they laughed, and beat their hands and danced.

We were eating the asado that morning, no sleep, but I felt I had to tell Rhin before he went to his toldo, and I waited till we finished, and told them all.

Rhin stood, and he seemed to have gone very old.

"If the Chief of Police told you that, he knew more than he would say," he said, and stretched his arms, tired. "There's real danger to every one of us. They could poison the water. They could infect us with measles or anything else. I am sure in my soul that's the way Lliutro died. I will take the women and children out tomorrow. They will be safe."

"You could wait a bit, boy," Vyrnwy said, shaky in the voice, a reproach. "Till Brother Little Mountain do take the roof to his heart and give a Blessing, anyway. Good God, what have they worked for all this time, then?"

"If I am not careful, to die here," Rhin said, quiet. "Poor

little souls, they have worked harder here than I ever saw. Because it was for them and the children. Did you see them inside there, this morning, and the sun putting the colors everywhere? They were crying, boy."

"Look," I said. "Catriel will go now for Brother Little Mountain. He is bound to come if we tell him we need him. Is it sense to give a man a school and a church and nobody about?"

"He might have only ghosts," Rhin said.

"But, Rhin," I said. "Good God, boy, I thought the whole idea behind this was to put them back on their own land? Each one in a house. Tractors, harrows, everything is ready to come here. Gendarmes will be here. I will see the Governor and have a patrol, one place to another."

Rhin looked about the pampas, flat to the horizon, nothing moving, with the roof of the belltower showing to the right, and behind us, far away, the foothills green and brown, and everywhere the blue, blue sky.

"You will make it very easy for Mr. Barramendiz," he said. "Three miles or more between houses. Who would hear anything? Who would find anything? Put a body outside. In an hour it is bones. Most of the bones chewed shapeless, and who was it?"

"O, Christ, Rhin, stop," I said, and turned from him, because I could see my Lal, dancing up there at the waterfall, and I wanted to murder not to think any more of a red alerces box that rattled. "Enough. If you have got to take them, very well. But why can't you wait till Brother Little Mountain gets here?"

"Thousands, tens of thousands of Indios are dead because somebody waited for somebody else to go somewhere, and they never did," Rhin said. "If the gendarmes come, it might only be to drive out undesirables. I will take them out while they are desirable, and healthy. In Chile, they can live their years in peace. It is only over the mountain, see."

Sitting here, now, I know that Over The Mountain used to be only a couple of miles across gorse and wildflowers, though when I was small even the Himalayas seemed not so high or so far away. A shift in miles of slag has done a lot to alter the shape of the land, but friendly Mr. Weed worked his best to hide what nakedly would be heartache, if only at distance, for gorse and grass are gone, and wildflowers blow only in the dreaming mind, O Valley Mine.

Ceinwen used to deliver the Sunday joints over that little green bump, not far, and yet it might have been another country, an alien people. We were from Here, they were from There. They had their colliery, we had ours. Only now and again was any mixing, and then generally a fight to follow, though in these days it is hard to say why, or what poison was in those who did the fighting. Certain it is that if she and I, or any other boy from our side had been caught together, there could have been a funeral or two.

We are all fools down here, too much to say with the fist, not enough with the brain, too little with the heart. No lessons have been learned since I was a child, because the fist seems to be growing as the brain gets smaller and conscience has nearly gone. Often in those days I wondered how Barramendiz and his partners would feel if they were told somebody was ready to kill their wives and children only to take a piece of land. Kill them, or send them off, or anyway get rid of them. There was no fear in me that he would send out more men because I was sure Saiheque had taught him a lesson.

The chickens I counted were rotten from the egg.

Saiheque sent boys to watch along the valley to tell us when Brother Little Mountain would reach us. Groups of Indios were coming from everywhere, some called by Saiheque, though most were odds from the Territory, there for free food and wine. Many came over from the Bio-Bio but without women and children, and many a hundred more might have come, but Saiheque had sent warning. Only the hunters and the old men as good as dead, and everybody ready to fight. Perhaps that warning set the mental level because day after day while they were coming in I could feel the spark in the air.

They were camped near the tanks, and in early morning long lines of fires made pink starlight over the pampas, and they sang prayers, with pipes of bone, and drums and silver bells, not as we know singing, but strict in time, of half-and-quarter tones, a strange and beautiful gift to the Twin Brother of their god.

Yet I knew something was wrong, and Rhin knew better than me, but he waited against instinct for Brother Little Mountain.

We knew he was only hours away that morning when the first lookout rode in, and everybody went running, fires were stamped out, horses sent further off, nothing moved anywhere near, and Llangiñeu looked as it always had, a desert of pampas bush, a hill of rock under the clear blue of Patagonia's sky.

The church and garden lay behind the school in a hollow dug from a low hill. On the north side, with the steepest rise, we built two stone shafts with iron scroll gates painted white because the natural iron would rust too soon. Twelve long, wide steps led to a plinth, and only when you were there would you see the garden beyond the gates, and two hundred yards away, along paths and around the fountains, with all the flowers laughing at you, the northern grille of the church.

Rhin, Vyrnwy, Donato, and I were crouched under the bell-tower oxeye in the elbow of the south and east wings, and in all those gray-green miles nothing to be seen moving, and we were waiting for Vyrnwy to come up with the pot of coffee, but he hit his fist on the ladder, looking up.

"Well, there is a splendid church, this is, isn't it?" he whispered, as if Brother Little Mountain might hear thirty miles away. "O, there is a Hell of a fine church for you, aye. You can tell we are all Chapel here."

"What, now," Rhin said. "Where is the coffee with you?"

"Coffee, damn," Vyrnwy said, and disgusted. "I just noticed. How will he baptize, then? Uh? Baptism, boy. We forgot the bloody font, here."

Well, there was a scramble down that ladder as if we were all in sentence of the Pit. We found a root of alerces near the carpenter's shop, and Saiheque and his boys started with the bandsaw to flatten the base, and the rest of us cut and smoothed the roots and cleaned the bark with chisels and the sander. Vyrnwy made an eggcup in iron hoops and scrolls, and when the top of the root was sawn flat, I scooped a bowl in the middle, and the boys polished the surface to a deep red shine. The others had made five stone circles in the southwest corner, each smaller in five steps, and on top we put the iron eggcup. It took eight of us to lift the root in, and we cut and shaved until it sat solid on the hoop, and wood and iron got a last polish, and we swept up and ran. Mortar was still soft, iron was still warm, but we had a font on five steps when Brother Little Mountain pulled his feet from the stirrups and lay over the pony's neck to drop off in play of dust drifting from his clothes and the old shovel-brimmed hat.

Catriel had told him he would be met by a guide, so he made a fire and put on the pot, and all the time we were watching him from a bump among the little hills, and so were hundreds of Indios from behind every shrub or any ripple in the land.

Foyel waited in the belltower for a sign from us to ring the big bell but Saiheque put a hand on my shoulder and turned me to look the other way.

As an arrow, a woman in a red poncho trotted toward us, and a packhorse behind, and for moments I thought she was Kalata, and wondered where she could have been all that time. But everybody has a style of riding as they have of walking, and after a few moments I was sure she was not Kalata, and I thought she might be Solva. But then, even at that distance, I saw the shining gray of those eyes, and I knew, and I could have dropped.

Sûs.

Well, I was out and away and running like a madman and

not a breath in me, and she saw me and kicked to a gallop, arms out and laughing at the sky, and kneeing to a stop on the hinds in pour of dust, and off, running, and a clutch strong as any condor's talons.

"You shall not forget me," she shouted, in Arauco. "You shall not leave me. I am me. I am with you. Or let the fox and the rats enjoy me."

"I am your fox and all your rats," I said. "You shall never be from the reach of my hand. Come, you."

That *fssst!* was Vyrnwy waving to us from the oxeye to run, quick, and we let the horses go and hurried through the garden without a word. Sûs felt the sun and pulled off the poncho. She wore a blue blouse and a thin raw leather wrap-skirt with a belt, and slippers, and with the plaits hanging and the calm face, gray eyes in a smile, she looked to be too young, too innocent, and the fear that had kept me from sleep seemed to take me by the throat and I could barely breathe, thinking that the dream could break and she would go with someone else, younger, and my brain told me, more fit to live the young years with her.

Three little kisses on the chin she gave me as if she knew what I was thinking, and took my arm and went up the steps into the quiet church patched with color from the afternoon sun, and she stood as the Indios had, in wonder. Vyrnwy waited at the ladder, and shook hands with her and I saw more of the wonder in him, too. Up she went, into the tower, and Rhin and she spoke in Arauco, and he looked at me, happier than I had seen him for a long time.

"Well, you are home at last, boy," he said. "I am very glad. She will be a wonderful wife. Look, now then. He's had his tea and he's getting impatient. Will we ring the bell?"

Brother Little Mountain had walked a path, reading his little book down in the dip about five hundred yards away, a place we had chosen because we could see him from the tower, of stone, that was part of the rise and fall of the hills.

He closed the book and looked up at the sun, a black

stroke and a pink dot for a head, and yet even so far away his goodness came to us as something natural as sweat.

"The poor man has been patient long enough," Vyrnwy said, and reached for the bellrope. "We should have had the goodness to meet him."

"It would have been chat and noise from the beginning," Vyrnwy said, from the top of the ladder. "Huw was right. Let the man find it for himself, and take it to the heart. In good silence. When he is the master, then noise."

Rhin pulled the rope, and the bell sang a deep note.

Brother Little Mountain turned quickly, trying to fix direction, and Rhin let the rope go in a louder note, pulled again, and again, three bellnotes to scamp any notion of a dream, and the Brother started walking direct, holding up the soutane to climb to where El Pampero had brought the sound. The garden wall was above his eye line, but to his left he saw the stone columns and the gates. He stood there, looking, knowing well as anyone that Llangiñeu was a desert and gates were a dream, especially white gates on a rise leading nowhere.

Rhin pulled the bellrope and the sound hummed.

Brother Little Mountain put the book in his pocket and walked a strong pace as if he were angry that he could dream so much. He stopped at the steps, looking at them side to side, and went up, hidden from us until he was head and shoulders over the rise, and through the white scrolls he saw the church beyond the garden, and he put both hands to his face and closed his eyes to the sky.

Down the path he went as one in a dream, looking at blossoms, putting his face to them, touching the border plants, holding the bloom of a damask rose for moments, and he sat on the fountain step and loosened the soutane and put his head under the fall, and while he assured himself that the water was real, we went down the ladder and stood in the shadow of the south-east corner.

"Cruel, it is," Rhin said. "We should have met him. The

poor man is sure he is mad or dreaming. Not fair. Not right."

Sûs pressed my arm.

"What is this house?" she asked me, in my ear, and I felt her lips, and when I looked at her I knew she meant me to. "Who lives here?"

Solva had told me that Sûs was pagan, absolute, and to speak of religion was the same as talking about eskimos.

"Not a word, not an idea," she said. "I tried to tell her but we started to laugh, so silly it sounded, and she isn't sure of Castellano so we had a good cup of tea instead. Talking to that one about sin, of course is silly beyond words. It isn't in her. It will never be."

What, then, to say to her, eye to eye, and the warmth of her burning, was a puzzler, indeed.

"It is the house of the Brother of *Ranginhüenüchaü*," I said, for want of something better. "It is *Nguillatun*, and even more. This man in black is *ngen-toqui*. He is coming into his own House. We built it for him."

"Solva told me it was for Lal," she said.

"It is for Lal, and nobody else," I said. "It is her *rehue*. Later, he will put his saddle inside the door. Mine is already here, with hers and her peons, under that altar. When I die, here is where I shall come. When you die, be with us."

Three little kisses on the chin she gave me, and nodded, and we were close and even through rawhide I felt her warmth.

Brother Little Mountain's shadow darkened the church, and the prayer in Latin came to us, and he stood for a moment on the step, and pushed open the grille, and light flashed gold again, and we heard the sound of his knees hitting the stone, and the breath of a man in tears. Rhin nodded at Foyel in the tower, and we ran to the other side of the altar.

Brother Little Mountain lay face down, touching the steps with his fingertips.

In murmur of bells that shook the floor we lifted him, and he was helpless, wet through from the fountain, heavy to carry but we got him across to his room and Sûs found towels and dried his face, and went to make coffee.

Rupert von Gelsbach had sent everything a priest could want in vestment or furniture, and we made a bed and a couple of chairs, a wardrobe and desk, and a little bathroom to be cool after a dusty journey. We put him in the big chair, and he leaned his head, and only suddenly he seemed to see us.

"A journey with all angels," he whispered, as if he slept. "I know how it will be to enter Paradise. A taste. But enough. I know."

"It is yours," I said, and gave him the key. "It is gift of her, down beyond the fountain, there. Others are with her. They were all of another religion, but they are safe in the same Arms, now, I suppose. Whose, is small matter. We shall be there soon enough. She wanted this church to be for Indios. Where they could come without feeling ashamed, or pushed in at the back. Where they could sit down, even in the front. So we built the altar four ways for them to be nearer you. Lal, she was called. Beautiful she was. Do you remember her? Will you bless her name?"

He smiled in closed eyes, and then I think we heard the shouting outside between pealing bells, and I cannot forget the way Rhin looked at me with fear gone white in his eyes.

They were fighting out there.

Indios quarrel with the voice, but they never fight one to one. They save blood for a feast, perhaps one day in a year or more, and they eat their fill and drink enough, and then they call on hate, and shout every insult to the womb that gave life to the mother, and the male muscle that loosed the father, and friends join both sides, and at any show of a knife, or a throw of the Lost One, the fight will finish when a few are dead.

"Mixes fighting pure-bloods," Rhin whispered without voice. "I knew, I knew it when I saw them coming in. They were sent. Saiheque knew it. Dear Jesus, why didn't I go?"

"Two gendarmes came with me," Brother Little Mountain

said. "They called in at Hualjaina. They can't be far away."

Rhin looked at him with tears in his eyes.

"Nothing will stop them," he said. "The mixes will fight while they are ten to one or more. The moment they see less, they'll run. The pure-bloods will fight till not one is left. We are finished."

"O, come on, now, Rhin," Vyrnwy said. "Let's go there and use a hammer. Stop them."

"Come," Brother Little Mountain said, and out of the chair, quick.

The bells were quiet but the ropes still moved, and when we were at the door Rhin pointed to Foyel, running toward the dustcloud and the screams of women, and shouts.

"We haven't got a pony, my God Almighty," he said, beating hands in despair. "It will take twenty minutes to get over there. They will be dead."

"Wrong," I said. "The truck is below the wall. Come, you."

Hopeless to make Sûs stay. She had me by the arm, and that was enough, and she came in the cabin with Rhin. I drove, bumping over shrubs and roots for there was no path and I had to be careful because of the others in the back. The nearer we got, the more hopeless, and bodies were everywhere, and groups fighting with knives half-seen in thick dust, and women crawling, screaming, to pull men away and dozens of children crying and their little faces gaped in terror. A fist hammered on the cabin roof and I stopped, and Brother Little Mountain jumped down.

"Let these maniacs kill themselves," he shouted. "The children are mine."

Sûs must have understood, because Rhin was out, and so was she, and they were picking up the children and lifting them into the back, and I got down with a heavy spanner in each hand, and Vyrnwy had a long-handled spade. But the crowd was going away from us and in a lift of dust I saw Saiheque fighting with *boleadores,* holding off a pack of men with knives circling round him, and he had the smallest ball on a thong under the right foot, and he swung the midsize in the left hand and the largest he flicked in and out, too fast for the eye to see, and every time a man lifted a knife to throw he stepped nearer with that swing and flick, or side-stepped behind another body to spoil aim. While we were running he hit two in the face with the long ball, but he was bleeding from slashes and his eyes were tired.

Vyrnwy cut and whirled the spade with blacksmith's strength, and down they went, and my spanners hit two, and I had nothing to fight with, but the man coming for me with a knife got a crowner with the flat of the spade that will ring in my head as long as I live, and then they were running, and I held Saiheque in so much blood it was a wonder the boy was alive. We carried him back to the truck and Sûs unbelted the rawhide skirt to wrap him, and Brother Little Mountain knelt to do what he could. Fights were still going on, but few and distant, and most were running for their ponies in dust and shouts.

"Get him back for water," Vyrnwy said, breathless. "We'll look for the others."

Dozens of riders farther over were dragging bodies on lassos, and some carried men between them, and others were helped, but everywhere men were running, catching ponies and off.

"They will hide the bodies," Rhin whispered. "We will never find them. No evidence, no crime. How can I tell anybody they were desirable?"

"You have got witnesses," I said.

"That they were fighting?" Rhin said. "Self-defence? No excuse. They were all Indios. Enough. I will take the women and children and anybody left of the men, tonight. I wish to God I had gone when I knew I should. If Saiheque has got a boy left, it will be a miracle. If he dies, his people are finished."

The two gendarmes were walking through the garden when we lifted Saiheque out of the truck. Brother Little Mountain talked to them, and they ran back to their horses and galloped over to the tanks.

We put Saiheque on the floor of the bathroom and ran the hose over the dust and wounds, and Elvet took the truck back to Vyrnwy.

Sûs had gone out to pick bundles of leaves and roots, and she put the pot on for hot water. Other women came in, and we left them.

"Hopeless," Brother Little Mountain said, eyes red with dust. "The gendarmes are going to clear them out. There might be serious trouble between the two Governments, men fighting like this. What caused it?"

"Barramendiz sent in his peons, of course," Vyrnwy said. "A point of men from each *estancia*? No trouble. A couple of barrels of wine to pay, and who will be wiser? A lot of dirty Indios having a fight, there's all. And no witnesses."

The gendarmes were soon back. They found nothing except knives, *boleadores*, and blood. A long line of women and children wept a way from the tanks, and the girls were coming in with the ponies.

"But imagine the stupidity," Brother Little Mountain said, and put fists to temples. "I shall lose all these children."

"You're lucky to be alive," the corporal said. "They'd have killed the lot. Probably have burned this place, too. There're barrels of kerosene over there."

Brother Little Mountain folded his arms and looked down at him.

"Destroying a church?" he asked. "Why?"

"Then there's nowhere for them to go," the corporal said, as a matter of fact. "There's been a crowd here for a long time. More coming every week. Then they were going to start working the land? That'd bring more. Couple of years, how many? But a lot of people are after their titles. After this, logically, they'll get them. Must be twenty or thirty dead. Or more. That's it. They're dangerous. You've got no answer. Clear them out."

He looked at me.

"I wouldn't stay here tonight, if I were you," he said.

"We're going to ride everybody here back with us. Anybody won't come, we aren't responsible."

"I shall stay here," Brother Little Mountain said.

"They won't touch you," the corporal said. "Mightn't be so particular about anybody else."

Instantly, as El Pampero changes to a cold breath, I was in freeze of fear for Sûs. Any thought of her so much as scratched boiled the blood behind my eyes. To tell the truth, disgrace or not, I cared nothing for the church, or school, or anybody or anything, but only for the warmth that burned through me, and three little kisses on the chin.

For so much, the world can go to Hell.

Shame, because Saiheque was my excuse to go. We piled the truck with a couple of bales of tossed clover, and put him in the blankets, and I went to find Sûs. Families were crowded in the school, bedding on the floor, infants crying, women soothing, and Brother Little Mountain had a shouting circus of children round him waiting for biscuits from the box under his arm.

"You were good enough to leave them," he said, sorry, with a biscuit in his fingers. "But they're hungry."

"Anything here is yours," I said. "Look, then. I am not of your religion. But I know enough about you to be sure. Will you marry us, now, among these people?"

Down went the box, and from the soutane pocket came the little book, and without more words, we went out, and into the quiet church alive in light and color.

We knelt at the southern altar, and we heard the Latin, and the women gathered and children stopped play. Vyrnwy stood beside me, and we used the ring on Sûs' little finger, that would only go over the top joint of the third, but no matter, because the Hand was on our heads, and we were one.

Rhin opened the new register, and we were the first names in, and when I had signed, Brother Little Mountain wet Sûs' thumb with ink and she put her mark on the page. She took my right hand, and pressed her thumb on the scar Saiheque had made.

"Where is my house?" she said, loud. "Let us go there. *I-want-my-house.*"

I could hear Lal.

33

The man to deny an *Araucana* anything rightfully hers would be a fool because she wants so little. If his saddle is inside her door as hunter, then her place is equal as mother, and so, guardian of the family and time-to-come, which she tends in fire with her thoughts that burn with the little sticks and pieces of bark, for where a spark is, life is, and while she lives, all things will be done as she was taught, and nothing will be in fault or out of place.

The women would not let us go without the *conchotún*, feast of marriage, birth and death.

Even in grief they screamed refusal.

We had to wait.

Sûs was sister to all of them, and I was *pichamanque*, brother to Saiheque, and we had nothing to say, because we knew.

As well, for when the herbs were soft in poultice, they put Saiheque in a cocoon of steaming leaf and so saved his life, though before he slept, Foyel came in with his older brother Huentrép over the pommel, and leading a packhorse with Perquen and Catriel, and Cheuquen came after, leading a string carrying a dozen. The women ran to have them off and in poultice, and Saiheque smiled at me, and went to sleep in a long breath that I thought might never stop, and an old woman sang to us that *Ranginhüenüchaü* had put a thumb under his lungs to make him suck back more of his skein.

In that time I walked with Brother Little Mountain to show him where everybody was buried in the garden, if their families came, and down to the potting sheds to see what was ready for planting.

"There's only one matter not settled," I said. "If Lal were here I am sure she would not allow any statues in the church. Silver candlesticks and flowers on the altar, as it is now, and nothing else. Nothing on the walls. The sun, and often the moon, here, will give all the color through the windows. The Indio mind is bare and strong. Let their church also be bare. Put your saddle over the eastern door. There the sun rises, and El Pampero blows. The women will look for it, and lift the children to touch. They will feel surer."

Rhin came from talking to the hurt men lying in shadow of the garden wall. Others were riding in, some with broken bones and many cut, but they all seemed cheerful enough, and soon the air seemed to change, and instead of the black day we had all thought it was, in a few minutes it came happy and everybody was laughing.

"Thank God there were no firearms," Rhin said, while we were eating. "The story would be different. As it is, we have lost some good ones, but they lost many more. Victory for us. But never again. A few of the local men will stay behind to clear up, but the rest will come with me. I will never more be here. I never want to hear another word about land."

"Injustice to these children," I said. "When they are older, that land would be a patrimony."

"When they are older, where they are going, they will be alive," Rhin said. "Will you warrant the same here?"

"There must be a way of dealing with this Barramendiz," Vyrnwy said. "If I have got to throttle him."

"He isn't the only one," Rhin said. "Not the only one ready to pay either. There are plenty of ways to get rid of us. Drink is the easiest. How long would any of these last on their own? Their land would go just the same. They will come with me, and the children will learn to work. That is the first thing."

It was then, looking at him, all bones and clothes worn to cottons, that I saw his nearness to Brother Little Mountain. One was priest and scholar, and the other of little learning but how much other knowledge, yet there was a link. One served by prayer and the other in goodness of heart, and I am not sure there is any great difference. Nobody calls a priest a madman for devoting himself to the souls of men, but many thought Rhin a lunatic for helping his Indios, yet if that sense of duty were not alive and beautiful in some of us, there would be no priests or Rhinberry Wynns, and my life, for one, would have been the poorer.

Vyrnwy, of course, loved him as a brother but he could never see any sense in what he did, but then again, he had a tidy bit of Teg in him by then, and she, of course, could never even listen to the word. A war party had murdered an uncle of hers, and nothing anybody could say was the slightest use after. To her, they were all murderers, thieves and idle drunkards.

No sense to argue.

"Look," Vyrnwy said, and held out a hide pouch. "Spend this on the children. It will buy a few things, anyway. You've got a good six days to go, haven't you?"

Rhin shook his head at the pouch.

"No, thank you, boy," he said. "We aren't looking for anything except what we earn. I have taught them that, at any rate."

"You've all earned money here," I said.

"We worked for Lal, and you, and somebody else," he said. "If there's money, give it to the Brother. It will come useful, no doubt."

"Who is this somebody else?" I asked, but I was sure I knew.

"Lliutro," he said, and smiled direct, eye to eye. "Her saddle is also under that altar. I put it there. Will you curse me?"

"I should have been the one to think of it," I said. "I am ashamed I didn't."

"Saiheque brought it," he said. "He is sure she took you to Sûs."

But again Brother Little Mountain refused me.

"I don't need money," he said. "I haven't anywhere to keep it. If I have need of anything I shall be happy to apply to you. The workshop, for example. We need machines, lathes. Drawing tables."

"Leave it to me," I said. "Will you take charge here?"

Well, he smiled to warm the earth.

"It's mine," he said, no man steadier. "Here there are children. They need me."

"When you want to build more, let me know," I said. "I have got a big debt."

"What debt is this?" he said, frowning.

"My wife," I said. "I am in debt for life, and thankful."

That little hand came into mine, a strange new feeling, of fear and wonder equal, fear that I was dreaming, wonder I was not, and we stood arms about to see them all riding away, some of the women holding bandaged men in the saddle, all waving and shouting to us.

Rhin came on the golden palomino, a dear little horse, and the richest thing about him except his spirit.

"Goodbye, now then," he said, and I am sure he stayed in the saddle to turn quick and go. "We are always saying goodbye, boy. But this one will be for longer. I will never come on this side again. Up at the pass, there, I will shake the dust. But we will pray that you shall always go warm in the Light. God rest a Hand everywhere here. My prayer is in the heart."

Sometimes the throat is stuck, and no words will come, and there is only a look.

He went at standing gallop on a turn, and we stood to watch Brother Little Mountain handing up the children to mothers in the saddle, and they were all moving, and Rhin a waving shadow in the dust, and dust in rise, and children shouting to us, and shadows then, and gone.

Saiheque and the others were still asleep in the truck, with a couple of women and Elvet looking after them, and Brother Little Mountain came to the fountain with us because the gendarmes were waiting for him to sign a report.

"One thing is worrying me," I said. "How am I going to teach this one what a church is for? She knows nothing about prayer, or anything else."

He smiled at her, and I never saw two pairs of eyes so different that looked to be filled with the same light.

"Which language will you teach her, first?" he asked.

"She's got a baby-memory of Cambrian," I said. "Perhaps it will come easiest."

"It's the music of a godly people," he said. "Their mark is everywhere here. Don't teach. The faith is in her. Let it bloom. As these flowers. They can only grow to be what they are. Those are the eyes of truth. How could she be anyone except herself? I shall pray for you both. Remember me, here. Go with God, in peace."

We left him, that dusty one, walking through the garden, holding out his arms to the church and singing some happy little thing, and the gendarmes took off their caps and knelt, and he blessed them, and took them in.

"Only the church and him," Vyrnwy said. "What will he do, and no people?"

"Wait, you," I said. "When they know where he is, the late ones will have to stand. When the flowers are all out, they will drive hours to be here."

"Well, damn, I never thought of that," Vyrnwy said. "We will be here, certain. But I thought it was for Indios?"

"Indio," Sûs shouted to let everybody know, and nearly had us from our wits. "You are Indio. I am Indio. Kintú is Indio."

Instantly, then, Lliutro was near and smiling, for Kintú, floral coronet of the cacique was her name for me, so I knew some Indio woman had told, and I could feel my heart drowning, wondering what.

"Didn't take her long to find a nice little name for you, yes?" Vyrnwy said. "There is pretty, boy. Do you know what Teg calls me? Because I eat plenty, and I am dirty. Well, in work, anyway. *Môch*. That's me. I like it. I do like an old pig, indeed. Clean as the clouds, if let. Friendly he is, see, and a splendid taste everywhere."

Sûs was giving me that look sideways, with the smile.

"Kintú," she whispered. "Where is my house?"

"First we go to our sister's house," I said. "Tomorrow we shall ride the air. We will go to other *rehue*. When we come back, the place of your house will be ready. We will see it built. Even for a toldo, you must still find the place, and then guanaco. Now, we go to hunt. *Galôn fach-i, ty'n cofio?*"

She smiled the gray, gray light, and rested that head, and sat closer.

Nothing is nearer drunkenness.

We left Saiheque and his boys with the doctor at Indio Stones, and found a car at the garage, and loaded the truck with half the grocer's shop, and Elvet drove it back to Brother Little Mountain for a gift, so instead of a mule or horses he had a grandson of Henry Ford to ride, and he called it Enrico, and treated it as the old mule's daughter.

"But Huw, my dear," Olwen said, in that beautiful lazy English, when she met us. "Heaven above, why must you take the poor darling down there? What's she going to see? A lot of coal mines? Iron works? All smoke and filth? Those that are working, of course. Horrors, darling, really. I'd save her that. She'll get quite the wrong idea, don't you agree? I mean, really?"

"No," I said. "I will show her where I was a boy. Where I was taught to be myself. Where I had an extra lesson from Bron. Without only those little things, who would I be? I will see Mrs. Tom Harries and have the accounts in order. You might as well use the money. It's no use to me. Scholarships for girls from the Valley. What Angharad did for you, you can do for other little ones. And I'll try to save the houses on The Hill. Whatever you think, love was there. Love was under every step we took. If only we could have known."

We wish and we dream—*Ichabod!*—but the facts deny us.

We have been down here, and all through the back, and across the landslide since this morning, engineers, masons, carpenters, all veterans of the colliery, but there is nothing to be done.

I can see my good father and brothers out there, now, with Dai Bando and Cyfartha, and Hwfa and Old Twm, and dozens more, sitting in the first row and the others rank on rank behind, and the youngest cross-legged in front, all in Sunday best, bowler hats on the knee, a little flower in the button-hole, and Mama watching through the window, and Angharad and Ceridwen and me in fits here from what she was saying. But the annual photograph of our choir was an event, and some families had more than forty round the walls, and plenty of tales to tell about everyone in them, so every face was serious, though every eye had the same little smile, watching the photographer come from under black velvet, and hoping nothing would happen to make them laugh because if they did, their shapes went cloudy. Old Mrs. Hoggin, the Clock, refused three years running to buy one, because old Hoggin was always in a gust at the wrong time, and she said it was senseless to pay good money to hang up the picture of an old ghost, when in a little while she would have a real one for nothing.

Ghosts, yes, they all are now, but real and dear enough to some.

"Only ten days or a couple of weeks ago, we might have got a 'dozer to shift the weight," Emrys John, in school with me, said, and I have often wondered how small boys in blue jerseys with thin legs grow into fat little men with gold-rimmed glasses and a mustache like a bit of old thatch. "Now it's too late. With this rain, she will come down in a run. The wall at the back is strong. But when it cracks, there is nothing to hold. No hope, see."

Thinking of his life and mine, and Rhin's and Vyrnwy's and Brother Little Mountain's, and Saiheque's, all lived at the same passing of the clock, and Angharad and Olwen and Lal and Sûs, and the Indios still in the Bio-Bio, and the gendarmes patrolling the mountains, and Sam Ellis, grandson of Ellis, the Post, a fireman, and out there now, calling to me, I am in wonder that so many can live so strangely apart with not a single thought for each other, or a smile or wave of the hand across the grave we are all going to. Too many of us live as dead ones, and some have never been from the grave, and love is only a mood, a little byplay to bawl about with guitars, and forget.

"Mr. Morgan," Sam's voice is bubbling down the shaft. "The Super' says you have got to come out, now. Everything is very rumbly here. The rain is coming heavy, look."

This little house is shaking, and I wonder did it shake when my father was brought home in his box—and I can smell the wood now—even if we never saw or felt, though I am sure Mama did.

Because when he went, then so did the Valley.

A discipline, a strength, a Faith common to him and his kind went into that box, and that one, and Mama's, and all the others are down there now, under the slag, and them, brothers and sisters in that other Valley, wrenched from their piece of earth are with them, though I can see their eyes and hear their voices, and while I live, so shall they.

Little house, where so many of us were taught a way, and every board was blessed, and every stone soaked my Mama's goodness through the years, I must leave you. Another life is outside, and Sûs is waiting for me in Tossall's and I will take a warm hand ready for me, and I wonder is there a better feeling, and we shall go back direct, to Down Where The Moon Is Small. We said goodbye to Olwen over the telephone at Mrs. Tom Harries, though I am sure she has no idea we are off so soon, and I feel better than I should, perhaps, because it was in my throat that I would never see her again. But Sûs understood nothing of that beautiful English, and only smiled a brilliance of gray, and shouted to talk, but she will come better, and I love her more than there is hope in all the world to find the words.

This past couple of hours I have felt small, so much I have been given for so little in return. But there is nothing I can do, no help I can give to anybody here, little I can save, any more than in the Andes, or in New Gilgal or along the valley of the Camwy.

What I could have done, or might or should have done, is beyond me to know, and I see that tin with its lid in a lift like the agent's hat, and the straw and paper in bob of shining water getting wider, and the ship leaving shore, and everything leaving me, and nothing, no, nothing to be done.

We are condemned to be possessed of others, half-thralled through a lifetime, and the rest depending on the will of somebody else. How many tons or yards above the graves I wanted them to mark, but the rose cuttings I took to the cemetery were no stranger to the ground than I, born of a love that grew here.

This little blue cloth holds the secret. My mother could have run from the place and all of us many a time, but she never did. My father could have walked out and gone somewhere else, but never.

They came here and they loved.

They stayed because they loved, as those stayed because they loved along the Camwy, and over in the Cordilleras, and how green were those Valleys then, in whisper with prayer, quiet with work, quick with hope, green, yes, the Valleys of them that are gone.

Farewell, a biddance now, Valley mine, and farewell, my Camwy, O farewell. The anthem is gone from you, and a music is past.

Yet, as buds burst from a tree thought dead, there is hope.

Sûs lives, and beyond there she has many a sister, now, and in surety tomorrow. Women are the strength. Men can be flattered, bought, suborned.

Women, the Angharads, Lals, Sarahs, Dolis, Eirenes, Sûs's, no, never.

Of Cambria we are, and Cambria still is, because of them.

O, if we shall ever sing again as our Fathers, for melody and harmony and all glory unto God. Send soon the day, for we are not forever, and a deathwatch eats in the beam.

I will pack these shirts and socks, and this suit, that knew my Mama, and Bron, and Ceinwen, and so many beauties of my young time, in this little blue cloth my mother tied about her hair when she did the house, and then, I will be gone from the Valley.

Little Looking Glass
1965